Three in One
Ballet Stories

HI THERE, SUPERMOUSE!

Rose has pink cheeks, blue eyes and loves to dance.
Nicola has straggly arms and legs and loves football.
The two girls could not be more different, or so
they think, until Nicola meets someone who could
change their lives.

A PROPER LITTLE NOORYEFF

Jamie Carr doesn't mean to get involved at the
Thea Tucker School of Dance, but he accidentally
finds himself in the wrong place at the wrong time.

STAR TURN

As soon as she sees Karen, Jessamy knows she is a
dancer. But there is something mysterious about
her. Why is she so secretive about her lessons? And
who is the curious Madame Olga? Energetic and
passionate Jessamy is determined to find out.

Other Red Fox Story Collections

Cool School Stories
Three in One Animal Stories
Completely Wild Stories

THREE IN ONE
BALLET STORIES

RED FOX

A Red Fox Book

Published by Random House Children's Books
20 Vauxhall Bridge Road, London SW1V 2SA

A division of Random House UK Ltd
London Melbourne Sydney Auckland
Johannesburg and agencies throughout the world

Copyright © Jean Ure, *Hi There, Supermouse!* 1983, *A Proper Little
Nooryeff* 1982, *Star Turn* 1993

1 3 5 7 9 10 8 6 4 2

Hi There, Supermouse! and *Star Turn* first published in Great Britain
by Hutchinson Children's Books 1983 & 1993, *A Proper little
Nooryeff* first published in Great Britain by The Bodley Head 1982

Red Fox edition 1998

Printed and bound in Great Britain by
Cox & Wyman Ltd, Reading, Berkshire

Papers used by Random House UK Ltd are natural, recyclable
products made from wood grown in sustainable forests. The
manufacturing processes conform to the environmental regulations
of the country of origin.

Random House UK Limited Reg. No. 954009

ISBN 0 09 926582 6

CONTENTS

HI THERE,
SUPERMOUSE!

1

'*Honestly*, Nicola.' Mrs. Bruce regarded her elder daughter with the exasperated air of one who has very nearly reached the end of her tether. 'I just don't know how you could *do* such a thing. I don't know how you *could*.'

Nicola shook her hair into her eyes and stared down glumly at the carpet through the lank strands of her fringe. She supposed she ought to say something, only what was there to say? The thing that she had done was so indisputably *awful* – and she hadn't even been aware that she was doing it until it was too late. One moment she had been sitting there, at the dining room table, struggling to write an essay about 'Getting up in the Morning' for Miss McMaster, on Monday; the next, to her horror, she had been busily drawing a face on the toe of one of her sister Rose's tap dancing shoes.

What made it even worse (if anything *could* make such an evil deed even worse) was that the shoes were red leather and very nearly new, and the pen she'd used for drawing was deep dark black and wouldn't come out no matter how much she spat on it, nor how hard she rubbed. In fact, she'd only succeeded in turning what had been a rather good face into a great splotchy mess. If she'd left it as a face, she could at least have done a second one to match. She might have started a new fashion, shoes with funny faces. *She* wouldn't mind if someone drew faces on her plimsolls, or her gum boots. But then, of course, she wasn't Rose. Rose was Rose, and Rose was perfect. Rose was pretty. Rose was *good*. Rose couldn't go round with faces on her shoes.

Rose, at this moment, was screaming fit to bust. Nicola pushed her fringe back out of her eyes. Stupid thing. Making all that fuss over a mere shoe.

'Hush, now!' Mrs. Bruce, distracted, pulled Rose towards her and stroked her hair with a soothing hand. Rose's hair was bright chestnut and springy: Nicola's was dark, and limp, and straggled. She was rather a straggly sort of person. She was tall, for an eleven-year-old, and at a gangly stage, where her arms and legs seemed too long for her body. Rose was short and bouncy, with forget-me-not blue eyes and a round pink face full of freckles. Nicola's face was thin, and rather sallow, and her eyes were brown, and deep set. Nobody would ever have taken them for sisters. There was only a year between them, but already Nicola was like a walking beanpole beside small, compact Rose. Their father, fondly, called Rose his little Rose Petal; Nicola, for almost as long as she could remember, had been 'old Nickers'. Sometimes she wished that he wouldn't, but mostly it didn't bother her. She knew that she was her father's favourite. Not that he loved her any more than he loved Rose; just that really and truly he had hoped for a boy, and everyone always said that Nicola was 'as good as'. Rose was her mother's favourite – Mrs. Bruce didn't care for boys. She definitely loved Rose more than she loved Nicola. She looked at Nicola now, over Rose's copper curls, and said, 'How anyone could be so *wicked* . . .'

Rose wrenched her head away.

'She did it on purpose, just to be mean!'

'I did not!' Nicola was indignant. 'How was I to know it was your stupid shoe?'

'You could see it was my shoe! You only had to *look*.'

'Well, I didn't, and anyway it oughtn't to have been there . . . shoes on a *table*.'

'Don't be ridiculous, Nicola!' Mrs. Bruce spoke sharply. 'It's no use trying to make excuses, you've ruined a perfectly good pair of shoes. I don't even know if it'll clean. They'll probably have to be dyed.'

A wail broke forth from Rose.

'If she had the money, I'd make her pay for a new pair. As it is – ' Mrs. Bruce eyed Nicola, sternly ' – you can certainly pay for any repair work that needs doing. And *that's* letting you off lightly. It's about time, my girl, that your father started to take a sterner line with you. I've had just about as much as I can stand. Ordinary naughtiness is one thing; but when it comes to deliberate acts of vandalism – '

'It wasn't!' Nicola felt impelled to speak up in her own defence, though she knew that it was hopeless.

How could she expect her mother to understand, when she didn't even understand herself? She tried, nevertheless. 'It wasn't deliberate,' she said. 'It was an accident.'

Rose, in shrill tones, said, '*Accident?*'

Mrs. Bruce only pursed her lips.

'Trying to wriggle out of it won't help, Nicola. This isn't the first time this sort of thing has happened. What about the other day, when you threw ink all over the place?'

'That *was* an accident.'

'Well, maybe it was, but this certainly wasn't. You can hardly pretend not to have known what you were doing.'

But I didn't, thought Nicola. I *didn't*. She looked down at her English rough book, still lying open on the table. She looked at what she had written:

'Getting up in the Morning. I get up in the morning at seven o'clock when my dad brings me a cup of tea. I get up straigt away because of taking my dog Ben round the block. My sister Rose dos'nt get up untill our mum's called her three times Rose its time to get up or you'll be late for school but even then she doesn't always come imedeately. If I didn't come I would be told I am lazy and slothfull and who is to take Ben for his walk, but my mum says Rose needs her sleep because of going to be a dancer and so it is alright for her to stay in bed late and – '

And what? wondered Nicola. What had she been going to write next? She couldn't remember. She couldn't remember anything. Had she *really* been wicked enough to draw a face on Rose's tap shoe?

The tap shoe, unhappily, told her that she had. It sat there on the table, squat and accusing, with two eyes, and a nose, and a downturned mouth which seemed to say, 'This really is not amusing, you know.'

'I didn't *mean* it,' said Nicola.

'It's all very well saying you didn't mean it, but the fact remains that you *did* it. Didn't you?' Nicola munched glumly at her bottom lip. Mrs. Bruce shook her head. 'It's beyond me,' she said. 'It really is. If you were a stupid girl, I could understand it, but you're not. So why behave as if you were?'

Nicola said nothing: she was too busy trying to munch all the way down to her chin. If her teeth had been just a bit longer, or her chin just a little bit shorter . . .

'There's no point in being clever at school,' said Mrs. Bruce, 'if you're going to be stupid outside it. There, now, Rose, love.' She pulled a handkerchief from her pocket. 'You have a good blow and dry your eyes. And don't worry about the shoes; we'll get something done. It might be quite exciting, having them dyed another colour . . . how about blue? Blue would be nice.'

Rose, hiccuping into the handkerchief, wept afresh and declared that no one, but *no one*, had blue tap shoes.

'Well, then! You can set a new trend, can't you? Nice bright blue, to match your eyes.'

'But what about this morning?' Rose almost shrieked it. 'What will Madam Paula say?'

'You'll just have to apologize to Madam Paula and explain that your elder sister – ' Mrs. Bruce rested a moment, significantly, on the word elder ' – your *elder* sister, who ought to know better, thought it funny to deface other people's property.'

'I *didn't*,' said Nicola. 'I didn't *know*.'

Mrs. Bruce ignored her. She picked up the one good shoe and the one bad shoe and thrust them gently at Rose.

'Off you go! You don't want to be late. Tell Madam Paula we're thinking of letting you have extra classes next term . . . that will please her. She's always saying you're one of her star pupils. As for you, Nicola, you can get out from under my feet and take that dog for a walk.'

'I've already taken him for one.'

'Then take him for another!'

'But I'm doing my *home*work. I've got an essay to write.'

'You can write it later. Go along! Do as you're told. Saturday morning and sitting about the place . . . go out and get some fresh air. Blow some of the naughtiness out of yourself – and don't go over that building site!'

There were two building sites in Fenning Road. There was one close by, which was the one her mother didn't like; and there was another further down which Mrs. Bruce didn't yet know about because she always walked up towards the shops, in

16

Streatham High Road, instead of down the other way, towards the Common. Nicola made a quite definite distinction in her mind between the two: between *that* building site (which had been forbidden) and the *other* building site (which hadn't). It couldn't possibly be termed disobedience to clamber over the earthmound into the *other* building site. She wasn't doing anything wrong. No one had put up any notices saying 'Private' or 'Trespassers will be prosecuted'. They hadn't even put up a fence. In any case, it was better for Ben, because there weren't any motorcars for him to get run over by.

The building site was full of mud. Back in the summer there had still been some grass, and even a few flowers, but now it was autumn, and the rain had come, and men with bulldozers had been at their work, carving trenches and throwing up mountains. On the whole, Nicola preferred it this way. It gave more scope. Trenches and mountains could be anything you cared to make them, from battlefields to lunar landscapes. Grass and flowers were too much like the local park, with its 'Dogs must be kept under control' and its 'Keep to the path' and its 'No entry'. And anyway, they made her think of Rose. Rose had green fingers. (Rose had *everything*.) She grew geraniums in pots and cultivated her own corner of the garden, so that sometimes, when he wasn't calling her Rose Petal, Mr. Bruce referred to her as 'my little gardener'. Nicola hated gardening. The only part of it she enjoyed was stoking bonfires, and her mother wouldn't let her do that any more. She

17

said she couldn't be trusted – all because she'd accidentally set light to the fence and Rose had gone running indoors screaming.

Nicola stubbed her toe, viciously, into a pile of loose earth. Rose was so *stupid* – and she was a tell tale. 'Nicola's done this, Nicola's done that . . . Nicola's *hurt* me, Nicola's been *mean* to me . . . Nicola's *horrible.*' Well, and so could Rose be, when she wanted. She was just sly about it; always sucking up to people, putting on her airs and graces, prinking and preening – 'I'm little *Rose*mary, oh, aren't I *pretty* – '

Nicola, long-leggitty in black wool tights and a red plaid skirt that didn't reach her knees, did a little twirl, tiptoe in the mud.

'Such a *dear* little girl – such a *sweet* little girl – '

Prink, preen, simper, simper.

'Just *see* how she can point her toe! See her curtsey – see her pirouette – '

Nicola pirouetted vigorously on the top of her mud bank. '*See her fall flat on her silly fat face –* '

BANG.

Slap, thud, into the mud.

'Nicola's *hurt* me, Nicola's been *mean* to me . . . boo hoo! Now I'm all *dirty* – '

Absorbed in being Rose, Nicola covered her face and roared, dramatically.

'Yes, and serve you jolly well *right!*'

With a demonic yell, she sprang off the mound. She was back again, now, to being Nicola.

'Silly, simpering, self-righteous *cow!*'

Whooping and hallooing, she danced around the mound.

'Serve her right, serve her right, serve her – '

'Excuse me!'

Nicola came to an abrupt halt, in the middle of a whoop. Outside, on the pavement, a lady was standing. She beckoned to Nicola, and nodded; Nicola scowled. The lady cupped a hand to her mouth.

'May I have a word with you?'

She didn't *sound* as if she was going to make a scene; still Nicola was wary. In her experience grown ups – even youngish, glamorous grown ups, like this one – only ever wanted to have words with you for one thing, and that was to tell you that what you were doing was something you ought not to be (such as playing on building sites). Nicola slouched across, reluctantly.

'I've seen you somewhere before,' said the lady. 'I'm trying to think where . . . do you by any chance have a big black dog?'

Unfortunately, just at that moment, Ben chose to put in an appearance. If he hadn't, she would have denied all knowledge. (It was always safer to deny all knowledge where Ben was concerned: you never knew what he might have got up to when you weren't looking.)

'That's the one!' said the lady.

Ben grinned, and wagged his tail.

'Is he yours?'

Since Ben, at that point, was sitting companionably on her toe, she couldn't very well disown him. She mumbled, 'Yes,' in a way that might be taken for 'no' if any accusations were to be made.

'Then that's where I've seen you!' The lady seemed pleased. (Because she had solved a mystery, or because she had tracked down a culprit?) 'Going into the house with the green shutters ... I remember your dog trying to get a tree trunk through the gate with him and not succeeding! I live just there, by the way.'

She pointed to a large, ivy-clad house overlooking the building site. Nicola's scowl intensified. So what? It wasn't *her* building site. It didn't say 'Private'. It didn't say 'Trespassers will be — '

'Do you have dancing classes?' said the lady.

'No.' Nicola grabbed Ben's collar, to prevent him going off again. He was already plastered in mud from one end of himself to the other. 'That's my sister does that,' she said. She wasn't taking the blame for anything Rose might have done. Not that Rose ever *did*.

'I was watching you,' said the lady. 'I thought perhaps you might have come in here secretly to practise.'

Nicola stood her ground.

'It doesn't say "Private",' she said.

'No, it doesn't, does it? Rather amazingly — they're usually terrified of a few stray children getting in and managing to enjoy themselves. After all — ' she waved a slender hand at the sea of mud ' — just think of all the damage you could cause . . . what's your name, by the way?'

'Nicola Bruce,' said Nicola. Now she supposed there was going to be a complaint made, like the time she'd been caught climbing on the roof of the girls' lavatory at school. She hadn't been doing any *harm*. What harm could you do to a lavatory? *Or* a mouldy building site. It was stupid to say, 'Think of all the damage you could cause.' Nobody could cause damage to a bit of bare earth. It wasn't as if there was anything growing in it.

'Well, I'll say goodbye, then, Nicola. I expect we'll bump into each other again. Mind you don't get mud all over that pretty skirt!'

The lady turned, and walked off up the road, in the direction of the shops. She was tall and slim, in red velvet jacket and trousers. From behind, she looked almost like a boy. Quite often, when she was wearing jeans, people said that Nicola looked like a boy. That was one of the reasons why Mrs. Bruce wouldn't let her wear them very often; not only because she didn't like boys, but because she believed that girls should be girls. Rose was always a girl. Whenever she was taken to buy a new frock she inevitably chose something soft and frilly that would have made Nicola look like a piece of twig dressed up as a sugar plum fairy. Rose just *naturally* looked like a sugar plum fairy.

Nicola tossed her head. So, who cared? She certainly didn't. She had better things in life to worry about than stupid clothes. She let go Ben's collar and

21

he went hurtling off, joyously, through a trench full of dirty water. Nicola stomped back again to her mound.

'Look at *me* – I am *Rose* . . . Sugar Plum Fairy with a big red nose . . .'

She wished that grown ups would mind their own business. It just wasn't the same, when you knew that they were spying on you.

2

Nicola had forgotten all about the lady on the building site. A whole week had passed, and other things had happened in the meantime. Miss McMaster had praised her essay on 'Getting up in the Morning'. She had given her eight out of ten and read it aloud to the class as an example of a good piece of writing – 'even if it does dwell rather obsessively on your sister Rose *not* getting up'. Now she had given them another essay to write, on the subject of 'My Family'. Nicola had already composed the opening paragraph:

'My Family. My family is made up of my mum and dad and my sister Rose. There is also my dog Ben. My mum and dad sleep in the front bedroom in a large bed with a blue cover. My sister Rose sleeps in the backbedroom wich is the next biggest becuase she has to have spase for all her dansing things and to practise pleeays' (she wasn't too sure about this word) 'before she goes to bed wich means I have to have the very smallest room of all scarsely any bigger than a cupboard in wich to put myself and my belongings wich I have quite a number of.'

That had been on Wednesday. On Thursday Rose

had come back all cock-a-hoop from her ballet class saying that Madam Paula had said she would be ready to go on point next term and please, *please* could she go out and buy a pair of point shoes straight away, so as to have plenty of time in which to darn them and sew on ribbons? To Nicola's disgust, Mrs. Bruce had said that she might just as well, since 'sure as eggs' the price would only go shooting up if they waited. She hadn't said anything at all about the price of running shoes shooting up. She'd simply said that 'You'd better wait and see what Christmas brings.' She'd been quite cross when Nicola reminded her of it.

'There's a world of difference between shoes for ballet and shoes for running. If Rose is going to be a dancer, then she needs the right things. *You* can run in your plimsolls. In any case, I should have thought the less said on the subject of shoes the better, as far as you were concerned.'

In the end, she had relented and said that if Nicola could manage to keep herself out of trouble for just forty-eight hours, then maybe – 'I said *maybe*' – she would reconsider. It was now three o'clock on Saturday afternoon and Nicola hadn't done anything wrong since half-past seven on Thursday evening. That meant she had kept out of trouble for forty-three hours and thirty minutes. (She was ticking it off in a special notebook by the side of her bed.) Nothing, surely, could go wrong *now*?

She had forgotten about the lady from the building site – at least, not so much forgotten as dismissed her from her mind. After all, if she had been going to make a complaint, she would have done it ages ago. Nobody stored up grudges for a whole week; or did they?

Did they?

The front gate had been pushed open. Nicola heard it as she sat perched on her bedroom windowsill constructing a model Concorde from a model kit. Her bedroom windowsill was triangular in shape and wide enough for her to curl up on. If she peered out of the left-hand window she could just make out the porch over the front door and, if she was quick enough, see who it was coming up the path. She peered – and recoiled in haste. Not only in haste, but indignation, as well: it was the lady from the building site.

She was wearing a skirt, instead of the red trousers, and her blond hair was loose about her shoulders instead of being scraped back from her head as it had been before, but Nicola had no difficulty in recognizing her. She had the sort of face that wasn't easy to forget. It was bony, like a model's, and very pale, except for the eyes, which were huge and long-lashed with green sparkly stuff over the lids. In other circumstances, Nicola might have been impressed. All she felt now was a sense of outrage. To have waited a whole *week* –

The doorbell rang. In a flash, Nicola was out of her room and along the landing. As she reached the head of the stairs a door opened somewhere below and her mother came into view, wiping her hands on a towel as she trod across the hallway. Nicola crouched, spiderlike, at her post. She watched as her mother opened the front door. Almost at once, she heard the light, crisp voice of the lady from the building site, 'Mrs. Bruce? I do apologize for calling round unannounced! My name is Pamela French – I live just down the road. Number ninety-eight. I wondered if I might have a word with you about Nicola?'

'Nicola?' said Mrs. Bruce. Her voice was guarded. 'What did you want to – '

'I was watching her, last Saturday. I was really on my way to do some shopping, but I just had to stop. She was over on the building site – you know the one? Where the old hotel used to be? It's right next door to us, as a matter of fact. Anyway, she was dancing around, as children do, and I couldn't help noticing – '

'Miss French,' Mrs. Bruce breathed, rather deeply. Nicola could imagine how her forehead would be puckering. 'Mrs French, I beg your pardon . . . I think I'd rather like you to come inside and say what you have to say in front of Nicola's father, if you don't mind. If it wouldn't be putting you to too much trouble?'

'Oh! No, not at all.' Pamela French sounded surprised. She also sounded quite pleased. (How mean can you get? thought Nicola.) 'I'd be only too glad to.'

Nicola watched, with bitterness at heart, as her mother led the way across the hall and into the sitting room. She heard her say, 'Norman, this is Mrs. French − ' and then the door closed and all sound was cut off. Inch by inch, she squirmed her way down the stairs. It was a trick she'd learnt in the past; if you sat on the very bottom step and leaned as far forward as you possibly could, and provided the television wasn't turned on, you could hear almost every word that people were saying. Even if anyone came out when you weren't expecting it you weren't likely to be caught, because the banisters were the filled-in sort and gave perfect cover for a quick scamper back to safety. Rose had once informed her, in her goody-goody way, that it was a sin to eavesdrop, but Nicola didn't see why it should be. It didn't say anything about it in the Bible. They'd had to learn all the ten commandments by heart for RI last term, and there hadn't been a single thing about Thou Shalt Not Eavesdrop. They'd have said, if it was a sin. Anyway, she didn't care if it was or it wasn't. People *oughtn't* to talk about you behind your back. It was only an excuse for saying horrid things.

Nicola reached the bottom step and carefully lowered herself on to it. Mr. Bruce usually had the television turned on, for the sport, on a Saturday afternoon, but obviously he'd been made to turn it off, because she heard her mother's voice quite distinctly, '*Nicola*? You want *Nicola*?'

'If you think that she'd enjoy it − which I'm sure she would, if the way she was dancing around was anything to go by.' (That was Pamela French.) 'I've never seen a child so absorbed! It was quite magic to watch.'

'But *Nicola* – '

'What exactly – ' Mr. Bruce joined in the conversation ' – what exactly would you want her to do?'

'Let me explain . . . I belong to this little group called "The Silent Theatre". It's what you might call semi-professional. We don't perform for money, but we've most of us been in the business at one time or another – '

'Business?' said Mr. Bruce.

'On the stage.' His wife sounded impatient. She knew more about such matters than he did. 'Dancing, acting . . . that sort of thing.'

'Yes, that's right. A couple of us used to be actresses, I used to be a dancer, Ted – that's the man who runs the group – used to be a professional mime. We try to set our standards as high as possible. That's why, when I saw Nicola – '

'But Nicola can't dance!'

'Actually, I think she probably could, but in any case we don't really need a dancer. We just need a child who's expressive and can move well. What we do, you see, is put on little shows in mime and take them round to the old folks' homes and the hospitals – schools, orphanages – places like that. We've already got one planned for Christmas, which we're in the middle of rehearsing, but the trouble is we're short of a child. It's just for the one sketch – "The Family Portrait". It's great fun. I'm sure Nicola would enjoy it. It's all about this Victorian family sitting for their photograph. What we want Nicola for is the Bad Little Girl . . . we've got a Good Little Boy, but we just can't find a Bad Little Girl anywhere. I've been keeping my eyes peeled for weeks. We did have one, only her family suddenly moved out to Australia, which left us rather in the lurch.'

'But you can't possibly want *Nicola*.' Mrs. Bruce had recovered herself. Her voice was firm. 'Rose is the one you want. She's our little dancer.'

'Yes, Nicola said her sister took dancing lessons.'

'Rose will be only too happy to do it for you. Can't get enough of it, that one. Dancing all the day long . . . up on her toes ever since she was a tiny tot. It's a pity she's not here just at the moment, or you could see for yourself.'

'Yes! I'm sure. The only thing is – '

'I'd have kept her in, if I'd known you were coming. Unfortunately, she won't be back for another hour or so. She's gone off with a friend to watch an old Fred Astaire movie. Would you believe it? He's her idol. Fred Astaire! You'd think he was a pop star, the way she carries on . . . let me show you a photograph of her. Here . . . this is Rose.'

Rose, Rose, up on her toes,
Overbalanced by her big red nose . . .

'This is when she had her first ballet dress – that's her in the school play – that's the show they put on last term at dancing school – and that one was taken just a couple of weeks ago, on her birthday.'

'Ah – ' Even crouched on the stairs, Nicola could detect a certain lack of enthusiasm in the response.

29

Her heart began to warm to Pamela French. Perhaps, after all, not *everybody* thought that Rose was wonderful. 'Yes . . . she's rather a — a *pretty* little girl, isn't she?'

'Oh, she's got the looks.' That was Mr. Bruce. He was proud of the way Rose looked. Rose took after her mother, who had been what Mr. Bruce called 'a stunner' before she had had two children and grown plump. Nicola was more like her father, dark and wiry. '*Interesting*,' people said, when they wanted to be kind.

'Yes, she's a charmer, all right.' Nicola could see her dad shaking his head, with an air of satisfaction. 'No denying that.'

'That's the only thing that worries me, you see.' Pamela French spoke earnestly. 'If it was a *good* little girl that we were after — but it's a bad one we want! Nicola struck me as exactly the right type. I can just imagine Nicola being into all *sorts* of mischief.'

Mr. Bruce chuckled again. 'You can say that again! Drives her mother to distraction, the things she gets up to.'

'That's *precisely* the sort of child we want! Full of naughtiness, full of high spirits — '

'Rose is full of high spirits.' Mrs. Bruce was plainly nettled. 'You couldn't get anyone more high-spirited than Rose.'

'But is she full of natural wickedness?'

'She could act it — she's a lovely little actress. She nearly got a part in *Annie* last year. She got through the first audition. She was called back. It was a very close run thing. Besides – ' Mrs. Bruce hammered home the final nail in the coffin ' – Nicola's not reliable. She gets these fads and fancies . . . nothing ever lasts more than five minutes. You'd find she just wouldn't bother to turn up, or she'd roll in half an hour late. As for learning lines . . .'

'Oh, but there aren't any lines, Mrs. Bruce! It's all in mime.'

'Well, there you are . . . what does Nicola know about that sort of thing? She's never done anything like it in her life. Rose, now, has been at it since she was a toddler. Since she was four years old. You can rely on Rose. Nicola, I just wouldn't answer for. She's got no staying power, that's Nicola's trouble. In any case, it would be inviting disaster . . . she can't even walk across a room without tripping over her feet! No, Mrs. French. I wouldn't be happy, foisting Nicola on to you. Rose is the one you want. Suppose I ask her to pop round and see you when she gets in? That way you could tell her all about it – work out when she'd be wanted for rehearsals, and so on. I'm sure Madame Paula wouldn't mind her missing the occasional class, if it's in a good cause. You'll find her very professional. Very conscientious. She's had a lot of experience . . . you needn't worry that Rose will let you down.'

'Well . . . what can I say?'

Pamela French seemed at a loss. Nicola, still curled into a tight knot at the bottom step, dug her finger-nails hard into the palms of her hands.

Don't let her say yes. Don't let her say yes. Don't let her say —

'I suppose I shall have to bow to your judgement . . . if Rose is the family performer — '

'You won't regret it. Not with Rose. I can vouch for her. What time shall I tell her to come round? Five o'clock? Would that be convenient?'

'Yes, by all means. Five o'clock would be fine. I'll look forward to seeing her.'

'What number was it again? Number — '

The sitting room door opened and her mother appeared. Nicola didn't wait to hear any more: she fled back upstairs, monkeylike, on all fours. There was a general buzz of conversation, then the front door clicked, and from her bedroom window she could see Pamela French walking down the path towards the gate. The front door clicked again, and was shut.

For a second there was silence; then a volley of sound burst forth from the sitting room: her father had obviously turned the television on again. In spite of it, she heard her mother's voice quite clearly, 'Imagine that! Wanting *Nicola* . . .'

3

'Mrs. French,' said Rose, 'used to be with the Royal Ballet.'

'Mrs. French,' said Nicola, 'used to be with the Royal Ballet . . .' She said it in a high-pitched squeak, which was meant to be an imitation of Rose. She was sick of hearing Rose go on about Mrs. French. Mrs. French this, Mrs. French that . . . Mrs. *French* says I'm a natural. Mrs. *French* says I've got rhythm. Mrs. *French* —

'She used to be a soloist,' said Rose.

'So what?' Nicola swung her bag full of school books and caught a passer-by a sharp blow upon the shin. The passer-by turned, and looked at her, irritably. Passers-by always did look at Nicola irritably. There just seemed to be something about her which annoyed people.

'Being a *soloist*,' said Rose. 'With the Royal *Ballet*.'

'Big deal.'

'Some people never get out of the corps. I wouldn't stay if I was always going to be in the corps. Mrs. French says there isn't much danger of it . . . she says I've got too much personality. She says — '

I'll kill her, thought Nicola. If she says it once more, I shall *kill* her.

'She says people with strong personalities don't merge well. She says – '

I don't care what she says. What she says is piffle. Piffle and rubbish and *junk*. I shan't listen to it. I shall close my ears and think of something else.

All very well, but it wasn't that easy; not with Rose prattling nineteen to the dozen at her side. Rose had been unbearable, this last couple of weeks. Ever since she'd been given the part – *Nicola's* part – she'd been like a cat that had got at the cream. Even Madame Paula had faded into insignificance. Now it was all Mrs. French and rehearsal schedules and 'being called'.

'I've been called for next Tuesday . . . I've been called for Sunday morning . . .'

Nicola scowled. She slung her bag of books over her shoulder. It should have been her that was being called – it should have been *her* doing the part. She bet she could do it just as well as Rose. She'd watched her, at home, showing her mother how it went. 'We all come in like *this*, and then I have to do *this*, and then Mama shakes her finger at me, like *this*, and then – ' And then she had to pull a rude face, which was something that Rose couldn't do. Rose didn't know how to pull faces – not real, wicked, ugly faces. Rose only knew how to screw up her nose and look pretty. Nicola couldn't look pretty to save her life, but she did know how to pull a good face. She knew exactly how she would have

done it, if she had been given the part. She'd practised it, in secret, in front of the bathroom mirror,
sticking out her tongue and making her eyes go all
squinty so that she looked like one of the gargoyles
on the roof of the local church. That was how it
ought to look; not all simpering and soppy, as Rose
did it.

Rose was now skipping along the pavement,
getting under people's feet as they tried to do their
last-minute shopping. She had been 'called' for seven
o'clock that evening, which made her even more
unbearable than usual. She was only doing it to show
off. She liked people to stop and watch – she fondly
imagined that they were all thinking how wonderful
she was. Nicola's bet was that some people were
thinking how stupid she looked. Skippity-hopping
about the place. She wished just *one* person would
say something out loud. Something like, look at
that dreadful child showing off . . . Nobody did, of
course. She humped her bag of books, gloomily.
Perhaps they really *were* thinking how wonderful she
was.

Rose did a series of little twirls past a waiting
bus queue and turned, bright-eyed, with her feet
carefully posed in one of her ballet positions, to wait
for Nicola.

'Did I tell you?' Her voice rang out, shrill and
high, about six times louder than usual, so that
everyone could hear. 'Madam Paula's got me an
audition for *The March Girls* . . . if I get it, I'm going
to be Rosemary Vitullo!'

Half the heads in the bus queue turned to stare. A girl of about Nicola's age, wearing school uniform, looked slowly and scornfully from Nicola to Rose and back again to Nicola. Nicola felt her cheeks turn an uncomfortable brick red. Why did Rose have to be so *awful*?

'What d'you mean?' she said, crossly. 'Rosemary Vitullo?'

'In the programme. It's what I'm going to be – my stage name.'

'What d'you want a stage name for?'

'Everybody has one.'

'No, they don't. Some people don't.'

'Only if they're called something nice to begin with . . . Mrs. French used to be Pamela Weston, but her real name was Lake.'

'So what's wrong with that?'

'Pamela Lake in *Swan Lake*?'

'Why not?'

''Cos it sounds stupid.'

'So does Vitullo.'

'No, it doesn't.'

'Yes, it does, it sounds *stupid*. Anyway, I know where you got it from – you got it from that teacher at school. She'll probably sue you.'

'She can't, she's not there any more.'

'She could still sue you. There's probably a law against using other people's names.'

'Well, I'm not staying as Bruce. Bruce is horrible. It sounds like a dog.'

36

'I think it's wrong, changing your name,' said Nicola. 'I wouldn't change mine if I got famous.'

Rose spread out her arms to an imaginary audience.

'What could you ever be famous for?'

'Something.'

'What?'

'Haven't decided yet. Let's go and look in Beames's.'

Rose, momentarily diverted from her embarrassing antics, said, 'What's Beames's?'

'Shop that sells jokes — next door to the Co-op. Let's go and see if they've got any sneezing powder.'

Rose did a little hop.

'What d'you want sneezing powder for?'

'Makes you sneeze. Linda Baker had some at school, it's great. We were sneezing all the time in geography. Mr. Drew thought it was an epidemic.'

'I bet he didn't really,' said Rose.

'Yes, he did. He said, it seems as though we've got the start of an epidemic — and then he told Linda she'd better not do PE if she was as bad as she sounded.'

'I wish I didn't have to do PE,' said Rose. 'I wish I could go to the Royal Ballet School and just do dancing.'

'You're only saying that because of Mrs. French.'

'No, I'm not. I've *always* wanted to go there.'

'So why haven't you?'

''Cos you can't start till you're eleven, that's why.'

''Cos you never thought of it before, *that's* why . . . anyway, I don't expect you'd be good enough.'

Indignant spots of colour leapt into Rose's already pink cheeks.

'I bet I *would*!'

'I bet you wouldn't. You have to be *really* good to get into the Royal Ballet School. Linda Baker's got a cousin who's tried three times, and *she's* got gold medals.'

'So have I!' shrieked Rose. 'I've got gold medals!'

'Yours are only tap: *hers* were for ballet. You haven't got any for ballet.'

For one satisfying moment, Rose was silent; then sullenly she said, 'I bet I *could* get in, if I tried. I bet if I asked Mrs. French she'd say I could.'

Nicola tossed her head.

'Ask her, then.'

'I will!'

'Bet she'll say you need gold medals.'

'Bet she won't! Bet she – '

'Oh, shut up,' said Nicola, suddenly growing bored. 'Let's go in and see if they've got any of this sneezing powder.'

The sneezing powder was available: it was the money which was not. Nicola, as usual, was broke. She always spent her pocket money within hours of receiving it. Rose, on the other hand, quite often saved hers. Nicola looked at her, hopefully.

'Why don't *you* buy some?'

'Don't want any,' said Rose.

'But it's only fifty p.'

Rose considered a while.

'I'll lend it you,' she said, at last. 'But you'll have to pay interest. People always pay interest. You'll have to pay – ' she did some calculations on her fingers ' – five p. And I want it back on Saturday otherwise it'll be *ten* p.'

'All right,' said Nicola.

They walked up the road, with the packet of powder. Nicola took a quick look inside, just to make sure that it was the same sort as Linda Baker had had. Rose peered disparagingly over her shoulder.

'Is that all it is? Looks like curry powder to me . . . I bet that's what it is. I bet it's curry powder.'

'Tisn't!' Nicola snatched the bag away, jealously. 'It's special stuff that makes you sneeze.'

'Bet it wouldn't make me sneeze.'

'Course it would! They couldn't sell it if it didn't work. Here – ' She pushed the bag back again. 'Try it and see.'

Cautiously, Rose dipped her nose inside. In fairness, it was quite a small nose. It wasn't really the big, red, beaky thing that Nicola liked to sing about.

'There you are!' Rose raised her head, triumphant: not even the suspicion of a sneeze. 'Told you it wouldn't do anything.'

'That's because you didn't get enough. You have to *sniff* at it, not just hover over it.'

Rose puckered her lips uncertainly.

39

'Miss Joyce says it's not good for you, sniffing things.'

'That's glue, stupid! She didn't mean sneezing powder . . . go on! Do it properly.'

Still, Rose hesitated.

'I don't like the smell of it.'

'You won't *notice* the smell once you're sneezing – anyway, you've got to, now. It wouldn't be fair if you didn't.'

'Oh, all *right*.'

None too happily, Rose plunged her nose back into the bag. Nicola waited, in expectation. Quite suddenly, Rose gave a scream. The bag fell to the ground as both hands flew up to her face.

'What's the matter? What's the matter?'

Nicola stared at her sister in alarm. The forget-me-not eyes had gone all big and swimmy. Tears were coursing down her cheeks, mingling with the traces of powder to form great yellow-brown stains. Nothing like this had happened at school. What they'd done at school, they'd all sprinkled a bit on the backs of their hands and sniffed at it just before going into class. They'd started sneezing almost immediately – Mr. Drew really *had* thought there was an epidemic. Everyone had sneezed and sneezed. Rose wasn't sneezing so much as wheezing – as well as she could, for sobbing.

'What is it?' said Nicola. People were beginning to stare. Trust Rose to make a scene. 'What's the *matter*?'

'It hurts! It hurts!'

Rose roared the words at a hundred decibels. Heads turned, in all directions, and a lady who had stopped to watch now came over and said briskly, 'Where does it hurt? Can you breathe properly?' which Nicola couldn't help thinking was rather a silly question, seeing as Rose was yelling at the top of her voice. Rose, however, who always responded to an audience, only sobbed the louder and dramatically declared that she could hardly breathe at *all*.

'But where does it hurt? Not your chest?'

'Everywhere!' shrieked Rose. 'It hurts the back of my nose and it hurts my eyes and it hurts my throat and – '

The lady turned sternly to Nicola.

'Where does she live? Do you know?'

Nicola swallowed, and pointed down the High Street.

'Just over there. Fenning Road.'

'Then we'd better take her home straight away. Come along, little one! Let's get you back to Mummy.'

Nicola felt slightly sick – partly at Rose being addressed as little one, and partly at the thought of what Mrs. Bruce was likely to say when she saw the state she was in.

Mrs. Bruce said exactly what Nicola had feared she would say, 'For goodness' *sake*, Nicola! What have you done *now*?' Unfortunately, that was not all that she said. When Rose had been pacified and tucked into her bed with an aspirin and a mug of hot chocolate, and when the doctor had been telephoned and had made reassuring noises about no harm being likely to have been done, and agreeing noises about it being criminal that shops should sell such things, and certainly it ought to be looked into, she said a great deal more.

'I don't blame you for buying the stuff – I blame the shop for selling it. What I *do* blame you for is bullying Rose into sniffing at it.'

'I didn't *bully* her. She wanted to know if it worked.'

'Well, now you've discovered that it doesn't, so perhaps you'll be satisfied. Another time, just think before you do these things. It could have been disastrous. Surely to goodness you're old enough to know that you don't go about sniffing substances that could be dangerous?'

'I didn't know it was dangerous! A girl at school had some. We – '

'Oh, so it's going round the school, is it?' Mrs. Bruce pursed her lips. 'In that case, I think I'd better come up and have a word with Mr. Henry before someone really gets themselves hurt.'

'It's only *sneezing* powder.' Nicola was growing desperate. Her mother coming to see Mr. Henry was the last thing she wanted. Linda Baker would be furious. 'It doesn't *do* anything.'

'What do you mean, it doesn't do anything? You saw what it did to Rose.'

Nicola felt like saying, 'Oh, well, *Rose*.' It would do something to Rose. Everyone knew that Rose enjoyed being the centre of attention. She only had

to fall over in the playground to stand there blub-
bering until a member of staff came running up and
made a fuss of her.

'It could have been extremely nasty.' Mrs. Bruce
sounded cross. She obviously didn't think Nicola was
showing sufficient repentance. 'It could have affected
her breathing – she might even have had to go to
hospital. Then how would you have felt?'

Nicola looked down at the floor and didn't say
anything.

'You wouldn't have felt very good, would you?
No. Well, then . . . you just think about it. As it is,
we've been lucky. The doctor thinks she'll probably
have nothing more than a sore throat and a bit of a
headache, though goodness knows that's bad
enough. She won't be able to go to rehearsal tonight,
that's one thing you've achieved. Mrs. French isn't
going to be very happy with you.'

I bet I'd go to rehearsal, thought Nicola. I bet I
wouldn't let a sore throat stop me. I bet I'd go if
I was *dying*.

'You'd better run down the road,' said Mrs. Bruce,
'and explain to her what's happened. Tell her that
you're very sorry, but your sister won't be able to be
there – and you can tell her why, while you're about
it.'

'What, me?' Nicola was resentful. It wasn't her
fault Rose was lying in bed pretending to be ill. *She*
hadn't told her to sniff half the bag up her nose.
Anyone with any sense would have known. 'Why
should I have to go and do it?' It was bad enough,

43

knowing that Rose had pinched her part – *her* part, that *she* had been wanted for – without having to go and make excuses for why she couldn't turn up. 'Why can't you telephone?'

'Because I don't wish to telephone! I wish you to go round there and explain, as politely as you can, what has happened. I should think in the circumstances it's the very *least* you can do. You can eat your tea, then you can get straight round there – and mind you give her the full version. Just remember . . . I shall be checking!'

4

The house that Mrs. French lived in was old and
tall, with a broad flight of steps leading up to the
front door and others that went down to a basement.
Nicola wasn't sure whether she ought to go upwards
or downwards. She had a vague idea that basements
were strictly for delivery boys and servants (in the
days when there had been such things) but the front
door seemed far too grand for common-or-garden
mortals such as herself to use. She wondered what
Rose would do, if Rose were here – and knew at
once that Rose, without the least hesitation in the
world, would go marching up to the front door. All
right, then: if Rose could do it, so could she.

Determinedly, she climbed the steps, taking them
sedately one at a time instead of at her usual full-
tilted gallop. The front door had two stained glass
panels and a big black knocker in the shape of a
lion's head, the actual knocking part being an iron
ring which the lion held clamped between his teeth.
Look as hard as she might she couldn't find any signs
of a bell, so gingerly, scared of setting up too much of
a racket (Mrs. Bruce was forever complaining of the
noise she made) she took hold of the iron ring and

let it fall back against the door. It didn't seem to make much of a sound, but obviously somebody must have heard it, for a light had been turned on in the hall and was shining through the stained glass panels. The door opened and there was Mrs. French, dressed in a sweater and jeans, with her hair in a pony tail. She looked surprised to see Nicola.

'Hallo, Nicola! Did you knock?'

'Yes,' said Nicola.

'Really? I didn't hear it – you'll have to learn to be a bit bolder! I only came down because I thought I heard the gate go. So, what can I do for you?'

'My mother said I was to come and say that I'm very sorry but Rose won't be able to be at the rehearsal tonight.'

'Oh, dear! That's a blow. I hope she's not poorly?'

'She took sneezing powder,' said Nicola, 'and made herself ill.'

'Took sneezing powder? Good gracious! That doesn't sound a very Rose thing to do. Is she going to be all right?'

'She's just got a bit of a headache and a sore throat. And actually – ' she had to force herself to say it ' – actually, it was my fault. She said I was to tell you. She said she was going to check.'

'Did she, indeed?' Mrs. French pulled a face. 'Then I must remember that you've faithfully carried out instructions . . . in what way was it your fault?'

Nicola hesitated. She didn't really believe that it *had* been her fault. Not altogether.

46

'I suppose,' she said, grudgingly, 'because it was my sneezing powder.'

'Ah!' Mrs. French laughed. 'That sounds more like it . . . I couldn't imagine *Rose*!'

'She didn't have to sniff it,' said Nicola.

'No, I'm sure she didn't. But since she did, and since it *was* your sneezing powder, I really think you ought to pay penance, don't you?'

Nicola frowned, not quite certain what penance meant. If it meant handing over money, then she couldn't, because she hadn't got any. Specially not now that she owed Rose fifty p — fifty-*five* p — and all for nothing. That was the really bitterest part of it. A whole packet of perfectly good sneezing powder just left there, lying on the pavement, for nine and a half million feet to trample on. It'd probably be ground into dust by now. Why the silly thing couldn't have held on to it —

'How about taking her place?' said Mrs. French. 'At the rehearsal? We really do need someone there, even if it's only to get the timing right . . . how about it? Just for this evening? I'm sure you could do it.'

Nicola was sure she could, too. She didn't know whether to scowl and mumble, or stand on her head by way of jubilation. In the end, she didn't do either, but simply pushed her fringe out of her eyes with one finger and said carelessly, 'All right, I don't mind.'

'Good! I'll pick you up in about — ' Mrs. French looked at her watch ' — about quarter of an hour.

Tell your mother I'll bring you back again, of course, as I do Rose.'

'All right,' said Nicola.

As she reached the bottom of the steps, Mrs. French called after her, 'You don't by any chance have a pair of ballet shoes, do you? No? Well, not to worry . . . bring some plimsolls. They'll do just as well.'

Mrs. Bruce didn't believe it when Nicola said that she was to take Rose's place at the rehearsal.

'You? What's she want you for?'

'She says she needs someone to be there even if it's only to get the timing right.'

'Well, she won't get it right with you around, that's for sure.'

'Why won't she?' said Nicola.

'Because you don't know anything about it . . . what do you know about counting bars?'

Nothing; she didn't know anything. She didn't even know for certain what a bar was. Rose was the one that was musical. Rose always had been, right from her cradle. She *hated* Rose. Sullenly, she said, 'I might as well not go, then.'

'Oh, you'll have to go if you've said you will. Just try to behave yourself and do what you're asked to do. It's only the one night. Rose will be back again on Sunday.'

The rehearsal took place in a room attached to one of the local churches (the one with the gargoyles). It had big coloured pictures of Jesus hanging on the walls, which just at first Nicola found rather off-putting. It didn't seem right to be pulling faces and sticking out her tongue in front of Jesus – it seemed almost as bad as if she were doing it in front of Mr. Henry, at school. But then, after a while, she became so absorbed in the story that she didn't really care. She forgot about Jesus, and concentrated all her attention on being a bad little girl – *the* Bad Little Girl. The part that by rights should have been hers. She was sure Rose couldn't do it properly. Rose simply didn't know anything about being bad.

To her great relief, she found that there wasn't any question of counting bars. The music – played on an old upright piano that stood in a corner by a fat lady wearing hundreds of cardigans – was the busy, bouncing sort where you knew automatically when you had to come in and when you had to do things.

She was rather surprised to find that it wasn't Mrs. French who was in charge of the rehearsal, but a small, bandy man called Mr. Marlowe. Mrs. French was playing the part of the Elder Sister. There was Mama and Papa, Elder Sister, Elder Brother, Nurse-maid with Baby (Baby was only a doll), Bad Little Girl, Good Little Boy and Photographer. Mr. Marlowe played the Photographer as well as conducting the rehearsal. Nicola thought it was hilarious. He was pretending to use an old-fashioned camera, which meant that he had to keep pulling an imaginary cover over his head whenever he looked through the lens. Every time he stopped being the Photographer in order to go back to being the man in charge of rehearsal, he would solemnly pause to remove the non-existent cover from his head before addressing them. The lady playing Mama, seeing Nicola convulsed with giggles, explained that it wasn't quite as silly as it might seem.

'One of the secrets of being a successful mime is really to *feel* the object that you're miming; so that if you were miming a jug of milk, say, and the front door bell suddenly rang, you wouldn't just let go of it in mid-air, you'd put it down on a table. That's why Ted has to keep taking his cover off . . . he really does *feel* that he's got his head underneath it, and obviously, if he has, then he can't speak properly, can he? We wouldn't be able to hear him.'

Nicola was much struck by this view of things. She tried very hard to remember it when her turn came. Mr. Marlowe had explained to her that what she had to do was take an imaginary mouse out of the pocket of her imaginary dress (Mrs. French had already told her what sort of dress it would be, and where the pocket was to be found) and she was to hold it up to the camera so that it could have its picture taken. At a certain point in the music – the bit where the piano did a sudden twiddle and went PLONK – the mouse was going to escape, on-purpose-by-accident, into the room. Nicola and everybody else had to follow it with their eyes, so that the audience would know where it was and what it was doing. (What it did in the end was run up Elder Sister's dress, so that Elder Sister screamed and jumped on her chair.)

'Remember, Nicola,' said Mr. Marlowe, 'we really have to *see* that it's a mouse. Not a doll, or a ball, or anything like that. It's got to be a mouse, or people won't understand what's going on.'

Nicola didn't have any trouble at all imagining a mouse. She had had a mouse of her own once upon a time. Unfortunately, she had forgotten to shut his cage properly one day and he had got out and frightened Rose into hysterics, so that Mrs. Bruce had said that if she wasn't going to look after him properly he would have to go, but she could still remember the way he had felt in her hands, all warm and tiny and quick-moving. She wondered why Rose hadn't mentioned anything about this particular bit. She'd mentioned almost everything else. It was odd, thought Nicola, considering this was one of the most important bits there was. After all, if the mouse didn't escape then the Elder Sister wouldn't scream and jump on her chair, and Papa wouldn't hold the Bad Little Girl up by one ear and shake her, and the Elder Brother and the Photographer wouldn't go running round the room brandishing fire irons; and if nobody did any of that, then half the fun would be gone.

Nicola concentrated very hard, therefore, on making her mouse into a real mouse — so much so that when Mr. Marlowe, emerging from his cover, suddenly cried, 'Cut! Polly, darling, could you move a bit further in? That's better . . . all right, let's take it again,' she was very careful to restore him to her imaginary pocket before folding her hands once

51

more in her lap and resuming her pose. She knew that the mouse was real for *her*, because when he finally escaped she could actually see him scurrying across the floor, so that it was all she could do not to go chasing after him. Whether or not she had made him real for other people she wasn't sure, but she thought perhaps she must have done because at the end, when the photograph had at last been taken and the scene was over, Mr. Marlowe called out, 'Splendid mouse, Nicola! Well done! What colour was it?'

Nicola answered without hesitation, 'White, with brown ears,' because that was what her own mouse had been; and everybody laughed except Mr. Marlowe, who said, 'No, seriously, it's important . . . if she hadn't known what colour it was, I'd have been extremely disappointed. OK, everyone! Let's have a quick coffee, then run it once more.'

The lady with the cardigans, whom everyone called Marge, was already busy with a kettle and an array of mugs which stood on a table near the piano. For Nicola and the Good Little Boy (his name was Mark and he was six years old and looked almost too good to be true) there was a choice between hot milk and lemonade. Nicola had lemonade, because she thought that Rose would probably have had hot milk. Mark also had lemonade, because he said he'd had hot milk once and there'd been a skin on it.

'Ugh!' said Nicola. 'Horrid!'

'Rose always drinks hers,' said Mark.

'Rose *would*.'

Mark looked at her, solemnly. He had huge grey eyes in a small, heart-shaped face topped by a cap of thick gold hair. Nicola could quite understand why it was that he had had to be a *good* little boy. He was even more unsuited to badness than Rose.

'Isn't Rose coming back any more?' he said.

'Don't know.' She did know, of course. To say that she didn't simply wasn't true. Still, she'd said it now.

'I wouldn't mind,' said Mark, 'if she didn't. I'd sooner have you. I like your mouse better than I like hers.'

'*Do* you?'

'Yes. I do,' said Mark; and he nodded, to emphasize the fact. 'I think it was a super mouse. I could see that it was brown and white.'

'Brown ears,' said Nicola.

'Brown ears,' said Mark. 'I could see it.'

Nicola beamed. Really, she thought, in spite of looking so terribly good, Mark was quite a nice little boy. That was something else that Rose had never mentioned.

Mrs. French, who had taken her coffee away into a corner with Mr. Marlowe, suddenly turned and beckoned to her. She had a smile on her face, so Nicola knew it couldn't be that she'd done anything wrong. She bounced across, still beaming.

'Nicola – ' Mrs. French held out a hand. 'We wanted to ask you something . . . how would you feel about playing the part of the Bad Little Girl all the time?'

Nicola's beam turned into a half-witted gape.

'Instead of Rose?'

'It's the mouse, you see.' Mr. Marlowe sounded apologetic. 'We've never been too sure that your sister actually likes mice.'

'No, she doesn't,' said Nicola. 'She goes into hysterics.'

'Ah! That would account for it.'

Account for what? wondered Nicola. Had Rose been going into hysterics at rehearsals?

'Tell me,' said Mrs. French. She leaned forward, on her chair. 'Would Rose be very upset, do you think, if you did the part instead of her?'

Nicola thought about it.

'Yes,' she said. 'I expect so.'

Mrs. French and Mr. Marlowe exchanged glances.

'Suppose we wrote Rose in as something else?' That was Mr. Marlowe. 'We could always use another sister.'

'A good little sister to go with the good little brother?' That was Mrs. French.

'Why not? They could come in together, holding hands.'

'And what would she do while the mouse chase was going on?'

'Well – ' Mr. Marlowe made a gesture. 'She could always run across to Nurse and hide in her petticoats.'

'Mm . . . yes. That's not a bad idea. It wouldn't be such a good part as the one she's got now, of course.'

'No, but it would still be a part. It would be up to her what she made of it.'

'True.' Mrs. French turned back to Nicola. 'How do you feel about it, Nicola? Would you like to play the Bad Little Girl?'

'*Would* she? She'd been playing it in secret for weeks. Mr. Marlowe laughed.

'I can see by her face that she would . . . all right, then, Supermouse! The part's yours.'

'But don't forget,' said Mrs. French, quickly. 'We want Rose as Youngest Sister. You'll tell her that, won't you?'

Nicola nodded, breathlessly. She was too delirious for speech.

'We mustn't make it sound as if we don't want her any more. It wouldn't be fair just to discard her. She's put in a lot of hard work, after all.'

'Oh yes,' said Mr. Marlowe. 'She's a proper little trouper. No denying that.'

'Just not right for this particular part.'

'Unlike old Supermouse here.' Mr. Marlowe grinned: Nicola grinned back. 'Come on, then, Supermouse!' He set his coffee cup to one side. 'Let's be having you . . . time we got stuck in again.'

It was half-past nine when Mrs. French dropped Nicola off in Fenning Road.

'Don't forget,' she said. 'Tell Rose we definitely still want her.'

'Yes. All right.' Nicola, in her eagerness, was already through the gate and half way up the path. 'I'll tell her.'

She hopped up the step into the front porch and jabbed her finger on the bell, keeping it pressed there till someone should come.

'What's all the panic?' It was her father who eventually opened the door. 'Don't tell me they've landed at last?'

'Who?' Nicola paused impatiently, already poised for flight.

'The little green men,' said Mr. Bruce.

'Oh!' She didn't have time, just now, for her father's jokes; she had news to break. She tore across the hall and into the sitting room. 'Mrs. French wants me to – '

The words died on her lips: Rose was there, curled up in pyjamas and dressing gown on the sofa. She had obviously been allowed to come downstairs and watch television to make up for having missed the rehearsal.

'Mrs. French wants you to what?'

Her mother twisted round to look at her. Nicola stood awkwardly on one leg in the doorway. Somehow, with Rose there, all triumph had gone.

'She wants me to – '

'Well?'

'She wants me to do the part – '

She tried not to look at Rose as she said it, but her eyes *would* go sliding over, just for a quick glance. A quick glance was enough: Rose's pink cheeks had turned bright scarlet, her freckles standing out like splotches of brown paint carelessly flicked off the end of a paint brush. Nicola forced herself to look at something else. It seemed too much like spying, to look at Rose.

Mr. Bruce came back in, closing the door behind him. He gave Nicola a little push.

'Born in a field?'

Nicola didn't say anything. He was always saying 'Born in a field?' when she didn't close doors behind her. Mrs. Bruce, leaning forward to see round her husband as he crossed back to his arm chair, said, 'What do you mean, she wants you to do the part?'

'She wants me to do it – instead of Rose. But it's all right,' said Nicola. 'She still wants Rose. She wants Rose to play another part . . . she wants her to be the *good* little sister.'

'There isn't any good little sister!' Rose's voice was all high and strangulated. 'There isn't any such part!'

'They're going to write it in,' said Nicola, 'specially for you. Mr. Marlowe said you were a proper little trouper, and Mrs. French said you'd done a lot of hard work and it wouldn't be fair to – to discard you. So they're going to make this other part, and you're going to come in with the Good Little Boy, and hold his hand, and – '

'I don't want to hold his hand! I don't want another part!' Tears came spurting out of Rose's eyes. 'I want my own part!'

'Hush, now, Rose, there's obviously been some mistake. Did you tell Mrs. French, as I told you – ' her mother looked at Nicola, mistrustfully ' – that the reason Rose couldn't come to rehearsal this evening was because you'd made her sniff powder up her nose?'

Nicola nodded.

'*Did* you?'

'Yes! I did! That's why she made me take her place. She said I'd got to pay pence.'

'Pay pence?' Mrs. Bruce looked bewildered. 'What are you talking about?'

'What she said . . . she said I'd got to pay pence.'

'Penance,' said Mr. Bruce. 'Do I take it we have some sort of crisis on our hands?'

Mrs. Bruce tightened her lips.

'Nothing we can't get sorted out. Rose, do for heaven's sake stop making that noise! How can I get to the bottom of things if I can't hear myself speak?'

Rose subsided, snuffling, into her dressing gown. Mr. Bruce, shaking his head, disappeared into his paper. He usually washed his hands of it when it came to what he called 'female squabbles'.

'Now, then!' Mrs. Bruce turned back again to Nicola. Her voice was brisk and businesslike. It was the voice she used when she suspected someone of not telling her the entire truth. It meant, *let us get down to brass tacks and have no more of this nonsense.* 'What exactly did Mrs. French say?'

'She said, how would I feel like playing the part of the Bad Little Girl all the time.'

'Instead of Rose?'

'It's because of the mouse. Rose can't do the mouse the same as I can.'

'Yes, I can!' Rose sat bolt upright on the sofa.

'No, you can't,' said Nicola. 'You don't like mice.'

'What's that matter? It's not a *real* mouse.'

'But you have to pretend that it is! You have to *feel* it – '

'I do feel it! I feel it all wriggling and horrible!'

'If you thought it was horrible,' said Nicola, 'you wouldn't have it with you in the first place.'

'Yes, I would!'

'No, you – '

'Do they have to?' said Mr. Bruce.

'No, they don't.' Mrs. Bruce spoke scoldingly. 'Be quiet, the pair of you! This is ridiculous. How can Nicola possibly take over the part at this late stage? Rose has been rehearsing it for weeks.'

'Anyway, what's *she* know about it?' Rose jerked her head, pettishly, in Nicola's direction. '*She's* never acted.'

'Quite. I really think, Nicola, you're being just a tiny bit selfish. When it's Rose who's done all the hard preliminary work – just to come waltzing in and reap the benefit. It's not very sisterly, is it?'

Nicola stuck out her lower lip. Her mother, seeing it, changed tack. Her voice became coaxing.

'You know how much it means to Rose. For you, it's just fun. For Rose – well! For Rose it's everything. After all, she's the one who's going to make it her career. It really means something to Rose. Surely – '

She broke off and smiled, hopefully. Nicola said nothing. She could be stubborn, when she wanted; and now that she'd got the part, she certainly wasn't going to be talked into giving it up just to satisfy Rose.

'Make her!' Rose's voice rang out, shrill and accusing from the sofa. 'Make her say she won't do it!'

'I can't make her,' said Mrs. Bruce. 'It must be Nicola's own decision.'

Her father lowered his paper and looked at Nicola over the top of it.

'I suppose you couldn't just say yes and keep them happy?'

Why should I? thought Nicola.

'After all . . . anything for a quiet life.' Mr. Bruce winked at her. He quite often winked at Nicola over the heads of Rose and her mother. It was supposed to convey a sense of fellow feeling: Us Lads against Them Womenfolk. Usually she responded, but today she did not. She just went on standing there, stony-faced, in silence.

'No?' said Mr. Bruce. 'In that case — ' he raised his paper again ' — there's nothing more to be said. She's been offered the part, she obviously wants to do it, so let's not have any argument. Rose will just have to take a back seat for once.'

Mrs. Bruce looked at her husband, frowningly.

'It really isn't playing fair, to take away a part that's already been given to someone else . . . I'm surprised that Mrs. French would do such a thing.'

'But I was the one she wanted all along!'

The words had slipped out before she could stop them. Mrs. Bruce turned, sharply.

'How do you know?'

'Because – because she told me.'

'She didn't,' screamed Rose. 'It's a lie!'

''Tisn't a lie!'

'It is! It is! Why should anyone want you? You can't dance! You can't – '

'Rose, be quiet! *And* you, Nicola. Brawling like a couple of alley cats. You can both get up to bed.'

It was rare for Mrs. Bruce to grow as cross with Rose as she did with Nicola. Rose pouted, but none the less humped herself off the sofa. She trailed rebelliously in Nicola's wake to the door.

'Good,' said Mr. Bruce. He rustled his newspaper. 'If that's all settled – '

'It's not all settled.' Mrs. Bruce plumped up the cushion where Rose had been sitting. 'As soon as you two get back from school tomorrow we're going down the road to talk to Mrs. French. We'll see what *she* has to say about it. In the meantime, you can both of you get upstairs and put yourselves to bed . . . I've had quite enough of your bickering for one evening!'

5

The next day, after tea, both Rose and Nicola were
marched down the road to Mrs. French. They stood
on the front steps behind their mother as she
knocked at the door with the lion's head knocker.

'Now you'll see,' said Rose.

They were the first words she had addressed to
Nicola all day. Nicola didn't deign to reply. She was
thinking, if Mrs. French lets her have the part back,
it will be the meanest thing I ever heard . . .

It was Mr. French who opened the door – at least,
Nicola assumed that it was Mr. French. He was
youngish, and good-looking, with long, curly black
hair and a gold chain round his neck with a med-
allion hanging from it. When Mrs. Bruce explained
that they had come to see Mrs. French, he twisted
round to look at a grandfather clock in the hall and
said, 'Can you bear to wait five minutes? She won't
be long, she's just giving a class. Due to finish any
time now.'

He led them through into a front room which
was cluttered with books and stacks of gramophone
records.

'Sorry about the mess – we've never quite got

around to finding a home for everything. We're still having the place done up, which means only half the rooms are habitable. Now, what can I offer you? Can I offer you coffee? No? You're sure? Well, in that case perhaps you'll excuse me if I slope off. She shouldn't be too long.'

As Mr. French left the room, Rose turned excitedly to her mother.

'I didn't know Mrs. French gave *classes*.'

'I expect they need the money. Big place like this . . . must cost a lot to keep up.'

Rose clearly wasn't interested in what things cost to keep up: her mind was running on quite other lines.

'Do you think *I* could have classes with her?'

'You?' Mrs. Bruce looked at her in surprise. 'Why should you want classes with her? What's wrong with Madam Paula?'

'Nothing,' said Rose. 'But Mrs. *French* used to be with the Royal Ballet.'

'That doesn't necessarily make her a good teacher. In any case, you don't want to specialize in ballet. You've always said you want to be in musicals.'

'She's changed her mind,' said Nicola. 'She wants to go to the Royal Ballet School now.'

'*Do* you?'

Rose had turned pink beneath her freckles. She shot Nicola a venomous glare.

'I've always wanted to.'

'I never knew that! Why on earth didn't you say so before?'

''Cos she never thought of it before.'

'Yes, I did! I thought of it — '

'Enough!' Mrs. Bruce held up a hand. 'Don't for heaven's sake start that again.'

'But I did think of it before! I thought of it *ages* ago.'

'Then you should have said ages ago. We could have done something about it.'

'We still could,' said Rose. 'You don't start there till you're eleven. If I could have classes with Mrs. French — *can* I have classes with Mrs. French?'

'But what about Madam Paula? She mightn't like it.'

'It wouldn't matter about Madam Paula if I was going to the Royal Ballet School . . . *can* I? *please*? Say that I can!'

'Well . . . I don't know. I suppose, if you're really set on it — '

'I *am*,' said Rose. '*Honestly*. I really *am*. I've been set on it for *years*. I've — '

'All right, all right! You've made your point. I believe you.'

'So will you ask her? This evening? *Will* you?'

'Yes, yes. I'll ask her this evening . . . as your father would say, anything for a quiet life.'

Rose beamed, triumphantly, in Nicola's direction: she'd got her own way again. She was *always* getting her own way.

Mrs. French came in wearing black tights and a sweater, with her hair pulled back into a knot, the way it had been that first day, on the building site.

'Hallo, Mrs. Bruce! Rose, Nicola . . . what's all this?' She laughed. 'A deputation?'

Nicola, embarrassed, sat on her hands on the extreme edge of an arm chair, whilst Rose moved up closer to her mother on the sofa.

'I hope it's not inconveniencing you.'

Mrs. Bruce made it sound as though even if it were she had no intention of going away again. Nicola cringed. If the arm chair had had a cushion she would have put it on her head and pretended not to be there. As it hadn't, she kept her eyes fixed firmly on a pile of books which had been stacked in the hearth. The top one was called *Theatre Street* by somebody whose name she couldn't pronounce: Tamara Kar-sav-in-a. She heard Mrs. French say, 'No, not at all! As a matter of fact, I'd just come to the end of a class, so you chose a good moment – that's a very famous book, by the way, Nicola. Written by a famous Russian ballerina. You can borrow it, if you like.'

'Can I?' Nicola looked up, avidly. She liked it when people offered to lend you their books: it showed they trusted you.

'Remind me to let you have it before you leave.' Mrs. French perched herself amiably on the arm of another chair, similar to the one that Nicola was sitting in. 'You might like to read it as well, Rose. It's all about life in a Russian ballet school.'

Rose looked dubious: she wasn't much of a reader. She tugged, impatiently, at her mother's arm. Mrs.

Bruce, who had been starting to say something, broke off.

'What?' She bent her head. Rose whispered, urgently. 'Oh, yes! All right. Let's get that out of the way first . . . Rose is nagging me to know whether it would be possible for her to take some classes with you. Apparently, she's set her heart on going to the Royal Ballet School – '

'The Royal *Ballet* School?'

The way Mrs. French said it, Nicola was pleased to note, she made it sound as if Rose were asking to have tea with the Queen. She couldn't have made it clearer that in her opinion Rose didn't stand a chance. A warm glow of satisfaction slowly spread itself through Nicola's body. So much for Rose. Maybe she *wasn't* so wonderful, after all.

'It's an extremely difficult place to get in to, you know.'

'I know,' said Rose. She sounded complacent: if anyone could get in there, *she* should be able to.

'Did you know that out of every four hundred applicants only about thirty are chosen? And at least ten of those will be boys?'

Rose made a little pouting motion with her lips.

'She has been dancing a long time,' said Mrs. Bruce. 'Ever since she was four years old. She's had a lot of experience.'

'Ah, but it's not just a question of experience, Mrs. Bruce – '

'You need gold medals.' Nicola couldn't help it: she *had* to say it. 'You need gold medals, don't you?'

'Well, no, as a matter of fact, you don't! You not only don't need gold medals, you don't even need to have done a step of ballet in your life. In fact, sometimes they prefer it if people haven't because it means they won't have been able to develop any bad habits.'

'I'm sure Rose hasn't developed any bad habits,' said Mrs. Bruce.

'Well, no, it's quite possible that she hasn't. I'm just pointing out that a totally inexperienced girl stands every bit as much chance of getting in as one who's been doing it since she was a baby . . . Nicola, for example.' Mrs. French paused. 'She'd stand just as much chance as Rose.'

Rose didn't like that. Nicola could see that she didn't. Mrs. Bruce, quite plainly, didn't believe it.

'Surely,' she said, 'there has to be natural talent?'

'Oh, yes! Yes, that's the very thing they're looking for — that plus the right physique. Lots of girls are turned down simply because they don't meet the physical requirements. It doesn't mean they can't still go on to be dancers. There's no reason on earth why Rose shouldn't have a go, if she wants. I'm just warning her not to be disappointed, that's all.'

'Perhaps if she were to take a few classes with you first — '

'I'm afraid that wouldn't be possible, Mrs. Bruce. You see, I don't teach full time — I only take a very few selected pupils. Usually girls who are already in the profession. I very very rarely work with the younger ones. Only in the most exceptional cases.'

Mrs. Bruce bristled slightly: she was accustomed to think of Rose as being exceptional.

'You know what I feel?' said Mrs. French. 'I feel that Rose is far too much of an all-round performer to tie herself down to just one branch of show business. Especially ballet, which is so restricting. Where does she have classes at the moment?'

'She goes to Madam Paula's. It's where she's always gone.'

'Then I think that's exactly where she ought to keep on going. It'll not only give her a good general grounding as a dancer, it'll provide her with the opportunity to develop any other talents she may have, as well. Who knows? She might have potential as an actress, or a singer – '

'Oh, she has.' Mrs. Bruce nodded. 'Madam Paula's already told us. In fact, she's going up to London for an audition later this month. It's for *Little Women – The March Girls*, they're calling it. We're hoping she might stand a chance as Amy.'

'I'm sure she'd make a lovely Amy.' Mrs. French smiled. Rose smiled back, uncertainly. Nicola could tell that she was trying to make up her mind whether the thought of making a lovely Amy was sufficient compensation for not being considered exceptional enough to have classes with Mrs. French.

'Even if she doesn't get one of the leads,' said Mrs. Bruce, 'I keep telling her, there's bound to be lots of other parts.'

'Well, of course.'

'I always think it's worth trying. It'll stand her in good stead later, when she's doing it for real.'

'Yes, indeed. I'm all for people having a go.'

There was a silence. Nicola looked down again at the pile of books. She didn't know why, but she had the feeling Mrs. French wasn't really very interested in Rose. It was odd, because people usually were. You'd have thought, being a dancer, that Mrs. French would be.

'Anyway — ' Mrs. Bruce cleared her throat. 'The thing we really came about was this part that Rose is doing for you. Nicola said something about you wanting her to take over. I told her, it's ridiculous, at this late stage. She must have got it wrong.'

'She hasn't got it wrong, Mrs. Bruce. I did ask her if she'd like to, but only because we have something else in mind for Rose — we do definitely still want Rose. Did Nicola not tell you?'

'Yes!' Nicola's head jerked up, indignantly. 'I did tell her! I told her you wanted Rose for the youngest sister.'

'That's right.' Mrs. French nodded. 'We decided that what we'd like was a Good Little Girl to go with the Good Little Boy — Rose struck us as being the very person. As you say, it is rather late to be changing things round, but Nicola already seemed to know most of the Bad Little Girl's part, and I have every confidence in Rose being able to pick things up just as quickly as if she were a pro — which, indeed, she practically is! Certainly she will be if she gets into the West End.'

Mrs. Bruce looked round, doubtfully, at Rose.

'The only thing is, she seems to think it's not a proper part.'

'Oh, but it is! I assure you . . . we're writing it in specially.'

Rose, burying her head in her mother's shoulder, made some utterance that only Mrs. Bruce could hear. Mrs. Bruce patted her hand, consolingly.

'I'm sure Mrs. French will do what she can. You must remember, though . . . it's not always the largest parts that are the best parts. Not by any manner of means. Isn't that so?' She appealed to Mrs. French, who said, 'Any professional will tell you, Rose . . . a part's what you make it.'

'Not if it's not a real one.' The words came out, muffled, from Rose's buried head. 'Not if it's just a *pretend* one.'

'But it's not a pretend one! Mrs. French has already told you . . . she's writing it in specially.'

'I don't want it! I want the other one — the one I had before!'

Mrs. Bruce looked up; half apologetic, half accusing.

'It is very upsetting for a child, to have something that's been given her suddenly taken away.'

'Yes, I do realize that, Mrs. Bruce. That's why I've made sure she's being offered something else.'

'I don't want something else!'

'Not even if it's something that's far better suited to you? Just think! No more horrible mice!'

'She's worked very hard at that mouse,' said Mrs. Bruce.

'Yes.' Mrs. French sighed. 'We really do appreciate all the work she's put in. That's why we don't want to lose her. But you do know, don't you, Rose – ' leaving her perch on the arm of the chair, Mrs. French sank down, gracefully, on to her heels beside the still sniffling Rose ' – you do know that if you're going to go into the profession you'll have to be prepared to take some pretty hard knocks? It won't do you any good just sitting down and crying – you have to learn to take the rough with the smooth. Things don't always work out just the way we'd like them to. Suppose, for instance, you were offered the part of Amy, and then suddenly the director decided that the girl playing Beth would be better as Amy, and that you'd be better as Beth – '

'I wouldn't mind playing Beth! Beth's a *real* part.'

'But so is the Youngest Sister . . . I promise you! You'll have plenty of things to do.'

'I don't want to play the Youngest Sister! I want to be the Bad Little Girl!'

Mrs. French sat back on her heels. Mrs. Bruce looked at her, challengingly, as if to say, 'Well? And what now?' Rose just sat there, weeping. Nicola regarded her sister with contempt. All this fuss over a mere *part*.

'Dear oh dear!' Mrs. French shook her head. 'The last thing I wanted to do was cause any unhappiness. I'd hoped I'd managed to find a satisfactory solution . . . now what do we do? I can't very well ask Nicola to play the Youngest Sister, can I?'

There was a silence, broken only by Rose's snuffles. Nicola could guess what she was thinking. She was thinking that as far as she was concerned there wasn't any reason why Nicola should be asked to play anything at all. Mrs. Bruce was probably thinking exactly the same thing.

'I suppose – ' Mrs. French spoke pleadingly to Rose ' – I suppose you couldn't possibly think of the production as a whole? How much better it would be if we had a really *bad* Bad Little Girl and a really *good* Good Little Sister?'

Rose buttoned her lip.

'No.' Mrs. French pulled a rueful face. 'I suppose not. I should have stuck to my guns right at the beginning – it's my own fault. I just didn't want to cause any ructions in the family. Now it looks as though I've caused one anyway.' With an air of somewhat weary resignation, she rose to her feet. 'I honestly don't know what to say, Mrs. Bruce. I've offered Rose another part; what more can I do? I can only repeat that we should be extremely sorry to lose her – and that the part *is* a real part, if she cares to make it one. It's entirely up to her. If she's as professional as I think she is . . .'

There was a silence, while everybody looked at Rose, and Rose looked at the carpet.

'I'll tell you what.' Mrs. French crossed to the door. 'I'll go and make us all a cup of coffee, while Rose sits here and has a think. I'm sure when she's done so she'll realize that things aren't anywhere near as bad as they seem. It's simply a question of changing one part for another. Nothing so very catastrophic.' She held open the door, looking at Nicola as she did so. 'Coming?'

Nicola jumped up, gladly: she was only too pleased to escape. She followed Mrs. French down a passage and into a large, Aladdin's cave of a kitchen, with stone flags on the floor and a sink the size of a bath tub, with two of the most enormous taps she had ever seen. In the middle of the flags stood a wooden table about ninety feet long – well, say fifty feet long – at any rate, a great deal longer than the table in Mrs. Bruce's kitchen. This table wouldn't even fit *into* Mrs. Bruce's kitchen. Mrs. French pressed a switch attached to something which looked like a large thermos flask.

'Tell me – ' she began unhooking mugs from a row of hooks on the wall ' – does Rose always get whatever she wants?'

'Yes,' said Nicola. 'Usually.'

'What about you? Do you?'

'Well – ' She considered the question, trying to be fair. 'Sometimes.'

'Haven't you ever wanted to learn dancing, as Rose does?'

Nicola frowned, and ran a finger along the edge of the table. Once, ages ago – ages and *ages* ago – she had thought that perhaps she might. She had mentioned it one Christmas, when her grandparents had been there. Her grandfather, teasing, had said,

'What! A great lanky beanpole like you?' Her grand-mother, trying to be kind, had told her to 'Come on, then! Show us what you can do'; but when she had, they had all laughed at her. Rose had laughed louder than anyone. Mr. Bruce, afterwards, feeling sorry for her, had pulled her on to his knee for a cuddle and said, 'She might not be any good at waving her legs in the air, but she makes a smashing centre-forward – don't you, me old Nickers?' She'd given up the idea of dancing classes after that. Dancing was stupid, anyhow. She'd far rather play football.

'No?' Mrs. French was looking at her. Nicola hunched a shoulder. 'What made them send Rose for lessons?'

'Don't remember. 'Spect they thought she'd be good at it.'

'And they didn't think you would be?'

'S'pose not.'

'Do *you* think you would be?'

'Don't know.'

'Well, let's have a try,' said Mrs. French. She suddenly left her coffee mugs and advanced upon Nicola round the table. 'How old are you?'

'Eleven,' said Nicola.

'Eleven and how much?'

'Eleven and two months.'

'Right. So let's see what you're like on flexibility . . . if I support you, how far back can you bend?'

Nicola didn't need support – she could bend as

far back as anyone wanted her to. She could go right over and touch the floor. But that wasn't dancing, that was gymnastics. She was quite good at gymnastics. She could turn somersaults and do the splits and walk on her hands, and all sorts of things.

'What about frog's legs?' said Mrs. French. 'Stretch out on the – no, wait! It'll be cold. Lie on this – ' she snatched a coat off a peg and spread it out. 'Lie on your back, as flat as you can . . . that's it. Now, put the soles of your feet together and bend your legs outwards as far as they'll go, making sure your knees are touching the floor . . . that's not bad at all! Quite a lot of natural turn out. What are your feet like?'

'Just feet,' said Nicola, bewildered. Even Rose didn't have special sort of feet. At least, she didn't think she had. She was sure her mother would have mentioned it if she had.

Mrs. French laughed.

'Don't look so worried. I'm not looking for extra toes – though if the first three did happen by any chance to be more or less the same length, it would be a distinct advantage. Makes point work far easier. Let's have a look. Come on! Up on the table and get your socks off . . . mm, well, two the same length. Good high arches. Any trouble with your ankles?'

Nicola shook her head. This was all very strange. She was sure Madam Paula had never made Rose sit on a table and take her socks off.

The door opened and the curly black head that

belonged to Mr. French peered round. At the sight of Nicola, bare-footed amongst the coffee mugs, he groaned and said, 'Why is it one can never get away from feet in this house?'

'Because feet are important.' Mrs. French handed Nicola her socks back. 'I'm glad to say that Nicola's passed the test with flying colours.'

'Bully for Nicola . . . can I scrounge a coffee?'

'Oh, God, I forgot about it!' Mrs. French flew back across the room to the thermos flask. 'Nicola, I didn't ask you . . . do you drink coffee, or would you rather have milk?'

'Rose has milk,' said Nicola.

'How about you?'

'I don't mind what I have.'

'Spoken bravely,' said Mr. French.

They went back to the front room to find Rose still red-faced and tearful but at least no longer weeping.

'I've been telling her,' said Mrs. Bruce. 'She's still got her audition to look forward to. She might well get something from that.'

'Indeed she might,' said Mrs. French. 'And then think how grand she'd be . . . we'd have to count ourselves lucky if she even passed the time of day with us!'

Rose puckered her lips, to indicate that she knew very well she was only being humoured. She didn't join in any of the conversation which followed, but kept her head bent over her mug of warm milk, not even looking up when Nicola, rather shyly, asked

Mrs. French what it had been like to be a soloist with the Royal Ballet. Mrs. French shook her head.

'I'm afraid I was only a very minor soloist . . . I never aspired to the Lilac Fairy or Queen of the Wilis, or anything like that. Peasant pas-de-deux from *Giselle* was about as far as I ever got. I wasn't really the right physical type. My thighs were always too fat, and my knees were too knobbly.'

'I can hardly believe *that*,' protested Mrs. Bruce.

'Oh, I promise you, it's quite true . . . they may not look particularly fat or knobbly just at this moment, but put them under a tutu and you'd soon see what I mean! One really needs legs like Nicola's – nice and long and straight.'

Nicola had never given much thought to her legs. She knew that they were long, because her mother always said she would make a good wading bird, and sometimes she'd heard people describe her as gangling. She hadn't known that they were *nice* and long – or that they were straight. She glanced at them, now, surreptitiously, as they hung down over the edge of the chair. They just looked like ordinary legs to her. Her mother also glanced at them, not quite so surreptitiously.

'Nicola's legs are too thin,' she said. 'Make her look like a crane.'

'Well, it's better than looking like a female hammer thrower . . . female hammer throwers don't get anywhere; not in ballet. Cranes sometimes do.'

Mrs. Bruce didn't say anything to that. There was

a pause, then she leaned forward to place her mug back on the tray.

'Come along, you two. It's time we were off.' She took Rose's half-empty mug away from her. 'We've imposed on Mrs. French quite long enough.'

'You haven't imposed at all,' said Mrs. French. 'I'm glad that you came. I just hope we see both Nicola *and* Rose at our next rehearsal – oh, and by the way, you may be getting a call from our wardrobe mistress some time during the week. She wants to come round and measure up for costumes. I gave her your number. I hope that was all right?'

'Of course. Though whether they'll both – well! We shall have to see. Nicola, if you're taking that book, you make sure you look after it.'

They walked back up the road in silence, Mrs. Bruce in the lead, Nicola, clutching her book and thinking about her legs (nice and long . . . *and* straight) a few paces behind, and Rose, who usually skipped and hopped and danced about, morosely dragging her feet in the rear. As they reached the house, Mrs. Bruce, holding the gate, said, 'Well?' It seemed to be directed at Nicola. It couldn't really be directed at anyone else – Rose was still trailing, several yards behind. Nicola looked at her mother, warily.

'What?'

'You're determined not to let Rose have her part back again?'

'It's not her part.' Jealously, she hugged *Theatre Street* to her chest. Mrs. French had lent it to *her*, just as she'd given the part of the Bad Little Girl to her. 'It's my part.'

'It *was* Rose's before.'

No, it wasn't, thought Nicola. It was always mine. She walked through the gate.

'She can do the other one – the one they're writing in for her.'

'I won't!' Rose's voice came shrilly from somewhere outside in the road. 'If I can't do the part I want, I won't do any!'

Under cover of the darkness, Nicola pulled one of her squint-eyed faces and stuck out her tongue; then she turned, and stumped off up the path. If Rose wanted to cut herself out entirely, then that was her problem.

6

The problem may have been Rose's, but Rose being
Rose meant the rest of the house were not denied
their share in it. Someone had only to mention the
word ballet, or dance – or even just *performance* – for
the tears to come spurting. For three whole days she
walked round red-eyed, with a wet handkerchief
permanently screwed into a ball, and at mealtimes
sat in silence, toying with her food and saying, 'No,
I couldn't, it'd make me *ill*,' when exhorted by Mrs.
Bruce to try and eat something. She wouldn't speak
to Nicola at all. She wouldn't even say please or
thank you, or ask her to pass the salt, let alone make
any sort of conversation.

Nicola tried hard to tell herself that *she* didn't care
– she wouldn't care if Rose never addressed another
word to her as long as she lived – she didn't even
like Rose; but it was difficult, when it was your own
sister, and you not only had to live under the same
roof but go to the same school and walk the
same corridors. It was difficult not to be affected by
it. One way and another, there was so much reproach
being cast round that it quite soured any personal
triumph she might have felt. Mrs. Bruce had said

her piece and didn't intend saying any more: *she* just looked, and occasionally pursed her lips. But then Mr. Bruce, too, felt the need to join in. He was waiting in the hall one morning, as Nicola came clumping back in her gum boots after taking Ben for his walk.

'Tell me,' he said, 'this part you're doing – the one that Rose was going to do . . . means a lot to you, does it?'

Nicola frowned.

'Mrs. French asked me to do it.'

'Yes, I know she did. I was just wondering . . . how much it meant to you? Whether it was really all that important?'

Nicola concentrated on removing her gum boots before she could be accused of treading mud into the carpet. How could she explain that it wasn't the part in *itself* which was so important – though the part was fun, of course. She enjoyed conjuring up imaginary mice and pulling rude faces, and she rather thought she was going to enjoy doing it in front of an audience as well; but what was more important was the fact that Mrs. French had wanted *her. Her* instead of *Rose*. That was what was really important. Nobody, in the whole of her life, had ever preferred her to Rose before.

Her silence obviously made Mr. Bruce uncomfortable: he never liked having to speak seriously to her about anything.

'I just thought I'd ask.' He ruffled her hair with clumsy affection. 'Don't you worry about it. It's your part, you go ahead and do it. Rose will get over it. Not the end of the world.'

On Saturday afternoon the wardrobe mistress came round to take measurements. Her name was Miss Harris, and she reminded Nicola, rather unpleasantly, of a teacher she had once had at primary school. The teacher had been thin and waspish, with big globular eyes, and had disliked Nicola from the word go. Miss Harris didn't have globular eyes, but she was certainly thin and waspish. Furthermore, she was most put out when she discovered that it was Nicola she had come to measure and not Rose.

'Where's the other one?' (Her voice was *definitely* waspish.) 'The little one with the freckles? I thought she was the one that was doing it.'

Mrs. Bruce looked at Nicola rather hard.

'She was doing it, until Mrs. French changed the parts around.'

'Oh? So what part is she playing now? I didn't know there *were* any other parts. I thought I'd already measured for them all. What part is she playing?'

'She isn't,' said Mrs. Bruce, 'any more.'

Miss Harris made an irritable clicking noise.

'It would help if they'd keep a person informed . . . I've gone ahead and chosen all the materials now. Arranged all the colour schemes.' From out of a large plastic carrier bag she pulled a length of buttercup yellow material. 'This would have suited the other little girl beautifully. I don't know how it's going to look on this one.'

82

'Yellow doesn't really suit Nicola,' said Mrs. Bruce.

'No, it doesn't. She's far too sallow.' Miss Harris draped the material over Nicola's shoulder and turned her towards the light. She tutted again, impatiently. 'It's going to make her look as if she's got jaundice.'

'That's what I've always found,' said Mrs. Bruce. 'I never buy her anything in yellow if I can help it. Or pink. Blues and browns suit her best.'

'Well, she can't have either blue *or* brown, I'm afraid. They wouldn't go with my colour scheme. It'll have to be the yellow . . . my goodness! You are a skinny one! Where's your waist? You don't seem to have any.'

Nicola was affronted. Of course she had a waist! It was there, in the middle of her body, the same as everyone else's. What was the woman talking about?

'I suppose this must be it, here.' Resigned, Miss Harris wrapped a tape measure round her. 'There isn't any difference between your waist and your hips. I shall have to bulk you out. It doesn't matter so much about the top half, but you've got to have *some* shape . . . what are you going to do about your hair?'

Nicola looked instinctively at her mother for guidance. Mrs. Bruce sighed.

'I never know *what* to do about Nicola's hair.'

'It ought to be long, if it's Victorian. That's another expense . . . I'll have to hire a wig – unless we could get away with a hair piece.' Miss Harris picked up a handful of Nicola's hair and regarded it doubtfully. 'Hm! There's not much of it, is there?'

'I try to keep it fairly short,' said Mrs. Bruce. 'It looks better that way.'

'Yes; it would.' Miss Harris, disparagingly, let the hair fall back where it belonged, on top of Nicola's head. 'No body, that's the trouble.' Rose's hair, of course, had plenty of body. It sprang about all over the place. Even when it was wet it was all thick and bunchy. When Nicola's was wet it just clung limply about her face in hanks. 'Oh, well!' Miss Harris squared her shoulders. 'We shall just have to do the best we can.'

From the tone of her voice, it didn't seem that she held out much hope of the best being anything very satisfactory. Nicola began to feel like an undersized chicken that wasn't even fit to have its neck wrung.

'I suppose they must know what they're about,' Miss Harris grumbled to herself as she took down measurements. 'They wouldn't switch parts for no reason. I must say, the other little one always looked all right to me, but then I'm only wardrobe. Nobody ever considers wardrobe. First they expect you to operate on a shoestring – '

Shoestring? thought Nicola. What on earth was a shoestring? Did she mean shoelaces? Perhaps when she'd been young people *did* tie their shoes with bits of string. Come to think of it, they probably did. Shoelaces most likely wouldn't have been invented at the turn of the century. She still didn't see how

you could *operate* on one. She came to the conclusion
that Miss Harris was loopy. What with not knowing
where people's waists were, and then thinking that
someone wanted her to operate on a tiny bit of
string . . .

'It's always the same,' Miss Harris grumbled on.
'They seem to think you can work miracles. They've
got no idea how much things *cost* these days.'

Mrs. Bruce nodded, sympathetically.

'They ought to try buying school uniforms —
they'd learn soon enough. You take a simple thing
like a blazer — '

Miss Harris wasn't interested in simple things like
blazers. She seized Nicola's hand and crossly jerked
her arm out straight.

'Materials have gone up and up — and *then* there's
all the sewing to be done. They don't take into
account the reels of cotton one has to buy. Keep
still, child, and don't wriggle! How can I measure
you if you're moving about all the time? In future,
I shall tell them, you go to a theatrical costumier.
It's all very well, saying they want to build up their
own wardrobe, but who has to do all the work? I
wouldn't mind if they'd just keep me informed. But
when they go round changing parts at a moment's
notice — '

Nobody (except, presumably, Miss Harris) ever
knew what happened when they went round changing parts at a moment's notice, because at this point
the door crashed open and an apparition burst in.
Miss Harris broke off in mid-grievance. She stared,

slack-jawed, across the room. Nicola and Mrs. Bruce also stared. The apparition stood and simpered. It was wearing a pink net party frock and had its face plastered in make-up, the mouth a red gash, the eyes bright green surrounded by thick rings of black, some of which had been smudged and transferred itself to neighbouring portions of the face. A strong aroma of perfume filled the air.

'What on *earth* – ' Mrs. Bruce took a step forward. 'Is that my Chanel you've been at?'

For just a second, the apparition showed signs of uncertainty. The simper faltered – as well it might, thought Nicola. She was awed, in spite of herself. Mrs. Bruce's Chanel was more precious than the Crown Jewels. More precious than *gold* dust. It had been a present from Mr. Bruce on their last wedding anniversary. It was in the tiniest bottle that anyone had ever seen, and Mrs. Bruce had told them repeatedly that 'If I catch *either* of you, *ever*, touching my Chanel – '

'My goodness!' cried Miss Harris. She giggled. 'It does smell nice!'

Confidence reasserted itself: the apparition broke into a happy beam.

'Rose, this is not funny!'

Mrs. Bruce, all too obviously, was not finding it so; neither was Nicola. It was the first time she could ever remember that Rose had really done something awful. It didn't seem right, coming from Rose. Nicola was the one that did the awful things: she was the one that got slapped and told off and had her pocket money stopped. This was turning everything topsy turvy. Only Miss Harris still seemed to find it funny. Even Rose had stopped beaming and was beginning to quiver. Mrs. Bruce advanced upon her wrathfully.

'How much have you used? Half the bottle, from the smell of you!'

'I should think she's bathed in it,' said Miss Harris. She giggled again. 'At least she's got good taste!'

Mrs. Bruce was too cross to be amused. Nicola could see that she was cross – her lips had gone all pinched and her cheeks were sucked in. When that happened, it meant trouble. Nicola had observed it all too often.

'How many times have I told you that you are *not* to touch my Chanel? And what's that make-up doing, smeared all over your face? Where did you get it from? Out of my bedroom! You have no *right* to go into my bedroom, helping yourself to my things. Look at the mess you've made! You've got lipstick all over that frock. If you've got it on my bedroom carpet, I'm warning you, there's going to be trouble. What for goodness' sake did you think you were doing?'

To this, Rose made no reply – probably couldn't, thought Nicola, from the depths of her own experience. Already the tears had come gushing. Two black rivulets were slowly rolling down the rouged cheeks, leaving dirty trails behind them. Nicola turned away, not liking to look. She knew what Rose had thought she was doing: she had thought she was making an impression on Miss Harris. She had thought Miss Harris was going to turn round and say, 'Oh! What a dear little girl! We *must* have her in the show instead of the other one.' She hadn't got the least idea that she looked ridiculous. She'd done her eyes like Mrs. French did hers — *tried* to do her eyes like Mrs. French did hers — and put on her best dress and come prancing downstairs without a doubt in the world but that she was going to be crooned over. Nothing else could have given her the courage to drench herself in Chanel — although, upon reflection, it probably hadn't been a question of courage, with Rose. Rose was always so sure of herself — always so *sure* that she was pretty, so *sure* that everyone was going to approve of her — that very likely she'd just have gone marching straight in and helped herself without even giving it a second thought.

Nicola watched, in awed silence, as a weeping Rose was led away. For once in her life, she was glad she wasn't in Rose's shoes. Pinching Mrs. Bruce's Chanel was almost the worst thing that either of them had ever done. (Not that Rose ever *did*.) It was far worse than just smashing windows or setting light to the fence. It was even worse than when Nicola had scrubbed the dining room table with bleach and taken all the polish off. At least on that occasion she'd had the quite genuine excuse that she thought she was helping — she'd only been six years old. You didn't know any better at six years old. Rose was ten, and certainly knew better.

She wondered if she felt like gloating. She tried a

few gloating thoughts, by way of experimenting . . .
Rose, getting whacked . . . *Rose*, getting told off . . .
Rose, having her pocket money stopped . . .
Somehow, the gloat wouldn't come. All she could
think of was Rose standing there looking ridiculous
with eye make-up running all over her face.

'Well!' Miss Harris seemed in better humour than
she had before. 'What a little monkey! That's what
I should call a *really* bad little girl.' She laughed,
tinnily, as she ran the tape measure down Nicola's
leg. 'Good gracious, child, you're all limbs!'

Nicola glowered beneath her lashes. What did she
mean, all limbs? She only had four, didn't she, the
same as other people? And Rose *wasn't* bad. Nicola
was the one that was bad. That was why Mrs. French
had wanted her.

'I wonder,' mused Miss Harris, 'if we might be
able to get you a *blond* wig? Anything to make you
look less sallow . . . it's a pity you haven't got your
sister's colouring. We could have got away without
make-up, with her. You're definitely going to need
something on those cheeks, especially standing right
next to Mark. He's such a very *fair* little boy. You're
not going to look a bit like brother and sister. Still
– ' she rolled up her tape measure and with an air
of fatalism stowed it away in the plastic bag ' – I
suppose they must know what they're doing.'

Mrs. Bruce came back, looking flustered.

'Honestly! That's nearly half a bottle of expensive
perfume gone. I simply cannot imagine what came
over her.'

'Oh, they get the devil in them at times.' Miss Harris spoke with the air of one who knows. 'We can't expect them to be little angels.'

'Well, I wouldn't say that Rose is a little angel, but she's certainly never done anything like this before. I can only excuse her on the grounds that she has been very upset just lately. It came as quite a shock when Mrs. French suddenly decided to take the part away from her like that – she's been sobbing her heart out for the last three days. The poor child couldn't understand what she's supposed to have done wrong.'

'She didn't do anything wrong,' said Nicola, 'she just wasn't *bad* enough.'

'Well! Not bad enough!' Miss Harris echoed the words, with another of her tinny laughs. 'I've never heard that one before!'

'She was supposed,' said Nicola, 'to be playing a bad little girl.'

'It seems to me, she is a bad little girl!'

'She's not as a rule,' said Mrs. Bruce. 'She's usually good as gold. As a matter of fact, I'm really rather worried about her. She hasn't eaten anything for – '

'Oh, if she wants the part as badly as all that she might as well *have* it.' Nicola stalked across the room. '*I* don't care.' She tore open the door. 'I didn't really want it, anyway.'

'Nicola!' Her mother's voice stopped her as she was half way up the stairs. 'Come back a minute . . . I want a word with you.'

If she was going to have a go at her for being *rude* –

'Come on!'

Sulkily, Nicola went back down.

'Did you really mean that?' said Mrs. Bruce. 'About letting Rose take over the part again?'

No . . . *no*! She didn't really mean it, she shouldn't ever have said it, it was *her* part, Mrs. French had given it to *her* –

'Did you?' asked Mrs. Bruce.

Nicola clenched her fists tight behind her back. She nodded.

'Are you quite sure? It's not something you're going to regret?'

She was already regretting it. She *hated* Rose. Rose had *every*thing.

'It would certainly make life a lot easier,' said Miss Harris.

'It would certainly make Rose a lot happier.' Mrs. Bruce smiled at Nicola. 'I'll tell you what . . . as a reward, I'll buy you those running shoes you wanted. How about it? Would that please you? We might even stretch to a new top, as well, if you like. You deserve something. Suppose I meet you after school on Monday and we go down the road and have a look?'

Nicola tried to feel enthusiastic at the prospect, but it wasn't any use. She couldn't – not now. It had come too late. She'd wanted the running shoes in September. She didn't really care about them any more. She hunched a shoulder.

'All right.'

'*Thank* you,' prompted Mrs. Bruce.

'*Thank* you,' said Nicola.

She supposed she should have known better than to expect any gratitude from Rose. When she went downstairs at four o'clock to have tea (having spent the past hour seeking solace in her bedroom with Ben — not that Ben was terribly good at solacing: he tended to think life was just one big joke) she found her father watching football and Rose stuffing herself with buttered crumpets.

'Where's mine?' said Nicola.

Rose beamed greedily. She had trickles of melted butter running down her chin.

'You weren't here, so I ate them.'

'Pig!'

'You should've have come earlier. They go flabby if they're left.'

'Don't want any, anyhow.'

'You'd better.' Mr. Bruce spoke without taking his eyes off the football. 'Your mother's out in the kitchen right now doing some more.'

Nicola knelt down on the hearthrug with Ben. They both of them looked accusingly at Rose, stuffing the last piece of crumpet into her mouth.

'You'll get fat,' said Nicola.

'No, I won't. Miss Harris said I've got a nice little shape.'

'*Yuck.*' Nicola made a being-sick noise.

'She said it was just as well I was doing the part again . . . she said you'd have looked all wrong in it.'

'She's just stupid.'

'No, she isn't.' Rose had obviously found an ally in Miss Harris. 'She said she couldn't understand why they'd ever changed the parts round in the first place . . . she's going to tell Mrs. French that now I've got it back again I've got to keep it because she's going to run the costume up this evening. She says Mrs. French'll probably be quite glad, secretly. After all – ' Rose, with relish, licked buttery fingers ' – I was the one she originally wanted.'

Nicola's face turned scarlet with indignation.

'*I* was the one she originally wanted. She wanted me *ages* before she wanted you. You've only got it back again because *I* said you could.'

Rose was not one to be easily shaken: when it came to her own self-esteem, she always had an answer ready.

'I s'pose you got cold feet. Amateurs usually do.'

The *cheek* of it. It almost took one's breath away. Nicola leaned forward and hissed furiously in Rose's face.

'If you want to know the truth, it was because I felt sorry for you, making such an *idiot* of yourself.'

'You'd have made an idiot of yourself, if you'd gone ahead and done it!'

'I jolly well wouldn't have made such an idiot of myself as you did . . . you had *eye* black all over your *face*. You looked *ridiculous*.'

'No, I didn't!'

'Yes, you did!'

'No, I – '

'For heaven's sake!' Mr. Bruce snapped off the television set. 'Can't you two ever conduct a civilized conversation? Just give it a rest for five minutes!'

They subsided, glaring at each other. Ben, evidently feeling the occasion called for a comic turn, rolled over on to his back and lay there, grinning, with his legs in the air.

'That's better.' Mr. Bruce picked up the *Radio Times*. 'Bit of peace and quiet for once.'

Mrs. Bruce came into the room carrying the teapot and a dish full of hot buttered crumpets.

'Ah, Nicola, there you are.' She put the teapot in the hearth and the dish of crumpets on a small side table. 'Has Rose thanked you nicely for letting her have the part back?'

Nicola looked, and said nothing. Rose, with a pout, muttered something that might or might not have been 'Thank you'.

'Well! That wasn't very gracious, was it?' Mrs. Bruce settled herself into an arm chair. 'Surely you can do better than that?'

Rose turned slightly pink (with vexation rather than embarrassment).

'Thank you very much,' she said, 'for letting me have the part back . . . but I *was* the one they originally wanted.'

'Rose! That's quite enough. Nicola's been very generous, don't go and ruin it. Pass her the crumpets.'

Rose, with bad grace, did so. Nicola took one and dropped it without much enthusiasm on to her plate. Squidgy fat crumpet. It made her feel sick.

'Eat up, then.' Mr. Bruce was watching her. 'No danger of *you* putting on weight . . . you don't really mind too much about this part, do you?'

Nicola swallowed.

'Not particularly.'

'Not going to make you unhappy, is it?'

She forced back tears.

''Course not.'

'I shouldn't like to think you'd been pressurized.'

Nicola didn't know what pressurized meant. She only knew that she certainly wasn't going to let *Rose* see she cared.

'Didn't really want it, anyway. It's soppy, all that sort of thing.'

Rose's voice rang out, shrill and piercing, from the other side of the hearth, 'You won't think it's soppy when I'm famous . . . when I'm rich and on television and everybody's heard of me!'

Nicola felt a large wodge of crumpet moving slowly down the centre of her chest towards her stomach.

'Who wants to be rich and famous?' said Mr. Bruce. 'There's more to life than that, you know. I'll tell you what, me old Nickers!' He leaned towards her, and tweaked companionably at her hair. 'How about you and me going down to Selhurst Park next Saturday? Eh? See Palace at home to West Ham? Should be a good game. What d'you reckon?'

He was trying to be nice to her. Nicola choked. She didn't *want* people to be nice to her – she didn't *want* to go down to Selhurst Park, she didn't *want* to see Crystal Palace at home to West Ham. All she wanted was to play the part that she had been chosen for. And now she couldn't because she'd gone and given it back to Rose, who was nothing but a mean and hateful pig and didn't deserve it.

'So how about it?' said Mr. Bruce. 'Long time since we've been to a game together . . . shall we make it a date?'

Nicola pushed the remains of her crumpet towards Ben.

'S'pose we could,' she said. 'If you want.'

7

The week that followed was disastrous: everything went wrong that possibly could. Miss McMaster, in English, told her that her latest essay was 'a *sad* disappointment . . . not at all what I've come to expect of you' (she'd been too busy thinking about Mrs. French and the mime show to concentrate properly on writing essays). Mr. Drew, in geography, said that her map drawing was a 'most miserable effort', and that if that was the best she could do she had better stay in at break and trace the outline of Italy six times by way of practice. In singing she was told off for making up what Miss Murray called 'stupid and ridiculous words' to the song they were supposed to be singing – instead of *Sleep on a little while, and in thy slumber smile*, Nicola had sung, *Sleep on a wooden door, and in thy slumber snore*, which everybody else had thought quite funny, but Miss Murray notoriously had no sense of humour. She had said that if Nicola persisted in such juvenile behaviour, she would have no option but to report her. Finally, just to round off the week, she had been sent out of an RI class by Miss Joyce for being 'impertinent and unwholesome'; and while she was standing under the clock in the front hall, which was where sinners were traditionally sent to stand, Mr. Henry had come out of his study and said, 'Good heavens alive, Nicola! Not you again?' Her form mistress had said that if there was any more of it, she would seriously have to consider talking to her parents.

'I hear nothing but reports of how you refuse to co-operate, or how you've been a disruptive influence. It really isn't good enough, Nicola. You're a bright child — why can't you behave like one?'

Because she didn't want to, that was why. She didn't want to be a bright child, she wanted to be a stupid, pretty, fussed-over, *spoilt* child. She wanted to be a child who always got what she wanted. You didn't get what you wanted by sometimes coming top in exams or being given good marks for essays. Nobody cared about that sort of thing. If Rose went home and said that Madam Paula had told her her pirouettes were the best in the whole class, Mrs. Bruce would instantly stop whatever she was doing and demand to be shown the wonderful pirouettes there and then; but if Nicola went home and said she'd got nine out of ten for an essay and offered to read it aloud, it was, 'That would be lovely, let's wait till I can really sit down and concentrate,' only she never *did* sit down and concentrate because she didn't really *care*. Nobody cared. And if nobody cared, then she couldn't see that it mattered whether she behaved like a bright child or an idiot child, or even like a juvenile delinquent, if that was how she felt. She would behave exactly as she wanted to behave.

On Saturday morning, when Rose had gone to her tap dancing class, she took Ben for a walk.

'Just remember,' said Mrs. Bruce, 'you keep away from that building site.'

Why should she keep away from the building site? She liked the building site. She'd go on a *million* building sites, if that was what she wanted.

Defiant in blue jeans and her gum boots, Nicola stumped up the road and clambered over the earth mound into the mud. Ben slithered joyously at her side – he was already caked all over with clay. He lumbered out of the ditch and shook himself, vigorously: filthy droplets spattered Nicola's sweater. It was the new sweater which she had been bought as a reward for being nice to Rose. Five seconds ago, it had been snowy white, with red ribbing at the waist and cuffs; now it was more a kind of dirty grey, with brown blobs speckled over it. Mrs. Bruce had been doubtful at the time as to the wisdom of buying anything white. Rose had white: Nicola was more a brown and navy type. She had only given way because Nicola for once in her life had been good and deserved a special treat. She was going to be furious when she saw the state she had got herself in.

Nicola scowled. So what? It was her sweater. If she wanted it to be a dirty grey, then it was no one's business but hers.

She played for a while on the mound, while Ben

went splashing off on his own. She tried singing rude songs about Rose — Rose, Rose, wobbling on her toes, Falling in the mud on her big red nose — but somehow the game had lost its charm. It wasn't as much fun as it had been. She had just abandoned the rude songs in favour of seeing whether she could jump the ditch at its widest point, when a voice called out to her from the other side of the earth works. *Splat*, went Nicola; straight into the mud. She hauled herself out and slopped boggily across the sea of clay.

'My goodness!' said Mrs. French. 'You are in a mess!'

So what? They were her clothes, weren't they? It was her skin. If she *wanted* to get herself into a mess —

'I was very sorry,' said Mrs. French, 'to hear that you won't be playing the part for us after all . . . I'd rather been hoping this was one occasion when Rose *wouldn't* get her own way. They didn't make you feel guilty about it, did they? It wouldn't be fair if they did. After all, Rose *was* offered something else.'

'She wouldn't do it,' said Nicola.

'So you had to sacrifice your part? That doesn't seem right.'

Nicola struggled for a moment with self pity.

'Didn't really bother me.' She stuck her thumbs into the back pockets of her jeans and took up an aggressive stance, legs apart, chin tilted. 'Didn't really care all that much.'

'Didn't you?' said Mrs. French. 'I thought you

looked as if you were thoroughly enjoying it that one night.'

Tears pricked at the back of Nicola's eyes. She stubbed the toe of her gum boot into the mud.

'It was all right.'

'I see. So you're not desperately upset about not being in it?'

'Not upset at all. I'm going to see Crystal Palace play West Ham.'

'Are you, indeed? You like football, do you?'

'It's better than dancing . . . dancing's wet.'

Mrs. French pulled just the slightest of faces.

'I'm afraid I don't know anything about football. What is it? A cup tie, or something?'

'*League*,' said Nicola. She couldn't altogether keep a note of scorn out of her voice. Cup tie! Where would Mr. Bruce be likely to get tickets for a cup tie? Anyhow, Crystal Palace were already out. They'd gone out in the first round.

'Well! Let's hope it's a good match,' said Mrs. French.

She smiled, and went on her way. Nicola was left by herself to do battle against a sudden and terrible desire to burst into tears. She mustn't – she *wouldn't*. Crying was ignoble. Crying was what Rose always resorted to. Nicola was tough: *she* didn't care.

'Hi, Nickers!'

Nicola looked up, and through a faint blur saw three of the boys from her class at school – Kevin Batchelor, Denny Waters and Terry Pitsea. They weren't particular friends of hers, though sometimes, as a mark of respect, they let her kick a football around with them. Kevin had once said that she was almost like a boy, and 'heaps better than that stupid sister of yours'.

"Lo.' She turned and whistled at Ben, as an excuse to hide her face until all traces of possible tears might be gone. Nicola could whistle by putting two fingers in her mouth, a feat of which she was justifiably proud. Not even Kevin could whistle like that. She whistled a second time, just for good measure. Ben, needless to say, took not the slightest bit of notice, but at least the tears had dried up. She turned back again. 'Didn't know you lived round here?'

'Bin to see someone.'

"Cept they wasn't in.' Terry scrambled up the earthworks to join her. 'What you doin'?'

'Nothing special.'

'That your dog?'

Nicola looked, and saw Ben on his back, energetically rolling. She nodded.

'What's 'is name?'

'Ben.'

'Come 'ere, Ben!' Kevin, jumping up beside Terry, snapped his fingers. Ben went on rolling. 'Any good at doin' tricks, is 'e?'

'He can beg,' said Nicola. 'Sort of. Sometimes,' she added.

'Does 'e sit, an' stay, an' all that sort o' thing?'

'I expect he would, if he was trained.'

'Let's train 'im now . . . sit, Ben.' Kevin pointed sternly to the ground. Ben stood up and wagged his tail. '*Sit* . . . well, stay, then . . . *stay* . . . there! 'E's stayed. I know a thing or two about dogs, I do. Got one o' me own. All right, Ben, now you c'n sit . . . *sit* . . . 'e's not quite sure of it yet, 'e thinks it means lie down.'

''E thinks it means roll,' said Terry. 'What is 'e, anyway? Sort o' sheepdog, or something?'

'He's a mongrel,' said Nicola.

'They're the best,' said Kevin. 'Look, 'e's learnt already . . . 'e's sittin'. Good boy, Ben! Good boy!'

A small, virtuous voice suddenly piped up from the road outside. 'You'll catch it, you will, playing on that building site.' It was Rose, self-important, on her way home from Madam Paula's. Nicola stuck her tongue out: Kevin put two fingers in the air.

'You just wait,' said Rose.

She trotted on down the road, her hair (full of body) bouncing self-righteously behind her as she went. Denny jerked a contemptuous thumb over his shoulder.

'What's her problem?'

'I'm not meant to play here,' said Nicola. 'She'll be mad when she finds out.'

'Who? Your mum?'

Nicola nodded, gloomily. Rose was bound to tell. It would be the first thing she said, the minute she got indoors: 'I saw Nicola playing on the building site . . .' She grabbed Ben by the collar and snapped on his lead before he could make a break for freedom.

'Let's go somewhere else.'

'Where?'

'We could go up the Common,' said Terry.

'I'm sick o' the Common.' Kevin heaved a lump of rock: it fell with a satisfying *plash* into the ditch full of muddy water. 'Let's *do* somethin'.'

'Let's go and steal a chicken,' said Nicola.

They stared at her; impressed, but wondering.

'Where from?' said Kevin.

'Butcher up the road. He's got hundreds of them, all lying about.'

'But what we stealin' it *for*?' said Denny.

'Steal it for your mum.'

She knew that Denny's mum liked chickens because Denny had written an essay about it which Miss McMaster had read out to the class on the same day that she had told Nicola her work was 'a sad disappointment'. Denny's mum had had a sad disappointment. She had saved up her money for a whole fortnight in order to buy a chicken to make some special West Indian dish for Denny's brother's birthday, and on the way home in the bus her shopping bag had been stolen, so that instead of having chicken for his birthday Denny's brother had had to have a boiled egg, and his mum had made a joke about it and said that instead of having chicken *roast* they were having chicken *boiled* (a joke which some of the dimmer members of the class, having apparently quite forgotten that chickens came out of eggs, had had to have explained to them).

'I ain't never stolen nothin' before,' said Denny.

'Neither have I,' said Nicola. Stealing was wicked:

she suddenly felt excited. 'Wouldn't your mum *like* a chicken?'

'Yeah, but – '

'Denny's chicken,' said Terry; and doubled up laughing at his own wit. 'D'yer get it? Denny's chicken 'cos he's scared to steal a chicken – '

'Even for his own mum,' said Nicola.

'I don't want to get into no trouble,' said Denny.

'You won't get into trouble: *I'*ll get into trouble. *I'*ll steal the chicken and you can just stand and watch . . . come on!' Nicola jumped over the earth works on to the pavement. Now that she'd had the idea, she wanted to put it into practice. 'All those who aren't chicken, follow me!'

Terry ranged himself at her elbow; Kevin, who always liked to be the leader in any joint endeavours, strode a few paces ahead; Denny, still reluctant, brought up the rear. They cut across Fenning Road, went up a side street to avoid any possibility of bumping into Mrs. Bruce, and turned into Streatham High Road.

'Where's this butcher, then?'

'Further down. He's all hidden away by himself. Be easy as pie.'

The butcher may have been all hidden away by himself – he was one of four shops in a tiny passage called Islet Court – but Nicola had forgotten that it was Saturday morning. The shop was crowded with customers, all pushing and cramming. Obviously impossible, even for someone as thin as herself, to wriggle her way through to the front, snatch a chicken from the window, and wriggle out again without being caught.

'So now what we gonna do?' Kevin's voice was challenging. He looked pointedly at Nicola as they stood in a bunch on the opposite side of the road. 'Thought you said it'd be easy as pie?'

Various desperate possibilities flashed across Nicola's brain. She was about to suggest hurling a brick through the window (except that she knew that, when it came to it, she wouldn't dare. Stealing a chicken was one thing: breaking a window was quite another) when Terry, pointing, said, 'What about one o' them?' At the entrance to the butcher's, hanging from a hook, were some brownish-coloured birds with bright tail feathers, vivid blues and greens and reds. They certainly weren't chickens, but they were, presumably, meant for eating.

'What are they?' said Kevin.

Painstakingly, Terry spelt out the hand-written notice propped beneath them.

'*Peasants*?'

'Pheasants,' said Nicola. 'Like in photographs.'

Kevin turned to Denny.

'Your ole lady fancy a pheasant, Den?'

Denny's face was troubled.

'I dunno about no pheasants . . . she never said nothin' about no pheasants. Let's go, man!'

'Can't,' said Kevin. 'Not till ole Nickers's nicked somethin'.'

'Only reason we come 'ere,' said Terry. 'What's the matter? You still chicken?'

'I don't want no trouble.' Denny repeated the words obstinately. 'I already bin in trouble once. You ain't.'

'I bin in trouble!'

'Not with the cops, you ain't.'

'Look, shuddup!' said Kevin, fiercely. 'It's Nickers what's doin' it, not you.'

'Well, she jus' better get a move on, else I'm goin'.'

Everybody turned to look at Nicola.

'Go on, then,' said Kevin.

Nicola swallowed. Now that it had come to the point, she was rather beginning to think that she might be a bit chicken herself. She had just remembered that Mr. Archer, who stood behind the counter in his striped apron, hacking up the joints of meat with his meat axe, sometimes delivered things to Fenning Road in his van. He sometimes even delivered things to Mrs. Bruce. He would know who Nicola was – he would know where she lived –

'Well? Go on!' Kevin was growing impatient. 'You gonna nick a pheasant for Denny's mum or aincher?'

'Yes.' Nicola felt a surge of defiance. From now on, she was going to do just exactly whatever she wanted, no matter *how* wicked it was. In fact, the more wicked, the better.

'What about Ben?' That was Terry, showing sudden and rather belated concern. 'Want me to stay 'ere and 'old 'im?'

'Tie 'im to the lamp post.' Kevin snatched at the lead. ''E'll like that. Dogs go for lamp posts.'

The die was cast. Three abreast, they marched across the road, leaving Ben secured to his lamp post, Denny hovering at a safe distance.

"'Ang about,' said Kevin. 'Someone's comin'.'

He bent, elaborately, to do up his shoelace as one of Mr. Archer's assistants came walking out to the front of the shop. Calmly, the assistant unhooked a couple of pheasants, cast a casual glance at the three children standing on the pavement, and went back inside.

'There y'are,' said Terry. 'Piece o' cake.'

'Wanna leg up?' Kevin cupped his hands together. 'We'll give yer one two three . . . OK? You ready, Tel? One – two – *three* – '

Nicola found herself suddenly thrust up into the air. Wobbling perilously, she made a snatch at the nearest pheasant: the pheasant remained firmly attached to its hook. Nicola struggled, began to overbalance, and clutched in her panic at the entire bunch. As she did so, a voice came booming from inside the shop, 'What the blazes do you kids think you're up to out there?'

Kevin and Terry didn't wait to offer explanations: with one accord, they dropped Nicola and ran. Denny ran with them. Nicola was left, dangling two feet above the pavement, her hands full of dead pheasant. Across the road, Ben barked excitedly. Ben would: he was that sort of dog.

'Well, well!' Two brawny hands reached up and plucked Nicola out of the air. She was set down with a bump on the pavement, at Mr. Archer's feet.

'I seem to recognize you, young lady . . . number nine Fenning Road, if I'm not much mistaken? I think you and I had better pay a little visit to your mother . . .'

'I don't know, Nicola.' Mrs. Bruce came back from closing the front door behind Mr. Archer. Her voice sounded weary. 'I just do not know what we're to do with you.'

Nicola eyed her mother uncertainly. She had braced herself for a scene – a really big, unpleasant sort of scene; the sort of scene that only came once in a lifetime. Stealing was so absolutely and utterly the worst crime that she had ever committed (eclipsing a hundred times Rose's raid on the Chanel, which now seemed almost puny in comparison) that she would not have been surprised if she'd been put on bread and water and shut up in her room for a week.

'I suppose there's no point in asking what made you do it?'

'It was just a sort of – joke, really.'

Joke?

'Well . . . a sort of game. We couldn't think of anything else to do.'

'I see.' Mrs. Bruce compressed her lips into a thin line. 'You couldn't think of anything else to do – *and* you've been playing on that building site again. Even though I specifically told you not to. Well, from now on your father can deal with you. As soon as he gets in from shopping I intend to have a word with him; what happens next is between him and you. I've done my share. I can't do any more. It's about time he shouldered some of the responsibility.'

Mrs. Bruce left the room. A few seconds later, Nicola heard the sound of saucepans rattling in the kitchen. She stood a moment, undecided. She had been prepared for bread and water – she had even been prepared for the police. It wouldn't be the first time Mrs. Bruce had threatened her – 'I'll get the police to you, my girl, if you don't mend your ways.' She had been prepared for almost anything except having her father brought into it. Mr. Bruce never intervened in domestic affairs. He was the one that went out to work and earned a living: Mrs. Bruce was the one who did all the telling off and the managing.

With dragging steps, Nicola trailed up the stairs, with Ben, to her bedroom. Her sole consolation was that at least Rose wasn't there to gloat over her. Rose had gone across the road to play with a friend: Mr. Bruce had gone to get a hair cut and buy some new bits for his electric drill. She wondered what would happen when he came back – whether he would be very angry with her. She could hardly ever remember him being angry; not really *toweringly* angry like Mrs. Bruce sometimes was. He would almost certainly tell her that this afternoon was cancelled. He wouldn't be taking her to Selhurst Park to see Palace; not now. He might never take her again. He might even *beat* her. Mr. Bruce had never raised a finger to either of the girls – he left that sort of thing to Mrs. Bruce. Mrs. Bruce quite often dealt out a sharp slap or a box round the ears, and had once, when Nicola was little, chased her round the garden and halfway up the stairs with a stick. She didn't *think* that Mr. Bruce would do that; but she couldn't be sure.

At midday she heard the front gate click, and peering cautiously out of the left-hand window saw the familiar figure of her father, in his weekend tweedy jacket and brown trousers. He was carrying a small package, which was presumably his new drill bits, and had an expression of happy anticipation on his face. Nicola suddenly felt sorry for him: *he* wasn't to know that in only a matter of seconds he was going to be confronted by the awful news that his elder daughter was a thief. He thought that he was going to sit down, as usual on a Saturday, to one of Mrs. Bruce's casserole stews, followed by rhubarb pie and custard, followed by a trip to Selhurst Park to watch Crystal Palace at home to West Ham. Two stray tears trickled mournfully down Nicola's cheek: why did she always have to go and ruin things for everyone?

Ben, who had also heard the front gate, was already at the bedroom door vociferously demanding to be let out. She opened the door and he was off, bounding down the stairs to give Mr. Bruce the sort of greeting that might have been thought more appropriate for someone who had been away a whole month instead of a mere couple of hours. Nicola watched, over the banisters. She saw her mother come up the hall – saw her say something to Mr. Bruce. It was too low for her to hear, but she was almost certain she saw her mother's lips form the word 'Nicola'. Mr. Bruce's happy expression changed to one of glum apprehension. Together with Mrs. Bruce, and Ben, he disappeared into the front room. The door closed.

It was some while before Nicola could nerve herself to creep downstairs to her listening post. It wasn't so much that she was scared of being discovered as that she was scared of hearing what was being said. She didn't *want* to hear – but she knew that she had to. She had to know what terrible things her father was being told.

By the time she reached the foot of the stairs he had obviously been told the most terrible thing of all: he had been told about her being a thief, and being brought home in disgrace by Mr. Archer. She heard her mother's voice. The tone was slightly raised, and she spoke with an air of finality, 'I told her, from now on I wash my hands of you . . . it's between you and your father.'

There was a pause; then Mr. Bruce said something, too low and rumbling for her to make out the words. Her mother's voice came back at him, sharp and accusing, 'Perhaps you'd have been happier if she *had* been a boy . . . heaven knows, you've done your best to make her one. I suppose you think that stealing pheasants from a butcher's shop is nothing but a mere boyish prank?'

'You did say she did it as a joke?'

'Joke! If that's your idea of a *joke* . . .'

'Well, I don't think it's quite as serious as all that.' Mr. Bruce was obviously moving about the room: his voice kept coming and going. There was a gap, then, 'The girl's no thief. Not in the ordinary sense of the word. What's more important as far as I'm concerned is what's behind it all.'

'What's behind *any* of the things she does?'

'That,' said Mr. Bruce, 'is what we have to try and find out.'

Nicola heard what sounded like a snort from her mother, then more low rumbling noises from her father, amongst which she managed to distinguish the phrases 'drawing attention to herself' and 'sure sign she's not happy'.

'I really don't see why,' said Mrs. Bruce. 'We've always treated them exactly the same.'

'But have we?' Her father had come back within earshot. 'Haven't we tended to make far more of Rose, simply because she's the pretty one?'

'Not at all!' Mrs. Bruce was indignant. 'As if I'd let a thing like that colour the way I treat them! I've treated them *exactly* the same.'

'It's still been Rose who's had all the attention . . . I mean, in the first place, why was it only her we sent off to have these dancing lessons and not Nicola, as well?'

'*I* don't know . . . I suppose at the time we couldn't afford to pay for two lots.'

'So it had to be Rose?'

'Well – yes! She was obviously the one who was going to benefit the most.'

'How do we know that Nicola mightn't have benefited, if she'd been given the chance? This Mrs. French – ' more rumbling: Nicola strained her ears almost to bursting point ' – she seems to think pretty highly of her. Suppose she's right? Suppose the lass has got talent? And we've been crushing it all these years?'

Mrs. Bruce stuck firmly to her guns.

'She's never shown the least sign.'

'Or we've never shown the least interest.'

'She's the one that's never shown the interest . . . *she'd* far rather go off and kick a football around. The only reason she hung on to that part for as long as she did was to keep it from Rose. *She* didn't want it: she just didn't want Rose to have it.'

'I still think she should have been given the chance. We should have let her show what she can do. It wouldn't have hurt Rose, to suffer for a bit.'

'You say that *now*?' Mrs. Bruce sounded bitter. 'You were the one who said you didn't like to see her so upset.'

'Oh, I admit it! I was as much at fault as anyone. I see now that I was wrong – we were *both* wrong. We should never have – '

Never have what? Nicola's ears, distended to about twice their normal size, flapped in vain against the banisters. The next words were from her mother, 'Well, I don't know . . . you may be right. Unfortunately it's a bit late in the day to do anything about

114

it now. We can't take the part away from her a
second time – anyway, the costumes have already been
made.'

More rumbling.

'What about this audition you're taking Rose to?
Couldn't she go with you to that?'

'What? You mean actually do an audition herself?'
Mrs. Bruce spoke doubtfully. 'I suppose she *could*.'

'Well, and why not? Why shouldn't she? You said
when you went along to that *Annie* thing there were
kids who couldn't even sing in tune.'

'I'm not altogether certain that Nicola can.'

'So give her a chance! She might surprise us all.'

There was a pause; then: 'Are you going to talk
to her?' said Mrs. Bruce.

'Yes, yes, leave it with me. I'll attend to it.'

'When?'

'Oh . . .'

Nicola could see her father humping his
shoulders, in the way that he did when her mother
was nagging at him to do something that he didn't
want to do. *When are you going to cut that grass? When
are you going to change the washer on that tap?* WHEN
ARE YOU GOING TO TALK TO NICOLA?

'I'll do it this afternoon,' said Mr. Bruce. 'In half-
time.'

'Half-time? What half-time?'

'Selhurst Park . . . we're going to the match. Had
you forgotten?'

'Actually, I had.' Her mother's tone was dry. 'I've
had rather more important matters on my mind –

115

such as apologizing to Mr. Archer. Speaking of which, I shouldn't have thought that a child who steals pheasants *deserves* to go to football matches.'

'Oh, let her be . . . she's had enough to put up with just lately. She did give Rose her wretched part back; you've got to grant her that. She could quite easily have hung on to it – after all, she *was* the one they originally wanted. Not only that – '

Not only that, someone had just come in at the front gate. It must be Rose. Nicola sprang up from her hiding place and went to open the front door, as a person might do who had just been casually coming down the stairs and just happened to be passing.

Rose looked at her, triumphantly, as she walked up the path, balancing on the cement rim which bordered it.

'Did you catch it?'

'Catch what?' said Nicola. 'Housemaid's knee?'

'Catch it for playing on the building site.'

'No. Did you expect me to?' Nicola waited until Rose had almost reached the front door. 'Stupid *tell* tale.' She thrust her face into Rose's: Rose toppled over, with a shriek, into the flower bed. 'Serves you right,' said Nicola. 'I hope you take root and get eaten by *toads*.'

8

The auditions for *The March Girls* were being held
the following week, in a theatre up in London.
Madam Paula had arranged for Rose and Nicola to
go on Friday morning at eleven o'clock – Mrs.
Bruce was to go with them, as chaperone. There
hadn't been any difficulty about including Nicola.
Madam Paula had been quite willing for, as she said,
if she *did* happen to land herself a part it would all
be added publicity for the Madam Paula Academy.

'Not to mention,' said Mr. Bruce, drily, 'ten per
cent of her earnings.'

Nicola couldn't imagine having earnings – even
Rose had never had *earnings*. It somehow didn't seem
quite real. In fact, nothing seemed quite real except
for missing school on Friday. She hadn't told anyone
where she was going, not even her own particular
gang. Her form mistress had had to know, of course
– Mrs. Bruce had written a note, explaining – but
her form mistress wasn't one for making a fuss or
splashing bits of information around. Half the school
knew where Rose was going: Nicola preferred to
keep the news to herself.

On Friday morning, at half-past nine (so as to run no risk of being late) they set off for the station.

'I've told Mrs. French,' said Rose, self-important, 'that she isn't to worry . . . even if I do get a part the rehearsals don't start for nearly a month. I'll still be able to play the Bad Little Girl.'

She shot a glance at Nicola, to see how she was taking it: Nicola preserved a stony silence. She wasn't giving Rose the satisfaction of knowing that she still had a sore place inside her.

Rose skipped happily, several paces ahead. She was wearing her pink net party dress, with white socks and black shiny leather shoes which buttoned over the instep. Over the pink dress she had on a pink tweedy coat, with a pink furry muff for her hands, while her hair was held back with a big, pink, satin bow. She looked, thought Nicola, like something off the top of a chocolate box. Nicola herself was wearing a dress of brown velvet, with bits of lace at the collar and cuffs. It was a dress she most particularly hatred. She'd wanted to wear her new top (now that it had been washed and restored to its original whiteness) but Mrs. Bruce wouldn't hear of it.

'Not for an *audition* . . . the aim is to make yourself look pretty.'

She couldn't see how the brown velvet dress was supposed to make her look pretty: her neck stuck out of the top of it like half a yard of broom handle, and the sleeves were about two inches too short, which made her wrists dangle. At least she had been spared the white socks. She had refused point blank. In the end, after much grumbling, Mrs. Bruce had let her wear her black wool tights.

'Makes you look like little orphan Annie . . . they're not *looking* for orphans. You look like something that's come out of an institution.'

At any rate, thought Nicola, it was better than looking like something that had come off the top of a chocolate box.

'P'raps I could be a Hummel,' she said.

'What's a Hummel?' That was Rose, ignorant as usual.

'The *Hummels* . . . the poor people they take food to on Christmas morning. Where Beth catches the fever . . . don't you know *anything*?'

Nicola had spent the last few evenings rereading *Little Women*. Rose hadn't read it at all. All she knew was that there were four leading parts, called Amy, Meg, Beth and Jo, in the first few scenes (after that, they grew up and were played by older people) and she was determined to get one of them. She wasn't interested in minor characters such as Hummels. All the way up to Victoria in the train she kept saying, 'I wonder if Susie Hamilton will be there . . . I wonder if there'll be anyone from Maude Foskett . . . I wonder if we'll see that awful girl with the squint . . . I wonder if they'll want us to dance . . . I can dance in these shoes almost as well as in my tap shoes, so it doesn't really matter if they do . . . d'you remember how awful it was in the *Annie* audition when that girl burst into tears and ran away? I wonder if anyone'll do that today? I hope they don't. It makes me feel so *awful* . . . it makes me feel really embarrassed for them.'

Never mind *Rose* feeling embarrassed: it made Nicola want to curl up and die, just listening to her. If there'd been a corridor, she'd have gone and stood in it. She tried concentrating her thoughts on things outside the window, but there wasn't any escaping Rose's voice. It filled the whole carriage.

'I wonder if the Tots Agency will send anyone . . . I wonder if we'll see that girl we saw last time . . .'

The theatre was in Shaftesbury Avenue, which meant they had to take a tube from Victoria to Green Park, and then another from Green Park to Leicester Square. Nicola liked travelling by tube. She liked looking at all the people. They were quite different from the sort of people who lived in Streatham High Road. Some of them were so strange – she saw a man with his hair in two long pigtails down to his waist, and a boy with red finger nails and lipstick – that they made Rose look quite ordinary. It was a relief, for once, to find Rose reduced to ordinariness. It seemed to subdue even her, because she actually sat in silence all the way from Green Park to Leicester Square, a journey which must have lasted very nearly five minutes. Not until they arrived at the theatre did she regain her normal bounce.

'This is where we came before . . . that time we came for the dancing thing and they said what a pity it was I was too young else I'd have got the part.'

'That's right,' said Mrs. Bruce. 'Nicola, come along and don't dawdle!'

'She's probably scared,' said Rose. 'Most people are. *I'm* not.'

'We all know you're not,' said Mrs. Bruce.

'Neither am I,' said Nicola. 'I'm not scared.'

It was quite true: she wasn't. She didn't see what there was to be scared of. It was only an audition. She'd heard enough about auditions from Rose to know what to expect. You got up on a stage, with lots of other girls, and people came and looked at you, and measured how tall you were, and wrote down what colour hair you had, and what colour your eyes were, and then they asked you to do something, like sing a song or perform a little dance. Sometimes Rose had had to learn a song beforehand, or have a dance already prepared, but this time they'd been told there wasn't any need. If there had been, Nicola knew what she would have done. She'd have sung the song Miss Murray had told her off about, and she'd have sung it with the funny words – *Sleep on a wooden door, and in thy slumber snore* – and after she'd sung the word snore, she'd have put her head on her hands and made a loud snoring noise. And if she'd had to prepare a dance, she'd have done the sailor's hornpipe, which they'd learnt in PE last week when it had been raining and they'd had to stay indoors. Miss Grant had said that hers was the best hornpipe of anyone's, and that had included Janice Martin, who did ballet.

'I expect they'll give us something to improvise,'

said Rose, knowledgeably. 'That's what they sometimes do.'

Nicola wasn't sure what improvise meant. She
thought perhaps it might mean making things up on
the spot, but she certainly wasn't going to pander to
Rose's vanity by asking. She was already quite
swollen-headed enough. When she had first heard
that Nicola was to come to the audition with them,
Rose had been inclined to flounce and be resentful.
She was the one who went to auditions, not Nicola.
What did Nicola want to come for? What was the
point? She couldn't sing, she couldn't dance – it was
stupid. Since then, her attitude had changed. It
was no longer Rose resentful, but Rose benevolent,
Rose patronizing – and Rose patronizing was almost
harder to bear than Rose anything else. If she had
told Nicola once that it would be 'all right,' because
everyone was always 'ever so nice to beginners', she
had told her a dozen times, just as she had promised
a dozen times to stand next to Nicola on stage, so
that if she got lost – 'if they give us some steps to
do, or anything' – she could watch what Rose was
doing and pick it up from her. Now, in her bossy
way, without waiting for the stage door man to give
them directions, she went skipping off ahead, calling
out to Nicola and her mother to follow.

'It's down here . . . I remember from last time.'

Nicola and Mrs. Bruce walked sedately behind
her. There were times when Nicola felt quite adult
compared with Rose. Rose really was such a *child*.
Always showing off and trying to attract attention.

'In here!' She flung open a door, and went prancing through into a long, narrow room with mirrors and dressing tables all down one side. 'Goody! We're first!'

Rose did an exultant pirouette before one of the mirrors. Nicola looked at her own reflection and screwed up her face: she *hated* the brown velvet dress.

'Don't do that,' said Mrs. Bruce, 'it makes you look ugly. Try smiling for once.'

She smiled – and Rose giggled. Nicola sat down with her back to the mirror. It was just affectation, looking at oneself.

Other people started to come in; soon the room was quite crowded. Nicola thought there must be at least forty bodies in there, although half of those, of course, were mothers. She looked around at the other girls, trying to see if there were any like herself – any who *weren't* pretty and chocolate-boxish. It was a comfort to discover that there were one or two. In particular she noted a large, flabby girl with long yellow hair and a face like a horse, and a small spidery child with buck teeth. (Rose informed her, in a whisper, that 'that was the one that ran away and cried'.) Rose had met most of the girls before, at other auditions. She kept waving and calling out across the room.

'Hallo, Susie! Hallo, Dominique! Hallo, Kate!'

At last, at eleven o'clock, a lady in blue dungarees appeared and checked off their names on a list. Rose, self-important, in penetrating tones, informed Nicola that 'I expect we'll all go up on stage now.'

'That's it,' said the lady. She nodded at Rose. 'I seem to recognize you . . . have you been here before?'

Rose beamed, and blossomed.

'We were here last year,' said Mrs. Bruce. 'For the *Great Charlene* auditions. Unfortunately, she was a bit too young then . . . she was only nine at the time.'

'Ah, yes,' said the lady. 'I remember . . . quite a baby, weren't you?'

All the mothers and most of the girls turned to look at Rose, but they didn't look at her as people usually looked, with indulgent smiles and stupid simpers. Instead, they looked at her quite coldly, almost disapprovingly, as if she had done something wrong. It was a pity, thought Nicola, that a few more people didn't look at Rose like that. It was bad enough when she only drew attention to her*self*, but now she'd gone and drawn attention to Nicola, as well. Not that Nicola had anything against attention; not as such. Attention was all right when you'd done something to deserve it — when you'd just turned a double back somersault in gym, or just had an essay read out by Miss McMaster (or just been told off for singing 'stupid and ridiculous' words in a singing class). What she objected to was when people stood and stared for absolutely no reason.

The mothers were all starting to bunch up together: they were going to go and sit in the auditorium and watch. As Mrs. Bruce departed, she gave Nicola's hand an encouraging squeeze and whispered, 'Just do your best . . . nothing to be scared of.' Nicola wondered why everybody kept expecting her to be scared. It wasn't as if it was anything important, like exams.

The mothers disappeared, and the lady in the dungarees escorted her charges – some of them, like Rose, giggling and chattering; others, Nicola noticed, grown suddenly strained and silent – along a stone corridor and up a flight of stairs towards a swing door at the end. Another moment, and they were on stage and being told to form into a line. Nicola had never been on a stage before, except for the one at school, which was scarcely any more than a glorified platform. She was surprised at how large it was – far larger than the gym: even larger than the assembly hall – and also how dirty-looking and shabby. There were some bits of scenery dotted about, and they looked pretty dim and shabby, as well. She couldn't quite make out what they were supposed to represent, but there was no time to study them because already things were happening.

A bald gentleman in a funny coat with fringes was walking slowly down the line followed by the lady in the dungarees and another lady, wearing baggy Turkish trousers and a floppy blouse. Every now and again the bald gentleman would stop and say 'Amy' or 'Beth', or just occasionally 'Meg' or 'Jo', and then the lady in the dungarees would make a mark on her list and hand over a large white label with a letter and a number written on it. When he came to Rose, the bald gentleman hardly even bothered to look: he just said 'Amy' and passed straight on to Nicola. He looked at Nicola long and hard, through narrowed eyes, seemed about to move on, then suddenly, over his shoulder, flung an instruction at the lady in the dungarees, 'Try her as Jo.' Nicola was given a label with a big red 'J' in the middle of it, and a small black '2' in the bottom right-hand corner. The label had a loop that went over the head, and strings that tied behind. It wasn't very elegant, but anything that helped cover up the hideous velvet dress could only be good. She bet Rose wasn't too happy, having to ruin the effect of the pink net party frock.

Rose had a label with an 'A' on it, and a '4' in the corner. It seemed there were more Amys and Beths than there were Megs and Jos, because when he had reached the end of the line the bald gentleman turned to the lady in the dungarees and said, 'OK, we've got enough As and Bs; do you want to make the numbers up?' and the lady in the dungarees went back to the beginning and began handing out Js and Ms to people who hadn't been given anything first time around. Nicola was glad she wasn't one of them. She thought that it must be rather depressing, just being there to make the numbers up.

When all the labels had been allocated, they had to divide into four groups, according to which letters they were, and arranged themselves in height order; and when they'd done that, the tallest from each group had to come forward, and then the second tallest, and then the third, and so on, until in the end they had formed themselves into six different groups of four, each with a Jo, a Meg, an Amy and a Beth. Nicola had been the second tallest in her original group, while Rose had been next to bottom in hers, so fortunately they finished up in different 'families'. Nicola definitely hadn't wanted to be in the same family as Rose.

'All right, people!' The bald man in the funny coat clapped his hands for silence. 'Now, you all know what parts you're doing – right? OK. So we've got a little song here that we want you to learn – no need to look worried, it's only a few bars. It goes like this . . . *We are the March girls, We're not stiff and starch girls, We're Amy, Meg and Beth, and Jo* . . . got it? You see, it's quite simple. Let's try it with the music. Sandy! Can we have some music, please? Right! All together, now . . . *We are the March girls, We're not stiff and starch girls* – '

It took a few minutes for everyone to get it right. It wasn't that the tune was difficult, but that some people couldn't seem to remember which order the names came in, or even if they remembered they kept getting them in a muddle. Rose was one who got them in a muddle. She kept singing, 'Amy, Beg and Meth' – then clapping a hand over her mouth and giggling. When at last even Rose was able to do it without collapsing, the lady in the Turkish trousers showed them some steps which they had to do as an accompaniment.

'It's just a little march, really – the March march,

as you might say – but it'll be your first entrance, so we want it to look impressive.'

The march was jolly, and swaggering. Each group came on in turn, in a line, and went swinging across the stage, heads held high, arms and legs going like pistons, as they sang their song. Nicola enjoyed it – she could have gone on marching all day. She was quite sorry when the bald man said he thought he'd seen enough, and that it was time they moved on.

'Back you go, into your original groups . . . scurry, scurry! Time is precious! We'll take the Jos first. Barbara, will you do the honours? I'll be getting on with the Megs. Amys and Beths, you can have a bit of a breather.'

The six Jos all went off into a corner with the lady in the Turkish trousers.

'Another little song,' she said. 'This is the Jo song. Not *quite* as simple as the other, but I don't think you should have too much difficulty. It goes like this . . . *Jo, Jo, Jo, I wish I WERE a Jo. A REAL Jo, Go Jo, proper boyish JO Jo.*'

Nicola didn't like the Jo song. She tried telling herself that the reason she didn't like it was that Jo wouldn't ever sing anything so stupid, but she knew that it wasn't really that. The real reason she didn't like it was because she couldn't do it. It wasn't the words that defeated her so much as the tune – she simply couldn't get the notes right. She could *hear* them all right, in her head; but what she heard in her head wasn't what came out of her mouth.

When all the Jos had done their song and the bald

man had listened to them, Nicola was told that she could go. All the Jos were told that they could go except for Jo 1 and Jo 3. Jo 1 was the girl Susie Hamilton, whom Rose knew, and Jo 3 had long chestnut hair and looked exactly *like* a Jo. Nicola knew enough about auditions to know that these were the two who still stood a chance: the rest of them had been dismissed as useless. As she left the stage (not trailing or pouting like Jos 4–6: that would be showing one's feelings too much) the bald man crooked a finger at her and said: 'Jo 2! Here a minute . . . you're a nice little mover – very nice little mover. But whoever told you you could sing?'

Nicola grinned, in spite of herself.

'Nobody.'

'Nobody, eh?' The bald man grinned back at her. 'Well, I'm afraid nobody's quite right . . . you can't! You concentrate on the dancing. That's where your talent lies.'

Somehow, after that, Nicola didn't mind so much about being dismissed. After all, it was nothing new that she couldn't sing – she had *always* known that she couldn't sing. No one had ever told her before that she was a nice little mover.

The lady in the dungarees took back their labels, then led the four discarded Jos round to the auditorium to collect their chaperones. As Nicola slipped into a seat next to her mother, Mrs. Bruce whispered, 'That wasn't bad at all. I thought you were quite good. Far better than that last girl.' The last girl had been the spiderlike child with the buck teeth. Nicola pulled a face.

'I can't sing.'

'Never mind. You can do other things.'

There was a pause.

'What sort of other things?' said Nicola, hopefully.

She waited for her mother to tell her that she was a nice little mover, but Mrs. Bruce only clicked her tongue against the roof of her mouth and said, 'That terrible child with the yellow hair! Why *will* they let them do it? Some parents simply have no sense of responsibility.'

I don't care, thought Nicola. The bald man in the funny coat thought she was a nice little mover – a *very* nice little mover. She bet he knew more about it than Mrs. Bruce.

Up on stage, four of the six Megs had just been told they could go, and one had burst into tears.

'Really!' said Mrs. Bruce. 'Thank heavens Rose doesn't behave like that.'

Six Beths had now come forward and one after another were singing their Beth song. Nicola didn't take too much notice of them: she was too busy thinking about what the man in the funny coat had said. *A nice little mover . . . a VERY nice little mover . . .*

Not until it was the turn of the Amys did she sit up and pay attention. When all was said and done, Rose *was* her sister, and she supposed she *ought* to want her to do well. The Amy song might almost have been written for Rose. It went:

> *How fine to be pretty*
> *And witty*
> *And cute!*
> *How fine to be me —*
> *Ah me!*
> *A-my!*

Rose not only sang it with great gusto — Rose had a voice that both kept in tune *and* could be heard all over the theatre — but she also sang it in an American accent, which hardly anybody else had dared to try, or maybe they simply hadn't thought of it. Nicola had to admit that it hadn't occurred to *her*, even though she had read the book and knew perfectly well that it was set in America. She had a moment of grudging admiration for her sister. Rose might be horrid, but she could certainly do a song and dance routine.

No one was surprised when Rose was one of the two Amys asked to stay behind; and probably no one was surprised when a week later Madam Paula rang to say that Rose had been offered the part. Rose herself made a great show of pretended amazement — 'I never thought I stood a *chance* . . . Katie's so much *better* than I am . . . she's so much *prettier*' — but it didn't ring true. She was only saying it because she thought it sounded humble.

Mr. French declared that they must have a celebration, and took them all up the road at Saturday lunch time for beanburgers and milk shakes, while Mrs. French made a cake in the shape of a book and wrote AMY on it, in curly, icing-sugar letters. All the neighbours were told, and the local newspaper, who came round to take a photograph. Their grand-parents, both lots, sent telegrams saying WHO'S A CLEVER GIRL? and WELL DONE ROSE. Even Nicola went out and bought a special *Congratulations* card and wrote 'Love from Ben and Nicola' in it. (It cost her an effort, but she was glad when she'd done it: it made her feel pleasantly generous and noble.)

On the Saturday evening, after tea, when they'd demolished half the cake and Nicola and her mother were doing the washing up – Rose having been let off, as a special treat, and Mr. Bruce never doing it because of doing other things, like putting new washers on taps, and Mrs. Bruce, in any case, not considering it 'man's work' – her mother suddenly said, 'Your father and I have been thinking . . . Rose is going to be earning money, doing something that she likes doing, and I daresay we shall let her spend some of it on herself. We shan't insist that she saves every single penny of it . . . now, what about you?' She stopped, and looked at Nicola. 'Is there anything special that you would like? Anything you'd like to do? Like to buy? Anywhere you'd like to go?'

She was only asking her because she thought that Nicola would be feeling left out – because she didn't want her getting jealous. But she wasn't jealous. She honestly didn't care that Rose had got the part of Amy. Rose deserved it, because Rose was good at it. What Rose wouldn't be good at was the Bad

Little Girl, and that was the only thing that Nicola wanted. She wanted her own part back again.

'Well?' said Mrs. Bruce. 'There must be something!'

Nicola shook her head. She knew it wasn't any use asking for what she really wanted. They'd say it was too late, and that in any case the costumes had already been made.

'Oh, now, come on!' Mrs. Bruce took a handful of cutlery out of the water. 'I can't believe there isn't *any*thing . . . how about a new bicycle?'

Politely, Nicola said, 'I like the one I've got already, thank you.'

'Well, then, how about a portable television set for your bedroom? Then you could watch whatever you wanted.'

'I don't really like watching television,' said Nicola.

'You don't really like watching television . . . all right, then! How about taking lessons in something? Ice skating — how about ice skating? You're quite good at games and gym . . . you'd probably be a winner at ice skating.'

A thought flashed across Nicola's mind: she didn't particularly want to learn *ice* skating —

'Something else?' said Mrs. Bruce.

'No.' She dismissed the idea. It had already been laughed at once: she wasn't running the risk a second time. 'It's really quite all right.' Composedly, she picked up a plate from the draining board. 'You don't *have* to give me anything.'

Mrs. Bruce seemed taken aback.

'I know we don't *have* to – we just thought that we'd like to. Why don't you think about it? Then if anything strikes you, you can let us know.'

'All right,' said Nicola. 'But it's not actually *necessary.*'

9

Now that she was a genuine professional (or 'pro', as she and Mrs. Bruce preferred to call it) Rose had become somewhat condescending in her attitude towards the part of the Bad Little Girl. One might have thought, listening to her, that she was already a big name and really ought not to be wasting her valuable time appearing on the same stage as a bunch of mere amateurs. Needless to say, she made no move to offer the part back to Nicola. She said that she had 'given her word', and that once you'd given your word it was very important you should keep it: Madam Paula had said so.

'I couldn't let them down *now* . . . not after saying that I'd do it.'

Not after sulking and sobbing for a whole week because you thought you weren't going to be *allowed* to do it, thought Nicola, sourly.

Word had got out at school, in spite of Mr. Henry's policy of not announcing individual achievements until the last day of term. Everyone knew that Rosemary Bruce had been given a part in a West End show. Some people were predictable, and gushed, 'She's ever so clever, your sister, isn't

she? She must be *ever* so good.' Others, equally predictable, tried to make out that it wasn't really
anything so very wonderful. Janice Martin, who did
ballet, said loftily that *her* dancing teacher wouldn't
let her try for 'that sort of thing', and Linda Baker,
whose cousin had gold medals and had failed three
times to get into the Royal Ballet School, sniffed
and said, 'Of course, it's only a musical . . . *anyone*
can do *musicals*.' One or two, however, looked at
Nicola with a mixture of sympathy and curiosity
and asked her whether she didn't mind, having a
sister who was going to be famous.

'I don't expect she's going to be famous, exactly,'
said Nicola. 'Not playing Amy. She's only got three
scenes.'

On the other hand, Rose probably *would* be
famous, one of these days. She was always saying
that she would be, and Nicola saw no reason to
doubt her.

'She'll be *quite* famous,' said Sarah Mason, who
was one of Nicola's special friends.

'She is already,' said Cheryl Walsh. Cheryl was
neither friend nor foe, but stood on strictly neutral
ground in between. 'Everybody's talking about
her . . . I wouldn't want to have a sister that everybody talked about.'

Nicola frowned. People had always talked about
Rose. She had grown used to it by now – just
as she had grown used to the idea of Rose being
famous.

'Wouldn't *you* like to be famous?' said Sarah.

'Not particularly,' said Nicola.

'But won't you absolutely hate it if she's famous and you're not?'

'Imagine if she keeps being on television,' said Cheryl, 'and you're stuck working in a lousy shop.'

'I'm not going to be stuck working in a lousy shop,' said Nicola.

'How d'you know?'

''Cos I know.'

'*How* d'you know?'

''Cos I'm going to be doing something else.'

'What?'

They looked at her, challengingly. Nobody in their class knew what they were going to be doing after they'd left school except for one boy who was going to be a soldier because that was what his father was. It was too far ahead for anybody else. Mostly, they hadn't even thought about it.

Nicola hadn't thought about it, either; not until that moment.

'I'm going to be a doctor,' she said.

They considered the idea.

'That'd be all right,' said Sarah. 'Then when Rose got ill through being so famous she could come and be your patient.'

Nicola tossed her head.

'I'm not having *Rose* as my patient . . . not *ever*.'

The mime show was going to have four perform-ances in all – one in the church hall, one in an old people's home, one in a centre for the disabled, and one in a local hospital. The one in the church hall, which was the one the public were invited to, was on a Saturday evening, just two days after the end of term. Nicola couldn't make up her mind whether she wanted to go or whether she didn't. To go would be agony – but then, so would not to go. In any case, it really didn't matter a jot which way she decided, since Mrs. Bruce had already decided for her.

'Of course you're coming! You can't stay at home by yourself all evening.'

'I could always go next door.'

'Go next door? What on earth for?'

'So I wouldn't have to be by myself.'

'Oh, don't be so silly, Nicola! You'll enjoy it once you're there.'

She would have enjoyed it more if she hadn't had to wear the brown velvet dress – and even *more* if she hadn't had to face the dismal prospect of watching Rose ruining her part. (She still thought of it as 'her part'; she couldn't help it. It *was* her part.)

The Family Portrait came right at the end of the programme, which meant she had it looming over her the whole of the evening. In spite of that, there were moments when she almost managed to forget it. One of those moments was in a sketch called *The Reading of the Will*, when Mr. Marlowe, who had christened her Supermouse and was playing the part of an Angry Relation, banged very fiercely with his fist upon an imaginary table and then sat down with a painful *thump* on an imaginary chair which wasn't there. Nicola giggled so much that her insides began to hurt, and Mrs. Bruce had to put a finger to her lips and say 'Sh!'

Another moment was when Mrs. French, all by herself, did a mime called *The Awakening*. The programme didn't say what it was an awakening *of*, but explanations weren't really necessary, because anyone could see that it was a flower, gradually pushing its way up through the earth and unfolding towards the light. Nicola was quite shocked when at the end, under cover of the applause, her father leaned towards her and whispered, 'So what was all that supposed to be about?' Surely if she could see that it was a flower, then he ought to be able to? After all, he *grew* them. She tried explaining to him, but Mrs. Bruce said, 'Be *quiet*, you two!' which made Mr. Bruce pull a henpecked face and close one eye at Nicola in a naughty grimace.

At last it was time for *The Family Portrait*. The curtain swung back, and there was Mr. Marlowe, dressed up in a frock coat and funny check trousers, setting up his imaginary camera, fussily moving it from one position to another, diving under his imaginary cover to peer through the lens. And now here came all the others, just as Nicola remembered. First Papa, with a big bushy beard, then Mama, wearing a lace cap on her head, followed by Elder Brother and Sister, Nurse with the Baby, wrapped up in a white shawl, and finally, hand in hand, the Bad Little Girl and the Good Little Boy. Rose looked angelic. She looked as if butter wouldn't melt in her mouth. She was wearing a buttercup yellow dress, with frilly pantaloons which peeped out beneath, and a pair of black ballet slippers decorated with rosettes the same colour as the dress. Her hair had been parted in the middle and hung enchantingly on either side of her face in bunches of ringlets. Mark, playing the Good Little Boy, was dressed in a sailor suit and long white stockings. It was hard to say which of them looked the more saintlike, him or Rose.

Nicola waited impatiently for the moment when Mama shook her finger and the Bad Little Girl had to pull a hideous face: Rose beamed, adorably, and half the audience made little crooning noises; at which Rose, ever conscious of the impression she was making, beamed even more. She knew that if she beamed long enough, she could make dimples appear in her cheeks. Nicola felt somewhat nauseated.

She waited for the next moment – the moment when the Bad Little Girl had to produce her pet mouse and let it escape. The moment came. Rose dipped a hand into her pocket and brought out something that was small and wriggly. It might have been a guinea pig, perhaps, or a kitten. What it quite definitely was not was a mouse. Nicola could see that it wasn't a mouse. It was too *big* for a mouse. Mice weren't just small, they were absolutely tiny. The thing Rose was holding was more like a teddy bear. More like an *elephant*. The elephant broke loose

140

and went bounding like a kangaroo across the floor. Rose's ringlets bobbed violently as she followed its progress. Up and down, it went; up-and-down, up-and-down. It might almost have been a beach ball. Or a frog. It bounced as far as the Photographer, and then, quite suddenly, it disappeared. One minute it was there, and the next minute it wasn't. Perhaps it had changed into an ant, thought Nicola, and been trodden on. The audience were plainly puzzled. It wasn't until the Elder Sister screamed and jumped on to a chair with her skirts clutched round her legs that they understood what was supposed to be happening and began to laugh. Papa went marching across to the Bad Little Girl and shook her angrily by the ear; but Rose, instead of squirming and pulling a wicked I-don't-care face, only bit her lip and quivered and looked pathetic. An old lady sitting near Nicola made a sentimental cooing noise. Nicola wanted to lean across and shout, 'You aren't *meant* to feel sorry for her – she did it on *purpose*. She's *always* doing things on purpose!' It wouldn't have made any difference. The audience thought Rose was wonderful. Audiences always would; Nicola suddenly saw it, quite clearly. It didn't matter that what Rose was doing was all wrong for the part: she was being herself, and that was enough.

At the end of the show, when all the cast were lined up for their applause, Mr. Marlowe stepped forward, and holding up a hand for silence said, 'Ladies and gentlemen . . . thank you for coming along on this cold night. Your support has been much appreciated. We only hope that you've enjoyed yourselves. Before you go, we thought you might be interested in a little snippet of information about one of the members of our cast . . . Miss Rosemary Vitullo.' (Rose of *course* had got her own way about changing her name.) 'Rosemary is shortly going to be starting rehearsals in the West End, no less . . . she's to play the part of the young Amy, in the musical version of *Little Women*.' He held out a hand, to a pink-cheeked Rose. 'Come along, young lady! Come and take a bow . . . no need to be shy.'

Rose was never shy. If she was pink-cheeked, it was through gratification. She stood there, dimpling, while the audience clapped and clapped. Mrs. Bruce clapped as loudly as anyone. Nicola and her father clapped as well, but not quite so loudly.

'I'm sure we all wish her the very best of luck,' said Mr. Marlowe. 'May it be the start of a long and illustrious career.'

Rose bowed, prettily, and stepped back into line. (Why was it, wondered Nicola, that Rose always seemed to know instinctively what to do? It didn't matter what situation she was in, so long as she had an audience she couldn't go wrong.) The curtain came down for the last time, and Mrs. Bruce, with a bustle, stood up.

'Come on, then!' She handed Nicola her coat — a tweedy one, like Rose's, only brown instead of pink, to go with the brown velvet dress. 'Let's make our way backstage.'

'If you're going backstage,' said Mr. Bruce, 'I'll see you outside.'

Mr. Bruce didn't like having to go backstage. He didn't very much like the theatre at all. He worked as an accountant in a firm of surveyors and he liked life to be stable and ordered, as it was in his ledger books. He didn't enjoy excitement and crisis and never knowing whether tomorrow was going to be the same as yesterday. Rose and Mrs. Bruce thrived on it. For her part, Nicola rather thought that she took after her father. Her school exercise books were always neat and tidy (unlike Rose's, which tended to be a sprawling mess) and she kept the books on her bedroom shelf in strict alphabetical order, becoming quite upset if even her mother, for any reason, chanced to move them. Rose kept *her* books — not that she ever read them — all jumbled up in a heap on top of a cupboard. Probably, thought Nicola, that showed that Rose had an artistic temperament. It was probably very artistic to keep books jumbled up in heaps on the tops of cupboards, and to leave all one's things lying about, and . . .

'Come along, dozy!' Her mother gave her a little push. 'What are you dithering for?'

'I'm not dithering.'

'Well, come along, then! Let's get a move on.'

She would rather have gone to wait outside with her father, but she had left it too late: he had already disappeared. She had no option but to trail backstage behind Mrs. Bruce.

Backstage was a turmoil, as usual, though it wasn't

nearly as bad as after one of Madam Paula's shows. At Madam Paula's you got mothers — dozens and dozens of mothers — and half a million children, all showing off. Here, at least, it was mostly grown ups; husbands and wives and friends of the cast, with just the occasional younger person like herself. There was only one person showing off, and that was Rose, who was dashing about shrieking in her yellow dress. No one was making any attempt to check her. Even Mrs. Bruce, who usually made at least a token effort, only smiled indulgently and said, in apologetic tones, to a complete stranger whose ear Rose had just shrieked down, 'She's a bit over-excited, I'm afraid'; and the complete stranger, instead of suggesting that Rose be required to keep her voice down to a more acceptable level, simply smiled back and said, 'Perfectly natural . . . anyone would be, getting a part in the West End. Is she your daughter? You must be very proud of her.'

'Oh, we are,' said Mrs. Bruce. 'Aren't we?'

She turned to Nicola, for confirmation.

'Yes,' said Nicola.

'We always knew she'd make it one day, but I must say we never expected it quite so soon. Did we?'

'No,' said Nicola.

'How old is she?' said the stranger.

'She was ten in October. Just thirteen months younger than my other daughter here.'

'And does your other little daughter do anything?'

144

'Not theatrically,' said Mrs. Bruce. 'She's the clever one, aren't you, Nicola?'

'Don't know,' said Nicola.

'Of course you are! You write essays, don't you?'

Nicola picked at a button on her coat. She wished her mother wouldn't. She knew she was only trying to be kind, but people didn't *want* to hear about her being clever or writing essays. They wanted to hear about Rose.

'It must all be very exciting,' said the stranger. 'Has she ever done anything professionally before? The other little one, I mean?'

While Mrs. Bruce was explaining that Rose had very nearly but not quite got a part in *Annie*, and how she would have got a part in the *Great Charlene* except for being just a few months too young, Mrs. French's husband appeared. He had a harassed expression on his face. Perhaps he, too, like Mr. Bruce, didn't care for coming backstage. Unlike Mr. Bruce, however, he was looking extremely dashing, in a black velvet jacket and trousers, with a bright red shirt and a silk scarf tied about his neck. Nicola thought he was the handsomest man she had ever seen. She smiled at him, hopefully, not really expecting him to recognize her, but he stopped, at once, and said, 'Hallo! It's the girl with the feet . . . Nicola, isn't it? That your sister they're all making eyes at?'

Nicola nodded, suddenly bashful. Mr. French pulled a face.

145

'Don't envy you,' he said. 'Never mind . . .' He winked at her. 'Keep your pecker up!'

'Was that Mrs. French's husband?' said Mrs. Bruce, a few minutes later. 'What was that he was saying about feet?'

'It was just something Mrs. French said.'

'Oh? What was that?'

'She said that feet were important . . . she said I had good high arches and two toes the same length.'

'Two toes the same length?'

'For point work,' said Nicola.

'But you're not going to — ' Mrs. Bruce broke off. 'There's the man that played the Photographer.'

'Mr. Marlowe,' said Nicola. She wondered if he would remember her. Probably he wouldn't. People didn't always; not once they'd seen Rose.

'Someone said he used to be a professional,' said Mrs. Bruce.

Mr. Marlowe suddenly caught sight of Nicola, and waved.

'Hallo, Supermouse!' He blew her a kiss: Nicola blushed. 'How's Supermouse getting on?'

'All right, thank you,' said Nicola.

'Basking in reflected glory? Or aren't you the basking type?'

Nicola wasn't quite sure what he meant by that. She wrinkled her nose, uncertainly. It was Mrs. Bruce who said, 'She's very happy for Rose. Aren't you?'

'Yes,' said Nicola.

'I should hope we all are,' said Mr. Marlowe. He

chucked Nicola under the chin. 'Attaboy, Super-mouse! Keep up the good work!'

'Strange man,' said Mrs. Bruce, as soon as Mr. Marlowe was out of earshot.

'He's nice,' said Nicola.

'What's all this about Supermouse?'

'That's what he called me,' said Nicola. 'Because of – '

She had been going to say, 'Because of me doing such a good mouse,' but fortunately, perhaps, Mrs. French arrived in time to stop her. (It wouldn't have been the right thing to say at this particular moment. Tonight was Rose's night: no one wanted to hear about Nicola.) She listened, patiently, as Mrs. Bruce related yet again the story of the audition, explaining how Rose had come to get the part, and what a wonderful thing it was for her career. She heard Mrs. French agree that it was, indeed, wonderful for Rose's career, and Mrs. Bruce say that of course it was only the first rung on the ladder, and Mrs. French say that everyone had to start somewhere, and Mrs. Bruce say that Rose had been extremely lucky, and Mrs. French say that she had indeed, and Mrs. Bruce say that they were thinking, after *The March Girls*, of sending her to a full-time stage school, and could Mrs. French perhaps recommend any? Madam Paula had suggested the Italia Conti or Barbara Speke. What did Mrs. French think? Mrs. French said she thought that either would be per-fectly splendid. She couldn't really make any other recommendations. She didn't know that much about

147

stage schools; only ballet schools. But she was quite sure that both the Italia Conti and Barbara Speke were thoroughly reputable. What one had to avoid were the one-horse establishments which operated from two rooms and a cupboard in the back streets of suburbia.

'Oh, we shouldn't dream of letting her go to one of those,' said Mrs. Bruce. 'We shall check most carefully. After all, it is her career.'

'Exactly.' There was a pause, and Nicola thought that Mrs. French was going to move on; but then, suddenly, she heard her say, 'Well! That seems to be Rose taken care of . . . now, what are we going to do about Nicola?'

'Nicola?'

Mrs. Bruce sounded as startled as Nicola was.

'I always hate to see good talent go to waste,' said Mrs. French. 'Of course, I do realize that Nicola thinks ballet is wet, and that she far prefers a game of football — '

Nicola, who up until now had kept her eyes fixed firmly on the ground, risked a quick glance and found to her surprise that Mrs. French was smiling. She had thought, after the things she had said on the building site, that Mrs. French wouldn't ever want to talk to her again.

'Oh, Nicola's football mad,' said Mrs. Bruce.

No, I'm not, thought Nicola. I'm not football *mad*.

Mrs. French laughed.

'I'm sure there's nothing wrong with football —

my husband tells me it's an excellent game. *He* says it beats *Swan Lake* into a cocked hat any day of the week. I suppose it's always possible that Nicola might agree with him.' She raised a quizzical eyebrow in Nicola's direction. 'The only trouble is, there's not really very much future in it, is there? Not for a girl. Not even in this day and age. You're hardly very likely to end up playing centre-forward for England!'

'Are you saying – ' Mrs. Bruce spoke hesitantly ' – that she's any more likely to end up dancing *Swan Lake* for – ' she spread out her hands ' – the Royal Ballet?'

'Well, it's far too early to make predictions, of course, but . . . I always believe in giving things a go; don't you?'

Mrs. Bruce puckered her lips.

'You're suggesting she should take classes? I suppose, perhaps, Madam Paula – '

'Not Madam Paula.' Mrs. French spoke quickly. 'Not that she isn't excellent, in her way, but – not for Nicola. I was rather wondering whether you would let Nicola come to me.'

'To you?'

'For classes. I thought maybe just twice a week, to begin with, until we see how she develops – '

'Forgive me,' said Mrs. Bruce, 'but I was under the impression you didn't take younger people?'

'I don't, as a rule. But just occasionally I make exceptions. I'd very much like to make one now, if Nicola was agreeable.'

Mrs. Bruce looked down at Nicola, dubiously.

Nicola's heart was pounding so hard she could hear the blood roaring in her ears.

'You really think that *Nicola* — ?'

'I think she has potential. At this stage one can't say very much more than that. But she's exactly the right build, she's supple, she's musical — '

'Musical?' said Mrs. Bruce. She laughed, a trifle nervously. Nicola could understand her bewilderment. Perhaps, after all, Mrs. French was only teasing?

'Very musical,' said Mrs. French. 'The one night she was with us she picked up several quite complicated cues with no difficulty at all. Rose, of course, has been doing it all her life; but for someone who's had no training . . . mind, I'm not necessarily saying that she'd end up as a leading ballerina. She might not even make it as far as the corps — she might not even *want* to make it. She might decide she wants to do something different. On the other hand, she could turn out to be a second Pavlova. We just don't know until we've tried. But either way, it would seem a pity if she was never given the chance to find out.'

'Yes. Well — ' Mrs. Bruce seemed slightly bludgeoned. 'Perhaps if we could talk it over and let you know?'

'By all means. But the sooner the better — she's just at the right age. I wouldn't want to leave it any longer. Another few months and it would really be too late.'

'I see.' Mrs. Bruce shifted her bag from one hand

to the other. 'Well, in that case . . . if we could let you know first thing Monday morning?'

'Monday morning would be fine. I'll look forward to hearing from you.'

With another smile at Nicola — who this time, rather shyly, smiled back — Mrs. French went on her way. There was a moment's silence, then: 'We'd better collect Rose,' said Mrs. Bruce. 'Your father will be wondering what's happened to us.'

Rose was still running about shrieking in her yellow dress.

'Go and get changed,' said Mrs. Bruce. 'And make it quick . . . we'll wait for you outside.'

Slowly, Nicola and her mother walked back down the passage that led to the exit.

'Well, I suppose if you really wanted to,' said Mrs. Bruce. She stopped. '*Do* you really want to?'

'Wouldn't mind,' said Nicola.

'You'd rather have ballet lessons than ice skating?'

She hunched a shoulder.

'What does that mean?' said Mrs. Bruce. 'Yes? Or no? There'd be no point in doing it if you weren't going to enjoy it. Do you think you *would* enjoy it?'

''Spect I might.'

'You're not just saying that because you think you've got to please Mrs. French? We don't want you pushed into doing something against your will — any more than we want to waste money on something that's not going to give you any pleasure. But if you're really quite sure — ' She waited a moment. 'If you really do think that you'd like to try it — '

'Might just as well,' said Nicola. Even if she *was* going to be a doctor. There wasn't any harm in just trying.

'Well, I'll go round first thing Monday morning, then,' said Mrs. Bruce.

Mr. Bruce was pacing up and down outside the church with his hands behind his back. He turned, as he saw his wife and Nicola.

'You've taken your time. Everyone making a fuss of Rose, I suppose.'

'And Nicola,' said Mrs. Bruce. 'It appears we've got two gifted daughters . . . Mrs. French wants her to go and take dancing lessons with her — seems to think she's going to be another Anna Pavlova.'

'Is that so?' said Mr. Bruce. 'Well, and who knows?' He ruffled Nicola's hair, affectionately. 'Maybe she will.'

Maybe I will, thought Nicola. Not that she was going to be a dancer, she was going to be a doctor; but still, there couldn't be any harm in just *trying*.

A voice came piping from somewhere behind them, 'Who's going to be another Anna Pavlova?'

'Nicola,' said Mrs. Bruce. 'Not you.'

'Nicola?' said Rose. She giggled.

Just for that, thought Nicola, I jolly well *will*.

That is, of course, if she didn't decide to become a doctor.

A PROPER LITTLE NOORYEFF

1

Cautiously, keeping one eye on Mr. Hubbard, busy scrawling cabalistic symbols over the entire length of the blackboard, Jamie reached out for his pen. With the flat of his hand, he edged his geometry rough book towards him; between finger and thumb, turned the page. Old Mother Hubbard had ears like a lynx: if you only stopped breathing for five seconds he wanted to know what you were up to. Over on the far side of the room some great gormless prat was cracking his fingers. Crack, crack, flaming crack. They were going off like pistol shots. Any minute now and the Hubbard would be spinning round demanding to be told 'Which of you louts is playing the percussion?'

He eased the top off his pen. It was the new felt tip he'd purloined from his little sister's pencil case that morning. A new felt tip always inspired confidence. Boldly, in big black capitals, he wrote WHAT ABOUT TOMORROW?, underlining each word very heavily three times, that there might be no mistake. Next to him, Doug Masters, who was supposed to be his best friend, craned over to see what he had written. He put his arm across it: this correspondence was private, even from best friends.

He waited till the next jet plane went thundering overhead, then with practised hand ripped out the page, at the same time as Doug stuffed his mouth full of biscuit and half a dozen whispered conversations were hurriedly resumed. Mr. Hubbard, who hadn't been born yesterday, whipped round from the board.

The jet passed on, the roar died away. Mr. Hubbard nodded, and went back to his symbols. Doug's jaws worked silently on undigested biscuit. Jamie folded his paper into a compact square and leaned across the gangway to prod at the nearest girl. (Old Mother Hubbard was a stickler for segregation. He said teenage boys were lower than beasts of the field, and that if he had his way they would all be kept in cages and regularly thrashed.)

The girl looked up, vacantly; disturbed, no doubt, from some private daydream. Jamie thrust the note at her. He pointed urgently at Sharon, sitting prim and upright in the front row, making as if the cabalistic symbols really turned her on. The girl shrugged her shoulders. Her name was Coral something. It always sounded like Coral Flashlight, but he supposed it couldn't really be. People just weren't called things like Flashlight. Anyway, it didn't matter what she was called, all he wanted was for her to get that note to Sharon.

Furtively, overdoing the cloak-and-dagger bit, she stretched an arm across the gangway, twisting her palm back to front like something out of a second-rate spy movie. The note, not surprisingly, fell to the ground. Jamie pushed at it with the toe of his shoe: maladroitly, she raked it in with her ruler, a feat ten times more difficult than simply leaning over to pick it up. Anxiously he watched its passage down through the ranks to the front row. He saw it placed on Sharon's desk. He saw her glance at it – cool, disparaging. What is this rubbish? He could imagine the disdainful lift of the eyebrow. Sharon was good at disdainful lifts of the eyebrow. Jamie put a finger in his mouth and tore at a flap of loose skin. The note lay where it was, in full view of the Hubbard should he choose to turn round and cast his gaze in that direction. For one agonizing moment he thought the little cow wasn't even going to bother reading it – thought she might even be going to humiliate him in front of the whole goggling harem by simply screwing it up; but then, slowly, with an air of bored condescension, as if the whole business were too utterly childish for words, she slid it off the desk and down into her lap. He saw the dip of her head as she switched her eyes away from the board, and he knew that she was at least going to look at it. That, at any rate, was something.

Mr. Hubbard, going a bit manic, started banging chalk against the board, viciously stabbing letters of the alphabet into the various nooks and crannies of his symbols, droning some geometric liturgy to himself as he did so. Some gobbledygook about hypotenuses. Jamie spared the thing one quick glance, then returned his attention to Sharon. She seemed to be writing a reply. He hadn't expected that. At worst he had expected her to ignore him; at best, if she happened to be in a good mood, he had thought she might perhaps turn round and nod; but he hadn't expected the favour of an actual reply. Sharon thought old Mother Hubbard was the cat's whiskers. That was why she always sat up straight and studied his symbols and tried to pretend she was some kind of mathematical genius. She wasn't given to messing about with notes, as if they were still in junior school.

By the same devious route as it had gone out, his sheet of paper made its way back to him. Sharon was already doing her little Goody Two Shoes bit again; not even bothering to turn round in her seat. Somehow, he felt that it did not bode well. Coral Flashlight, with her eyes fixed firmly to the front, leaned across the gangway and dropped the folded square upon his desk lid. Just in time, he pushed it under his rough book, as Mr. Hubbard spun round and said: 'Right! Pay attention! Given that angle A is 110° – '

Never mind angle A; there were more important things at stake. Like, what about tomorrow? If that little cow were going to let him down –

He wiped a lock of hair out of his eyes. Mr. Hubbard turned back again, to embellish angle A. Doug, who had plainly been awaiting his opportunity, instantly nodded in Sharon's direction, and pulling a face like a demented gorilla began making a series of unmistakable gestures, right hand placed in the crook of his left elbow, left hand clenched into a fist. Broad grins ran like an attack of mumps about the classroom. Even some of the harem were giggling; others, as usual, were looking down their noses like rows of affronted dowagers. Some of the girls thought Doug was a riot. Some of them didn't.

Sharon herself remained oblivious, though had she seen she would not have been embarrassed. She would only have tossed her head in that way she had, full of female contempt for male stupidity. Jamie was the one who stood in danger of embarrassment. He could do without Doug's crudities, just at this moment. In any case, he'd got hold of the wrong end of the stick where Sharon was concerned. Straight up and down, that was Sharon. Strictly no funny business. It was hands off and a quick peck on the cheek if you were lucky. Not that he'd ever particularly wanted anything more. Really he only kissed her because it was the thing to do; he'd have been quite happy without. Sometimes he thought that so would she.

Doug, encouraged by the mump-like grins, was growing pornographic. The big blue soup-plate eyes of Coral Flashlight protruded like globules: she tittered, into her hand. Jamie felt his cheeks turning brick colour. Savagely, he hacked at Doug's ankle beneath the desk. Doug only leered; and with maddening affability stuck his fingers in Jamie's face. There were times when having Doug for a best friend could be a real pain. Goaded, Jamie gave him a sharp shove in the ribs and mouthed two words, very succinctly. They were the sort of words which at home would have brought him a stiff clip round the ear and the advice to 'Watch that language! You're not in a barrack room.' Now they brought only the sarcastic invitation from the front of the class to 'Feel quite free to express yourself, lad . . . no need to be bashful. If you've something to say, let's all have the benefit.'

Coral Flashlight tittered again. Jamie squirmed.

'Well?' Mr. Hubbard waited, expectantly. '*Do* you have something to say?' A pause. Doug wrote BALLS on the cover of his rough book. 'You do not have something to say. Strange − I could have sworn I saw your lips move. Perchance you were but practising the art of silent ventriloquy? If that is the case, then I would strongly advise you for the future to stick to one of the lesser known foreign languages. Preferably Serbo-Croat. Not everyone is as robust as your friend Douglas. Now, I wonder, if it's not putting you to too much trouble, whether I might tempt you to direct your attention to the angle marked C in the far corner of the figure marked (i) upon the blackboard and advise us as to its probable size? − You note I say probable. I am well aware that a wild guess is about to be unleashed upon us. Just strive, if you will, to apply at least a modicum of intelligence.'

Sharon had half turned in her seat. He could feel her eyes upon him, round and brown and bright like a sparrow's. He wondered if they contained any faint glimmerings of sympathy, or only scorn.

'You have one in 180 chances,' said Mr. Hubbard. He said it bracingly. 'That is a great deal better than the football pools.'

'Football pools are a load of crap,' said Doug.

One of the harem said: 'That's all you know. My dad won fifty quid on them last year.'

Someone else said: 'My dad once got a postal order for a fiver and my mum went mad and stuck it on the mirror and couldn't get it off again.'

Doug said: 'It's a mug's game, doing the pools.'

'Yes, and it's a mug's game not paying attention in my geometry lessons.' Mr. Hubbard picked up a piece of chalk and lobbed it across the room at Jamie. 'Come on, dozy! Look alive.'

Mechanically, he fielded the piece of chalk. A faint, derisive cheer went up. Someone shouted: 'Owzatt?' Mr. Hubbard thumped on his desk.

'Shut up! I'm waiting for the Professor over here to set his powerful intellect in motion . . . angle C, Professor! Enlighten us, if you please.'

Jamie wondered if little Goody Two Shoes sitting so smug in the front row knew what size the flaming angle was supposed to be. He certainly didn't. Taking a stab at random, he said: 'Forty-five degrees.'

'*Wrong!*' Mr. Hubbard intoned it triumphantly, booming his voice like a gong. From somewhere down the front of the class came the sound of sycophantic sniggering. He knew, then, that whatever she had written in that note he wasn't going to like it. Mr. Hubbard, playing to his audience, waved a careless hand. 'Oh, sit down, lad! Sit down! Take the pressure off your brain . . . you'll do yourself a mischief, standing there like that.'

Jamie sat down. Under cover of the laughter which greeted this latest shining example of wit and repartee, he slid the sheet of paper from under his rough book. Surreptitiously, he prised open a corner of it. A corner was enough. Under the big bold capitals of his WHAT ABOUT TOMORROW? Sharon's small, tight hand came back at him, insolently: *What about it?*

He seethed. It was only what he had half been expecting, but still he seethed. He spent the rest of the period seething. He would like to have gone marching down the gangway, lifted her bodily out of her seat, and shaken her till the teeth rattled in her little pea-brained head. He'd thought something was up, the way she'd been avoiding him. She'd been on her high horse all week, refusing to talk. She got like that, sometimes. Moody; spiteful. He didn't know why he bothered with her. She wasn't anyone special. There were plenty of other girls just as pretty, *and* with nicer natures. A pity she couldn't contract something hideous and disfiguring, like a plague of boils or an attack of mumps. He'd like to see her with her face all swollen up. That would show her. That would take her down a peg or two. Primping little madam.

He was still seething when the bell rang for break. Sharon, who usually stayed behind to ingratiate herself with the Hubbard, was up and out of the door before Jamie had even got his books together. By the time he had fought his way through the harem and out into the corridor, she had disappeared. He ran her to earth five minutes later, seated on a bench in the sunshine, safely surrounded by a gaggling horde. He glared at her from a distance: she stared back at him, haughtily. Later on, during the dinner break, he hung around outside the door of the girls' cloakroom, which was strictly not allowed, and tried to collar her as she came out, but she had obviously been anticipating an attempt of some sort because she had taken the precaution of arming herself with a friend. This time, the friend stared at him haughtily as well. He ignored her, and jerked his head at Sharon.

'Coming up the road?'

'Can't,' said Sharon. 'Got things to do.'

'Can't,' said the friend. 'Got things to do.'

They went off together, arm in arm. He heard them giggling, as they turned the corner. Why did girls always have to be so unpleasant?

A day which rounded itself off with a double dose of physics couldn't really be expected to have very much going for it, not even if it did come right at the end of the week. Her Highness didn't take physics. If she had, he could at least have sat there and execrated her. As it was, he could only sit there and brood. Doug, slouched next to him on one of the lab's high stools, at the furthest end of the extremest back bench, which was their usual slouching place, drew

obscenities in his phys. and chem. book and tried to
interest him in a game of Filthy Limericks.

'There was a young woman from Bude — '

'Belt up.'

'Who stood at a bus stop quite nude — '

'Look, I said belt up, didn't I?'

Doug stuck his fingers in his face.

'What's your problem?'

'Haven't got a problem.'

'Old Prissy Knickers given you the elbow?'

So what if she had? Jamie humped a shoulder and
gazed moodily down the lab. to where Miss Spender
was doing things with a bell jar and a bit of limp
balloon. What if she had? What did he care? He'd
never really fancied her all that much. She was just
someone to knock around with. You had to have
someone, you couldn't tag along on your own; but
truth to tell, he'd never been what you might call
struck on her. She didn't exactly turn him on. Come
to that, he couldn't think of any girl who did. He
wasn't a raving sex maniac like Doug. He could take
it or leave it. All the same, no one liked being stood
up, and furthermore he didn't see why she was doing
it to him. There wasn't anything wrong with him,
was there? He didn't have bad breath, or body odour,
or — for a ghastly moment he thought that he did,
but it was only that great hulking idiot next to him,
messing about with the Bunsen burner. Blow the
place up, if he wasn't careful.

He looked at him, frowning. No girl, as far as he
knew, had ever stood Doug up. What had Doug got

that he hadn't? He wasn't any brainier, he wasn't an athlete, he hadn't got any hair on his chest. He had admittedly started shaving, but you had to look pretty hard to notice, and anyway, to counterbalance that he had pimples. Great red pimples that sometimes turned yellow. Jamie didn't have pimples. He didn't have a face like an old boot, either. A short while ago he'd actually overheard his Auntie Carol say to his mother that 'Jamie's going to be quite nice-looking, isn't he?'

He scowled. The fact that she'd said *going* to be meant that she still regarded him as just a kid. Smooth, unformed. In that case he wasn't sure that he wanted to be 'quite nice-looking'. Sooner be mature and have a face like a boot. He bet if that little cow had been going out with Doug she wouldn't have dared treat *him* that way.

Doug caught his eye and winked.

'Cheer up . . . plenty more fish in the sea.'

Well, *that* was an original remark.

On his way down to the cloakrooms at the end of the day he made a special detour via the Assembly Hall, where the house notice boards were to be found. He always did it, every Friday; never actually stopping to study them, in case people should see him and think 'There he goes, poor mug, looking for his name again', but just casually strolling past and nonchalantly glancing as he did so. Today he glanced so nonchalantly that he had to go back and glance again, to make quite sure that he wasn't hallucinating.

He wasn't. It was up there, in black and white.

> *Team for Interhouse Match Wed. 12th May*
> *R. Pearson* (cap.)
> *D. Jones*
> *J. Carr* —

He'd made it! He'd flaming well *made* it! Out of the corner of his eye, he saw the swish of something yellow. He turned, quick as a flash, and caught the tail end of Sharon, whisking herself through the door. Emboldened, he ran after her, cornering her where she couldn't escape, at the top of the stairs that led down to the cloakrooms.

'Well?'

She faced him, brazenly.

'Well what?'

'You never answered my question.'

'What question?'

'I thought we were supposed to have a date tomorrow?'

'Oh?'

That 'oh' maddened him. It really did madden him. Exasperated, he said: 'Look, I already told Doug we'd see him down the disco, didn't I?'

'Did you?'

That maddened him even more.

'You know I bloody did!'

Sharon said: 'Don't swear. I've told you before.'

She was enough to make you swear. He clenched his fists. It was lucky for her he wasn't given to violence. 'Look – ' He moderated his tone. 'Look, when you tell someone you'll do something, you can't just back down at the last minute.'

Sharon tossed her head.

'Who's backing down? I don't remember being consulted.'

What did she mean, she didn't remember being consulted? Nobody had been consulted. It had just been a general arrangement. She'd been there, she'd been part of it. If she hadn't wanted to come, she should have said so.

'Seems to me,' said Sharon, 'some people round here take things a bit too much for granted.' A blush suddenly appeared on her cheek. He turned his head to discover the cause of it, thinking perhaps it might be the Hubbard, but all he could see was Bob Pearson, coming in from net practice with his hair all sweaty and damp patches on his shirt. Sharon dimpled a smile, shy and almost coy. 'Hi, Rob.'

Bob Pearson flapped a hand and said: 'Hi, Sharon.'

So, he knew her name, did he? Second-year sixth, and knew the name of a fifth-form nobody? Jamie swung back, jealously.

'You needn't think *he*'ll look twice at you.'

Already the blush had subsided. With an airy gesture, she slung her bag over her shoulder.

'That's all you know.'

He narrowed his eyes.

'Are you going out with him?'

'Might be. Might not be.'

She was. He knew that she was. She was jacking

him in for that self-satisfied gigolo. That was why she was being pert and unpleasant. She was feeling guilty. Guilt got people that way. As if suddenly repenting, she said: 'Sorry about Saturday. You should have asked me earlier. If you're stuck for someone to take, there's always Coral.'

Jamie said: 'Stuff Coral.'

He wasn't so desperate for a bird that they could palm him off with just anybody. Sooner go without. Sooner stay at home and read a book or give a hand humping crates of beer. He wasn't all that crazy about discos, anyway. He wasn't all that crazy about *girls*.

'Perhaps another time,' said Sharon.

He felt a strong temptation to say, 'Oh, get knotted!' It might not have been particularly intelligent, but it would have given a momentary satisfaction. He wondered, afterwards, why he hadn't.

As he mooched back home, along the wire-netted footpath that bordered the playing fields, he indulged himself in a vision. The scene was the interhouse cricket match, and the vision was of a certain R. Pearson being out for a duck (preferably on the very first ball of the very first over) whilst a certain J. Carr, with cavalier disregard, smote sixes to the right of him and sixes to the left . . . yes, and she needn't think he was going to take her back again, because he wasn't. Not even if she came on her bended knees and begged him. He was through with that little cow. Once and for all, and that was *final*.

2

The day being Friday meant that at eight o'clock he had to stop what he was doing (which on this particular Friday was staring glazed-eyed at the box whilst mentally sticking pins into a waxen image of Sharon) and go over the Common to pick Kim up from her ballet class. It was one of his regular tasks. He'd been doing it for the past three months, ever since she'd got her own way about having two classes a week. Before that, it had just been Saturday mornings, and Saturday mornings she could get there and back under her own steam, because the Common was full of kids and dogs and people taking short cuts, but come the evening it tended to get a bit hairy, what with nutters flashing in the bushes and yobs on motor-cycles frightening the life out of her. She'd come back crying her eyeballs out the first time she'd gone by herself, saying that 'some big boys had chased her'. Now Jamie had to play escort, at least on the journey home. He didn't really mind. There were some evenings when it could be a drag, like when he had other things to do, but on the whole he preferred it to cleaning the car or humping crates of Guinness. It was Sharon who'd minded.

Looking back to last Friday, he realized that that had been the cause of it all – all the flouncing and the head tossing. There'd been a film she wanted to see which started at 7.45. He'd offered to take her on the Saturday, but the Saturday wouldn't do. The Saturday wasn't good enough. It had to be Friday. She'd nagged at him all through the dinner break.

'Why's it have to be you? Why can't someone else go and do it? Why can't your Dad go? It'd only take him five minutes in the car.'

When Jamie had said that his father was busy in the shop, she'd said: 'Well, your Mum, then! What's wrong with her?'

Jamie had said there wasn't anything wrong with her, except that she couldn't drive.

'Well, so why can't *she* stay in the shop and let *him* go?'

He had shaken his head.

'Not on a Friday. Not by herself.'

Sharon had stared at him; as if his mother was loopy, or something.

'Why not?'

Patiently, he had tried to explain that running an off-licence wasn't the same as running a newsagent's or confectioner's.

'You get some pretty dodgy customers. Real screwballs. Specially on a Friday.' And specially in their part of town. They didn't exactly live in one of the most salubrious areas, tucked away as they were between the flyover and the gasworks, with the Common (the shabby bit, where people dumped their rubbish and scattered Coca Cola tins) straggling past the doorstep. 'He wouldn't go off and leave her alone. Not unless I was there.'

'But it would only take him *five minutes.*'

'Yeah – that's if she's on time.' Just lately she hadn't been. They were putting on some kind of show for half term, which meant special rehearsals and classes running over. Last week he'd had to kick his heels for almost twenty minutes out on the Common. He'd torn strips off her for that – and Sharon, afterwards, had torn strips off him. She'd sulked all the rest of the evening.

'Why's it have to be *you?*' She'd kept saying it, over and over, as if it were his fault. As if he could have conjured up another member of the family if only he'd been prepared to try hard enough. 'Why can't she get the bus, for heaven's sake?'

'Bus only runs once every hour.' And in any case, he was getting paid for it. An extra pound a week on his pocket money. He needed that extra pound, he was saving up for a guitar. He was almost half-way there. His mother said it would be a sheer waste of money – 'just a craze, like all the others'. Like the skateboard and the trumpet. It was perfectly true that the skateboard and the trumpet hadn't lasted very long, but there was a limit to the amount of satisfaction you could get out of a thing like a skate-board, and as for the trumpet, that had been second-hand and half the valves hadn't worked properly. The man in the shop had said it was because it was Chinese. The guitar was going to be different. He was really determined to crack the guitar. Even Sharon had thought it was a good idea – but not if it meant he had to go trailing over the Common at eight o'clock every Friday.

'*Honestly*,' she said. 'It's *ridiculous*. Anyway, what's she want to do ballet for? Stupid thing to do. Not as if she's ever going to get anywhere. You have to be slim, for ballet. What's she want to go and do it for?'

He hadn't the faintest idea what she wanted to do it for. It didn't seem to him to matter very much *why* she wanted to do it: the important thing was that she *did*. Like he'd wanted to play the trumpet, and now wanted to play the guitar. She could have picked on something different – swimming, or gymnastics, or ice skating, or something – but she hadn't, she'd picked on ballet; and if that's what gave her a buzz, wobbling about on her toes and contorting her feet into odd positions, then so what? Why shouldn't she? No call for her Highness to get all snooty about it.

He scowled, as he scuffed his way through the usual litter of Coke tins and Kentucky Fried on to the clear ground beyond. It was typical of Sharon: anything *she* couldn't see the point of, nobody else ought to be able to. As a matter of fact he thought ballet was pretty wet himself, just as he thought art and opera were, but that didn't mean he jeered at people who spent their time walking round art galleries or going to see whatever the name of an opera was. *Madame Butterfly*, or something. *Carmen*, or something. It was a question of what turned you on. Kim was crazy about her ballet. Other kids worshipped footballers and pop stars, but not her. She'd got her bedroom walls all plastered with these photographs – sylph-like females in white skirts pretending to be swans or whatever – and she had this old, grotty ballet shoe she kept wrapped in cotton wool and occasionally took out to show people, so long as they promised not to touch it, and practically not even to *breathe* on it, on account of it had belonged to someone special like Pavlova, except that it wasn't Pavlova, it was someone he'd never heard of, but anyway someone famous nonetheless. Kim hadn't believed him when he'd said he hadn't heard of her. She'd said he couldn't possibly not have heard of her.

'She was *famous* – she was an asso*luta*.'

'An asser what?' Jamie had said.

Kim had rolled her eyes.

'Asso*luta*. That means she wasn't just an *ordinary* ballerina – she wasn't even just an ordinary *prima* ballerina – she was a prima ballerina asso*luta*, and *every*body's heard of her – and if they haven't, then they're ignorant as pigs. It's like not having heard of Queen Victoria.'

Sometimes, now, when she embarrassed him at bus stops or in the supermarket by suddenly twirling about or sticking her legs out at daft angles, he'd get his own back by saying in a high, squeaky voice 'Prima ballerina asso*luta*' so that everyone would turn round to stare and Kim would get all red and selfconscious. For all that, he only ever did it to tease; he never sneered at her. He never said she wouldn't get anywhere. That Sharon could be a right little cow at times.

He walked past the wooded area where the nutters flashed and sometimes hard porn magazines were to be found, on to the chalk pit where the motor cyclists held their illicit rallies, up to the crest and on to the flat land at the top. This was the better area – Park side, as opposed to Town side. In this area you saw girls in blue velvet riding hats mounted on their own ponies and women in silk scarves walking retrievers. All round the perimeter were large old houses still inhabited by families. (Down in the scrublands any large old house that wasn't derelict was automatically split up into bed-sits.)

It was in one of these houses, the one called The Elms, though since Dutch elm disease they'd all been cut down, that Kim's ballet classes were held. There was a board outside which said THEA TUCKER SCHOOL OF DANCE *Director: Thea Tucker*. Inside it was just an ordinary house, with a long, dark hallway and a few strategically placed chairs where people like himself could sit and wait when they had to. If it hadn't been for the board outside you wouldn't ever have known that it was supposed to be a school. There was a place in the centre of the town that was far grander. It even sounded grander: it was called the Benton Academy of Dance & Drama, and every year, for the Christmas pantomime, it provided a troupe of dancers called the Benton Bluebells. Furthermore it taught tap and ballroom as well as ordinary ballet. Thea Tucker only did the classical stuff. He could never understand why Kim had insisted on coming to such a one-horse establishment, when she could have gone to something called an Academy. He'd tried asking her, once. He'd said: 'There's a girl in my class goes to the Benton Academy — ' It was as far as he'd got. Kim had instantly screwed up her face, with its absurd button nose, and said: '*That* place!' She'd managed to pack more scorn into the words than you'd have thought a twelve-year-old with a button nose was capable of. He hadn't said anything more after that.

This evening when he pushed open the heavy front door, which was always left on the latch during class times, the hallway was empty. Had the class ended when it should, there would have been a stream of small girls rushing up the stairs in their practice costumes, or down again with bags full of ballet shoes, all changed and ready to go. Instead, from behind a closed door further down the passage, he heard the tinkling of a piano, accompanied by a rhythmic clopping and thumping which he had learnt to recognize as the sound of feet in what Kim called 'blocked shoes'. He clicked his tongue, irritably — more to convince himself that he *was* irritated than because he actually was. He didn't really object to wandering about the Common for another thirty minutes. In fact, he quite enjoyed looking at all the rich people going in and out of their rich houses. It was the principle of the thing rather than the thing itself. If the brat thought she could keep him hanging around like this every week, then she had another think coming. Unless, of course, he were to charge *waiting* time?

The door at the far end of the passage had opened and a girl had come out. She looked at him and said: 'Have you come to collect someone?'

She was the sort of girl who always made him tongue-tied. She obviously belonged to rich people, because her voice was what a young Kim had once called 'lardy dardy', really meaning Laurel and Hardy only now they tended to use it for anything that was at all posh. 'Oh, very lardy dardy' his Dad would say, when Mum got done up in her best for family occasions. He would have said it now, looking at this girl. She was dressed in a black leotard thing and tights, with blonde hair (the silver kind, not yellowy) pulled straight back into a bun, the way Kim was always trying to do hers except that it hadn't yet grown long enough, and even when it had it wouldn't suit her, because Kim had this little round squashy face like a currant bun. The girl who had appeared at the far end of the passage was all thin and sculpted. She might have stepped straight out of one of Kim's ballet photos. She said again: 'Have you come for someone?'

Jamie found his tongue.

'My sister — Kim Carr.'

'They're just running something through. I should think they'll be about another ten minutes.'

'Oh. Well, in that case – ' He snatched at the front door. 'I'll come back.'

'You can wait inside if you'd like.'

'No. That's all right.' He'd rather be out on the Common than shut up here with nothing to look at but a pile of ballet magazines.

'The thing is,' said the girl, 'they might be longer than ten minutes – they might be half an hour. They're doing their Dewdrop routine.' She paused, looking at him. 'Why don't you come along and watch?'

Come along and watch? *Him*? Watch a pack of small girls doing a Dewdrop routine? She must be joking!

'They wouldn't want me in there,' he said.

That was a mistake: he realized it the minute he'd said it. He should have told her he had other things to do. Now he'd laid himself wide open.

'Actually,' said the girl, 'it would do them good to have someone there. It would give them an audience – someone to play to. Give them an incentive to get things right.'

He muttered: 'I wouldn't know if they got things right or if they didn't,' but he'd left himself without a leg to stand on. The girl said seriously: 'Ah, but they're not to know that, are they? Do come! I'm sure you'll like it.'

It seemed he had no alternative. Limp with embarrassment, he shambled down the passage; sheepishly, as she flung open the door, he slunk in at her heels.

177

'Take a seat.'

She waved him into a chair. He slumped down on to it, legs flung out before him, arms folded across his chest, trying to look as if he couldn't care less, which in the circumstances wasn't that easy. He'd never been alone in a whole roomful of females before, especially half-naked ones; and just to add to his discomfiture, when at last he felt strong enough to risk a quick glance he found that the room was surrounded on three of its sides by full-length mirrors, which meant that you could hardly help staring at yourself whether you wanted to or not.

He shuffled on his seat, and his reflection shuffled with him. It looked stern, and ill at ease; shabby, too, in washed-up jeans and an old blue sweat shirt with *University of Illinois* printed across the chest. He wondered what on earth had possessed him to get a sweat shirt with *University of Illinois* splashed all over it. For crying out loud, he didn't even know that Illinois *had* a university.

The clopping and the thudding was still going on. Clop-*thud*. Clop-*thud*. At close range it sounded like a herd of three-legged buffaloes. He raised his eyes a fraction, and the buffaloes turned into a dozen small girls in pink tunics all leaping about in a circle. Some of them were looking solemn, and some of them were wearing bright, fixed, toothy grins, but each and every one had her arms held up in the air and her head tilted to one side, making like mad to be dewdrops. Kim was making like mad along with the rest. The circle dissolved and then re-formed itself

into a line, and there was Kim, bang in the middle,
all beaming and porky with her fingers splayed out
stiff and straight with the effort she was putting into
it. Good old Kim! Even he could see that her fingers
weren't *supposed* to be all stiff and straight. Not if it
was a dewdrop she was being. Maybe if it had been
a streak of lightning or an icicle or something; but
not a dewdrop. He wished there were some way of
getting it across to her: 'Relax those fingers!' It was
what Mr. Butterworth was always bellowing at them
in the gym, only with him it was shoulders – *'Relax
those shoulders!'*, accompanied by a vicious chopping
up and down with both hands that left you sore for
days afterwards.

The girl who was responsible for his being there
had gone across to the piano and was talking earnestly – he could tell that it was earnestly, from her
expression – to an elderly lady who he supposed
must be the famous Thea Tucker that Kim was
always on about. For months past it had been 'Miss
Tucker says this' and 'Miss Tucker says that'. She had
become almost a household god.

He gazed at her, covertly, through the mirror.
At first glance she didn't seem anything particularly
special. She must have been at least as old as his
Dad's mother, yet she was plastered in make-up and
wearing a black pleated knee-length skirt over a
boat-necked leotard and flesh-coloured tights. It was
a get-up which would have looked positively ridiculous, not to say downright indecent, if his Gran had
tried wearing it – positively ridiculous if his *mother*

had tried. On Miss Tucker it somehow looked OK, perhaps because she hadn't gone shapeless like most old people. Her face was all wrinkled, he could see that even at this distance, and the veins on her neck were knotted like cords, but the rest of her might almost have passed for a young girl.

She suddenly glanced across at him, and he looked away, confused. Were they talking about him? Out of the corner of his eye he saw the girl nod in his direction. He saw Miss Tucker frown. It was a frown that contained more of doubt than of active disapproval, but all the same he felt himself grow hot. What were they talking about? Why did they keep looking at him like that? What was supposed to be the matter with him?

Selfconsciously, he sat up straighter on his chair. He unfolded his arms, tried crossing his legs, found the washed-out jeans had grown too tight, and hastily uncrossed them. Miss Tucker and the girl stood watching his antics judiciously, as if he were giving a performance for which he was to be awarded marks out of ten. He half turned, on his chair, so that they only had him in profile. In front of him, the Dewdrops thundered to a halt, more or less in time with the music. Miss Tucker detached herself from the piano and moved forward into the room. She walked with a strange, duck-like waddle, her feet splayed out at right angles. It should have looked graceless, but in fact it didn't: she had too much regality about her for that.

'All right, children!' She clapped her hands. 'That

was better than last time, but do try to remember that you're meant to be dewdrops. Not cart-horses . . . Kim, dear, watch those fingers. They look like bunches of twigs. Deirdre, remind me I want to take a look at your ankles some time. Andrea – yes.' Her lips tightened. 'Andrea I shall have a Word with tomorrow.'

At this, an exceptionally tiny child with a cheeky elfin face grew very pink and looked as if she might be about to burst into tears. Jamie felt sorry for her. He wondered what terrible crime she had committed. Later, when he asked Kim about it Kim went all big-eyed and said: 'She forgot her belt . . . her elastic belt, you know. To wear round her tunic. *And* she did it last week. Miss Tucker was *furious*.'

Miss Tucker, now, having bestowed upon the unfortunate Andrea a look which would have quelled a lump of granite, said: 'Very well, then. Off you go. Ten o'clock sharp in the morning – we'll take it straight through to Anita's solo.'

All the little pink Dewdrops chorused: 'Yes, Miss Tucker. Good night, Miss Tucker', bobbed themselves up and down like corks on a high sea as they curtsied (why did they do that, Jamie wondered? She wasn't royalty) and went clip-clopping off towards the door. The girl, he noticed, had already gone. He made to follow, and found himself detained by Miss Tucker. She said: 'Anita tells me that you're Kim's brother.'

Anita. So that was her name – and they *had* been talking about him. He knew that they must have

181

been. Now he supposed he was going to be told off
for being there. He opened his mouth to defend
himself, but before he could say anything Miss
Tucker, abruptly, had said: 'Are you musical?'

'Musical?' The question took him by surprise. He
considered it a moment. He had once sung in the
church choir, when he was too young to know
any better, and Miss Hargreaves at school had never
actually asked him to shut up or told him that he
must be tone deaf, as she had Doug. On the other
hand, discretion was always the better part of vain-
glory. After all, why did she want to know?
Cautiously, not committing himself, he said: 'Not
specially.'

'You don't play anything?'

He thought of the second-hand trumpet, and the
guitar, and said: 'No.' And then, as an afterthought,
in case that sounded ungracious: 'Kim does.' Kim
had had piano lessons once a week until she'd started
clamouring for ballet instead. The family couldn't
afford both – that was why Jamie had never learnt.
It was music and ballet for Kim, football and cricket
for Jamie. Just as well, really. He wouldn't have
wanted to spend hours thumping about on a piano.
He wouldn't have minded a bit of encouragement
over that trumpet, though. He bet with a bit of
encouragement he could have learnt how to play it.
As it was, every time he'd tried putting it to his lips
his mother had complained of a headache and his
father had said: 'If you blow that down my ear
once more I'll confiscate the perishing thing.' They'd

never made all that fuss about Kim and her piano, even though it had lived in the same room as the television set. Still, he didn't mind giving her a plug, if it was likely to raise her stock with the formidable Miss Tucker. 'Kim can play pretty well,' he said. 'She did it for two years. She passed these exams.'

Miss Tucker didn't seem very interested in Kim or her exams. She only went on looking at Jamie, and said: 'What about your sense of rhythm? Do you have a sense of rhythm?'

He shrugged a shoulder. How should he know? It wasn't something he'd ever given any thought to. Miss Tucker grew impatient.

'Can you move in time to music? If you hear a piece of music – Marjorie!' She turned, with a peremptory snap of the fingers, to the little mouse lady who had been playing the piano. 'Give him something to move about to.'

The little mouse lady, who had been on her way out through the door, obediently turned and pattered back again. She sat herself down, opened the lid of the piano and began to play. He wondered if she'd charge overtime, or if she didn't mind being exploited.

'There you are.' Miss Tucker jerked her head. 'See what you can do.'

He stared at her, bemused.

'Well, go along,' she said; and she shooshed at him with her hands as if he were a chicken. 'Go and do something.'

Reluctantly, he shuffled a few paces forward.

'Do what?'

'Whatever you feel inspired to do.' (Cut and run. This place was a mad house. The woman herself was obviously a raving lunatic.) 'Just move about, in time to the music.'

Feeling the biggest idiot this side of the moon, he slouched pigeon-toed across the room. Her voice called imperiously after him: 'Come along, come along, young man! You can do better than that! Listen to the music — what is it telling you? It's telling you to *move*, isn't it? Well, then . . . move! Let's see some action. *Yum*-pum, *yum*-pum, *yum*-pum, put some animation into it! Lift up those feet! Shake out those shoulders! Good gracious me, anyone would think you were suffering from sleeping sickness . . . you haven't got anything wrong with you, have you?'

He was nettled. Did he look as if he had?

'If this is the way you carry on when you go to discos — '

'It's not the way I carry on when I go to discos!' Goaded, he turned on her. 'It's different at discos.'

'How?' said Miss Tucker. 'In what way is it different?'

The music was different — everything was different. For one thing, you had a bird.

'For one thing,' he said, 'you have a — ' The word died on his lips. 'You have a partner,' he said.

'Oh! So that's what's bothering you. Well, that's easily remedied.'

Before he knew what she intended, Miss Tucker

184

had come waltzing out into the middle of the room. Gaily, she seized him by the hand.

'There we are, then . . . let's get with it!'

3

It ought by rights to have been the most embarrassing thing that had ever happened to him — disco
dancing to the wrong sort of music with a daft old
bat as old as his grandmother. Oddly enough, it
wasn't. He was even managing, reluctantly, by the
end, to get some sort of a kick out of it. He was
pretty sure Miss Tucker was, too, the way she
was flinging herself about. Really, you had to hand
it to her: she might be a daft old bat, but she'd
certainly got spirit. Her enthusiasm was such that it
would have made him look even sillier standing on
his dignity than stepping down and joining in. He
was glad, all the same, that Doug wasn't there.

'Well!' said Miss Tucker. She was hardly any more
out of breath than he was. 'That was something
different.'

She could say that again. He wondered, now, if
she would let him go. He began sidling towards the
door, but before he could get there it had opened
and the girl, Anita, had reappeared. She had changed
out of her black leotard into T-shirt and jeans, with
her hair pulled back into an ordinary elastic band,
but still you could tell that she belonged to rich

people. She had that sort of an air about her. As soon as she saw Jamie she said: 'Has he agreed to – ' at the same moment as Miss Tucker said: 'Do you know, I really think he'll do?'

Do? He froze. Do for what? What was this? Some kind of a set-up?

Miss Tucker, taking him by the arm, said: 'Come over here and stand by Anita.'

He didn't know why he let himself be pushed around like this, he really didn't. She had absolutely no right – *he* wasn't one of her pupils. The habit of obedience was too strong, that was the trouble. Meekly, he allowed himself to be ranged by the side of the girl. She'd looked tall, at first, on account of she was so skinny, but in fact she didn't come much above his shoulder. Miss Tucker measured them both with her eye.

'Yes,' she said. 'The match is perfect. Heightwise he couldn't be better.' Better? For *what*? 'And I must say he is excellently proportioned.' By now, the girl was also measuring him with her eye. They stood before him, the pair of them, critically raking him up and down. He began to feel uncomfortable, like a prize bull in the market place. Perhaps they were white slave traders, shipping young men off to distant parts for nefarious purposes. Doug said things went on in some countries you'd never believe. Perhaps they ran a *brothel*.

'Do you do a lot of athletics?' said Miss Tucker.

Defiantly, he said: 'Yes.' He didn't know why he

said it defiantly, except that it sounded better that way. Miss Tucker nodded.

'I thought you must do – swimming, probably.' She squeezed at his upper arm. 'That's why your muscles are so well developed.'

He didn't bother telling her that the reason his muscles were developed was because he'd spent the last few years humping crates of booze up from the cellar.

'Well, now,' said Miss Tucker. He stiffened. Here it came. The moment of truth. 'How would you feel about helping us out?'

He looked at her, guardedly. Not with any brothel, he didn't help out. If they wanted a strong arm guy, they could look elsewhere. Doug, for instance. It was the sort of thing that Doug would probably enjoy.

'Do say you will!' Anita was looking at him beseechingly, both hands clasped to her bosom (what there was of it). 'The show's going on in six weeks.'

'Show?'

'Yes! We're getting absolutely desperate.'

'What we need,' said Miss Tucker, 'is a man.'

'Oh – ' He relaxed. So that was all they wanted him for: the show. Presumably to shift scenery, or something. He said: 'We-e-ll – ' He supposed he wouldn't actually mind. Lugging bits of scenery about would be as nothing besides hefting those everlasting crates up the cellar steps, and it wasn't as if he had much else on just at present. Not now that he'd finally chucked Sharon. On the other hand –

'You wouldn't have to *do* much,' said Anita. 'Only just *be* there. You'd never believe how difficult men are to come by.'

Miss Tucker explained.

'Our only really *mature* young man, unfortunately, broke his arm last week in a motor-cycle accident. I warned him time and again, such machines are lethal, but of course he wouldn't listen. Now he's in a plaster cast and quite useless.'

'All we're left with are kids,' said Anita. 'And, of course' (a note of scorn crept into her voice), 'and, of course, *Garstin*.'

Miss Tucker sighed.

'Poor Garstin. He does try. But I'm afraid that no amount of trying will compensate for lack of physique.'

'Not to mention being able to keep time to the music,' said Anita. She said it with a certain bitterness.

'Oh!' Miss Tucker beamed. She laid a hand on Jamie's head. 'Kim's brother has an excellent sense of timing! He is naturally rhythmical. I have already made sure of *that*.'

Jamie was growing uncomfortable again. What was all this about 'naturally rhythmical'? They weren't expecting him to shift scenery in time to *Swan Lake*, were they? He looked suspiciously from one to the other of them; from Anita, whose eyes, he saw with surprise, were actually green — not blue-green, or grey-green, but real greeny-green — to Miss Tucker, who was studying him again in that

189

way he didn't like, the white-slave way, taking in all the details.

'Yes,' she said. 'One must have the physique. Without it, one has no bearing. I'm afraid poor Garstin is rather like a beanpole. I knew that it would happen. He's shot up too fast – outrun his strength. Not that it would make a great deal of difference if he hadn't. If one isn't musical, one isn't musical, and that's about all there is to it.'

'Look,' said Jamie. He cleared a frog out of his throat. 'What exactly – '

'If I've got to dance with Garstin,' said Anita, 'then I'd rather not dance at all.'

Dance? *Dance*? The message, suddenly, got through. He backed away, indignantly. *Him*? *Dance*? Oh, no! No, no! They weren't getting him on that lark. No way. Not a chance.

'Actually,' he said, 'I'm pretty busy just at the moment.' He had exams the end of this term. One 'O' and some CSEs. They couldn't expect him to mess about on some tinpot little show. Anyway, *him*?

'It's not as if we should want you here every night,' said Miss Tucker. 'Only just now and again, and occasionally for a private session with Anita.'

In other circumstances he might not have objected to a few private sessions with Anita – he wouldn't have minded going to the cinema with her, for example. He wouldn't have minded taking her to the disco. He wondered if she was the sort of girl who went to discos. Probably not. Probably considered it not cultural enough. He bet she'd rather go to the opera or an art gallery.

'You needn't worry that we'd want you to do anything complex,' said Miss Tucker. 'There are only a couple of small lifts involved. I'm sure you wouldn't have any difficulty with those – I'm sure you could lift Anita with no trouble at all.'

Lift her? He could throw her about like a sack of coals, if that was what they wanted. There was hardly anything of her, she couldn't weigh more than about six stone. But anyhow, the question wouldn't arise because he wasn't going to do it.

'Naturally, if they were too much for you,' said Miss Tucker, 'we should have to modify them. But I don't foresee any difficulty. Not with that physique.' He squirmed. 'And then, of course' – she spoke briskly – 'one has to consider the presentation aspect. It's a distinct advantage, your being so dark – seeing as Anita is so fair. It will make a good strong contrast.'

'And after all, it is for a *cause*,' said Anita.

'Oh, yes. We always support a Cause. Last year it was Save the Children, this year it's Spastics.' Miss Tucker shot Jamie a shrewd glance. 'Didn't Kim say you had a little cousin who was a spastic?'

He glowered. Trust Kim. She *would* have to go shooting her mouth off, wouldn't she? He mumbled, grudgingly.

'What?' said Miss Tucker. 'Speak up, young man, and don't swallow your words!'

'I said yes,' said Jamie. 'She goes to Fairfield.'

'*Fair*field.' A look of triumph settled itself on Miss

Tucker's face. 'The very institution to whom we are giving the proceeds!'

He felt himself becoming trapped. Anita, quite obviously, had already decided that that was that – there could be no further grounds for argument. Fairfield had clinched it, as far as she was concerned.

'Well, there you are, then!' She turned, excitedly, to Miss Tucker – 'It means we could put the Russian dance back in!' – spun round again, to Jamie – '*You* could do a Russian dance, couldn't you?'

He said stolidly: 'Russian dance?'

'Yes! You know! Like the Red Army do – like the Cossacks – like this!'

All of a sudden she was down on her haunches with her arms folded across her chest, flinging her legs out. He had to admit that it looked pretty good – but he was willing to bet it was quite easy. He daresay he could do it, if he really felt inclined. He was almost impelled to get down there with her and try it, but before he could be betrayed into any such display of weakness he had intercepted a warning frown from Miss Tucker to Anita. He knew very well what the frown meant. He wasn't an idiot. It meant, we've nearly got him, don't frighten him off . . . one thing at a time: let's get the fish hooked first . . .

That did it. He hardened his resolve.

'I reckon I ought to be going,' he said. 'Kim'll be waiting for me.'

'But you will agree to do it,' said Anita, 'won't you? *Please!*'

'Let him think about it,' said Miss Tucker.

He seized at the suggestion, gratefully.

'Yeah,' he said. 'I'll think about it.' He wrenched open the door. 'I'll let you know.'

The only reason he couldn't let them know there and then was that he was too much of a coward. He couldn't tell them, straight out, I wouldn't be caught dead dancing in your crummy little show. He'd get Kim to do it for him tomorrow. On second thoughts, he wouldn't get Kim to do it for him tomorrow. He'd rather Kim didn't know anything about it, she'd only start nagging at him. He could just hear her. 'But, Jamie, it's for *spastics*.' Perhaps it would be easier if he simply let it slip his mind. Simply forgot about it.

Accordingly, he did so – but not before he'd spent ten minutes in his bedroom having a go at the Cossack thing. Just out of interest, that was all. Just to see if he could do it. (He could, but his mother didn't like it. She yelled at him up the stairs to 'Stop that, whatever it is you're doing! You'll have the ceiling down!') After that, he didn't think of it any more.

On Saturday evening, for want of anything more intelligent to do (he didn't really feel like going down to the disco by himself, and in any case he might bump into Sharon mooning over Bob Pearson, and that would just about finish him) he was sitting slumped before the box with the rest of the family when the telephone rang and it was for him. His mother came back from the hall and said:

'Jamie, there's a young lady wants you.' He'd known at once that it couldn't be Sharon. Sharon had never been 'a young lady'. She'd only been 'that Sharon'.

'Talks very nicely,' said his mother. 'Asked if she could have a word with you.'

It was, of course, Anita. He might have known she wouldn't give up that easily. She said: 'Hallo! Is that Kim's brother? I do hope you don't mind me ringing, but I've been on tenterhooks all day. I knew if I didn't find out I'd never be able to settle to anything . . . *are* you going to be able to help us? With the show?'

He was a fool. A dolt. A clod. A weak-kneed, lily-livered, yellow-bellied *clod*. Why couldn't he have said no, very firmly, right at the outset? Why couldn't he say no, very firmly, right now?

Because he was a clod, that was why.

He said: 'Well — '

'We'd really be most *terribly* grateful,' said Anita. 'Oh, I do hope you can! I simply don't know what we'll do if you can't.'

By the time he went back to the box, he had committed himself.

4

'The square of the sum on the hypotenuse – ' Jamie floundered, came to a halt, tried again. 'The *sum* of the squares on the hypotenuse – '

'Yes?'

'In a right-angled triangle – '

'Yes?'

He took a breath.

'In – a – right – angled – triangle – the – sum – of – the – squares – on – the – hypotenuse – is – equal – to – the – sum – of – the – squares – on – the – other – two – sides.'

'Oh!' said Mr. Hubbard. 'It is, is it?'

No; obviously it wasn't. It had obviously gone wrong somewhere. It was all a load of blithering rubbish, anyway. Mr. Hubbard regarded him with interest.

'How many squares, exactly, were you proposing to have on this hypotenuse of yours?'

'Er – two?' said Jamie.

'Two?'

'Well – ' He shrugged. It seemed as good a number as any.

Doug, in his rough book, wrote: ARSEOLES.

'I suppose you do know what the hypotenuse is?' mused Mr. Hubbard.

Now that he came to mention it, he wasn't at all sure that he did. As far as he was concerned, it was just a thing that was found in right-angled triangles – a thing which for some reason he couldn't fathom had squares attached to it, which squares, for another reason he couldn't fathom, were held to be equal to certain other squares also to be found in right-angled triangles. And what the use of it was was more than he could say. He wondered if the Queen would know, if someone were to ask her. If someone were to go up to her and say, 'Excuse me, your Queen, but do you know what the hypotenuse is – '

'*Well?*' said Mr. Hubbard.

The creep was actually expecting a reply.

'Well,' said Jamie. Sharon turned her head to look at him. 'Well,' he said, 'it's – it's something you get in a right-angled triangle.'

Oh, ha ha. Very funny. Titter titter. What a joke. Sharon had turned back again, her shoulders shaking. He scowled. He bet *she* couldn't get down on her haunches and kick her legs out. Couldn't even run for a bus, that one, without tripping over her own feet. Couldn't even dive two inches off the side of the pool without doing a belly flop.

He became aware that Mr. Hubbard was studying him. His face wore an air of puzzled wonderment, as if he were gazing upon some new species of earthworm hitherto unknown to man.

'Tell me, laddie – ' He leaned forward, across the

196

desk, towards him. 'Is it that you are bone idle, or are you just naturally thick?'

'One, two – *up* – hold – balance her with the right hand – round, three, four – down, gently – good – pause for the arabesque – two, three – now, give her your left hand – *left!* – good – lead her forward – three, four – pause – prepare to support – yes, that's good! That's good! That's excellent!'

At least there was *some*thing he could do right. Old Miss Tucker was as bucked as if he'd just scaled the north face of the Eiger. All he'd done was lift some strip of a girl up into the air and then put her back down again so that she could use him as a balancing post while she stood on one leg. He was glad that they were happy (remembering the incident of the small girl and the missing elastic belt he thought that taken all in all he would rather face the scorn of a Mr. Hubbard than the wrath of a Miss Tucker) but still he couldn't really see that he'd done anything so wonderful. He obviously had, however. Old Miss Tucker was beaming away like mad, and Anita had both her hands clasped to what passed for her bosom.

'Jamie,' she said, 'that was *super*. It really felt *super*!'

He grinned, in spite of himself. It hadn't felt too bad to him, either. In fact, if he was to be honest, he'd got quite a kick out of it. For all she was so skinny she hadn't felt bony, as he'd half expected. Instead, she'd been quite firm and warm, like next door's terrier, which might be tiny but was nevertheless all muscle. (Unlike his Gran's King Charles, which was just a lump of yielding flesh into which your fingers, unpleasantly, sank fathoms deep as you tried to lift it.)

'It would seem,' said Miss Tucker, still beaming, 'that you have a natural instinct.'

'*Honestly*,' said Anita, 'it felt as if we'd been working together for *weeks*.'

Even now he couldn't think what they were making all the fuss about. He tried to feel pleased with himself, but how could you bask when you still didn't know what you were supposed to have done? Miss Tucker attempted to enlighten.

'The art of partnering is not as easy as you obviously think. It is not simply a question of being on hand at the right moment – anyone can be taught to do that.'

('Anyone except Garstin,' muttered Anita.)

'What *cannot* be taught is the ability to work in harmony. For that one needs a degree of mutual sympathy which is either there or not there. Fortunately, in your case' – the beam returned – 'it evidently is.'

Well, if that was what she chose to believe. He couldn't say he'd noticed himself feeling in any particular sympathy with Anita. Not that he felt *out* of sympathy. She was pleasant enough, and at least she didn't have that maddening female habit of giggling. He hated it when they giggled. It always seemed to him that they were doing it on purpose to create feelings of insecurity. Anita certainly wasn't guilty of that; but even so – even discounting the fact that she belonged to rich people and that he didn't – it was difficult to see what they could ever have in common to feel sympathy about.

'It has always been my contention,' said Miss Tucker, 'that great partnerships are born, and not made. You have only to look at Markova and Dolin – '

'Or Fonteyn and Nureyev,' said Anita.

'Or Fonteyn and Nureyev,' said Miss Tucker.

Jamie wanted to say, 'Or Hobbs and Sutcliffe?' but thought perhaps it might not be appropriate. Miss Tucker and Anita probably wouldn't know who they were – worse still, might not even have heard of them. Come to that, he'd never heard of Markova and Dolin. He'd heard of Margot Fonteyn, of course, because everybody had, and he'd heard of Rudolph Nureyev till he was sick of the very sound of him. Rudolph Nureyev was one of Kim's idols, coming second only to the prima ballerina assoluta of the shoe. Sometimes, when he felt that she deserved taking down a peg, he'd rib her about it and ask 'How's the old Red-Nosed Reindeer, then?' It never failed to make her mad.

'You know – ' Miss Tucker was giving him the old slave-trader look again, through half-closed eyes with her head to one side. 'You know, I cannot help feeling that you should be doing something on your own account. Something simple, but spectacular – '

'David's solo!' cried Anita. 'He could do David's solo!'

Jamie stared at her in alarm. He hadn't agreed to do anyone's solos: he had only agreed to act as fork-lift truck and balancing post. They weren't getting him out there all by himself.

'Mm . . .' Miss Tucker sounded thoughtful. 'Possibly if we were to scale it down – '

'It's not as if there's anything madly technical. Only right at the end.'

'Yes, we couldn't expect him to manage fouettes.'

Instantly, he wondered why not. (He asked Kim, later: 'What's a fouette?' Kim said: 'It's what Odile does in *Swan Lake* . . . she does *thirty-two*, and all on the same spot.' 'Yes,' said Jamie, 'but what *are* they?' 'Well – ' Kim wrinkled her button nose. 'They're a sort of turning thing, when you whip one leg round the other.' 'Show.' 'I can't,' said Kim, and she giggled. 'I fall over . . .')

'Let me think,' said Miss Tucker. 'Can you jump?'

Could he jump? Once won medals for it, hadn't he? He said so – rather more boastfully, perhaps, than he had intended. Anita immediately said: 'Long jump, or high jump?' Pride carried him away.

'Both,' he said, carelessly. One year it had been one, one year it had been the other. 'I'm OK at either.'

'Yes, but not in those trousers.' Miss Tucker suddenly bent down and twitched at the leg of his jeans. 'Ridiculous! It's a wonder you can move at all. Remind me, for next time, to look out some tights for you.'

His blood ran cold. He saw himself, through the

medium of the obtrusive mirrors, backing away in
something like panic. *Tights?*

'You'll find them much more comfortable. Far less
restricting. Nobody can dance in skin-tight jeans.'

Desperately, he said: 'I've got some others at
home. These have shrunk a bit. The others aren't so
tight.'

'They'll still be too tight to dance in. Look at
you! Can't even bend your legs properly.'

'Yes, I can,' he said.

'Nonsense! Of course you can't.'

'I can!'

Miss Tucker gave him a look: it was the sort of
look she had given the small girl, Andrea.

'I have been in this business,' she said, 'for almost
forty years. I have taught Household Names. I know
what I am talking about.'

There was a silence. Anita, diplomatically, studied
her nails.

'What is your objection,' said Miss Tucker, 'to
wearing tights? Is there something wrong with your
legs? Or are you simply prejudiced?' His cheeks
flared: he mumbled, inarticulately. 'Simply prejudiced,' said Miss Tucker. 'How sad! I thought
modern youth had grown out of that sort of thing.
I thought you were more liberated. Evidently not.
Well, in that case, all the more reason why you
should start wearing them now. It will give you a
chance to get used to them by the time of the
performance.' His horror must have shown in his
face. 'My dear boy,' said Miss Tucker, 'you surely

201

didn't think you were going to be allowed to *perform* in jeans?'

He walked part of the way home with Anita, who lived in one of the big new houses that bordered the golf course, over on the south side of the Common. She obviously felt him to be in need of comfort and reassurance, for suddenly, in the middle of a silence, when he had been wondering what he ought to talk about, she said: 'Did you know that soldiers in the British Army sometimes wear tights?'

He looked at her, sideways.

'Oh, yes? Special issue, I suppose . . . for when they do *Swan Lake*.'

'No.' She rode his sarcasm quite calmly. 'Not special issue, just ordinary women's tights. And not for when they do *Swan Lake*: for when they're going off on route marches and the temperature's sub-zero . . . I know you don't believe me, but it's perfectly true. My uncle told me. He said there's nothing to beat a pair of tights for keeping out the cold. And he ought to know,' she added. 'He's been up Everest in them.'

He felt like saying: '*I*'ve got this uncle goes in for ladies' stockings . . . wears 'em over his head every time he does a bank job.' It was the sort of thing that Doug would have said. Instead, he only humped a shoulder and made a grumping noise. Everest was one thing: disporting yourself on stage before a gaping crowd of people was another.

'But in any case,' said Anita, kindly, 'I shouldn't

worry too much if I were you . . . you'll have a nice long tunic to go over the top.'

He wasn't sure whether she was teasing him or not. Her voice was serious enough, but he thought he caught a hint of laughter in the green eyes. He grunted, and said nothing. They'd just better think themselves lucky if he deigned to turn up next week, that was all.

The interhouse cricket match was a farce. He was sent in at number three and he made three runs and dropped about the same number of catches (two of which would admittedly have been pretty spectacular in anyone's book, but for one of which there was simply no excuse) and altogether made about as big an exhibition of himself as even Sharon could have wished. She came up to him afterwards and said: 'That was rotten luck, getting run out like that.' He wondered if she were gloating, or if she really meant it. Probably gloating. Probably only too glad to see him humiliated. She was still making goo-goo eyes at Bob Pearson, great self-important oaf that he was, strutting up and down in his First Eleven pullover, with his cap jammed over his eyes, making like he was W. G. Grace and Don Bradman and Len Hutton all rolled into one. Jamie shrugged a shoulder and said, 'Oh, it happens' – lofty, offhand, couldn't-care-less – and slunk away to nurse his grievances in private.

It hadn't been all his fault. The one catch that he'd muffed, that had been his fault; but not the running out. That had been the Pearson, that had. Selfish great lout – talk about hogging all the bowling. No one else had had a look in. From the moment Jamie had joined him at the wicket it had been nothing but a constant stream of orders bawled down the pitch – 'Now, partner!' 'Come along, partner!' 'You can make it, partner!' – with Jamie tearing to and fro like a stuck pig from one set of stumps to the other and him bagging all the honour and glory and knocking up all the runs. Thirty-nine not out, he'd ended up with (out of a paltry total of sixty-nine). Jamie had managed to scrape three, off a short ball at the end of an over, which would have left him facing the bowling. Mister Pearson hadn't liked that. He'd yelled: 'Yes, yes, and another one, partner!' And then, too late, on a note of panic: 'No, get back! Get back!'

Abandoned between wickets, Jamie hadn't stood a chance. He'd had no alternative but to turn and make a mad dash, in a despairing attempt to get his bat over the crease before a well-flung return sent the bails flying. Only inches from safety, he'd fallen flat on his face. He never wanted to think of it again. Never as long as he lived. From now on he wouldn't even bother to make his ritual detour through the Assembly Hall on a Friday afternoon and throw his casual glance at the notice board. He wouldn't even go through the actions. There wouldn't be any point; not after this.

Doug, next day, as they slouched round the field together during the morning break, said: 'That cretin. Deserves to be shot, getting you run out like that.' The sore patch in Jamie's heart became at this just a tiny bit less sore. If Doug had noticed, then surely others must have done? 'Guy's an idiot,' said Doug. 'Know what you want to do, next time he tries it . . . dig in your heels, and just don't move. That's what I'd do.'

Jamie kicked glumly at an empty Coca Cola can.

'Don't s'pose there'll be any next time.'

'Course there will,' said Doug. 'You weren't given a fair chance. Everybody's got to be given a fair chance. Stands to reason.'

Nevertheless, his name wasn't there when he walked past the notice board on the following Friday. He'd known that it wouldn't be; but still, the injustice smarted.

He had been hoping against hope that Miss Tucker would have forgotten her threat of finding him a pair of tights to wear, but of course she hadn't. He had known that she wouldn't, just as he'd known his name wouldn't be on the notice board; but if the injustice of the one continued to rankle, the embarrassment of the other very nearly annihilated. It wasn't so much what it *looked* like – he wasn't knock-kneed, or anything; he wasn't bandy-legged – as what it *felt* like. What it felt like was walking about naked, almost. He didn't know how people could. Not unless they were exhibitionists, which he was not, in spite of falling flat on his face in front of half the school: not unless they actually *enjoyed* being stared at and pointed at and sniggered about. He felt an absolute idiot, and just to make matters worse she'd gone and given him these stupid shoes. He'd been wearing trainers up till now. He didn't see how she could complain about trainers. If you could run in them, there wasn't any reason why you couldn't dance in them — except that he wasn't going to be doing any dancing. He'd come to a firm decision on that point. He was going to make it very clear. He'd agreed to help Anita do *her* bits and pieces: he hadn't agreed to do any on his own account. And furthermore, if there were any snide remarks on the subject of *tights* —

There weren't. When he entered the room, scowling to cover up his discomfiture at being seen abroad in such absurd and inadequate attire, Anita was ,already there, doing knee-bends at the rails ('*Plies*,' she said, later. 'And it's a barre, not a rail') while Miss Tucker was conferring at the piano with the little mouse lady, whose name was Miss Harrell. At the sound of the door, they all glanced up. Anita waved a casual hand and went on with her exercises; Miss Harrell smiled and nodded; Miss Tucker said: 'Good boy! You're on time.' Nobody gave any signs of thinking he looked odd or peculiar. The only reference made to his change of costume was by Miss Tucker, who said: 'Well! Now that you're dressed properly, we can get you doing things.'

He tried his best to explain that he didn't want to do things — that *doing* things had been no part of his agreement. Miss Tucker, impatient, brushed all objections to one side.

'Don't be so silly, of course you want to do things. What's the matter with you? You're not shy, are you? You shouldn't be, looking like that. You should be only too happy to show yourself off. A little bit of healthy exhibitionism never hurt anyone. That's what a solo's designed for, you know. After all' – she said it briskly, as if there could be no possible doubt in the matter – 'you don't just want to be a clothes prop, do you? Of course you don't. That would be very poor spirited. Now, when you've led Anita off, what I want you to do is to come back on – can we have the music, Marjorie? – with a series of grands jetes right around the stage – what are you puckering your forehead for? I suppose you don't know what a grand jete is? Well, that's soon remedied. It's nothing in the least alarming. Just a rather spectacular kind of jump. But perfectly simple . . . Anita, dear, could you show?'

Anita obligingly peeled herself up from the floor, where she'd been sitting slumped against the wall in a crumpled lotus position, and before Jamie's helpless gaze took off across the room in a series of flying leaps.

'There, now,' said Miss Tucker. She beamed at him, triumphantly. 'With all those medals for jumping? Don't tell me you can't do *that.*'

'Want to see something?' said Doug.
'Not particularly.'

They were sitting out on the field, where Jamie was struggling to get Doug's maths homework copied into his own book before it was time to go and face the Hubbard for another session of public scourging and humiliation. Not that Doug's maths was any more sparkling than his, but a page full of rubbish was a safer bet than a page full of nothing at all. In any case, when Doug said: 'Want to see something?' it usually meant something pornographic that he'd picked up on the Common. Jamie could live without it. It certainly wouldn't break his heart.

'Get away!' Doug nudged at him. 'Do you good.' He took a quick look to make sure there were no staff in the vicinity, then with an evil leer pulled a square of crumpled paper from the back pocket of his jeans and thrust it under Jamie's nose, obscuring the maths homework. 'Get a load of that, then!'

Jamie glanced at it – but only because he had to; and then as briefly as possible. He said 'Yeah', and pushed it to one side.

'Not bad, eh?'

'Not bad,' said Jamie. He couldn't think what it was that Doug got out of this everlasting porno of his. Sometimes he wished he'd got the guts to say 'Stuff your dirty pictures, they bore me,' but of course he hadn't. 'Look,' he said, irritably, 'what the hell is this supposed to mean? If $x^2 = 8,000$ square metres, how in God's name can x end up equalling 8,944?'

208

'I dunno.' Doug was lost in contemplative day-dreams of his piece of porno.

'Well, it can't. Even I can see that.' Grumbling, Jamie went back to the beginning and checked through Doug's arithmetic. 'Got the flaming point in the wrong place, haven't you?'

'Yeah?' Miss Hargreaves was coming towards them, along one of the gravel paths. Doug stuffed his piece of porno back in his pocket, waited till she'd passed, then rolling over on to his front said: 'You and Sharon jacked it in permanently, then?'

He grunted; non-committal.

'She was down the disco with that Pearson creep the other night.'

'Oh?' Just as well he hadn't gone there, in that case. Spared himself the aggravation.

'Beats me what they see in him,' said Doug. 'Apart from the obvious.'

He wondered what the obvious was.

'Sure as hell hasn't got anything else going for him.'

There was a pause. Jamie copied '$ax^2 + bx + c = o$'.

'Know what I reckon?' said Doug. 'I reckon you weren't giving her enough, that's what I reckon.'

He grinned, to show that he was joking. But was he joking? Jamie frowned. He copied '$x = -b \pm b^2 - 4ac$' (whatever the hell that meant). Did Doug know that he and Sharon had never — that *he* had never — that the furthest he'd ever got with her was a quick kiss and a cuddle down by the rabbit hutches in her Dad's back yard? It was the furthest he'd ever seriously tried to get with her. He'd always believed that it was the furthest she'd let him get. Maybe he was wrong. Maybe underneath the little goody-goody exterior she was a mass of seething passions, just waiting for some masterful male (B. Pearson?) to enfold her in his powerful embrace and wreak his wicked will.

Viciously, he copied 'Either $x = +6 + 7.746 = 13.746 = 2.291$' — the trouble was, he wasn't masterful enough: he wasn't *positive* enough — 'Or $x = -6 - 7.746 = -13.746 = -2.291$' (what a load of meaningless twaddle). But then again, how could you be positive when you weren't absolutely certain what it was that you wanted? Or even, come to that, whether you really wanted it? That was the trouble: he couldn't be certain. If only he could, he'd be as positive as anyone.

'Tell you what,' said Doug. 'We're going down the Folk Club Friday night. I bet if I asked Sandy, she could get Marigold Johnson to come along. How about it?' He winked. 'Be all right there. Doesn't give herself airs and graces like old Prissy Knickers.'

No, of course she didn't, thought Jamie. Didn't have anything to give herself airs and graces about, did she? School bicycle, that's what Marigold Johnson was. Practically every boy in the fifth had been out with her at some time or another, except for him. Not that he had anything against her. She was a good sort, was Marigold; he just didn't fancy her, that was all. And anyway, why did people keep

210

trying to push him into going out with people he didn't want to go out with? First it had been Sharon, trying to palm him off with Coral Flashlight; now it was Doug, urging Marigold Johnson on him.

'I can't come Friday,' he said. 'I'm doing things.'

Doug raised his head to look at him.

'Doing things?' How could Jamie be doing things that *he* didn't know about? 'What things?'

'Just things,' said Jamie.

'What just things?'

'Got to pick my kid sister up from her ballet class.'

'Oh! Is that all? Well, that's OK . . . come afterwards.'

$$4^2 - 8n - 1 = 0 —$$

'Can't.'

'Why not?'

'Can't, 'swhy not.'

Normally he could have done, because normally he only picked up Kim and took her back home: his sessions with Anita were in the middle of the week. It was only this particular Friday. They were having what Miss Tucker called 'a general run-through', and he had already promised to be there. He felt less than enthusiastic about it (exposing himself in a pair of tights in front of *Kim*?) but at the same time he didn't feel inclined to go letting people down at the last minute only for the sake of an evening spent with Marigold Johnson.

'Come off it!' said Doug. 'What d'you mean, you can't, that's why not?'

'If you must know – ' (n = – b $\pm$ b^2 – 4ac) – 'I said I'd stay on and give a hand.'

'Give a hand? With a ballet class?' Doug's voice rose to a screech. 'You're giving a hand with a *ballet* class?'

'No, you blithering idiot. I'm giving a hand with a show they're doing.'

'Oh!' Doug relaxed. 'You had me worried for a moment . . . I thought it was a touch of the old monkey fur jock strap and pink hairnet brigade.'

'Ha ha,' said Jamie.

'Yeah, well, you must admit . . . it would be a bit off. Mind you, with your hair you could almost do with a hairnet. Not surprised old Hubbard had a go at you.'

He frowned. There was nothing wrong with his hair; old Hubbard was an ass. He had told him the other day to 'go and get that wig lopped before I get a pair of scissors and do the job myself.' He had no intention of getting it lopped. He wasn't a skinhead, for God's sake. Anyway, Miss Tucker had said that it was just right. He reckoned she knew a sight more about such things than old Hubbard.

'So what you doing, then?' said Doug. 'Electrics?'

'Something like that.'

Doug thought about it a while.

'Ballet class, eh?'

Jamie bent his head over his maths book. He hoped they weren't going to harp on it.

'Good place for birds,' said Doug.

'Yeah.'

'Next best thing to a harem.'

'Yeah.'

'That what you're doing it for?'

Exasperated, Jamie sat up. He pushed his hair out of his eyes.

'No, it is not, you sex-polluted slob. It happens to be for charity. Some of us round here have minds that rise above the merely animal – and you can take your lousy stinking maths.' He slapped the book against Doug's head. 'I don't know why I bothered copying it in the first place . . . it's so bloody awful, I could have done better myself.'

5

The general run-through on Friday evening hadn't been anywhere near as bad as he'd thought it was going to be. In fact, if he were strictly honest with himself, he would have to admit that he'd got quite a kick out of it. Far from giggling at the sight of him wearing tights, Kim had gone round excitedly telling everyone that 'That's my brother'; and all the little girls had stared at him goggle-eyed and accorded him what amounted to almost a sort of reverence. He thought that very probably it was a case of reflected glory, since Anita, quite obviously, was the star of the whole set-up, but nonetheless it made a pleasant change from the open contempt with which the brat-like juniors at Tenterden Road Comprehensive were wont to treat their elders and betters.

On the way home, afterwards, across the Common, with Kim skipping ahead doing her Dewdrop routine, Anita said: 'You will be able to come next Sunday, won't you?'

He said 'Sunday?' and then 'Oh, yeah! Sunday', as if he'd forgotten. He didn't want her getting complacent about it. The only reason he'd agreed to

Sunday was because Miss Tucker had asked him specially. 'I know you're very busy and probably have things of your own to do, but you needn't stay for the whole rehearsal. Not if you don't want to. It's just that I would have liked to go through your bit with Anita, if at all possible.' And then, when she'd thought that he was going to make excuses: 'It does mean a great deal to her, you know.'

He'd already gathered that for himself. He'd thought Kim had got it badly enough, but Anita was a positive nut case. He'd never yet heard her talk about anything that didn't have some connection with the ballet – he'd noticed that it was always *the* ballet, like it was always *the* opera, which had to be pronounced 'oppra' if you were going to be really classy. Anita called it oppra. It was only common people like Jamie who said opperer. Not that Anita seemed to mind. There were some girls in her position who wouldn't have been seen dead with a boy from Tenterden, but to Anita it obviously didn't matter where he came from. So long as he could keep in time to the music and be there on hand when she needed him, that was all that mattered to her. Sometimes he wondered whether she was ever actually aware of him as another human being.

Now, eager, but seemingly just a bit embarrassed as well – which was odd, because he wouldn't have thought her capable of embarrassment – she said: 'Are you by any chance doing anything tomorrow?'

What was it with him, that he could never learn the simple lessons of life? Even a cretin would have known to hedge his bets. The correct answer was a cautious 'Depends' – and then see what she had to offer. Old Muggins goes and says, 'Nothing in particular. Why?'

Well, yes. *Why?* That was the question, wasn't it? Why, for starters, was he such an abject, grovelling buffoon? Did he really expect her to say 'Come to a party with me? Come to a disco with me?' Perhaps, poor mutt, he actually did.

'I was wondering,' said Anita – and her cheeks, which were usually pale, grew ever so slightly tinged with pink. 'I was wondering whether you'd mind awfully putting in a bit of extra rehearsal? The afternoon would be best, but we could make it the morning if you'd rather. It doesn't matter terribly, it's only that I did promise Mummy I'd go up to town with her. We've got this beastly wedding, and she wants to choose outfits, but it's not desperately important. Not nearly as important as being able to rehearse. It's that second lift I'm bothered about. I haven't quite got the timing of it right. I thought – ' Her voice faded, uncertainty. He was glad she was uncertain. He felt that she ought to be. 'I thought, if you could manage it, that maybe we could do it at my house. There's a proper studio, and everything, and I've got the music. I've got a tape of Marjorie playing it. I did it specially, the other day, just in case.' Again, she faltered. 'I wasn't sure how you'd feel about it.'

He wasn't sure how he felt about it, either. He wouldn't mind seeing inside her house, seeing what it was like, where the rich people lived; on the other hand he didn't want to do anything which would encourage her to start taking his co-operation for granted. This was a favour he was conferring.

'I guess I could come for an hour,' he said.

Her face cleared.

'An hour would be perfect! When could you manage it?'

If she was prepared to be humble, then he was prepared to be magnanimous.

'Any time would do me,' he said. 'Afternoon, if that's what's best.'

'About three o'clock? Would that be all right?'

He indicated that it would.

'Oh, that's super!' said Anita.

'So which house do you live in?'

'The one over there – ' She pointed, in the direction of the golf course. 'The one right at the end, with the green roof. If you're coming over the Common, you'd better use the back entrance, otherwise you'll have to walk for miles. But if you're coming by bus, then you have to get out at Delmey Close and cut up the passage, then walk along. It's all a bit complicated.'

'That's OK,' he said. 'I'll find it.'

The house Anita lived in was very new and clean and spacious. He had never seen anywhere so clean and spacious. He was used to the Victorian gloom of the flat above the off-licence, with its long, narrow passages, high-ceilinged but cramped, and its antiquated bathroom with the lead piping all naked and the cast-iron bath which his Mum always swore was going to 'come through that ceiling one of these days, sure as eggs is eggs'. His Mum had a thing about ceilings. Not surprising, really, since half the floorboards and most of the beams were eaten away with woodworm. A woodworm wouldn't have survived five minutes in Anita's house. It was all metal and plastic and spotless.

He walked there over the Common and went in through the back garden, which was also spotless, with a lawn that looked as if it were rolled up and put away in a cupboard every night to keep it from getting dirty, and all the flowers all bright and polished in their weedless flower beds. He marvelled at it: not an empty Coca Cola tin or cigarette pack in sight. The off-licence didn't have a back garden, only a bit of yard where they unloaded the crates; but he bet that if it had it would be like a garbage tip, buried fathoms deep under other people's rubbish.

Anita, already changed into her leotard and tights, came running out to meet him through some long French windows which opened on to a paved area full of trailing things in tubs.

'You came!' she said – as if she'd feared perhaps he wouldn't. The thought gratified him. 'Come in and get changed. You can use my bedroom, the studio's right next door.'

He said: 'That's all right. I don't need to change.'

She looked at him, doubtfully.

'You're going to stay as you are?'

218

Yes: he was going to stay as he was, in sweat shirt and jeans. It was his own personal act of assertion.

'You'll get awfully hot,' said Anita; but at least she didn't try offering him a pair of tights.

'Where are your parents?' he said, as she led the way indoors.

'Oh, somewhere about . . . I think Daddy's on the golf course. I'm not sure where Mummy is. She might be lying down, she always says going up to town exhausts her.'

'Won't it disturb her, then? Us thumping about?'

'We don't *thump*,' said Anita. 'And anyway, she's right at the other end.'

It was only then that he realized: the house was, in fact, a bungalow. He'd never been in a bungalow before. It seemed strange, having everything on one floor. The flat above the off-licence was on two (or two and a half if you counted the bathroom, which had been added on later). He thought that really a bungalow was probably more sensible, except of course that it would take up far more ground space, so that you'd need to be pretty rich if you were going to be able to pay the rates. Great, though, not having to run up and down stairs all the time. His Mum would like that, she wouldn't have to worry herself about the ceilings.

They rehearsed for an hour, in Anita's studio (what Kim wouldn't give, to have a place like that!). They worked as hard as ever Miss Tucker worked them: after only ten minutes, Jamie could feel the perspiration running in rivers down his back. He stuck it

219

for as long as he could, then with a defiant 'Hang on a sec' stripped off his sweat shirt and flung it across the room. He dared Anita to say something. He tensed himself, waiting for it. 'I told you so, I said you ought to change, I knew you'd get too hot . . .' Sharon couldn't have resisted it. She'd have been right in there, crowing at him. He didn't know whether Anita was more tactful or whether she was so absorbed in what she was doing that she simply didn't notice, but at any rate she made no comment. Only afterwards, when they had worn themselves to a standstill, she gestured towards some pink curtains at the far end of the room and said: 'You could have a shower, if you wanted.'

There was nothing he would have liked more; but one did, after all, have one's pride. He wasn't admitting he'd made a mistake.

'That's OK,' he said.

'Well, if you're sure . . . here!' She flung a towel at him. 'You'd better dry yourself.'

He wasn't averse to that, since she was doing the same. His hair was so wet it felt as if he'd been in the swimming baths.

'You ought to wear a sweat band,' said Anita. 'Stop it getting into your eyes.'

He looked at her. Innocently, she looked back at him. She hadn't been criticizing: only trying to be helpful.

'I thought that was pretty good, didn't you? I really thought we made some progress. Don't let's tell Thea about it — let's see if she notices. Then if she does we'll tell her. I know that lift was the one thing she was really worried about. She was wondering whether we ought to do something to simplify it. I told her it would be all right – and now it is! Isn't it?' She regarded him, anxiously. 'Don't you feel that it is? Don't you feel happier with it? I do. – You ought to put your jumper back on, by the way. You'll get cold, otherwise. I'll just go and change. I shan't be a minute.' She went through into her bedroom, and called out to him through the closed door: 'Would you like some tea and biscuits? Or a glass of orange, or something?'

'Wouldn't mind a glass of orange,' said Jamie.

Anita reappeared, almost within the promised minute, wearing a plain white dress with a pleated skirt and no sleeves. She looked fresh and cool and smelt faintly of flowers. Jamie, by contrast, felt hot and sticky. His sweat shirt was clammy and clinging to him, and the steam rose up from his jeans as he walked. He thought he probably stank like a thousand armpits. Anita, as usual, seemed not to notice: she was very good at not noticing. He wondered again if she were tactful, or simply self-absorbed. He couldn't quite make her out.

In the huge airy kitchen with its Vent Axia fan (his Mum had always wanted one of those: she was always on about her Vent Axia) they helped themselves to real fruit juice from the refrigerator and took it out with them into the garden. There were still no signs of Mummy and Daddy, for which, in his present state, he was thankful. He could just imagine their joy at seeing *him* out there — probably take one look and order him straight off the premises. Couldn't have nasty common boys like that around, polluting the atmosphere.

Anita walked across the smooth green lawn; gingerly, he followed her. It seemed almost sacrilege to step on the stuff.

'What are those things?' he said, trying to make conversation. He jerked his head at some brightly coloured flowers, nid-nodding in a nearby bed.

'Oh — I don't know.' Anita spared them a quick glance. 'Mesmeranthus, or something.' Plainly, flowers held no interest for her. Perhaps she was too used to them.

'They're pretty,' said Jamie.

'Yes. I suppose they are.' She studied them a moment, as if seeing them for the first time. 'Bracey does all the gardening. He'd know what they were. I could ask him for you, if you like — if you're really interested.'

He wasn't as interested as all that. It was just something to talk about. He wasn't sure what one did talk about, with a girl like Anita. She solved the problem for him.

'Tell me,' she said. 'Did you ever discover whether you *could* do that Russian thing?'

'Russian thing?' he said. He remembered, as he said it, that that was what he'd said last time.

'You know,' said Anita. 'Like I showed you.'

She set down her glass and showed him again, in her plain white dress with the pleated skirt.

'Oh, that,' he said.

'*Can* you do it?'

'I should think anyone could,' said Jamie.

She tossed her head.

'Garstin can't.'

'Oh, well! Garstin.'

He had met Garstin last night – a tall, lank youth about the same age as himself. It had been so pathetically obvious, looking at him, that he was the sort of boy who would never be capable of doing anything that required even a modicum of physical strength or co-ordination – the sort of boy who would always, inevitably, be clean bowled first ball and drop every catch that ever came his way – that Jamie had almost felt pity for him rather than scorn. Still, he felt duty bound to say *oh, well, Garstin*: it seemed the accepted response.

'The thing is,' said Anita, 'that if you *could* do it, we could put the Russian sequence back in the first half. We had to take it out when David broke his arm. There wasn't any use trying to do it with Garstin. But now that we've got you – '

She looked at him, hopefully. He frowned into his orange juice. He didn't care for this 'now we've got you' business. They hadn't *got* him. He was there purely as a favour. He could back out right now, if he felt inclined.

'It's tremendously exciting,' said Anita. 'Thea did the choreography herself. The music's by Borodin – *Polovtsian Dances*. Do you know it?'

'No,' said Jamie.

223

'Oh, I'm sure you do! I'm sure if you heard it — tchum DA dum, tchum DA dum, tchum DA dum — ' All of a sudden, she was whirling away across the grass, arms flying, pleated skirt twirling. 'Tchum DA dum, tchum DA dum — '

She was quite right, of course: he did know the music. He just hadn't known what it was called. As she danced, he could hear it in his head, all the timpani crashing and banging and the drums going bananas. For a moment he almost felt the urge to join in, but managed just in time to suppress it. This thing had gone far enough; it had to be checked, before it got out of hand.

'Imagine — ' Anita, breathless, her eyes bright, came whirling back to him. 'Imagine how super you'd look as a Polovtsian warrior! We could give you a moustache — we could make it out of creped hair — one of those ones that grows right down — ' She pencilled it in on his face with the tip of her right index finger. 'And you wouldn't have to wear tights! Think of that!'

He thought of it, and said grudgingly: 'Why? What would I have to wear, then?'

'Oh, there's a proper Polovtsian warrior get-up! A kind of bolero thing, and a band for your hair, and baggy trousers, and sandals with thongs . . . all fearsomely butch!'

He couldn't see anything fearsomely butch about dressing himself up in a 'kind of bolero thing' and sandals with thongs. On the other hand, it was certainly better than tights.

'Oh, do say you'll do it!' said Anita. 'Please!'

They had had this scene once before. On that occasion he had allowed himself to be talked round.

'I suppose' – he couldn't help saying it – 'I suppose *you* only want to do it because you'll be the star attraction.'

She fell back a pace.

'That's a mean thing to say – and it's not even true! If we *don't* do it I'll be the star attraction because then I'll have to fill in with the Sugar Plum Fairy, which I already did last year. And apart from the fact that everyone's probably sick to death of it, it wouldn't fit in nearly so well with the rest of the show. It's the *show* I'm thinking of – that and giving other people a chance. You're more likely to be the star attraction than me. It's a man's thing, not a girl's: I'd only be playing second fiddle. You'd be the one that got all the really exciting things to do.'

How could he say, after that, that he didn't want exciting things to do? He found that he was digging divots out of the lawn with the toe of his shoe. With guilty stealth, he began to flatten them back again.

'It seems such a waste,' said Anita. 'When God's given you a talent for doing something really well – '

He didn't believe in God. At least, he didn't think that he did. But perhaps it would be churlish of him to say so.

' – when there's something you can do that gives positive pleasure to people – '

Yes; jumping around in baggy trousers and a kind

of bolero thing. Give them all a big laugh, that would.

'The way I see it,' said Anita, 'it's like a sort of *duty*.'

She made it sound almost holy. Perhaps, to her, it was.

'Yeah. Well – ' He placed his foot firmly over the flattened divots. 'It's the time factor, you see.' Time factor: he liked that. He said it again. 'It's the time factor that screws it.'

Wilfully, she misunderstood him.

'There's still another four weeks to go, almost. You could easily learn it in four weeks! If we practised like mad – if you came round every Saturday and we really worked at it – '

'What, round here?' he said.

He felt himself weakening. Coming round here was a very different kettle of fish from going to Miss Tucker's. For one thing, he could tell Doug about it. 'I've got this new bird I'm going with. Lives in one of those big houses up by the golf course – '

'Of course,' said Anita, in thoughtful tones, 'I don't actually know that you can do it yet, do I? I've only got your word for it. For all I know, you could be just as useless as Garstin. I mean' – she looked up at him, demure in her plain white dress – 'you haven't actually shown me, have you?'

He had no objections to make: he knew perfectly well that he could do it. He could do it standing on his head.

It was a pity, perhaps, in the circumstances, that

he didn't; it would have saved a great deal of embarrassment. As he squatted on his haunches, there was a loud ripping sound. Momentarily, he forgot the company he was in: he gave vent to one of those four-letter words which if his Dad ever caught him at it brought retribution very swiftly in its wake. Anita didn't bat an eyelid. She didn't say 'Naughty naughty', or tell him not to use bad language; she only gave him a wicked grin and said: 'Just as well that didn't happen when Thea was around . . .'

He couldn't be sure whether she was referring to his jeans parting company, or to him swearing. Either way, it was embarrassing.

6

The following Saturday, at breakfast, Mr. Carr said: 'You coming down the road with me tomorrow, then?'

'Down the road?' said Jamie. 'What for?'

Mr. Carr looked hurt.

'One-day match, lad!'

'Oh.' He'd forgotten all about the one-day match. They always went to them together. Damn! He should have thought of that, before making rash promises. Now what was he going to do?

Before he could say anything, Kim's voice had come shrilling across the table: 'He can't tomorrow, we've got a rehearsal!'

'Now, come on, young lady – ' Mr. Carr wagged a finger at her. 'Fair's fair. You can get home under your own steam on a Sunday morning. Don't need your big brother to play escort all the time.'

'But he's *in* it!' said Kim.

'In it? In what?'

'In the *rehearsal*,' said Kim. 'In the *show*.'

'What, him?' Mr. Carr guffawed, happily. 'Doing what? Chasing Dewdrops?'

Jamie kicked out at Kim beneath the table. He

had made her promise that she wouldn't tell anyone. 'It's a secret. Understand? Just you and me. You let anyone else into it, and that's that. Finito. Right?' Kim had said 'Right' and solemnly nodded her head. Too late, he realized that he had not specifically included parents in the prohibition. Kim obviously didn't count parents as being 'anyone else': they were just parents. She took absolutely no notice whatsoever of his warming kick – probably thought he was just thrashing about for the fun of it.

'Jamie's *dancing*,' she said; and then, blissfully: 'He's partnering Anita Cairncross.'

The way she said it, she made it sound as if Anita Cairncross was the Queen, or Princess Anne, or someone. A minor royal at the very least.

'Is he, indeed? Well, well!' Mr. Carr seemed not quite certain how to take this piece of information. 'Good old Anita Cairncross! Let's hope she enjoys it. Can't say that I would . . . great clumsy oaf like that.'

Kim, who had strictly no sense of humour where her beloved ballet was concerned, said: 'Jamie's not clumsy. Miss Tucker says he's the most promising boy she's ever had.' Jamie choked on his Weetabix: 'She does, Jamie.' Kim, all unaware, reached out for a piece of toast and began smearing butter on it inches deep, taking advantage of the fact that Mrs. Carr was in the kitchen and couldn't see. 'Honest. I heard her talking to Anita. She said, he's the most promising boy I've ever had. And then she said something about, if we could only manage to convince him that it's – and then I couldn't hear any more because they walked away. Could you pass the honey?'

'Please,' said Jamie.

'Please,' said Kim. She turned, important, to her father. 'Jamie and Anita,' she said, 'are doing a classical pas de deux.'

'Oh, yes?' His father was eyeing him, quizzically. 'And what's a classical pas de deux when it's at home? Greek father of twins?'

Kim wrinkled her nose, not seeing the joke.

'It's when two people dance together. With lifts, and things.'

'Lifts?' said Mr. Carr. 'You mean the sort that go up and down? First floor, second floor – '

Kim looked at him, scornfully.

'That's in buildings,' she said. 'Lifts in ballet are something different. It's where the man has to pick the girl up and carry her.'

'Oh, is it?' said Mr. Carr. 'Ah, well, now you're starting to make sense! Picks her up and carries her, does he?'

'Yes, and then he has to support her when she does pirouettes and things.' Kim jumped up, over-turning the honey. 'Come and show him, Jamie!'

He shook his head, deeply embarrassed. This was worse even than splitting his jeans in front of Anita. Mr. Carr, goodhumouredly, said: 'Never tell me we're going to see those great hairy legs of yours encased in a pair of tights?'

230

They were back to those blasted tights again. He mumbled, incoherently, into his Weetabix.

'Swelp me Bob!' said Mr. Carr. 'That'll be a sight for sore eyes, and no mistake.'

Kim, sitting herself down again, began scraping honey off the tablecloth.

'Everybody wears tights,' she said.

'Yes, but everybody hasn't got great hairy legs, have they?'

'Jamie hasn't got great hairy legs. Miss Tucker says — '

They were spared, thank God, any more of Miss Tucker's utterances by the arrival of his mother bearing bacon and eggs. She had obviously caught most of the conversation, for she said at once: 'Who's Anita Cairncross? Is she the girl with the nice voice that rang you up the other day?'

'She's the one he's dancing with,' said Kim. 'She's the best dancer in the whole of the school. She's going to do it full time next year.'

'She sounded really nice,' said Mrs. Carr. 'Not like that other one. That Sharon, or whatever her name was. I never cared for that one. Always thought she'd lead you into bad ways. This one sounded quite different. Where does she live? Near?'

'Over on the Common,' said Kim. 'By the golf course.'

'One of the new houses. Well!' Mrs. Carr dished up bacon and eggs. Jamie looked at them unenthusiastically. 'Pretty, is she?'

Before Kim could say 'She's the prettiest girl in the whole of the school', he said: 'Not particularly.'

'Jamie, she *is*,' said Kim.

'No, she isn't. She's skinny as a rake.'

'She isn't skinny, she's slim!'

'Well, whatever she is, she hasn't got any sex appeal.'

'A likely tale!' Mr. Carr chuckled, as he leaned across to get the teapot. 'All I can say is, I wish you the best of British . . . I've heard of feats of derring-do, but this one takes the biscuit!'

'*Look.*' Jamie slammed down his knife and fork. Everyone, obediently, looked. They seemed startled – he was not one who was much given to wild outbursts. 'Look – ' He pushed his hair out of his eyes. 'It's for charity, isn't it? It's for *spastics*. What am I supposed to say? When they ask me? What do I say? Stuff spastics? Is that what you want me to say? Stuff Auntie Carol and stuff Linda and stuff Fairfield?' He glared at them. 'Is it?'

There was a silence. Even Kim was temporarily muted.

'No. Well – ' Mr. Carr cleared his throat. 'Obviously it isn't. We all have to do our bit, the best way we can. Only too glad you've got a social conscience. Better than vandalizing football pitches. So!' Some of his previous joviality returned. 'When is it happening, this great event? This classical father of two? I take it we shall be allowed to come?'

'You've *got* to come,' said Kim. '*Every*body's got to.'

'Everybody's got to! Well! That settles it, then, doesn't it?' Mr. Carr winked, and ruffled his son's hair – a gesture of paternal affection which Jamie could well have done without. He loathed it when people ruffled his hair. 'Don't worry yourself, lad! We'll take it seriously.'

With any luck, thought Jamie, they wouldn't get the opportunity: with any luck, they'd both of them be struck down with the shingles.

'Doesn't worry me,' he said. 'It's not my show.' He pushed his plate away. 'I'm only doing it to help out.'

On Tuesday morning, on the way to school, along the path that bordered the woods, he found himself overtaken by Sharon. Surprise, surprise, she stopped to speak.

'Hi, Jamie,' she said.

He looked at her, frowningly. 'Hi.'

She fell into step beside him, moderating her pace to his.

'Be late for school if you don't get a move on.'

So, he would be late for school. So it would be the second time in one week. So what? He had more important things to worry about. She had interrupted him in the middle of going through the steps of the Russian dance, which Miss Tucker had shown him last night. He had been seeing them in his mind, trying to fit them into their proper sequence. If she was so bothered about being late, then let her be the one to get a move on.

It seemed that she was not as bothered as all that. She was obviously disposed to talk and make overtures.

'Did you do that stuff for old Fossil?'

'What stuff?'

'That stuff about Elizabethan poets.'

'Oh, that. Yeah.' He'd cribbed it out of a book Anita had lent him. Anita went to the High School, which worked a year ahead of everyone else. She'd already done Elizabethan poets.

'I couldn't find anything to say,' said Sharon.

'No?' He kicked a stone. He wished she would go away and let him get on with things.

'I just couldn't think of anything – I mean, there *wasn't* anything. I only wrote half a page.' She looked at him, hopefully. 'How much did you write?'

'Dunno.' He shrugged a shoulder. 'Couple or so.'

'Couple of *pages*?' said Sharon.

'Yeah, well, I write big,' he said.

'I know, but *still* – '

For a while there was silence, as she pondered the awesomeness of it. Jamie went back to his Russian dance. He tried to pick it up where he'd left off, half way through, but it was like saying the alphabet when you were in infant school, unless you started right at the beginning – abcdefg – , hijkellamenno*p* – you couldn't get the rhythm of it, you couldn't get the pattern. Blast Sharon. Why did she have to come and talk to him at *this* particular moment? She hadn't been anywhere near him for weeks. Now

she'd gone and broken the sequence. He would have
to go all the way back and start again.

So. First there were the turning things – yaa-*dum*,
yaa-*dum*, yaa-*dum*, yaa –

'Don't seem to see you down the disco these days,'
said Sharon.

'What?' He jerked his head round, irritably. 'No.
I haven't had the time.'

On the morning air came the shrill sound of a
bell, marking the beginning of assembly.

'There's the bell,' said Sharon.

What did she think, he was deaf, or something?

'I knew we'd be late. If the butcher's open down
the bottom of Brafferton, I always know.'

Now what was she on about? Butcher down the
bottom of Brafferton, for heaven's sake! Exasperated,
he broke into a jog.

'Well, don't just stand there mouthing, then . . .
get a move on!'

In English, when the essays were collected, she
turned round and pulled a face at him. It was the
sort of face that implied some special kind of
relationship: he ignored it. In Civics, a bit later, she
patted an empty chair and invited him to sit next to
her. Loftily, he pretended not to have noticed and
went to sit next to Doug, in the back row, where
they passed an agreeable forty minutes seeing how
many dirty words they could make out of People's
Democratic Republic of Algeria. In spite of all this,
she still smiled at him as they went out through the
door; and to cap it all, as he sauntered up the road

with Doug during the dinner break, they ran into her coming out of the fish shop, and she smiled at him yet again and stuck a chip in his mouth.

''Oo's a lucky boy?' said Doug.

Next morning, after PE, when they were under the showers, he sidled up to Jamie, and out of the corner of his mouth muttered: 'Hey, Buster, you wanna hear sumpun? Woid's on the street that a certain little lady ain't got no gennelman friend no more.' And then, reverting to a more normal mode of expression: 'I reckon if you were to put in an appearance down the disco Saturday night you'd find she was a pushover.'

He toyed with the idea. He was still toying with it when he went round to Anita's on Saturday afternoon. As he stripped off in her bedroom (with her safely shut away on the other side of the door) he tried to imagine how it would be if he were stripping off in Sharon's bedroom (with Sharon very firmly on *this* side of the door). He couldn't make up his mind whether it appealed to him or whether it didn't. *I reckon you'd find she was a pushover* . . . but did he want her to be a pushover?

Well, and why not? He supposed that he ought, if only to show Doug – if only to prove to *himself*. He decided, quite definitely, that he would go. As soon as they had finished he would go straight back home and have a bath, change into something decent and go down to the disco to pick up Sharon. And this time he meant it. This time he really was determined.

He was still determined when they finished rehearsing; but then they went into the garden with their orange juice, and Mummy was out there sunning herself, and Daddy came back from the golf course, and everybody got talking, and he and Daddy talked about cricket, about which Daddy turned out to be quite knowledgeable, and Mummy wanted to know which school he went to, and didn't actually pass out on the spot when he said Tenterden, but instead said musingly: 'I've often wondered whether we shouldn't have chosen a comprehensive for Anita'; and then they had the garden to themselves, because Mummy had to go indoors to see about some food, and Daddy had to have a hot bath, to take away the aches and pains after his exertions on the golf course, and just as Jamie was thinking of saying, 'Well, I guess I'd better be off, then,' Anita said: 'Jamie, you *are* going to watch the ballet on television tonight, aren't you?' and before he had a chance to say 'What ballet?' or no, he couldn't, he was going out, had hurried on with: 'You really *ought* – especially if you've never seen any. *Have* you ever seen any?'

If he'd had any sense he'd have said 'Course I have. Loads.' (After all, he'd seen the Benton Blue-bells, hadn't he?) Instead, like an idiot, he said: 'Well, no. Not exactly. But – '

'Oh, but then you must! Jamie, you *must!* It's Fonteyn and Nureyev!'

Too late, he remembered: it was what Kim had been going on about for the past seven days.

'Fonteyn and *Nureyev* . . . Fonteyn and NUREYEV', until it had become a sort of ritual, every time she picked up the television paper.

'Honestly,' said Anita. 'It's not the sort of chance you can afford to miss.'

No, and neither was picking up Sharon at the disco. *That* wasn't the sort of chance he could afford to miss.

'The thing is,' he said, 'I was sort of thinking of going somewhere.' What did he mean, *sort* of? He *was* going somewhere. 'I was going to go down to the disco,' he said.

'But Jamie, it's Fonteyn and Nureyev! You can go down to the disco any time; but Fonteyn and *Nureyev* – surely just for *once* you could stay in?'

Seized with inspiration, he said: 'Wouldn't do any good if I did. We've only got the one telly. My old man'd go spare if anyone suggested watching ballet.'

It wasn't an absolute and total lie – Mr. Carr didn't exactly go spare, but he certainly grumbled quite a lot. On the other hand, not even he would have had the heart to deny Kim the opportunity of goggling at her beloved Nureyev, and if there'd been any really serious friction there was always the old black and white set down in the shop. Still, Anita wasn't to know.

'*I* wouldn't mind,' said Jamie. 'It's him. All he likes is international soccer and John Wayne shooting up Indians. Then he goes on about how it's him that pays the licence fee so it's him that ought to choose, and – '

'*I* know,' said Anita. 'You could come round here.'
He stopped, the wind taken out of his sails.
'Round here?'
'Yes! Why not?'
He couldn't bring himself to say: 'Because I'm going down to the disco to pick up a bird . . .' He mumbled: 'What about your parents?'
'Oh! They won't mind. Why should they? They only ever half watch, in any case. In fact, it would be quite nice,' said Anita, 'to have someone else who appreciated it, just for once. To have someone else who had a *feeling* for it.'
He was flattered, in spite of himself: five minutes later, he was going back home not to have a bath and change into something decent to go down the disco to pick up Sharon, but to have a bath and snatch a quick tea and go back over the Common to watch ballet with Anita.
Why, for goodness' sake, did he always have to be so *feeble*?

7

The ballet was *Romeo and Juliet*, with music by Pro-
kofiev, and according to the *Radio Times* it was going
to last most of the evening — a fact which Jamie
noted with the same sort of enthusiasm that he noted
a period of double maths or physics scheduled for
first thing on a Monday morning. He knew he was
supposed to be someone who had a feeling, but the
only feeling he could dredge up, as gingerly he
placed himself beside Anita on a velvet sofa that
looked far too fragile for actually sitting on, was the
glum anticipation of boredom. If he'd known it was
going to go on as long as this, he would never have
come; not even to please Anita. And if he'd known
it was going to be *Romeo and Juliet* — they'd been
subjected to *Romeo and Juliet* last term, with Miss
Fosdyke. It was quite the most futile play he'd ever
read. Really futile. He hardly imagined that the ballet
was likely to be any improvement.

It wasn't, to begin with. Just a load of people
pratting about in fancy dress, looking like something
out of a Christmas pantomime. Mrs. Cairncross,
glancing up from a nail-polishing session, said, 'Well,
it's quite pretty,' but one wanted it to be more than

just pretty. One wanted there to be some action. All these people in their fancy costumes were all very well, but what were they actually *doing*? Nothing, as far as he could make out. Certainly nothing that anyone else couldn't have done. At least with Benton's Bluebells there had been some real dancing.

He found that he was disappointed, in spite of not having expected very much. He had expected it to be better than *this*. Secretly, he'd been hoping that the old Nureyev guy that everyone raved about would be so impressive that even his Dad, watching back at home, would be forced to sit up and take notice. After all, the fellow must have *some*thing. Kim wasn't the only one to do her bits and pieces over him: even Anita tended to crumble at the edges. A few days ago, she'd been showing him how to do a thing called an entrechat (a complicated sort of leap where you were supposed to beat your heels together in mid-air – no mean feat, as he'd discovered when he tried it). Most people, she'd said, only managed to get as far as a six (pronounced sees) 'But as you're so good at jumping I shouldn't think you'd have too much difficulty with a huit (pronounced weet). Not once you've mastered the technique.' A trifle jealously, since he hadn't yet mastered it sufficiently to do a trois or even a deux, let alone a six or a huit, he'd said: 'What about this Nureyev, then? What can he do?' Her eyes had gone all glassy, sort of glazed over with a mist of reverence, and she'd said: 'Oh, well. *Nureyev.*' (But not at all in the tones that people said oh-well-Garstin.) 'I

241

shouldn't be surprised if *he* could manage a douze . . .'

Whether he could or he couldn't, it didn't seem to Jamie that he was getting much of a chance to show anyone; not in *Romeo and Juliet*. He might be impressing Kim, sitting with her stubby nose glued to the box (he bet she was: he could just picture her) but Kim was so far gone he'd probably only have to scratch his left ear and she'd think he'd performed some kind of miracle. He certainly wasn't impressing anyone else. Mrs. Cairncross, blowing on her nail varnish to help it dry quicker, wanted to know whether 'that was the one, then . . . the one you've all got crushes on?' And when Anita didn't deign to reply: 'When I was your age, it was all film stars. Tony Curtis, I remember.' She gave a little laugh. 'He was the one I went for.' Mr. Cairncross only poured himself a large bubble of brandy and said: 'Nice pair of legs he's got, I'll say that for him.'

It wasn't until the duel scene between Tybalt and Mercutio that things began to liven up. For the first time, Jamie found himself taking notice. This was more like! They were going at it, hammer and tongs, all over the stage. It was one of the best sword fights he'd ever seen. He crouched forward, on the edge of his seat, tense and absorbed, watching every move – not that he didn't know the outcome, because he remembered it perfectly well from last term with Miss Fosdyke. Mercutio had always struck him as being the one decent character in the entire play: he'd been disgusted when Shakespeare had killed him off half way through. What he was waiting for was the moment when it happened.

When it came, that moment he'd been waiting for, he was like Anita, beside him: eyes riveted, immovable. The death of Mercutio was fantastic. He didn't just lie down and die, he writhed, and rolled, and arched his back — thrashed with his limbs and curled up his muscles and bowled about the stage in hoops of agony. And yet, for all that, it was more than mere acrobatics. Watching Mercutio die he felt almost how he might feel if he were watching someone like, say, Doug. Someone with whom you had had fun, who was always good for a laugh, even if at times you could cheerfully have murdered them.

He wondered which part he would rather dance, if he were to be given the choice: whether he would rather be Mercutio, who at least was a real character, even if he did get nobbled earlier on, or Romeo, who lasted longer but was such a flaming wet, mooning about all the time like some love-sick chicken. He decided he would sacrifice the length and opt for Mercutio. He wouldn't half mind playing that death scene (he made a mental note to try it out in his bedroom some time when his Mum wasn't around). Of course, he would have to learn how to fence. He wondered how much lessons would cost; whether perhaps it might be a better idea to spend his savings on a fencing foil rather than the guitar he'd promised himself. If he were to buy the fencing foil —

He stiffened, sitting forward again on the edge of

his seat. Now it was Romeo's turn. He was having a right go at Tybalt – obviously determined to avenge himself for the death of his friend. That was what Jamie would do, if someone had just killed Doug. He saw himself doing it (he would definitely buy that fencing foil). Maybe Romeo wasn't such a flaming wet after all. He was really putting the boot in there. He'd really got old Tybalt on the run. Any minute now –

'Got him!' Mr. Cairncross reached out for his bottle of brandy. Mrs. Cairncross, coming back into the room with a tray full of something or other, said: 'Which one's that, then?'

'Tybalt,' said Anita.

'Tibble?' said Mrs. Cairncross.

Anita tightened her lips.

'*Tybalt*,' she said.

'Oh! Tybalt. Wasn't he the bullying one? Jamie, have a –

He wasn't quite sure what it was that she offered him. It sounded like 'Have a canopy', but when he took one, not wanting to be thought ungracious, all it was was a bit of toast with a dob of paste smeared on it. It tasted OK, but he was terrified of dropping crumbs and found that in any case you couldn't really concentrate if you were trying to eat at the same time. Perhaps that was why Anita wouldn't have one. He could tell, from the way she frowned and shook her head, without removing her eyes from the screen, that the constant interruptions were irritating her. He bet Kim was suffering in exactly the same way at home. Mr. Carr would be there in his armchair, drinking his Guinness and pretending to be watching a football match or a heavyweight title fight, every five minutes taking his nose out of his glass to shout encouragement ('Sock it to him, Rudi baby! Oh, nice one! Nice one!') while Mrs. Carr would be clicking with her knitting needles, yanking strands of wool out of crackling plastic bags and looking up at all the crucial moments to ask questions. 'What's happening now, then? What's he doing now? Who's been killed?'

Funny how all parents seemed to be alike. He'd have thought Anita's would be different, but obviously they were just as insensitive as everyone else's.

He swallowed his last piece of toast and sat forward, shoulder to shoulder with Anita, his elbows planted on his knees and his hands clamped either side of his head like blinkers, so that he couldn't be distracted. Having despatched the enemy, Romeo had at last come into his own. He'd really got it together now. He wasn't just mooning about any more, he really meant business. You could tell, the way they danced with each other, that he and Juliet had gone further than Jamie and Sharon had ever gone. No snatched kisses by the rabbit hutches in *Juliet's* back yard: when old Romeo had gone climbing up there to the balcony it had been for more than a good-night cuddle.

He began to revise his opinion of the great Nureyev. Maybe the fellow did have something going for him, after all. Maybe he'd been a bit too hasty, deciding that Mercutio was the part to have. Romeo's sword fight had been just as good as his, and he did still have a death scene to come. He thought that he would wait and see what the death scene was like; see whether it made up for all that mooning about at the beginning.

It certainly wasn't as spectacular as Mercutio's. Romeo didn't do acrobatics and bowl about the stage in hoops. He died quite quietly, by the side of Juliet. In the play, Jamie had thought only what a crass idiot the man was – and had noted with relief that there was only one more page of the rubbish to go. Miss Fosdyke had asked at the end if anyone had found it sad, but no one had; not even any of the girls. When she had applied to Doug to know why not, Doug, in his usual forthright fashion, had said: 'Load of cobblers, innit?' And then, when pressed to be more explicit: 'Well, I mean . . . her knocking herself out with sleeping pills and him taking poison and her sticking daggers in her chest . . . bloody stupid. Not the way people carry on in real life.'

He had spoken for the entire class. They had all voiced their agreement: it *was* bloody stupid: it *wasn't* the way people carried on in real life. Jamie had even added the rider that 'Fyou ask me, it ought to be done as a comedy . . . I bet that's what Shakespeare meant it for, originally. I bet if you did it as a comedy, it'd be one of the funniest things he ever wrote.'

Miss Fosdyke had obligingly let them try out the death scene, with Jamie playing Juliet and Doug acting Romeo: all the class had been in stitches. Even when she'd taken them, later, to see a London production with real professional actors, it hadn't been much better. Jamie had still sat stolidly unmoved from start to finish. He didn't know what should make the ballet any different from the play — maybe it was something to do with the music, and not having to listen to all those sloppy words — but whatever it was, when Nureyev as Romeo said goodbye to Juliet for the very last time and lay down by her side to die, he felt a strange burning sensation at the back of his eyes; and when Juliet woke up and found him there, and thought at first that he was just asleep, it really started to get to him. It really did start to get to him. It was like Ave Maria on the organ at his great grand-dad's funeral when he had been the same age as Kim was now. It had done terrible things inside him so that he had wanted to blubber like a kid, even though he'd hardly known his great grand-dad and had actually resented having to go to the funeral in the first place because it meant missing out on a football match. This flaming ballet was doing exactly the same sort of terrible things.

Mrs. Cairncross picked up her empty canopy dish.

'I think I'll make some coffee,' she said. She walked across to the door, passing in front of the television screen as she did so. 'What time, exactly, is this thing supposed to end?'

Mr. Cairncross cradled his brandy bubble.

'Any minute now, I should imagine.'

'Are you going to give Jamie a lift home?'

'By all means, if he wants one.'

Mrs. Cairncross paused, one hand on the door knob.

'*Would* you like a lift home, Jamie?'

Hunched forward on the edge of the sofa, seeing the screen through what had now become a definite blur, Jamie pressed so hard with his fingertips against his temples that it actually hurt. He took a breath – through his mouth rather than his nose, because his nose was all blocked up and snuffly – but before he had to risk saying anything, Anita, to his immense relief, had come to his rescue.

'You might at *least* wait until it's finished.'

Mrs. Cairncross pulled a henpecked face.

'Sorry, I'm sure! I thought it virtually had.'

'Well, it virtually *hasn't*. You haven't been watching. How can it be finished when Juliet's still alive?'

Afterwards, when Juliet had killed herself with Romeo's dagger and it really was finished and they were drinking the coffee that Mrs. Cairncross had made, they asked him again, 'How about this lift, then, Jamie?' but now he was ready for it, and although he still had to breathe through his mouth he was at least able to speak without making a fool of himself. He said, 'It's all right, thanks. I don't mind walking,' which was quite true, he didn't, but more than that he wanted to be by himself, to go over in his mind what he had just seen, to reconstruct those duel scenes before he had a chance to forget them. He didn't feel like having to make conversation, not even about cars or cricket. He rather thought that Daddy didn't feel like having to bestir himself, either, because when Mrs. Cairncross started having doubts about the Common – 'At *this* time of night? Jamie, do you think you ought?' – he said bracingly that Jamie was a well set-up lad and that he was quite sure he could take care of himself. 'Can't you, young man?' Anita just said: 'Honestly, Mummy, don't *fuss* so. There's almost a full moon out there.'

In spite of the full moon, as he was passing the wooded area where the nutters flashed and young love went courting, he managed to trip almost headlong over a couple of bodies concealed in the grass. They turned out to be Marigold Johnson and a boy from 5D, whose name he didn't know. The boy from 5D said: 'D'you mind watching where you're treading?' Marigold Johnson just looked at him and giggled. He muttered: 'Sorry, didn't see you,' and walked on, embarrassed. It always embarrassed him when he found people doing things like that. He only hoped to heaven that he hadn't been making mad fencing gestures all by himself. It would be round the school in next to no time: James Carr's going off his rocker. Walks the Common at dead of night making funny motions in the air . . .

He arrived home to find Kim still up, even though it was long past her bedtime. As he climbed the stairs, he heard his mother's voice, exasperated: 'Kim, did you hear me? I said, *go to bed.*' And Kim's voice, somewhat petulant, in reply: 'Yes, all *right*. I'm *going*.' There were sounds of feet crossly banging their way over the sitting-room floor, then the door at the head of the stairs was flung open and Kim flounced through, defiant.

'Anyway,' she said – it was obviously intended as a parting shot – 'football's only a *game*. Ballet dancers have to work *far* harder than *foot*ballers.'

'Get away with you!' That was his Dad, all masculine and jovial. 'Knees bend and point your toes . . . call that work? Load of old nannies! Wouldn't last five minutes.'

Kim turned red – she looked almost as though she might be going to burst. Jamie knew that she was wrestling with the urge to say something rude, such as 'Pig's *bum*', which was the worst thing she was acquainted with just at this moment. He sympathized with her, but hoped for her sake that she managed to suppress it. After a struggle that lasted several seconds, she said: 'You put one of your rotten footballers in one of Miss Tucker's classes and *he* wouldn't even last *one* minute.'

'You're dead right he wouldn't!' Mr. Carr chuckled. 'Be too busy running for his life.'

Kim opened her mouth to retort, but her mother got in first: there was a note of warning in her voice.

'If I have to tell you again – '

'Oh, all *right*,' said Kim. 'I'm going.'

Huffily, she left the room, elbowing her way past Jamie as if he wasn't even there. They heard her stumping up the stairs and along the passage overhead.

'You shouldn't tease her like that,' said Mrs. Carr. 'It's not fair.'

'Go on!' Mr. Carr grinned, unrepentant. 'Load of old nannies, the lot of 'em.' He winked at Jamie across the room. 'Where've you been, then? Out on the razzle?'

'Been out with Doug,' said Jamie. He didn't quite know why he said it, except that he wasn't in a mood for having his leg pulled, and if he said 'round at Anita's' his Dad would never be able to resist the temptation. 'Went down the disco. Down Bell Street.'

He only hoped Doug wouldn't ask him, Monday morning, why he *hadn't* been down the disco, down Bell Street. He had a sneaking sort of feeling, which he tried hard to suppress, that it was where he ought to have been. *Romeo and Juliet* with Anita was all very well, but it wasn't actually proving anything, was it? Chickening out at the last minute, that was how some people would have seen it. After all, Sharon was going to have been a pushover, wasn't she? Sharon was going to have been his for the asking. And he'd gone and chosen *Romeo and Juliet*, instead. Deliberately missed out on his chance. Turned his back on the sort of opportunity that might never come his way again, because by this time next week she'd probably have found herself someone else and be back to giving him the cold shoulder once more. She wasn't the sort of girl to hang about; not Sharon.

He decided, as he followed Kim up to bed, that first thing Monday he would ask her. 'Doing anything next Saturday?' And if she said no, or even if she just made faint noises, then he would go ahead and make a date. A *firm* date. This time he meant it. This time he *really* meant it.

8

He had hoped, next Monday, that he might bump into Sharon again on his way to school, but of course he didn't: no one was ever around when you wanted them to be. Instead, scuffing his way up the lane through the usual weekend debris, he found a page of porno. It was blowing about in the breeze, amongst all the rest of the rubbish, and it wrapped itself round his legs so that he had to bend down and peel it off.

Normally he would have given it a mere cursory glance and left it where it was: today, in his new role of Casanova–Don Juan, he picked it up to have a closer look. If it did things to Doug, then it ought to do things to him. Obviously naked ladies were what turned everyone else on (he'd even caught his Dad snatching a crafty glance at page 3 of the *Sun* when his Mum wasn't around) so maybe it was just a question of acquiring the taste, like with beer and whisky. The first time he'd swallowed half a pint of beer he'd thought he was going to bring up. He almost quite liked it now. Whisky still defeated him, but then whisky still defeated Doug, so he didn't feel too badly about it. It was this other thing that really bugged him. It was that he'd got to do something about. He guessed he might just as well start now, with a page of naked ladies.

To his unutterable astonishment, the naked ladies turned out not to be naked ladies after all, but naked men. He stared, unbelievingly. Doug had never shown him anything like that. To think that they actually *printed* that sort of thing – that real people actually *posed* for it. That other real people actually went into shops and *bought* it. He'd thought naked ladies were bad enough; but this –

'What's that you've got there, son? Something interesting?'

Jamie spun round, his face a crimson sunset. A copper was standing there. He must have crept up on him quietly, on purpose.

'Nothing,' said Jamie. He crumpled his hand, defensively, over the paper.

'Nothing, eh?' The copper advanced a step towards him. He was one of the young ones: they were always the worst. 'Won't mind if I take a look at it, then, will you?'

One ought to be able to say yes – one ought to be able to tell him to go and get stuffed, that it wasn't any of his business. Doug had tried that once, when they'd wanted to look in his bag and see if he was carrying stolen property (which he wasn't). He'd ended up down at the station being threatened with prosecution for obstructing the law.

'Come on, sunshine! Hand it over.'

Jamie did so.

'I found it,' he said.

'Oh, yes?' The copper took a look. His face grew a sort of mottled colour. Sort of dark purple with blotches. 'You dirty little bastard!' He said it contemptuously, almost viciously. 'You filthy dirty little bastard!'

'Look, I *found* it,' said Jamie.

'What difference does that make? You didn't have to stand there gawping at it, did you?'

'I wasn't gawping at it. I just picked it up. I didn't know what it was.'

'Didn't know what it was! Don't give me that. I saw you, feasting your eyes. Ought to be ashamed of yourself. Kid your age. Can't you think of anything more healthy to do? Have to stand about gorging yourself on obscenities? I tell you, sunshine, if I ever catch you at it again – ' He pulled a notebook out of his pocket. 'What's your name?'

Name? He was going to take his *name*? Just for picking up a bit of porno off the ground? Jamie swallowed. He'd heard about the police throwing their weight around. It had happened to Doug, it had happened to others. There was a black kid in his class had been hauled up on a breaking and entering charge when he hadn't been anywhere near the place and had half a dozen witnesses to prove it. Jamie had always sworn that if they tried it on with him he'd stand up for himself, he'd know what his rights were. Now it was happening and he found that he didn't; and even if he had he'd have been too scared to do anything about it. He was paralysed with the fear that his parents would be told – that his Head Master would be told – that he himself would be paraded before the whole school: the boy who gorged himself on obscenities.

'Well, come on, lad, I haven't got all day!'

If he had any nous, he'd give a false name. Christopher Marlowe, or John Milton, or something. That's what Doug would have done. He'd told them once he was Perkin Warbeck, and they'd actually believed him. Obviously, Doug had nous. Equally obviously, Jamie hadn't.

'James Carr,' he said.

'C–A–double–R?' said the copper.

It wouldn't have done any good, anyway. He knew which school he went to. They'd simply hold an identity parade.

'All right then, James Carr.' The copper closed his notebook with a snap. 'You have been warned. In future, you keep your perverted tendencies to yourself. There's decent kids use this footpath. I'm not having them corrupted by the likes of you. Now you can hoppit. Go on!' He jerked his head. 'Scoot!'

He scooted. He couldn't scoot fast enough. He realized, later, that the copper must have been a nut case. He wouldn't be at all surprised if the bloke weren't a bit kinky, getting all steamed up like that. They oughtn't to have coppers that were kinky. Not if it meant going round accusing people of things they weren't guilty of. Telling him to keep his perverted tendencies to himself – he hadn't *got* any perverted tendencies. He'd picked up what he'd thought were going to be naked ladies and they'd turned out to be naked men. It was a mistake that anyone could have made. Even Doug could have made it. Let them try accusing *him* of perverted tendencies. He'd have them up for slander.

By way of solace, when he approached Sharon during the mid-morning break and asked her whether she was going down the disco Saturday night, she was quite civil to him. Indeed, she was more than civil: she was positively effusive.

'Oh, Jamie,' she said, 'I wish I could. But I can't. Not Saturday.' She sounded genuinely regretful. 'We've got to visit these relations. I could make it Friday. Friday I'm not doing anything.'

Friday. He was supposed to be rehearsing on Friday. The show was going on in two weeks, and Miss Tucker was starting to grow anxious. Well, and so was he. *And* with more cause.

'OK,' he said. 'Let's make it Friday.'

'Go down the Folk Club?'

'If that's what you want.'

'Don't you like it there?'

'Yeah. I like it.' He was prepared, in the present state of truce, to like anywhere she chose to name. The Folk Club, besides, had the advantage that it meant walking back across the Common; and the Common late on a summer's night was notorious. You could hardly move for bodies in the grass.

'What about your sister?' said Sharon. 'Don't you have to pick her up?'

257

'She'll have to take the bus,' he said. 'It won't hurt her for once.'

He left it till the very last minute before he said anything. He ought to have told Miss Tucker, when he went along as usual on Wednesday, but she was all busy and bothered because one of the Dewdrops had gone down with the chicken pox and another had reported 'not feeling well'. At the end, as he was nerving himself, she put an arm about his shoulders and said: 'Good boy! That was excellent. We'll just give that ending a bit of a polish on Friday and it'll be fine.' That needn't, of course, have stopped him telling Anita as they walked home together afterwards. There really wasn't any excuse for not telling Anita. It was just that he couldn't stand the way she'd look at him, with her green eyes all reproachful, as if he were proposing to commit some heinous crime such as treason.

On Friday evening at tea he said to Kim: 'By the way, you'll have to get the bus back tonight. I won't be able to come and pick you up.'

Kim's eyes, round and brown in her little chubby face, were not so much reproachful as outraged.

'But it's a *rehearsal*,' she said.

'I know it is. I can't make it.'

'Why can't you?'

'Because I can't.' Why did everybody always have to question him? 'I've got something on at school.'

'You can't miss a rehearsal just for something on at school!' Kim's voice was shrill with accusation. 'You've *got* to come. You *said* you would.'

'I didn't say I would.' Everyone had simply assumed that he would. They seemed to forget that he was doing them favours. 'You'll have to tell Miss Tucker for me. Tell her it was something I couldn't get out of.' After all, whichever way you looked at it, school was a damn sight more important than some pisspot little ballet show. 'Tell her I'm sorry, but it came up at the last moment.'

'Why? What is it?' said Kim.

He wondered if she was really suspicious, or if it were just his guilty conscience at work.

'Something to do with exams. O levels.'

'*All night?*' said Kim.

'Someone's coming to talk to us. It'll probably go on for an hour or two. Then there'll be questions.' It was amazing how glibly you could lie once you got started. He even found himself half way to believing it. Growing cross, he said: 'Anyhow, never you mind. Just you make sure that you tell her, that's all.'

The Folk Club was hellish; nothing but a succession of nurdling idiots strumming on guitars and droning your actual authentic folk songs. With a hey nonny ho nonny, fol diddle di do, whey hey my lassie-oh. They all sounded exactly the same, and were all sung by middle-aged trendies with bushy beards and high-pitched voices which tended to wander off key and crack at all the crucial moments. There was positively nothing to relieve the tedium save thoughts of what was to come after, when they walked back home

across the Common. He had had a bath in preparation, and dressed all in clean clothes and borrowed
some of his Dad's after-shave. He felt ready for anything. He felt that tonight he really *could*. He would
be firm and masterful, and not take no for an answer.
According to Doug, that was how you had to treat
girls like Sharon.

'Push 'em about a bit. Show 'em you mean
business.'

He was hoping that she wouldn't need any
pushing about. He had these rose-coloured visions
of her gazing up at him out of eyes gone all liquid,
clasping both arms about his neck and whispering
sweet nothings in his ear. He knew it wouldn't really
happen that way. For one thing, eyes that were bright
and beady like a sparrow's couldn't possibly go
liquid; and for another, he couldn't imagine her
Ladyship under any circumstances whispering sweet
nothings. Not to him. Still, he hoped that she would
at least co-operate. It would be difficult to be masterful if she simply turned on her heel and walked
away. But if Doug were right, there wasn't much
danger. If Doug were right, she was screaming for it.

Certainly she had no objections to make when
he suggested that maybe they'd had enough of the
nurdling idiots for one night and ought to go off
and get a meal somewhere. She agreed instantly,
without even a show of hesitation; though whether
it was the prospect of food which enticed her, or
whether it was the prospect of walking home across
the Common – or whether, perhaps, she was simply

as bored as he was with all the hey nonny no-ing –
he had not the least idea. Sharon wasn't a girl for
giving things away: she liked to keep you guessing.

He stood her a milk shake and a king-size burger
and chips in a new hamburger bar that had just
opened up. It cost the earth, and meant that he was
going to have to plunder his fencing foil fund, but
for once he didn't begrudge it. Normally, with
Sharon, he would have done, because everyone knew
she received astronomical sums of pocket money.
Her mum went out to work specially in order to
provide her with it, and when she'd got it she spent it
all on herself, on clothes. She had the most extensive
wardrobe of any girl in the school. This evening she
was wearing a bright pink top with some sort of
sparkly stuff sewn round the neck and a black satiny
skirt with a slit down the side. He guessed she looked
pretty good in it. It wasn't the sort of gear which
Anita would have worn, but then Anita was different.
He supposed it had to be said that she was superior.
At any rate, she was well out of his league.

After the hamburgers, they walked back across the
Common. It was neither quite dark nor quite light,
but somewhere dusky in between. He wondered if
Sharon found it romantic. Experimentally he slipped
an arm about her waist: she let it remain there,
making no attempt to pull away. Emboldened, he
tightened his embrace.

'Know what?' said Sharon.

'No,' said Jamie. 'What?'

'I reckon I could've sung better than that lot.'

'I reckon you could,' said Jamie.

They reached the chalk pits, where a couple of young kids, they couldn't have been more than eleven or twelve, were messing about on motorcycles that didn't have either lights or licence plates. He and Doug had tried that once, on Doug's brother's bike, but it was a mug's game. There was always some busybody walking his dog or his bird who took exception and threatened to have the law on you.

'Honestly,' said Sharon. She sounded aggrieved. 'They oughtn't to be doing that. They might kill someone.'

'More likely kill themselves,' said Jamie, remembering the number of times he and Doug had ended up, minus bike, at the bottom of the pit. It had been a miracle they'd never broken anything.

'You ought to stop them,' said Sharon. 'You ought to say something.'

'Like what?'

'Like tell them you'll report them, or something.'

He was revolted.

'I'm not a flaming informer!'

'It's for their own good,' said Sharon. 'They oughtn't to be doing it.'

'Oh, let them alone!' He swung her in the other direction. 'They're enjoying themselves.'

'But they oughtn't to be *doing* it.'

So what? Had she never done anything she oughtn't? He wondered how it was that she had this knack of always managing to irritate.

'Shall we go into the woods?' he said.

'What for?'

'Be nice in there. Nice and quiet.'

'It'd be dark,' said Sharon. 'You couldn't see where you were going.'

'So who wants to?'

Sharon, apparently. She refused point blank to go into the woods. She said she'd rather walk up to the look-out and see all the lights marking the roads that led to London.

'Sometimes you can see St. Paul's, Mr. Hubbard says. If the conditions are right.'

He didn't believe that; St. Paul's must be all of forty miles away. Most likely what the Hubbard had said was that you could see as *far* as St. Paul's. Still, he wasn't going to argue with her; it wasn't worth it.

Duly they trudged as far as the look-out: duly they gazed upon the lights. At least they were alone up there. Perhaps it was quite a good place to have come. The hillside sloped away before them, invitingly covered in ferns and long grass. He wondered how one began.

'Want to come and sit down?' he said.

'Not particularly.' She was still searching in vain for St. Paul's. 'He said the sky had to be clear. I expect there's too much cloud.'

'Yeah, I expect so.' Anything to keep her happy. He caught her about the waist. 'Come and sit down.'

She wrinkled her nose.

'On the ground?'

'Why not?' What did she expect? A room at the Ritz? 'It's perfectly OK. It hasn't rained for decades.'

'It rained last Sunday,' said Sharon.

'Yeah, well, that was days ago. It's had a chance to dry out since then. See?' He bent down and rubbed his hand over the grass to show her. 'Dry as a bone.'

'Yes,' she said, 'but it might be dirty.'

Jesus! Some people. He peeled off his sweater.

'There! How about that?'

Yes; she liked that. Had a touch of the old Walter Raleigh about it. Graciously, she sat herself upon it. He sat down beside her.

'Of course, there isn't any moon,' said Sharon. 'That would probably make a difference.'

Oh, bound to, bound to. (How was one supposed to stop them *talking*, for goodness' sake?)

He slipped his arm back round her waist, and obligingly she wriggled closer. This was better, thought Jamie. He was obviously getting the hang of it. It was simply a question of being masterful.

He tried kissing her, and instead of presenting herself with lips all puckered and pursed like a prune she actually parted them slightly, as if to indicate willingness. He began to feel that Doug had, quite definitely, been right: this was what she had wanted all along. All it had needed with a bit of positivity.

Encouraged, he slid his hand inside her bright pink top with the sparkly things round the neck. Instantly, she pulled away.

'Ja-*mie*!'

'What's the matter?'

'*Don't.*'

She only said it because she thought she had to; because it would have looked bad if she'd just let him go ahead without making any form of protest. She was just playing hard to get, that was all. 'Push 'em about a bit – show 'em you mean business.' What she needed was someone to be masterful. Very well, then.

'*Do you mind?*' Something went stinging like a whiplash across his face: it took him a second to realize that it was Sharon, belting him one. 'You just keep your hands to yourself! I didn't come up here to be mauled about.'

He might have retorted, then what did you come for? (bearing in mind that the Common was notorious) but he was still reeling from the blow she had dealt him. He wouldn't be at all surprised if she'd broken his nose. For such a puny creature, she packed one hell of a powerful punch.

'You must be bonkers!' Already she was up on her feet, trampling with cold disregard all over his sweater. 'You must be out of your tiny mind!'

Jamie thrust a lock of hair out of his eyes.

'There's no need to get all uptight.'

'You've got a nerve!' shrieked Sharon. 'You bring me up here and maul me about and then tell me that *there's no need to get all uptight?*'

'Well – be reasonable.' He wondered if he had red marks across his face, and if so whether they'd be gone by Monday. 'There are some girls that actually like it.'

'If you think,' said Sharon, 'that I'm one of *that* sort, then you obviously don't know very much about girls, that's all I can say.'

They walked back home with half a yard of daylight between them. All his attempts at apology met with a cold rebuff; she kept saying, 'If you thought I was *that* sort of a girl – ' When he protested that he hadn't thought she was that sort of a girl (which was perfectly correct, he never had, it was Doug who'd told him she was screaming for it) she only looked at him frostily and said if he didn't think she was that sort of a girl then why had he done what he did?

'Done what?' said Jamie. 'What did I do?'

'You know,' said Sharon, with heavy emphasis.

'Well, all right, then, so I'm sorry. I made a mistake.'

'Yes: you thought I *was* that sort.'

You just couldn't win. He gave up trying, after that: they walked the rest of the way in stony silence.

He wondered glumly, as he deposited Sharon at her front gate (she unbent sufficiently to say 'If you promise on your *honour* to behave yourself, then I might manage to be free next Saturday,' but he wasn't interested any more) where he had gone wrong. Doug knew what he was talking about where girls were concerned. He might not be any great shakes at anything else, but he did know about girls. If he said Sharon was a mass of seething passions, then a

266

mass of seething passions she was, even if she hadn't yet woken up to the fact herself. Obviously what she needed was someone like Doug to come along and rouse her. Jamie, far from rousing her, had only repelled. Probably there wasn't another boy in the whole of Tenterden who could have botched it like he had.

He arrived back home to find the shop already closed for the night and his parents watching television. He stuck his head round the door and said 'I'm going upstairs' and disappeared again before his mother could start asking questions, like 'What did the man talk about?' and 'Don't you want any supper?' He didn't feel like telling any more lies, and he didn't feel like supper. He just wanted to go to bed; to creep into the privacy of his own sheets and brood.

He was in process of doing so when there was a perfunctory tap at the door and Kim came bursting in. He swore at her – partly because he was half naked and partly because how many times had he told her, 'You wait to be asked before you come into my room. Right?' Kim took no notice of his swearing. With an air of self-righteousness, she said: 'I told Miss Tucker about you not coming. She wasn't very happy.'

He grunted. He didn't want to know about Miss Tucker not being very happy.

'*And* I had to wait nearly forty minutes for the bus,' added Kim.

'Good.' Jamie took a flying leap into the middle of his bed and pulled the sheet up to his chin.

'I don't see why you say it's good.' Kim was obviously in an aggressive mood and spoiling for a fight. 'I don't see what's good about someone having to wait forty minutes for a bus.'

'Shove off,' said Jamie.

'No! Why should I? I had to wait *forty minutes*. And then when it came – '

'Look, I said shove off,' said Jamie. 'Go on . . . beat it!'

Kim beat it: but not without defiantly putting her head back round the door to say: 'Anyway, Anita sent a message for you. She wants to know whether you can make it by two o'clock tomorrow. Round her place.'

'No,' said Jamie, 'I flaming well can't!'

He was sick to death of the lot of them – and that included Anita. He must have been mad, ever getting himself mixed up in all this in the first place. He had a damn good mind to call a halt right now.

'You're to let her know,' said Kim. 'I said you'd phone her when you got in. That's now,' she informed him, in case he was too thick to have realized.

He picked up his pillow and hurled it at her. His mother ought never to have had that brat. She was nothing but a pain.

9

As always, he found himself pathetically unable, at the moment of truth, to say no: punctually at two o'clock the next day he was round at Anita's.

'Thank goodness you could come!' she said. 'Last night was an absolute shambles – poor Thea was practically tearing her hair. Karin's chicken pox was only an allergy, but Zoe's gone and got mumps and that wretched child Andrea turned up without her shoes and had to go all the way home for them, and what with one thing and another it was just absolutely *ghastly*. I said that you and I would get on and practise by ourselves, so that Thea could concentrate on the rest of them.' She hustled him indoors, as if there wasn't a minute to lose. 'The parents have gone out, they won't be back till six-thirty, so we can go on for just as long as it takes.'

'Oh, no, we can't,' he said. He said it purely as a matter of principle. When would these people ever learn? *He* was the one who was doing the favours. 'I can't stay any later than six, I've got to get back.'

'Oh! Well – six is all right. Just so long as we *work*. I want to get it really perfect – really spot on. So that when we show Thea tomorrow – '

'Tomorrow?' he said. 'What's with tomorrow?'

'There's a rehearsal, in the morning. At the Church Hall. Oh, Jamie, don't say you can't make it! Not again!'

He was nettled. What did she mean, not again? He was the one that should be saying 'not again'. It was the second Sunday running.

'I don't know that I can,' he said.

'But it's tomorrow morning! If you don't know *now* — '

'I might have something else on, mightn't I?' he said. 'I might have made other plans, mightn't I?'

Anita looked at him.

'*Have* you?' she said.

'No, I haven't! I just like to be asked, that's all.'

Her face cleared.

'Well, then, I'm asking . . . please, Jamie, will you come?'

He wasn't prepared to be that easily won round.

'What time is it?'

'Nine o'clock till two-thirty.'

'Nine *o'clock*?' He wasn't usually out of bed by nine o'clock on a Sunday.

Anita, anxious to mollify, said: 'I expect it wouldn't matter if you were a tiny bit late. You probably wouldn't be wanted right away.'

Jamie grunted. He knew he was being churlish, but that was the way he felt.

'Truly,' said Anita, 'we didn't mean to take you for granted. We would have asked you yesterday, only you weren't there.'

270

'I had something on yesterday.'

'Yes, I know. Kim told us. Oh, Jamie . . . *please.*'

Perhaps he had a power complex, he thought. Perhaps what he secretly wanted was for people to grovel.

'If you don't turn up I simply don't know what we'll – '

'Yeah, OK! OK!' Suddenly, he was bored by it. Mostly what he was bored by was his own pretence that he had it in him to say a firm *no* and to mean it. 'Don't keep on,' he said. 'You've made the point.'

In spite of feeling churlish, he didn't set out on purpose to louse things up. He tried his best – his heart just wasn't in it. As a rule, when once he'd got started, he was able to forget all his secret misgivings. So what if his old man did pull his leg? His old man was just a philistine anyway. As for Doug – well, Doug wasn't here, was he? Doug need never know. And even if he did, so what? What was so peculiar about people dancing? When you actually stopped to think about it? Where was the difference between dancing and running, or dancing and swimming, or even, if it came to that, dancing and playing football? They were all physical, weren't they? They all represented a challenge. The way he saw it, if some people could run a mile in under four minutes, then so could he; likewise, if Rudolph Nureyev could do an entrechat douze (*if* he could) then he would jolly well learn to do the same.

Today, he couldn't have cared less about Rudolph Nureyev and his entrechat douze. They were very far from the forefront of his mind. He was still brooding on last night, and the way that he had messed it up with Sharon. Even now he didn't know where he was supposed to have gone wrong. When he was masterful, she slapped his face: when he wasn't, she rejected him for louts like Bob Pearson. Even Doug said that Bob Pearson hadn't got anything going for him – 'except the obvious'. He never had explained what the obvious was; but whatever it was, it seemed pretty clear that Jamie hadn't got it. Doug had – Bob Pearson had –

'Jamie, what are you *doing*?' said Anita. 'That's the *second* time.' She jabbed the stop button on the cassette player and regarded him with an air of exasperation. 'What on earth is the matter with you?'

A good question, he thought. A very good question.

'*Well*?' Anita put her hands on her hips.

'Well – ' He didn't say 'well what?' There didn't seem much point.

'I thought we were supposed to be rehearsing?'

'So that's what we're doing, isn't it?'

'No, it is not!' She stamped a foot. 'What we're doing is just wasting time. I don't know why you bothered coming in the first place, if this is all the effort you're going to make.'

'Neither do I,' he retorted, 'if this is all the thanks I'm going to get.'

'Well, but Jamie, *honestly*. You might just as well not be here.'

He scowled.

'I'm almost beginning to wish that I wasn't.'

'Why? Just because you're not concentrating and I'm getting mad at you? I think that's rotten! I think that's really rotten! You wouldn't behave like it if Thea were here.'

No, he wouldn't. That was quite true. He felt a pang of conscience.

'The thing is – ' He kicked with his toe against the wall. 'The thing is, I don't reckon I ought to be doing this lot.'

She stared at him.

'Why not?'

He hunched a shoulder.

'Why not?' said Anita.

'I dunno. Just doesn't seem – right, I s'pose.'

'What do you mean, it doesn't seem right?'

Questions, questions. Always questions. He shook his head.

'Warriors dance,' said Anita. 'Look at Red Indians – look at African tribes. It's always the men.'

Jamie said nothing.

'What about Zulus?' said Anita. 'What about Cossacks? What about the Red *Army*?'

There was a silence. Perhaps if one were a Zulu, thought Jamie, it might be different. But one wasn't. One was a pupil at Tenterden Road Comprehensive, and if word of this ever got out one would be a laughing stock.

'I just don't see what the problem is,' said Anita.

No, of course she didn't. She was a girl – it was all right for girls. If *they* were good at dancing, everyone said 'how nice'. If, on the other hand, they wanted to do metalwork or play football, nobody turned round and said it wasn't right or it wasn't natural or there must be something wrong with them. Not these days. They wouldn't dare. Find themselves up before the Equal Opportunities thingummy before they knew where they were. They could scream till they were blue in the face about their flaming women's lib, he still reckoned they had it a damn sight easier.

Anita was looking at him; awaiting an explanation.

'My Dad' — he cringed, even as he heard himself say it — 'my Dad says dancers are a load of old nannies.'

'Oh, well! Your Dad!' Anita tossed her head, disdainfully. 'It's the stupid sort of thing someone's dad would say, isn't it?'

He supposed that it was. All the same, it didn't alter the fact: messing about in tights and ballet shoes wasn't natural. Not for a boy from Tenterden Road Comprehensive.

'I bet *your Dad*,' said Anita, 'doesn't know the first thing about it ... I bet he couldn't even tell an entrechat from an arabesque.'

Dead right he couldn't. Probably never even heard of them. He wished, though, that she wouldn't say 'your Dad' like that. It sounded wrong, coming from her lips; patronising, almost. He knew very well that she didn't call her own father 'Dad'.

'Anyway,' said Anita, 'you surely don't take any notice of what people *say*? Especially when it's not true. I mean, I know *Garstin*'s a bit of an old woman, but you can't judge everyone by him. In any case, Garstin's not a dancer. David was, and *he*'s not – an old woman, I mean. I think he might be gay, but that's something else. No one could say he was *wet*. As a matter of fact, he's a bit like you.'

He wondered, rather sourly, whether he was supposed to be comforted by this piece of information.

'It's all so *silly*,' said Anita. 'What on earth does it matter?'

He felt like saying, 'If you went to Tenterden Road Comprehensive you'd *know* what it mattered,' but the moment passed and he didn't. He didn't say anything; just frowned and tried to push his hair out of his eyes, only it wasn't in them because he'd taken Anita's advice and worn a sweat band. Anita sighed.

'Thea said we'd have trouble. She said you'd think it was compromising your masculinity.'

For crying out loud! What did they *talk* about, those two?

'I don't think it's – ' Irritably, he cleared a frog from his throat. 'I don't think it's *compromising my masculinity*.'

'All right, then! So why don't you want to do it? If you're not scared that it's soppy and that people are going to laugh at you, why don't you want to do it? Because you *are* scared that it's soppy and that people are going to laugh at you! You are, and you just won't admit it! You're such a *coward*.'

'No, I'm not.'

'Yes, you are! It bothers you, what other *people* might think. *You* don't think it's soppy, but – '

'How do you know?' he said. 'How do you know I don't?'

'Because if you did you wouldn't be any good at it – you couldn't be any good at it. And you *are* good at it. And anyway, you didn't think *Romeo and Juliet* was soppy, did you?'

He grunted, non-committally.

'*Did* you?' said Anita.

'It was all right. Bits of it.'

'Which bits?'

'Bits with the swords; they were OK. But they weren't ballet.'

'Yes, they were!'

'No, they weren't.'

'They were done by dancers – '

'Yes, but they weren't *ballet*.' He lunged, with an imaginary sword. 'They were fencing.' Feint – parry; cut – thrust. He'd got the whole of one sequence almost completely worked out by now. He'd been practising it in secret, in his bedroom. 'I wouldn't mind doing *fencing*.' Attack – two, three. Lunge – two, three. 'I'm thinking of saving up to buy a foil and have lessons.'

Anita stood watching a moment, then: 'I've got a fencing foil,' she said.

He stopped.

'Where d'you get one?'

'Had it for school. They said we could choose . . . either cricket or fencing. So I did fencing.'

276

His heart swelled. Some people, he thought, bitterly. Some people just had all the luck, didn't they?

'Hang on,' said Anita. 'I'll get it.'

She disappeared into her bedroom. He heard a cupboard door open, heard her rummaging about amongst what sounded to be a collection of tennis rackets and hockey sticks. It probably wouldn't be a real fencing foil; not the sort that real fencers used. Probably just some tinpot, half-size job fit for schoolgirls to mess about with.

'Here it is.' Anita had come back. She held something out to him: a real, bona fide, full-size fencing foil, with a button on the end of the blade and a proper metal guard between the blade and the handle. His heart swelled almost to bursting. Some people had *all* the luck. 'You can have it,' said Anita, 'if you like.'

He gaped at her, speechless.

'I won't be wanting it any more. I'm going to ballet school next term.'

'But – ' He gulped. 'What about the rest of this term?'

'Oh, I'll tell them I've lost it. I can always use one of the school ones. It really doesn't matter, you don't *have* to have your own. I've only got one because of this friend of Daddy's who used to be a professional. He gave it to me for my birthday.'

He was still uneasy – torn between the burning desire to possess, and the feeling that a fencing foil was not something to be given away lightly. Not, at any rate, without parental permission.

'Won't this friend of Daddy's object?'

'Don't suppose he'll ever know. Anyway, I *want* you to have it – I'd *like* you to have it. You ought to have a helmet and a jacket as well, really, but if you're going to take lessons they're bound to provide you with them.'

He grew excited.

'D'you reckon?'

'They'd have to. It's dangerous without. You could get stabbed in the eye, or almost anything. Shall I show you how to hold it?' She took the blade away from him, turning it over so that it seemed to him it was the wrong way up, but Anita said no, that was how you had to do it. 'Right in the palm of your hand, with your thumb placed flat . . . then you can either bend your wrist *this* way – or *that* way, depending what movement you're doing . . . see? It's quite easy, once you're used to it. Shall I show you the on-guard position? Like this. Look – ' She demonstrated, feet apart, at right angles, knees bent, sword arm extended, left arm raised, left hand gracefully curved. It looked almost like a ballet position. 'Shall I show you how to attack? I'll show you how to lunge – '

She showed him how to lunge, and how to parry, and how to riposte – she showed him the basic positions – prime and seconde, and tierce and quinte, and several others which he promptly forgot – she showed him how to engage, and how to disengage, and how to do a thing called a balestra, which was a method of attacking with a little jump forward, which he rather thought they had used in *Romeo and Juliet*. He decided, quite definitely, that he was going to save up and take classes.

'Yes, why don't you?' said Anita. 'You'd probably be quite good at it – seeing as you're good at ballet.'

He'd temporarily forgotten about being good at ballet. He tried his best to scowl, as an indication that he would rather not be, but somehow all ill temper seemed to have evaporated. When Anita, rather wistfully, said, 'It's almost four o'clock . . . I suppose we couldn't try just a *little* bit of rehearsing?' he felt an absolute heel. A whole solid hour he'd let her waste on him, even though he knew how worried she was about that second lift, which they'd never yet managed to get really right. *And* there was that bit in the middle, where he kept getting the timing wrong.

'Sorry,' he said. 'Didn't realize it was so late.'

They rehearsed non-stop until half past six, when Mummy put her head round the door and said: 'Good gracious me! Still at it? I just came to say that we're back.' Now it was Anita's turn to apologize.

'Honestly,' she said, 'I wasn't cheating you – I didn't do it on purpose.'

'Do what?' said Jamie.

'Make you stay longer than you should have. You said you had to be away by six.'

'Oh! That.' He grinned, rather sheepishly. 'I only said that 'cos I was mad at you.'

'You mean it doesn't matter?'

'Doesn't matter what time I go. Rehearse all night, if you like.'

For a moment, she looked almost tempted; but then, very firmly, she shook her head.

'No. Thea always says that one reaches a cut-out point. She says if you go on too long you undo all the good work that's gone before. But if you really *don't* have to get home' — she picked up a towel and held it out to him — 'then maybe you ought to stay and have dinner.'

She didn't say why he ought to stay and have dinner — a reward, perhaps, for being a good boy? — but whatever the reason he wasn't averse to it. (*There's this bird I know, lives up by the golf course. One of the big houses. I was round there last Saturday, stayed on to have dinner . . .*)

If Mummy and Daddy were put out to find themselves lumbered with an extra mouth at table, they were far too well bred to show it. Mummy simply opened the lid of her freezer cabinet (Jamie could hardly believe it: it was chock full of food, enough to feed an army) and said: 'Right. What do we all fancy, then?' while Daddy said: 'Cheers! Gives me a chance to crack a bottle', and went off to look in his wine cellar, which he kept in a cupboard under the stairs. Mrs. Carr hated having people sprung on her at the last minute. She always grumbled about 'not having anything in' and 'not being prepared'. It was one of the greatest crimes you could commit, bringing someone home without warning — except if it were Doug. She didn't care about Doug. He could just muck in with the rest of them and take pot luck. But once when Jamie had brought Sharon back she'd gone practically raving berserk. Still, he supposed it must make a difference, having a huge great freezer permanently full of food.

They talked, over the dinner table, of Anita going to ballet school. It appeared that Miss Tucker's was only a jumping-off point: as from September, she was starting full time, as a student up in London.

Mummy said: 'I've warned her, time and again . . . it's a dog's life. Nothing but slave, slave, slave. And then no guarantee of ever getting anywhere. But there you are, if it's what she wants.'

'It always has been,' said Anita.

'Oh! It always has been. Right from the time she was a little girl. There was never any stopping her. How about you, Jamie? What are you going to do?'

He had once thought of being a professional cricketer, but he had almost given up on that idea; especially after the last fiasco. He said he didn't know.

'You ought to try for ballet school,' said Anita. 'I bet they'd take you like a shot.'

'For goodness' sake!' Mummy laughed, merrily, as she ground salt out of a wooden salt cellar. Jamie watched in fascination, taking careful note so that he would know how to use it if anyone said 'Pass Jamie the salt'. Left to himself he would simply have tilted it upside down and felt stupid when nothing came out. 'There are other things in life,' said Mummy, 'besides ballet.'

'But he's good at it,' said Anita. 'And they're crying

out for men. They always are. There's about a thousand girls applying to every one boy.'

'I'm not surprised. Boys probably have more sense.'

'It isn't that. It's the fact that parents don't encourage them. Jamie's parents don't encourage *him*, do they, Jamie? His father still thinks it's a cissy thing to do. What was it you said he said? Something horrid.'

Jamie muttered: 'He was only joking.'

'Yes, but I bet he meant it, really. I bet he thinks if you became a dancer you'd turn into some horrid mincing creature with a lisp.'

Gratefully, Jamie took the salt cellar that Mummy was holding out to him and concentrated on grinding salt.

'*Honestly*,' said Anita. 'People are so *bigoted*.'

'I wouldn't say it's bigoted, so much.' Mummy reached across for another little wooden pot. 'More a question of not being able to rid oneself of the ideas one's been brought up with. It's not that easy. I daresay if *you* were a boy, we mightn't be quite so keen on the thought of your taking up ballet.'

'Why not?' said Anita.

'Oh! I don't know . . . I suppose because other things would seem more suitable. Pepper, Jamie? – Not that we'd stop you, of course. Any more than I daresay Jamie's father is stopping him.'

'*Would* he stop you,' said Anita, 'if you really wanted to?'

Grind, grind, grind. First the salt, and then the pepper. He bet his mum would go crazy over it.

'Dunno,' he said. 'I s'pose not.'

'Well, there you are, then! Why don't you?'

Why didn't he? Was she raving mad?

'Stop flogging everyone into balletomania,' said Mrs. Cairncross. 'Some people have better things to do with their lives. What does your father do, Jamie?'

'He runs an off-licence,' said Jamie.

'My God!' Daddy spoke for the first time. 'There's a useful chap to know! Champagne every weekend, eh?'

Actually, it wasn't even champagne at Christmas, because Mr. Carr didn't go for it. He reckoned it was overpriced. 'All gas and no substance.' Jamie was about to say that they occasionally had a bottle of table wine with Sunday dinner when Anita, who was not a girl to be easily deflected, broke in with: 'It seems such a *waste*. When someone's really got *talent* – and anyway, what else would he do?'

Mummy said briskly: 'I'm sure there are all sorts of things, aren't there, Jamie? I don't expect dancing's the only thing he's good at.'

'I suppose he'll go into a *factory*,' said Anita.

'Or an office,' said Daddy. 'Plenty of opportunities for bright young men. What O levels are you doing, Jamie?'

'History,' said Jamie.

There was a pause.

'No maths?' said Daddy.

'Not much good at maths.' He speared a chunk

283

of meat with his fork. 'Doing it for CSE – don't s'pose I'll pass, though.'

Old Hubbard had said it would be a miracle if he scraped any marks at all. He'd said Jamie was the nearest thing he'd ever encountered to a natural born cretin – if you excepted Doug, that is. He'd said if they had a Brainless of Britain contest it would be a close run thing which of them would win.

Daddy shook his head.

'Pity,' he said. 'Maths is a useful thing to have.'

'Why?' said Anita. 'What's useful about it? So long as you can add up and subtract . . . you don't have to have *maths* to *dance*.'

When he left, at nine-thirty, Anita came to the garden gate with him, smuggling his fencing foil in a cardigan. He had a sudden renewal of doubt.

'You quite sure it's OK?' he said.

'Oh, Jamie, of course I am! It's mine, isn't it? People can do what they like with their own things. If I want to give it to a friend, then I can give it to a friend . . . here!' She thrust it at him. 'Take it, and don't be stupid.'

He took it, holding it rigidly behind his back with one hand, in case Mummy or Daddy should be watching out of a window. He was sure, if they were, they would come running down the path to re-possess.

'If they ask you where it's gone – ' he said.

'They won't. They won't know.'

'But if they do – '

'I'll say I gave it away to someone who could

make better use of it. You mustn't get so hung up: it's only an *object*.'

'Yeah. Well – all right, then,' he said. 'If you're really sure.'

'Jamie, I *told* you. I *said*. I said I wanted you to *have* it.'

'Yeah! OK!' He stood a moment, uncertain; then awkwardly he said: 'Well, I – I guess I'd better be going. Thanks a million for the supper and everything.'

'Thank you for coming,' said Anita. '*And* for rehearsing all that time.'

''s all right,' he said.

He set off across the Common, carrying his fencing foil before him. He had just reached the first clump of trees and was about to disappear, when Anita's voice called after him: 'Don't forget about tomorrow morning . . . nine o'clock sharp – and don't be late!'

10

'Hey! You! Young Carr!'

Jamie, on his way across to the field with Doug, stopped in his tracks and turned. Bob Pearson was hollering at him from a distance.

'What's his problem?' said Doug.

'Dunno.'

'Tell him to get stuffed.'

At any rate, he wasn't going running to him. If Bob Pearson wanted to hold a conversation, then he could shift his fat carcase and come across and do so in a civilized fashion. He wasn't going to be bawled at over half a mile of playing field.

He stood waiting. Bob Pearson, looking not best pleased, began barging his way through a flock of juniors.

'What happened, then?' He reached Jamie and glared down at him. Jamie glared back. What was he talking about, what happened? What happened when? What was he supposed to have done now? 'Friday night!' Bob Pearson spoke impatiently. 'What happened?'

Friday *night*? The prickles broke out all up and

down Jamie's spine. Don't say that little cow
Sharon –

'There was a net practice! Four o'clock till seven!
Where the devil did you get to?'

Net practice. The irony of it. And there he'd been,
making up these lies – what he'd thought were lies
– about 'having something on at school'.

'What's the matter with you? Don't you ever look
at the notice board? Can't you read, or something?'

'Mental age of three,' said Doug.

The Pearson ignored him.

'There's a house match next Saturday. I've got the
nets booked for Tuesday and Friday. This time I
want you *there*. Understood?'

'Yeah.' Jamie nodded, feebly. 'Sorry about last
Friday. I didn't look.'

'No; obviously. Well, in future make sure you do.
I don't waste my time writing out lists just so people
can walk past and ignore them.'

'Creep,' said Doug, as he went steaming off.

Later in the day, Jamie made a detour via the
Assembly Hall and for the first time in weeks spared
a glance at the notice board. Sure enough, there was
his name: *R. Pearson (Cap.), D. Jones, J. Carr* –

It had been superimposed upon M. Chilvers,
which had in its turn been superimposed upon A.
Walker. M. Chilvers, he knew, because he had been
present to witness it, had broken his wrist in the gym
last Thursday. He didn't know what had happened to
A. Walker. Maybe he'd been struck by lightning
or got an ingrowing toenail; he didn't really care.

287

Whatever it was, it had given him a second chance he'd never thought to have.

'Marvellous, isn't it?' said Doug, craning over his shoulder. 'Expects you to come crawling back the minute he crooks his little finger . . . even has the diabolical nerve to yell at you for not keeping an eye on his poxy notice board. What's he think you're going to do? Chase up and down every five minutes looking at the flaming thing?'

It hadn't struck Jamie that way − he'd just been happy to find himself with a second chance. Doug was quite right, though. He tried to instil some indignation into himself.

'Know what I'd do?' said Doug. 'I'd tell him to stuff his lousy house match right up his − '

'Yeah, I know,' said Jamie. It was easy enough for Doug to say what he would do: Doug didn't have these dreams of being a professional cricketer. There wasn't any point in cutting off one's nose to spite one's face. 'I'll tell you one thing,' he said. 'He's not getting me run out again. No way. He tries any funny business, he's the one going to end up with egg on his face.'

The picture of Bob Pearson with egg on his face was a pleasurable one: it solaced him for any feeling of weakness he might have for allowing himself to be put upon.

'Matter of interest,' said Doug, 'what *were* you doing on Friday? Someone said they saw you with Sharon down the Folk Club.'

'Don't talk to me about that place,' said Jamie.

'And don't talk to me about Sharon, either. I've had it with that girl.'

'Not before time,' said Doug. 'I always told you you wouldn't get anywhere with her.'

'*You* always told me? *You* always told me – ' He stopped. What was the point? It didn't matter any more, what Doug had always told him. Maybe Doug didn't know quite as much about girls as they'd both thought he did. 'Anyway,' he said, carelessly, 'I've got someone else.'

'Who's that, then? Not old kinky Coral?'

'Nope.' He couldn't resist just a little bit of boasting. 'Doesn't go to Tenterden. Goes to the High.'

'Cor!' said Doug, playing awestruck. 'Mixing with the nobs! You wait till she takes you home to meet Mummy and Daddy . . . it'll be round the servants' entrance for you, mate.'

'I've already been home with her,' said Jamie. 'Had dinner round there, Saturday.'

'Dinner already!' Doug's tone was jeering, but he looked at Jamie with what seemed a new respect. As they parted company at the school gates, he said: 'You going to bring this new bird down the disco some time, then?'

'Might do,' said Jamie.

He wondered, on his way home . . . if Anita were to hear herself described as 'his bird', would she be indignant? Or did she now regard herself as in any sense belonging to him?

After some hesitation, when he got in, he looked

up Cairncross in the telephone book. After more hesitation – quite a lot more, as a matter of fact: it took him a full half hour of dithering before he could nerve himself – he picked up the receiver and dialled the number. It was Mummy who answered. She sounded quite friendly. She said: 'Hallo, Jamie. Do you want Anita? I'll get her for you.' And then he heard her shouting: 'Anita! There's Jamie on the telephone.' After a few seconds, Anita's voice came, breathlessly: 'Jamie? Oh, Jamie, you're *not* going to say you can't make it on Wednesday?'

'No,' he said. 'I was just ringing to find out if you were doing anything tonight?'

'Tonight?' She didn't seem to think it odd of him, or presumptuous. She seemed to think it quite natural. She said: 'Actually, I'm going up to Birdhurst Park to watch the Morris dancing.'

Jamie said: 'Oh.'

'I'm going with a girl from school . . . you could always come with us if you wanted.'

He might have done had it been Anita by herself, but not even for the sake of calling her his bird was he prepared to spend an evening watching Morris dancing in company with her and a girl friend. Men in tights was one thing: men with little bells on their ankles was more than he could take. He wasn't getting dragged into *that* scene. He asked her what about tomorrow, but tomorrow, it seemed, she had a class. She had classes Tuesdays, Wednesdays, Thursdays and Fridays – not to mention rehearsing all afternoon every Saturday. She was stark mad; not a doubt of it. He arranged that he would go and pick her up on Wednesday, so they could walk over the Common together to Miss Tucker's. He supposed that that was better than nothing.

He went round early on Wednesday, as soon as tea was finished. His mother had insisted he carry a bottle of wine with him, to make up for having stayed to dinner on Saturday. He'd done his best to wangle champagne, but she hadn't taken the hint, so now he was stuck with an end-of-bin Beaujolais, which he had a horrid feeling was probably the sort of wine that Mrs. Cairncross used for cooking in. He was in two minds whether to ditch the thing before he got there, but then he had visions of his mother seeking out Anita's mother at the fearful fiasco that Miss Tucker would insist on calling 'a divertissement' and asking her how she'd liked the wine, so he gritted his teeth and hung on to it. It was Daddy he handed it over to. Daddy said: 'Oh! A bottle of plonk! How perfectly splendid – this year's vintage, too,' which made it sound as if maybe it was all right after all.

Anita was in her school uniform. He'd never seen her in it before. It was salmon pink: a salmon pink dress, buttoned all the way down the front, with white collar and cuffs. It was the sort of dress that his Mum would have liked Kim to wear – all neat and tidy and little girlish. It ought by rights to have reduced its wearer very firmly to the status of a schoolgirl. Instead, it made her look almost grown up. It made him feel quite gauche and clodhopping –

291

possibly because he *was* gauche and clodhopping. Gauche and clodhopping and only taking one O level. He bet she wouldn't even look twice at him if it weren't for the fact that she needed him for her precious ballet. Probably wouldn't be seen *dead* with him. He wished there were something he could do that would impress her.

On their way to Miss Tucker's, across the Common, they came upon a gang of little kids from Jamie's street messing about with a bat and a ball, using a tree trunk with chalk marks for a wicket. If he'd been by himself they'd have clamoured at him to join in: because he was with a girl, and a girl whom none of them recognized, they obviously felt too shy. Magnanimously, he joined in anyway. This was his chance – the very chance he'd been waiting for. At least he would show her there was *some*thing he could do.

'Hang on a sec.' He snapped his fingers for the bat, took up his stance at the tree-trunk wicket, called casually down the pitch to Luke Gibbs, who was in the same class as Kim, to 'Toss us one up, then.' Luke obliged. Fortunately, he could bowl better than some of the kids: it was at any rate reasonably on course. With an air of satisfaction, Jamie stepped forward, opened up his shoulders and sent it smacking out through the covers for six. The crack of the bat meeting ball was music. Even if Anita knew nothing whatsoever of cricket, she could hardly fail to have recognized it as a classic stroke.

He stood back, smiling and benevolent: the professional cricketer surrounded by his admirers. One of the little kids had gone scampering after the ball. He picked it up, and in his excitement hurled it back towards the wicket. Jamie, reaching out a careless hand to arrest its flight, found himself suddenly attacked by a screeching virago.

'*Jamie!* Your *hands!*'

All the little kids stopped and stared. (He could just hear them, afterwards, amongst themselves: *Jamie!* Your *hands!*) Playing it cool, he tossed the ball back to the bowler, surrendered his bat and allowed himself to be dragged off. The minute they were out of earshot, he turned on her.

'What was that for?'

'Your *hands!*' She almost screamed it at him. 'That was a hard ball . . . you could have broken something!'

He looked at her stolidly.

'So what?'

'So you've got to *dance* on Saturday! You've got to *partner* me!'

'Is that all you ever think about?' he said. 'Dancing?'

'No, of course it isn't! But just at this *moment* – '

'So what else do you ever think about?' he said.

'Lots of things! Loads of things!'

'Tell me some.'

'*Tell* you some?' It was the first time he had ever seen her at all disconcerted. 'Well – '

'Do you ever think about the Bomb and people starving and what it's like not to have money?'

'Yes — sometimes.'

'You mean like about once in every blue moon?' She rallied slightly.

'Well, how often do you?'

'More than you, I bet. Do you know, I've never heard you talk about anything that wasn't ballet?'

A slight pinkness invaded her cheek. He noted it with satisfaction. Others before him, he thought, had had cause to complain.

'It's not that I'm not interested in other things.' She said it earnestly, as if trying to convince herself as much as him. 'It's just that when you want to do something like ballet there simply isn't *room* for anything else. If you want to get anywhere, you really have to dedicate yourself.'

'Crap,' said Jamie.

That took her aback — he bet no one had ever said crap to her in the whole of her pampered life.

'Jamie, it isn't crap!' she said. 'It's true! There's only one way you can ever hope to achieve anything, and that's by being completely single-minded. Imagine if you wanted to be a footballer, or a boxer, or a — a pop star, or something.' That's right, he thought. Bring it down to my level. Something that a common boy from Tenterden Road Comprehensive might just about be able to grasp. 'Imagine how hard you'd have to work,' said Anita. 'Imagine all the training sessions and the practice. Well, it's exactly the same with dancing. It's just no *use* thinking you can skip class every time you're a bit off colour or something a bit more interesting happens to turn up.' (Was that a dig at him?) 'It's no *use* thinking you can play football or cricket or do things that are going to develop muscles in all the wrong places. You have to put the ballet first.'

'That's if you're going to be a dancer,' he said.

'And you're not?' She shot a quick glance at him. 'Did you think any more about that? About what I said? I'm sure that if you tried for a ballet school – '

'I'm not trying for any ballet school!' His tone was tetchy: he could hear that it was. 'My old man would have a fit.'

'Is that the only thing that stops you?'

'No, it is not!' Whoever heard of a boy from Tenterden Road Comprehensive going to a ballet school? It was a ludicrous idea. Imagine standing up in a careers class and saying, 'Please, sir, I'm going to ballet school.' Doug would die laughing.

'You mean,' said Anita, 'that you would honestly rather spend the rest of your life doing some boring, soulless job in a factory than being a dancer?'

Why did she automatically assume that it had to be a factory?

Because he went to Tenterden Road Comprehensive and was only taking one O level, that was why.

He said: 'I'm not going into a factory.'

'Well, all right, an office, then! It's all the same – it's all boring and soulless. If you're not minding machines you're sitting at a desk writing letters. And you'd rather do that than *dance*?'

'I'm not going to do that,' he said.

'So what are you going to do?'

295

There were a million things he could do. He could join the army and learn how to kill people – he could join the police and harass all the black kids – he could run an off-licence and hump beer crates about –

'I'm going to play cricket,' he said. 'And what's more, I'm going to play it on Saturday.'

'*Saturday*?' Her voice rose, shrilly. 'But that's the day of the show!'

He enjoyed seeing her all out of control – she who as a rule was so cool and calm and superior.

'I know it is,' he said.

'Then how can you possibly play cricket?'

'It's all right,' he said. 'You don't have to panic.' (Privately, he thought it might do her good just for once.) 'The match is in the morning – it'll be over by two. Gives me bags of time. Show doesn't start till seven-thirty.'

'But your hands!' She screamed it at him. 'What about your *hands*?'

'What about them?' he said. 'I'm not a flaming concert pianist.'

'Jamie, I know you think I'm making an absurd amount of fuss, but honestly – ' she looked at him, pleading – 'honestly, I'm *not*. I'm really *not*. You've only got to have the slightest of sprains, or pull a muscle, or even just bruise yourself – '

'So what are you suggesting? I should wear a suit of armour?'

She bit her lip.

'Surely they could find somebody else? Just for this once?'

He was very certain they could; all too easily. And it wouldn't be just for this once.

'I'm not stopping playing cricket only for some lousy ballet show,' he said.

'Jamie! That's not fair!'

'It is fair.'

It was fair. Think of all the Saturday afternoons he'd sacrificed – all the Sunday mornings, all the Wednesdays and the Fridays. It was most certainly fair.

In a low, intense voice, Anita said: 'You don't seem to realize how important this is.'

Didn't realize how important it was? He was sick to death of being *told* how important it was. Come to that, he was sick to death of the whole thing.

'If anything were to happen and you couldn't dance – '

'Then you'd have to make do with Garstin, wouldn't you?'

Her chin went up.

'I wouldn't dance with Garstin if he were the last man left on earth! I wouldn't be seen dead on the same stage with Garstin!'

Such exaggerated over-reaction irritated him.

'Well, that's your problem,' he said. 'I can't guarantee I'm not going to be knocked stone cold. It's a chance you have to take.'

Anita, very pale, said: 'You mean, you're going to go ahead and play?'

She'd better believe it.

'Furthermore,' he said – the word sounded good, so he said it again: 'Furthermore, I don't even know for sure whether I'm going to be able to make the dress rehearsal Friday. We've got a net practice goes on till seven. If it ends on time I might be able to get there for half past. All depends how the light holds. Sometimes these things run over – might be nearer eight.'

Anita didn't say 'Oh, but Jamie, you *must*' – she didn't even bother saying her usual '*Please*, Jamie.' Maybe she was tired of it. Or maybe she guessed that in his present mood it would be a waste of breath. He'd been pushed far enough, he wasn't being pushed any further. Quietly, in a voice devoid of expression, she said: 'You'd better tell Miss Tucker.'

He didn't, of course. When it came to it, he couldn't. However mad Anita might make him, he just could never work himself up to the same pitch of indignation against Miss Tucker. When she went yum-pumming about the room ('*Yum*-Pum! *Yum*-Pum! *Yum*-Pum!') he wanted to laugh, but at the same time he wanted to join in, he wanted to do things that would please her. When she patted him on the head and said 'Good boy!' or 'Well done!' he didn't writhe and cringe as he would if anyone else had dared to take the liberty. She made him feel about three years old, but somehow he didn't mind. It amused him to humour her – and yet her praise, when it came, was very sweet. He decided he would tell Bob Pearson that he could only stay till five-thirty on Friday. When all was said and done, it was Miss Tucker who'd got in first. She ought, in fairness, to have priority.

He approached the Pearson on Tuesday, during a break in practice. Fortunately he was on form – he'd just been slamming the bowling right and left, even the great Pearson had been moved to murmur words of approval – so he reckoned it wasn't such a bad moment to ask.

'Will it be OK,' he said, 'if I leave at five-thirty on Friday?'

'No, it will not be OK!' The Pearson looked at him with the same irritation with which Jamie had looked at Anita. 'You need all the practice you can get. You already missed out on last Friday.'

'I wouldn't have done if I'd known. I didn't know that you wanted me.'

'So whose fault was that? You should have kept an eye on the notice board, as you're supposed to do.'

'What, every five minutes?'

'Don't be flaming impertinent!'

'I'm not being! I looked on Wednesday – ' That was a lie for a start, but it didn't matter: it was the principle of the thing. After all, he *might* have looked on Wednesday. 'I looked last thing. It wasn't there then.'

'What's that got to do with it? Anyone who was really keen would be down there every day, just checking.'

'Yeah, well, OK, I'm sorry, but – '

'But nothing! You either want to be in the team or you don't.'

'I do want to be in the team! It's just that Friday . . . I promised someone. Ages ago. I said that I would do something for them.'

'Yes, well, if it's some bird you're taking some-where, you can just forget about it.'

'It isn't a bird.'

'So what is it, then?'

He was damned if he was going to tell a creep like Bob Pearson what it was. (Please, I have to rehearse for a divertissement . . .) Defiantly, he said: 'It's helping out with a show. For spastics.'

'On Friday evening?'

'Yeah – well, that's when the dress rehearsal is. I told them that I'd be there.'

'You told them that you'd be there on a Friday evening? When you know perfectly bloody well that nine times out of ten Friday evenings are when net practices are held? Well, I'm sorry! I don't have people on my team with divided loyalties. To me, the House comes first. That's the way I expect it to be for everyone else. If it's not, then I'm not interested. You either play cricket, or you go off and do this other thing. It's up to you. You're going to have to choose.'

'But it's for *spastics*,' said Jamie.

'I don't give a damn what it's for! It could be for snow-blind huskies, for all I care. I've got a job to do, getting a team together. Like I said, you either want to be part of it or you don't; it's as simple as that. If you do, then you turn up on Friday and you stay till the end the same as everyone else. If you don't, you'd better tell me now, so that I can make other arrangements.'

He wondered, glumly, what the other arrangements would be. There was a kid in Class 4 who was said to be pretty hot stuff – for a kid. A fourteen-year-old taking his place! It would be more than he could bear.

'Well, come on!' The Pearson tapped impatiently with his bat on the coconut matting. 'Which is it to be? Us or Them? I haven't got all day.'

Desperately, Jamie said: 'I just don't like having to let people down.'

'Which people?'

'Well . . . *them*.'

'I see.' The Pearson nodded, coldly. 'You don't mind letting the House down: that doesn't bother you.'

'Yes, it does!' (Actually, it didn't. The only thing that bothered him was losing his place on the team.) 'It does, but – '

'But you'd rather give your allegiance elsewhere?' The Pearson turned away, in disgust. 'You're the sort that would sell his country down the drain in time of war. People like you I can do without. You needn't bother looking at the notice board any more: your name certainly won't be appearing there.'

He thought, afterwards, of a thousand retorts he might have made. He might have told the Pearson, for a start, that it was dumb clods like him that caused wars in the first place – all this Us and Them business. All this junk about the House coming first. The guy was a throwback. He wouldn't be at all surprised if he belonged to the National Front. It was just the sort of fascist organization that would appeal to one of his blinkered mentality. Of course, at the time, he couldn't think of a single thing to say other than 'Look, I'm *sorry* – ' which now he would have given anything not to have said. The Pearson hadn't taken a blind bit of notice. It had just been demeaning himself for no purpose.

He didn't even receive from Doug the sympathy he might have looked for. Doug, whilst not sub-scribing to the 'House first, last and always' business, nevertheless seemed to think he was raving mad. Putting some crummy dancing show before a cricket match?

'I wouldn't normally,' said Jamie. 'But when you've actually *promised* someone – '

He couldn't help feeling there'd been a bit of a change in Doug's attitude from earlier in the week, when he'd been all for telling the Pearson to 'stuff his lousy cricket match'. Now he wanted him to tell little old Miss Tucker to stuff her lousy dancing show. He just couldn't do it; not even for a place on the team. If he didn't arrive on time Friday evening it would louse everything up for her. She needed him there right from the beginning. She'd gone and put in this opening number (she called it a 'Grande Parade', pronounced Grond Parahd) where everyone had to come on and form themselves into a sort of avenue, and then he and Anita were going to appear in a spotlight and he was going to lead her down to the front of the stage and all the audience (hopefully) were going to look at them and think what a beautiful picture they made. He supposed, for Anita, it was a big moment. Not that it was for Anita he was doing it: it was for little old Miss Tucker, so that she could sit back and be happy.

As a matter of fact, he wasn't feeling very kindly disposed towards Anita just at this moment. He hadn't forgotten about the fencing foil, but the more he thought about it the more he felt certain she'd only given it to him as a means of keeping him sweet. It wasn't because she liked him, or thought him in any way special. She probably didn't like him. She probably thought he was an uncultured lout. Good enough to dance with, but definitely not One of Us. If only, just once, she would give some sign of appreciating him as a person. Even *acknowledging* him as a person. He didn't want her to fawn. He didn't want her prostrating herself, or anything like that. It was just that every now and again he had this corny vision of her throwing her arms about his neck. He knew it was corny. It was so corny it almost made him want to bring up. So why did he keep thinking of it? She wasn't going to do it. He couldn't imagine Anita ever doing it to anyone.

11

Friday evening, he walked over the Common with
Kim, who prattled the entire way about the costumes
she was going to wear. She didn't only have her
Dewdrop costume, but her Russian costume and
her Peasant costume, as well. Anyone would think,
thought Jamie, that it was a fashion show she was
appearing in.

She wanted to know what his costumes were like.
He said sternly, to discourage such frivolity, that he
couldn't remember; which actually wasn't true, since
he could remember all too well. He had spent half
the session on Wednesday being pinned into things
by Miss Harrell and paraded for inspection before
Miss Tucker. The Russian get-up hadn't been too
bad – at any rate, he didn't feel quite such a fool in
it as he'd thought he was going to – but the other
had been a decided embarrassment. Nobody had
told him that the tights were going to be *white*
(somehow he'd had it settled in his mind that they
would be black: black, and very thick) and the long
tunic that he'd been promised wasn't long at all, it
hardly came down as far as his hips. He'd asked if
it wasn't a bit on the small side, but Miss Harrell had

seemed surprised and said that on the contrary, it couldn't have fitted better: 'You must be about exactly the same size as David.' Hopefully, he'd tried suggesting that maybe he was *taller* than David – maybe the tunic ought to be a bit *longer* – but Miss Harrell had pooh-poohed the idea.

'It would ruin the line. Besides, it wouldn't be as comfortable.'

He'd nearly said that it could hardly be a question of its being *as* comfortable, since the way it was at the moment it wasn't comfortable at all, but he'd ended up just suffering in silence, with the result that he was now faced with the hideous prospect of actually having to be *seen* in the thing.

The Church Hall, when they arrived, was pandemonium. All the Dewdrops were running about shrieking – 'Miss Tucker, I can't find my *shoes!*' 'Miss Tucker, someone's stolen my *head*band!' 'Miss Tucker, Andrea's going to be *sick!*' Garstin was complaining to anyone who would listen, only no one had the time to do so, that he couldn't possibly wear the costume he'd been given because it had been sewn with nylon thread and he was allergic to nylon thread. A couple of mothers who'd come in to help with wardrobe were trying unsuccessfully to round up the Dewdrops and put them all in one place, even Miss Tucker was not her usual calm, brisk self but showed a tendency towards shouting and flying about. The only people who remained cool, so far as he could see, were himself, Miss Harrell, and a stray father who had volunteered to work the lights.

He didn't know where Anita was. He assumed she must be there, but if so she was keeping herself well hidden. Miss Tucker flashed past him, going like the Red Queen. She patted him briefly on the head with a 'That's right! Good boy! Go and get into your costume. Anita will come and make you up presently.'

He wasn't sure that he fancied the idea of Anita making him up; not after their last interchange. He wasn't sure that he fancied the idea of getting into his costume. He had to share a poky cupboard with Garstin, who was still fretfully complaining about his allergy to nylon thread.

'It's always the same. You buy things that say hundred per cent cotton and then you find they've gone and stitched them up with nylon. That's what's happened here. It's absolutely useless. I shall be itching all evening.'

Jamie had never spoken very much to Garstin before. He didn't particularly want to speak to him now, but in fact, apart from his obsession with the nylon thread, he turned out to be quite reasonable. The way Anita carried on, you'd think he was a complete dead loss. He understood about cricket, however, and he supported Surrey, so he couldn't be all that bad. Furthermore, he knew that he was hopeless when it came to anything physical. The only reason he'd come to Miss Tucker's, he said, was because he'd thought she did ballroom dancing. He'd wanted to learn ballroom dancing so that he could go in for competitions and meet girls. Then he'd found she only did ballet, and he'd thought that perhaps that would be even better – from the point of view of meeting girls, that is. He'd reckoned there wouldn't be much in the way of competition; not in a ballet school.

'And there wasn't,' he said. 'Well, I mean, apart from David, and he wouldn't have known what to do with a girl if he got one. Of course, they were all potty over him. Girls always go potty over his sort. Actually, you're a bit like him. They'll probably go potty over you pretty soon.'

Jamie shot him a hard look, but he seemed to have made the remark quite innocently. Garstin, he decided, was one of nature's babblers. Harmless enough; but a babbler.

'I've got to go and get made up,' he said at last, somewhat to Jamie's relief. 'Miss Harrell's going to do me. Anita won't. I get on her nerves.'

'Was Anita potty over David?' said Jamie.

'Anita doesn't go potty over people,' said Garstin. 'David said she was a cold fish.'

He thought about it as he tugged at his tunic, trying in vain to stretch it further down over his hips. He didn't think Anita was a cold fish, exactly. She wasn't cold to dance with, and she wasn't cold when she was talking about ballet. She became almost animated then. If she could only become animated about something *other* than ballet, she would be really quite a nice person to know. After all, she did have her good points. She wasn't mean or spiteful or petty-minded; not like Sharon. She almost never lost her temper or took offence – and after all, she had given him a fencing foil. Whatever her motives, it was still a pretty generous thing to have done. It was just a pity she was so one-track minded. It sometimes made it very difficult not to feel impatient with her.

He had just given up on the tunic (mainly for fear the material would rip if he tugged at it any longer) when there was a tap at the door and there she was. She was wearing a sort of wrapper thing, and her eyes were all done into fantastic shapes, with long lines sweeping out from the corners.

'I've come to do your make-up,' she said.

She didn't smile at him or say 'Thank you for being here' or 'I knew you wouldn't let us down,' or indeed give any indication at all that she was prepared to forgive and forget. If she had, he would have told her about not playing cricket tomorrow; but as she didn't, neither did he.

They hardly talked at all as she smeared make-up over his face. Jamie ventured the odd remark about 'Miss Tucker being all of a flap' and 'Garstin threatening to break out into a rash', but Anita only pursed her lips and smiled rather distantly. He wondered if she was sulking over what had happened on Wednesday. He wouldn't have thought she was the type, but maybe him saying crap had upset her more than he'd realized. Maybe she'd come to the conclusion that he was just a yob, and that she couldn't be bothered with him any more. Well, that was all right by him. After tomorrow, she wouldn't have to be.

That evening, for the first time, he met the great David. He knew at once who it was when he saw a youth with his arm in a sling standing next to Miss Tucker, talking with her, all matey-matey, as if on equal terms. He felt a momentary stirring of what might almost have been jealousy, except that that was patently absurd, because what was there to be jealous about? *He* didn't want to compete. Miss Tucker suddenly broke off her conversation and went scuttling away, with her dancer's ducklike waddle, to correct someone's port de bras (he'd learnt all the posh French names by now) or shove someone back into line. The youth slowly turned, and his eye fell upon Jamie.

'So you're the prodigy?' he said. 'I've been hearing great and wonderful things about you.'

'I got pressganged,' said Jamie. 'You want to take over again, you're quite welcome.'

The youth curled his lip slightly. Other than being of roughly the same height and build, Jamie totally failed to see any resemblance to himself. Simply because they both had dark hair and brown eyes, that didn't make them the same, did it?

'I fancy it's just as well,' said the youth, 'that I can't take you up on that offer. I might not find myself welcomed back with quite the rapturous enthusiasm you seem to think. At any rate, I'd rather not have to put it to the test . . . from all accounts, my son, you're something of a budding Nijinsky.'

Jamie scowled, suspecting sarcasm. In any case, he didn't want to be a budding Nijinsky. If he was going to be a budding anything, he'd rather it was a budding Botham.

'True as I stand here,' said David, 'Thea's just been singing your praises. If your ears aren't burning, they jolly well ought to be.' His ears weren't, but his cheeks were starting to. 'I tell you, she's falling over herself . . . I gather you're what's known as a natural – don't need to be taught like the rest of us. Lucky feller.' He winked. 'They'll be doing *Spectre de la Rose* next, just so you can leap through the window.'

'There isn't going to be any next,' said Jamie. He didn't know anything about *Spectre de la Rose*, whatever that was, but he did know that *he* wasn't going to be doing any leaping about in it. 'I'm only helping them out this once. Just until you come back.'

David said: 'Don't you kid yourself! Once Thea gets her hands on a bit of talent, she doesn't let go that easily. In any case, sorry to disappoint you, but I won't be coming back. That's what I came to tell Thea – in case she was missing me, which obviously she isn't. I've got a place at the Arts Educational. Starting next September. As far as I'm concerned, the field's all yours.'

'Thanks very much,' said Jamie, playing the heavy sarcasm bit.

'Oh, don't mention it! Only too glad I'm not going to be around – don't think I could take the competition. Not at my age. Not from a budding Nijinsky. Mind you' – he smiled, amiably – 'I personally shall reserve judgement until I've seen you in the Borodin ... seeing as Thea wrote that specially for me. She tells me she's had to modify it slightly – but only slightly. I shall be interested to see what you do with it.'

See if I fall flat on my face, thought Jamie. After all, it was no more than he would be hoping for, in David's position.

David's smile increased: it was as if he knew exactly what thoughts were going through Jamie's head.

'I'll let you know what I think of it,' he said.

He didn't really care two straws what David thought of it; not really. He wouldn't have had a sleepless night if the guy had come backstage afterwards and made some snide remark. On the other hand, when he looked round the door and said 'Hey, Nijinsky! That was bloody good!' he couldn't help warming to him. Not so much because he'd thought it was good, but because he'd actually come and told him so. That took some doing, Jamie knew. If whoever replaced him in the match tomorrow turned out to be a hero, he wasn't at all sure that he would be able to bring himself to go and offer congratulations.

Shortly after David, Anita turned up. She put her head round the door and said: 'Thank goodness for that ... he's gone.' He thought at first she was referring to David, but quickly realized that she meant Garstin. 'Daddy's coming in the car to pick me up,' she said. 'Would you and Kim like a lift?'

He might almost have been tempted to decline

(considering she'd said scarcely a word to him all evening) except that last Wednesday, when he'd gone to collect her, he'd seen Daddy's car standing in the drive, a big new Jaguar XJS: it was more than he could resist.

'Sure, OK,' he said. 'Thanks.' He said it as off-handedly as he could – to his ears, it sounded suitably ungracious. Anita, however, didn't seem to notice.

'Shall I take your make-up off?' she said. 'You look as if you're making an awful mess. I'm sorry, by the way' – determinedly, she removed the greasy lump of cotton wool with which he had been daubing at his face and threw it in the waste bin – 'I'm sorry if I've seemed a bit standoffish. I haven't meant to be. It's just that I always get absolutely paralysed before a performance – even when it's only a dress rehearsal. I'm all right once I'm actually on stage. It's all that hanging about beforehand. I get so wound up I feel I shall be sick if I even so much as open my mouth.'

'That's OK,' he said. Now he felt a louse. Really, she *wasn't* such a bad sort of girl. He grinned. 'I expect I'd have been too scared to talk to you, anyway.'

She looked at him, sympathetically.

'Did *you* get nervous?'

'Not of dancing,' he said. 'Of you.'

'Nervous of *me*?'

'In all that gear.' He'd seen her in a ballet dress often enough (Kim said he ought to call it a tutu, not a ballet dress, but he couldn't bring himself to do it: it sounded too stupid) but the one she wore to practise in was just some old, limp, floppy thing, rather like his Gran's lace curtains. The one she'd had on tonight had been all crisp and foaming, layer upon layer of net, with a stiff satin bodice which made it look as if she'd really got something there. He wouldn't have said it before, but he didn't mind saying it now: 'You looked' – he was about to say 'pretty good', but at the last minute he substituted 'smashing', instead – 'you looked smashing,' he said.

'Did I?' A blush appeared on her cheek. 'You looked super in the Borodin. Really fierce. And d'you know what Marjorie said when she saw you in the second half?'

'Cor blimey look at them legs?' said Jamie.

Anita laughed.

'Actually, no . . . she said, *that boy has a decided touch of the Michael Soames.*'

Jamie clapped a hand to his head.

'So that's what it is! I've been feeling a bit peculiar all evening. What do I have to do to get rid of it?'

'Nothing, if you've got any sense. Michael Soames used to partner Fonteyn. They were famous. I think secretly he must have been one of Marjorie's child-hood idols . . . she's always saying how Michael *Soames* did things, or how Michael *Soames* looked in the part. It's about the highest compliment she could pay you, saying you've got a touch of him.'

'Cripes,' said Jamie, imitating Doug.

'Well, she never said it about David,' said Anita, 'and *he* was the cat's whiskers – until you turned up.

You ought to be flattered. Aren't you, just a little?'
She eyed him, curiously, through the dressing-table
mirror. 'I know you *pretend* not to care, but surely
it's nice to be good at things?'

'I suppose so,' he said; and then, after a moment's
struggle: 'You can relax about tomorrow, by the way.
The cricket's off.'

'You mean it's been cancelled?'

'No,' he said. 'I mean I've gone and got thrown
out.'

She glanced at him with swift concern.

'Not because of this evening?'

'It was either coming here to rehearse, or staying
there to practise. They said I'd got to choose.'

'Oh!' For just a second, he thought she might
almost be going to throw her arms about him and
say how glad she was that he'd chosen to come
and rehearse; but then, reaching out for some cotton
wool, she said: 'Well, I'm sorry, and I think it's
absolutely rotten of them, but you mustn't feel too
badly about it . . . one has to keep these things in
proportion. After all' – she cupped a hand beneath
his chin, tilting his head back towards her – 'it is
only a game, isn't it?'

12

He didn't want to go and watch the interhouse cricket match on Saturday. The only reason he forced himself into it was because on balance he thought it would probably look better than if he stayed away. If he stayed away people might think he just couldn't take it: by turning up he was demonstrating to all and sundry that he really couldn't care less. After all, as Anita had said, it was only a game, wasn't it?

It may have been only a game: that didn't stop it being agony. Every nerve in his body twitched and writhed with the desire to pick up a bat and go marching out there. The pain of not being able to do so was almost a physical one. It didn't help that people kept coming up to him and saying 'Why aren't you playing?' and 'Why have they put that kid in instead of you?' The only thing that helped was that 'that kid' was clean bowled before he'd even had a chance to score. Jamie strolled across and commiserated with him, and for a moment felt pretty good, but then that idiot Doug had to go and ruin it all by prophesying glumly that 'We're probably going to lose, now. Thanks to you and that stupid show. If you'd been playing, you'd never have got out to a ball like that.' He was glad Doug had such faith in his ability, but at the same time he couldn't help feeling a faint twinge of irritation.

'You were the one that said I ought to tell him what he could do with his lousy house match,' he said.

'Figure of speech,' said Doug. 'Not meant to be taken literally.'

'Oh, yes?' said Jamie.

As they were leaving the field (the House having been duly beaten by four wickets and Bob Pearson looking like someone who'd just downed half a pint of sour beer) Jamie felt a prod in the ribs, at the same time as a high falsetto voice screeched in his ear: '*Jamie!* Your *hands!*' Spinning round, he encountered a baboon-like face split by a mocking leer. Another voice called from behind, in jeering echo: 'Hey, Jamie . . . what about your hands?' At this, Doug spun round as well.

'What's your problem, Roy Canary?'

Roy Canary (his name was actually Canaris. They called him Canary just to rile him) made a gesture with two fingers.

'Who pulled your string?'

Doug clenched his fists. Jamie could see that he was about to take a swing – knew that if Doug took a swing, they would both become involved – grabbed him by the arm and hauled him out of temptation's reach.

'Leave 'em. They're not worth it.'

He was not as a rule averse to a scrap, but

somehow he didn't reckon Miss Tucker would be too pleased if he were to turn up this evening with a black eye or a cut lip. Baboon Face, grinning, came dancing round in front of them. He flapped his hands, limp-wristed, in Jamie's face.

'Who doesn't want to hurt his puddy wuddies, 'en?'

Jamie took a deep breath. His fists, involuntarily, bunched themselves up. He could feel his muscles tensing, ready for action. Another crack like that —

'Who's afwaid the nasty hard ball might bweak his ickle wists?'

Just in time, he thought of Anita. Slowly — very slowly — he uncurled his fingers.

'Twist off, sunshine! You're not amusing anyone.'

He turned on his heel. He didn't care whether Doug was coming or not. There was a limit to the amount he could be expected to take, even for Anita's sake — even for Miss Tucker's. A second longer and he wouldn't answer for the consequences: a punch-up would be inevitable.

He heard Doug's voice, shouting a final obscenity; then, as he caught up with Jamie: 'What was all that about?'

'I dunno. Their idea of a joke, I s'pose. Because I wasn't playing.'

Doug, belligerent, said: 'Why don't we go back and work 'em over?'

'Not worth all the aggro. Not for those morons.'

'You mean you're going to let them get away with it?'

'Blokes like that are so thick,' said Jamie, 'you could mash 'em to a pulp and you still wouldn't reach grey matter.'

'I don't want to reach grey matter! I just want to give 'em a pasting.'

'No, you don't,' said Jamie. 'It'd demean you.'

Doug subsided, muttering. He plainly wasn't happy about it; neither was Jamie, if it came to that. He wondered if Anita would ever appreciate just how much it had cost him, not to lay one on that grinning ape – he wondered how the grinning ape had ever come to hear of the incident in the first place. He was in 5 Remedial, Jamie couldn't remember what his name was (if, indeed, he had ever known it) but he had an uncomfortable feeling that at some time or another he'd seen both him and Roy Canary knocking about with Luke Gibbs and the other kids. If they'd got hold of the story, it would be all round Class 5 in next to no time. *Hell.*

He kicked angrily at a stone. He'd got Anita to thank for that – her and her precious ballet. Nothing else mattered, did it? One-track bloody mind. Just so long as she could dance, everyone else could go hang. On the other hand –

On the other hand, she really *wasn't* such a bad sort. His bitterness against her subsided slightly. Anita was OK – and anyway, he reckoned he owed her. She'd not only given him that fencing foil, but in spite of all his moaning she'd shown him that there was at least *one* thing in life he could do better than other people. He guessed that was pretty important.

At any rate, it was more important than a couple of bug-eyed morons trying to be funny. If word got out, he could always make up some story. He could always say he'd got this new bird had had a relative died of brittle bones (his great grand-dad had died of brittle bones).

'Every time she sees a cricket ball it makes her think of him. Gets her all upset . . .'

Some sort of guff. They'd swallow anything, if you told it with enough conviction.

'That Canary,' said Doug. He said it in tones of deep loathing. 'That Canary's got it coming to him.'

Jamie suddenly cheered up.

'Monday,' he said. Monday he could get as many black eyes, bruise as many knuckles, as he liked. 'Any more lip on Monday, and we let 'em have it. Right?'

'You've got it,' said Doug.

The curtain went up strictly on time: seven-thirty to the very dot. Jamie, standing in the spotlight with Anita, on the high rostrum at the back of the stage, awaiting the moment when he must lead her down the steps, through the avenue of assorted Dewdrops and others, felt himself suddenly exposed to the critical gaze of a couple of hundred pairs of eyes and experienced a rush of pure panic. He had never realized it was going to be like this. Last night, at the dress rehearsal, it had been quite different. There hadn't been anyone out there then, save David and Miss Tucker and a small handful of parents. Now the place was jam-packed. Row upon row of upturned faces, bobbing whitely before him in the darkness like a field full of giant turnips. And all of them looking at *him* – or so it seemed. His throat grew dry, his tongue grew furry, his palms broke out into a cold sweat. Could this be stage fright?

Anita's hand felt for his and squeezed it, reassuringly. He remembered that Anita was all right once she was on stage. It was only beforehand that she became paralysed. Obviously, for him, it was the other way round. He was grateful for the physical contact, but he didn't know what good it was going to do him. His legs had turned to semolina pudding, all wobbly and uncertain. He'd never be able to get them downstage, and even if he did he couldn't remember what he was supposed to do with them. Every single step that Miss Tucker had taught him had gone – completely vanished – from his mind. Jesus! That was their cue!

Somehow (he afterwards had no recollection of it) he got down the steps and through the avenue. His legs, for all that they had turned to semolina pudding, must have taken over automatically from his brain, for when at last he came to his senses it was to find them carrying him about the stage of their own accord, faithfully executing all those steps which his conscious mind had rejected. He knew, then, that it was going to be all right. He didn't have to keep torturing himself with 'What comes next?' or 'What do I do after this?' He need only trust to his legs and they would do it for him.

From that moment, he began to enjoy himself.

By the time the Borodin was reached, at the end of the first half, he was feeling positively jubilant. A sort of exhilaration swept over him: almost a sense of power. He was up here, dancing, and they were down there, watching. *They* were watching *him*. It really was him, now. It couldn't be anyone else, because for just a few breath-taking seconds he had the stage all to himself. Tchum *da* dum, tchum *da* dum, tchum *da* dum – BAM! It felt good, it felt terrific, it could go on all night. He saw what it was that Anita got out of it. After all the long, weary hours of flogging oneself into the ground one was suddenly released, allowed to take off, to leap and soar and be ecstatic. This time it was for *real*. He felt almost drunk with the glory of it. It was like knocking up the runs at cricket. *Wham!* the boundary. *Wham!* through the covers. And everyone cheering, everyone applauding –

'I told you,' whispered Anita, 'that you'd bring the house down!'

His exhilaration sustained him throughout the interval – it sustained him even as he struggled into the hated tights and pulled on the too-short tunic. It didn't really bother him any more, that the tights were white and the tunic didn't cover anything. No one was going to laugh at him. He'd already shown them what he could do. Even his Dad was going to have to admit that there was a bit more to it than he'd originally thought.

The curtain went up again on the second half. The act opened with a thing that was described in the programme as a scena (pronounced by Miss Tucker as 'shayna'), followed by a Peasant Dance, with Garstin wearing his nylon thread (it had brought him out in a rash under the arms, a fact which appeared to give him no small amount of satisfaction if the number of times he had told people about it was anything to go by), followed by a solo from a girl who everyone said was 'awfully *good* – but not a patch on Anita,' followed at last by the Dewdrop routine. Jamie and Anita came on right at the very end. It gave him plenty of time to get nervous again, if he was going to, but although he felt odd twinges in his fingertips and a prickling sensation in the small of his back, it was from anticipation rather than from fear. He knew now that he could do it: he just wanted to be out there, getting on with it.

The Dewdrops cantered to their accustomed halt, broke ranks and re-formed, making a framework for him and Anita. He led her on, as Miss Tucker had taught him, walking as she had taught him to walk – 'Walk tall. Be conscious of yourself.' From the back of the hall came the sound of not very subdued laughter. Jamie froze. He felt Anita waver slightly, and then pick up. A high-pitched voice came shrilling at him from out of the auditorium: 'Hey, Jamie! What about your hands?'

It was the Baboon. The Baboon and Roy Canary. They were out there, in the darkness. They had come on purpose to jeer at him.

'Hey, Jamie . . . what about your hands?'

In his ear, he heard Anita's urgent whisper: 'Ignore them! Just carry on!' He danced mechanically, his legs coming to his rescue as they had before. The thoughts went seething through his brain. The Baboon and Roy Canary! How long had they been out there? They couldn't have been there in the first half, or they'd have started on their catcalls straight away. They must have slipped in during the interval. But how had they found out? Kim had been sworn to strictest secrecy, and none of the other girls went to Tenterden; he had made very sure of that. Maybe one of them had a brother, or a sister. A brother who knew someone – a sister who was going out with someone –

'Lovely pair o' calves you got there, darlin'!'

Loud shushes, now, were coming from the audience. It would take more than shushes, thought Jamie, to shut that pair up. He felt a kind of fury seize hold of him – not so much on his own behalf, as on Anita's. This was her big moment; the moment she'd been waiting for, working for. And now these loud-mouthed apes were doing their best to ruin it for her. He had an almost overpowering urge to stop dancing, to advance upon the footlights and yell at them to 'Sod off, the pair of you!'

'Keep going!' hissed Anita. 'Keep going!'

It wouldn't help her if he were to yell 'sod off'. It might bolster his own ego, if only temporarily; but it wouldn't help Anita. Reluctantly, he thrust the impulse to one side.

'Oh! Wot a tantalisin' twirl! Proper little Nooryeff,
innee? A right dark – '

The voice of the Baboon broke off in mid-sen-
tence. There were slight sounds as of a scuffle, a
door banged shut at the back of the hall; peace was
restored. The remainder of the show passed without
incident. If Jamie couldn't quite recapture the joy-
ousness of the first half, he had the satisfaction of
knowing that at any rate he hadn't let Anita down.
The applause at the end was tumultuous; he had to
lead her out four times. Her eyes were shining, her
face was flushed. She was really in her element, he
thought. He was glad, for her sake, that things had
turned out OK.

It was a bit of a let-down, afterwards, changing
back into humdrum jeans and sweater in his poky
dressing room, with Garstin still rabbiting on about
his rash.

'Look at it – look at it!' He held up an arm so
that Jamie could peer into his armpit. 'It'll take days
for that lot to clear up. Say, who were those yobs I
heard yelling? Some of your mob?'

'Just some casual acquaintances,' said Jamie.

'Strange people you know.'

'Yeah . . . it's the strange school I'm forced to go
to.'

He was playing it cool, in front of Garstin, but
deep inside him was a black pit full of yellow-bellied
slime. News travelled fast in Tenterden Road. Come
Monday morning there wouldn't be a boy in the
whole of Class 5 who hadn't got the message: proper

little Nooryeff ... He could imagine the sort of greeting he'd be given. He could imagine the jeers, the ribaldry, the jokes chalked up on the blackboard. As for Doug — he just didn't want to think about Doug. 'Any more lip on Monday and we let 'em have it. Right?' Jamie was still prepared to let them have it; he just had this horrid feeling that he might have to do it by himself. He hoped very much that he would be proved wrong, but he certainly wouldn't be prepared to place any bets on it.

There was a tap at the door and a head poked round. It was Anita.

'Can I come in?' she said. She was already halfway through the door before she'd finished saying it. Garstin, who had got down to his underpants in his eagerness to divest himself of the nylon thread, snatched prudishly at a towel, but he needn't have bothered: Anita scarcely spared him a glance. It wasn't Garstin she had come to see.

'*Jamie!*' She hurled herself at him, flinging both arms about his neck. It took him by surprise. He was, fortunately, standing fair and square upon his feet, or the impact would surely have sent him flying. Even as it was, he staggered slightly. 'Jamie, you were fantastic!' She spoke breathlessly: her eyes were still shining, her cheeks still flushed. 'You ignored them — you carried on — I just couldn't believe it!'

Neither could he: he just couldn't believe it. This was really happening? It took him a second or so to recover.

'I only did what you told me to.'

'Yes, but how many other people would have done? How many people would have had the *courage*? You kept everything going – you didn't even falter!'

He wondered if she knew how close he had come to holding up the action whilst he took time off to hurl invective.

'Truly,' said Anita, 'you were fan*TAS*tic!'

'Oh, I dunno.' He shrugged a shoulder, not quite comfortable under the weight of all this unaccustomed praise. 'I didn't really do anything so very great.'

'*I* think you did,' said Anita. 'I think what you did was the bravest' – under Garstin's slightly pop-eyed gaze, she went on tiptoe to press a kiss against his cheek – 'the bravest thing that anyone could ever do.'

She was wrong about that: the bravest thing that anyone could ever do was yet to come. It would come on Monday morning, when he had to go into school and face Doug. Still, he would cross that bridge when he came to it. This was his moment of triumph: he might as well make the most of it.

'Tell me,' he said. He closed his arms about her waist. 'You going home in the car, with Daddy?'

'Yes. D'you want a lift?'

'Not really . . . I was wondering if you'd fancy a bit of a walk across the Common, instead?'

Anita tilted her head back, considering the idea.

'It'll be dark,' she said.

'Yeah, I know,' said Jamie. 'But I am very brave . . . you just said so. Of course, if you don't trust me – '

'Oh, Jamie,' she said, 'of *course* I do!' She suddenly broke away from him, pulling open the door with such vigour that Garstin was very nearly flattened into the wall. 'Just give me ten minutes,' she said. 'I'll be with you.'

The door banged shut behind her. Garstin emerged, grumbling.

'I never thought *she* was the type,' he said.

Jamie looked at him, dangerously.

'What type?'

'Type for going potty over people,' said Garstin.

'She isn't,' said Jamie.

He grinned at himself, as he sat down before the mirror: he guessed you had to be pretty wonderful, for a girl like Anita to go potty over you . . .

STAR TURN

1

There were five new girls in Year 7 at the start of
the winter term at Coombe Hurst School. Jessamy
studied them, critically.

Four of them were quite ordinary – no different
from all the other Year 7s in their brown-and-orange
uniforms. Lumpy, Gangly, Clever and Beach Ball,
thought Jessamy, rapidly nicknaming them to herself.

Lumpy was rather plain and dim looking; Gangly
was tall, and beanstalk thin; Clever wore glasses and
a worried frown; Beach Ball was pretty, but rounded
and plump as a blown-up balloon.

Jessamy dismissed them; they held no interest for
her. The one who caught her eye, as they filed selfconsciously into morning assembly and tacked on to
the end of the Year 7 line, was the one at the back.

'There's a dancer if ever I saw one!' thought
Jessamy. She tended sometimes to think rather
mature thoughts for an eleven-year-old; it came from
being the youngest in the family, with a brother and
sister who were both grown-up.

Jessamy had only a quick glimpse of the girl-who-
was-a-dancer because Jessamy was at one end of the
line and the dancer at the other, and Miss Shergold,

the Head Mistress, would go all icy and sarcastic if she noticed Jessamy leaning forward and peering.

In spite of Miss Shergold, she saw enough to convince her: the girl *had* to be a dancer. She was tiny and trim and beautifully proportioned – a small, well-shaped head on a slender neck, which was exactly what you needed for ballet (no good being a pumpkin head and hoping to dance Giselle), with narrow hips and lovely long legs which Jessamy immediately envied.

Jessamy had good legs, but hers were made for beats and jumps rather than for the perfect *arabesque*. Jessamy had already, rather sadly, faced up to the fact that she probably wasn't ever going to dance Giselle. It wasn't only her legs. She had heard her mum and dad discussing it one day. Her dad had said, 'She has too robust a personality.' Her mum had agreed: Jessamy was more of a Swanhilda than a Giselle.

Jessamy didn't actually mind being a Swanhilda – *Coppelia* was one of her favourite ballets – though the part she really wanted to dance was the Miller's Wife in Massine's *Three-Cornered Hat*. That was something the new girl would never be offered, with her flaxen hair.

It was a pity about the hair. Blonde hair was lovely, of course, and one or two great dancers had been fair – Pamela May, for example, who had been with the Sadler's Wells Ballet long before Jessamy was even born – but black was best. It showed up better on stage. On the other hand, blonde was perfect for the Queen of the Wilis.

Jessamy whiled away the time during the usual beginning-of-term announcements ('No food to be eaten in the classrooms. Brown shoes with white socks or brown tights to be worn *at all times*') by mentally staging her own private production of *Giselle* with the new girl as Myrthe and herself, improbably, as Giselle. She was just deciding who she would have for her Albrecht – Erik Bruhn? Rudolf Nureyev? Her own brother? *Nijinsky?* – when the music started up for the end of assembly and Year 7, with the new girl now in the lead, filed out behind Mrs. Truelove, their form mistress.

By craning forward just a little, Jessamy could see that the new girl already walked like a dancer, even though she was only eleven. She had either been having ballet lessons for years or she was blessed with good natural turnout. Jessamy wasn't jealous because Jessamy had good natural turnout, as well.

'Do you mind?' hissed a Year 8, pushing at her.

Jessamy slipped back into the ranks and followed meekly behind the others – well, as meekly as she ever could. Jessamy wasn't really a meek sort of person. 'Assertive' was how she had been described on her report last summer.

Mrs. Truelove had already assigned the new girls to places at the front of the room, where she could keep an eye on them. Jessamy, as soon as she had arrived at school, had bagged three desks right at the back for herself and her two best friends, Sheela Shah and Susan Garibaldi. She couldn't see the new girl from where she sat, but when Mrs. Truelove took the register she started with the name 'Karen Anders', which was definitely new. A small but clear voice said, 'Yes, miss.'

Mrs. Truelove looked up from the register.

'I do have a name, Karen . . . it's Mrs. Truelove. Shall we start again?'

Sheela and Susan grinned, but Jessamy felt sorry for the new girl, being shown up like that. They had always heard, in Juniors, that Mrs. Truelove could be mean. Not that Jessamy cared two straws: teachers could be as mean as they liked and it just rolled right off Jessamy. It was rotten to be mean to a new girl, though. She could only hope that the new girl, like Jessamy herself, didn't care a fig for anything except dancing; that way, it really didn't matter if people had a go at you or accused you of being stupid at ordinary lessons. Jessamy was stupid at everything except English, art, music and French, and it didn't bother her in the slightest. Why should a ballet dancer need to be able to use computers and do mental arithmetic?

With all the business of electing monitors and filling in timetables, Jessamy didn't think about the new girl again until breaktime, when she looked round the playground and saw her standing with one of the other new ones, the one who looked serious and clever. The serious one was talking, very earn-estly; the dancer was listening politely, trying to pretend an interest. Jessamy could tell that she was pretending. She was standing with her arms in a low fifth, her hands loosely clasped, and her feet in third, and Jessamy just knew that she was itching to look down and check her position, check her ankles weren't rolling in (they weren't: she had a *very* good turnout). Her blonde hair was tied back in a pony tail. Jessamy had worn hers in plaits when they were in Juniors, but now she was in Senior School she wore it loose, with a hair band. Probably, one day quite soon, Mrs. Truelove would tell her to 'Do something about your hair, please, Jessamy.' They didn't like you having it all round your shoulders. Jessamy thought it made a nice change from having to scrape it back the way you did for ballet class.

'Hey!' Susan jiggled at her elbow. 'What are you goggling at?'

'Not goggling at anything,' said Jessamy, but she couldn't help a small backwards glance as she walked away, arm in arm with Susan and Sheela.

Jessamy had been best friends with Susan and Sheela all the way up through Juniors; they did everything together and almost never quarrelled. Jessamy certainly wasn't thinking of *not* being friends with them any more, but the small wistful thought occurred to her that it would be fun to have an ally – someone who shared her own passion for the ballet. Someone who knew what *entrechats* were and didn't go all silly and giggly when she talked of *ports de bras*.

'*Bra*?'

'Did you say *bra*?'

Ooh! Naughty! Squeak squeak giggle giggle.

Jessamy sighed. They couldn't help it; you had to

be patient. The only trouble was, Jessamy wasn't at all a patient sort of person.

'Let's go and sit on a bench,' said Sheela. 'I've got something to show you.'

Sheela had brought in a teen magazine which she had borrowed from the shelves of her dad's newsagent's. What she and Susan liked to do was turn to the problem page, which was always full of gigglesome (but highly spicy) questions about love and sex and *bodies*.

Sheela said, 'It isn't porn. It's learning about things.'

'It's being prepared,' said Susan.

Jessamy was quite interested in the love and sex, but didn't share Sheela and Susan's fascination with bodies – well, she *was* fascinated by bodies, her own principally, but not in any gigglesome sense. Jessamy was fascinated by the way her body worked and what she was able to do with it. She thought she probably saw it rather like a violinist saw his violin: as an instrument. For Susan and Sheela, bodies were exciting and giggly. Jessamy sometimes felt superior and sometimes felt that maybe she was missing out.

'Listen to *this*,' said Sheela, in tones of shocked delight. 'My boyfriend – '

The new girl was coming across the playground with the serious one. The serious one (Jessamy thought her name might be Portia Wetherall, except how could you call anyone *Portia*?) shambled, with slouched shoulders. The dancer – she knew her name was Karen Anders, but she didn't quite feel

336

ready to think of her as Karen; she was still too new for that — walked as if she were being pulled by an invisible string from the crown of her head. Good, thought Jessamy. She nodded approvingly, and smiled. The new girl, as if not quite sure the smile was intended for her, smiled back uncertainly.

Susan and Sheela, meanwhile, were sitting with heads bent over their teen mag. Jessamy could see that Susan's face was bright crimson. Sheela's almost certainly would have been had her skin not been too dark for it to show. They had obviously found something that excited them.

'Wow!' breathed Susan.

'Do you think that is *true*?' said Sheela.

'Must be, if it's in a magazine.'

'In that case,' said Sheela, 'I am not ever, *ever*, going to get married.'

'Safer to be a nun,' said Susan.

'Oh, but I can't be!' Sheela's wails rent the playground. 'I'm not a Christian!'

'You'll have to convert.'

'My dad won't let me! He'll make me get married! God, it's horrible,' moaned Sheela, enjoying herself.

They did this sort of thing, sometimes: frightened themselves silly. Secretly they loved it.

After break they had maths with Mrs. Allan, when Jessamy was predictably slow to grasp the principle of subtracting decimal fractions, and the new girl not very much better. If you gave Jessamy a complicated *enchaînement*, or series of steps, to perform she could pick them up immediately, no problem. Figures confused her. The serious girl, whose name *was* Portia, turned out to be some kind of mathematical genius, which confused Mrs. Allan: they weren't used to geniuses at Coombe Hurst.

The last period before lunch was gym. For years and years, Jessamy had been the star gymnast of her group. Miss Mayle, in Juniors, had wanted her to train seriously, but of course she couldn't do that. Jessamy's mother wouldn't hear of it. Sometimes she even grew twitchy at the thought of Jessamy just jumping over boxes or shinning up ropes.

'Your arms, Jessamy! Your arms! You'll end up looking like a coal heaver!'

Some day soon she would probably put her foot down, but she hadn't as yet, which meant that Jessamy was still free to bounce about and show off. The new girl didn't show off, and she didn't bounce, either, but she certainly challenged Jessamy's position as star gymnast. She was every bit as supple, every bit as neat, had just as good balance and landed just as lightly. Jessamy didn't mind. It only went to confirm her diagnosis: another dancer had come to Coombe Hurst.

At the end of the period Miss Northgate said, 'Well! Congratulations to Jessamy – and congratulations to Karen, too! I look forward to working with you two girls. I hope you all noticed how gracefully they did everything? How light they are on their feet? I'd expect it from Jessamy, of course – but it seems we have another little gymnast in our midst!'

Karen's cheeks grew slightly pink, as everyone turned to look first at her and then rather slyly at Jessamy, to see how she was taking it. Jessamy took it perfectly calmly. She had no ambitions as a gymnast, and anyway Karen's style was quite different from hers. Karen was obviously going to be one of those dancers who were blessed with line: Jessamy had elevation. They weren't in competition.

Afterwards, in the changing room, Jessamy said, 'You *are* a dancer, aren't you?'

Karen hesitated; then nodded rather bashfully as she pulled her T-shirt over her head.

'I knew you were!' Jessamy was triumphant. 'I said as soon as I saw you, that's a dancer if ever there was.' She turned and did a ballet dancer's walk the length of the cloakroom and back, toes pointed, arms in first. 'I can spot a dancer a hundred metres off!'

Susan chimed in: 'Her mother – ' she pointed dramatically at Jessamy ' – was Belinda Tarrant!'

She still was, of course, only her dancing days were long since over. Now she ran the Tarrant Academy of Dance.

'Yes, and her dad is Ben Hart,' said Sheela, who hadn't the faintest idea, when it came to it, what Jessamy's dad actually did, except that it was something to do with ballet. (In fact he flew about the world putting on productions for people.) 'And her *brother* – ' Sheela paused, importantly ' – her brother is Saul Hart of the City Ballet Company.'

Karen's face, by now, was bright pillar-box red.

She turned to Jessamy with eyes huge as satellite dishes (her eyes were bright blue: they would photograph beautifully, thought Jessamy). Karen obviously knew all about Ben and Saul Hart, and Belinda Tarrant, which was more than Susan and Sheela would have done if Jessamy hadn't told them.

'It's true!' said Susan.

Karen nodded, shyly. 'I can see it now.'

'She looks just like him,' said Sheela.

Jessamy did bear quite a strong resemblance to Saul — and to her dad. Both Saul and her dad were short and dark and compact. Belinda Tarrant, on the other hand, was long-limbed and red-haired (red-haired with a bit of help these days, as she ruefully admitted). Jacquetta took after her — the same glorious legs that went on for ever, the same burnished hair — only Jack had let the family down by throwing away her ballet shoes for a life of domestic bliss.

'Jessamy's going to be a ballerina,' said Susan.

'Prima donna ballerina,' said Sheela.

Jessamy did wish they wouldn't. She knew they were proud of her and liked to display her to people, but it wasn't in good taste to boast about her like that — especially when they got the terminology all wrong. Prima donna ballerina!

Jessamy tried to catch Karen's eye, but Karen, seemingly overwhelmed to think that she was at school with the daughter of Ben Hart and Belinda Tarrant, was struggling, scarlet-faced, into her skirt. Bother! Now she probably wouldn't dare to talk to Jessamy. She would think Jessamy was going to be too grand. There were some people – pushy people – who would instantly tap into her like leeches, but she could see already that Karen wasn't one of those. That at least was a relief. Ballet classes were full of them. *And* their mothers.

'Where do you learn?' said Jessamy, manoeuvring herself so that she was between Karen and the others. 'Somewhere local?'

'Mm.' Karen nodded, and ducked her head as she pulled on her sweater.

'In Chiswick?'

'Mm.'

'At a school? Or privately?'

There was a pause.

'Privately,' said Karen.

'What, individual lessons?' Karen's parents must be rich as rich! Even Jessamy, whose mother owned her own school, didn't very often have individual lessons. 'Who with?'

'I don't think you'd have heard of her,' said Karen, taking the elastic band off her ponytail, shaking her hair out and putting it back in the elastic band.

'I bet I would!' Jessamy knew all the dancing schools and all the teachers in the whole of Chiswick; practically the whole of London. 'Try me! What's her name?'

'I just call her Madame . . . Madame Olga.'

'Is she Russian?'

'Yes. She used to dance with Diaghilev.'

Heavens! She must be positively ancient.

'What's her surname?' said Jessamy.

341

'I can't remember. I can never pronounce it. Something like . . . Spess – '

'Spessivtseva? Olga Spessivtseva?'

'No, not her,' said Karen.

Jessamy relaxed. Olga Spessivtseva was famous. (Though come to think of it she probably wasn't still alive. She made a note to ask her mum.)

'Is she old?' said Jessamy.

'Quite,' said Karen.

'I'll see if my mum knows her. She knows everybody.'

They left the gym together, with Susan and Sheela close behind and Portia hovering.

'How many lessons do you have a week?' said Jessamy.

'Every afternoon after school and Saturday mornings.' Karen said it proudly, almost defiantly. Jessamy widened her eyes: she only had four lessons a week, and then not private.

'What syllabus are you doing?'

'Oh . . . just what Madame chooses.'

'So are you going to take it up professionally?'

Karen's face grew crimson again.

'I'd like to.' She looked enviously at Jessamy. 'I suppose you are?'

'Got to, haven't I?' said Jessamy.

Karen's blue eyes widened again, this time in shocked disbelief.

'Don't you want to?'

'Oh, yes,' said Jessamy. 'It's just that even if I didn't, it wouldn't make any difference. They're relying on me, you see, 'cause of Jack going and letting them down. She's my sister. She's only twenty-one and having *babies* already.'

Susan and Sheela groaned in unison.

'She won't ever go back to ballet,' said Jessamy. 'She says she's had enough of it. Mum was furious. She said she might at least have waited, like Mum did. Mum didn't start having babies till she was past her prime. That's what she always says . . . "*I didn't even think about you lot till I was past my prime.*" She didn't think about me at all,' said Jessamy. 'I was a mistake.'

'A night of mad passionate love,' said Sheela.

Portia looked at her rather wildly. Susan giggled.

'Take no notice,' said Jessamy. 'They've just discovered sex.'

Portia's eyes came out on stalks.

'They talk about sex all the time,' said Jessamy. 'They're obsessed by it.' She turned cosily to Karen. 'I must say, it'll be nice to have someone else here who's a dancer. There's a girl in Year 9 who does tap, and some of the kids do jazz dancing, but until you came I was the only one who did ballet. It'll be nice to have someone I can talk to and know they'll understand what I'm talking about. These two – ' she jerked her thumb at the still sniggering Susan and Sheela ' – they are just so dead ignorant it's unbelievable. They think *pose* means a bunch of flowers!'

Karen giggled, and then clapped a hand to her mouth as if she shouldn't have done.

'Oh, you don't have to worry about them,' said Jessamy. 'They know they're ignorant – I'm always telling them.'

'So what is a posy?' said Sheela.

Instantly, as one, Karen and Jessamy took up their positions, lifted a leg and stepped forward onto it.

'That's a posy?' said Sheela.

'Doesn't look like very much to me,' said Susan.

'It isn't very much. It isn't meant to be very much.'

'It just means to take a step, really,' explained Karen.

Susan and Sheela looked at each other. Susan tapped a finger to her forehead.

'It's French,' said Portia, coming unexpectedly to life.

'Ballet terms always are,' said Jessamy. 'I'll ask my mum when I get home if she knows your Madame Olga.'

'She won't,' said Karen.

'I bet she will,' said Jessamy. 'She knows everyone.'

2

'Mum,' said Jessamy, 'do you know a ballet teacher called Madame Olga?'

'Never heard of her.' Belinda Tarrant was checking the proofs of the new prospectus for the Tarrant Academy of Ballet. 'Look at that!' Crossly, she snatched up her red pen and made angry squiggles on the page. 'I sometimes think printers are halfwits.'

'She used to dance with Diaghilev,' said Jessamy.

'Who did?'

'Madame Olga.'

'Rubbish!' said her mum, making more marks.

'She did,' insisted Jessamy. 'Karen said so.'

Belinda Tarrant raised her head at last. She looked at Jessamy over the tops of her spectacles.

'And who may Karen happen to be?'

'Karen Anders.'

'And who is Karen Anders?'

'She's a girl at school. She just started, today.'

'And what does she know about anything?'

Losing interest, Belinda Tarrant went back to her proofs. It was sometimes very difficult holding any normal sort of conversation with her; she was always so busy. If she wasn't teaching, she was travelling up to town to meet people, or on the phone to Dad in Canada or Japan or wherever he happened to be, or auditioning new pupils for the Academy, or giving interviews for radio and television. Jessamy supposed that was what came of having a mother who wasn't quite ordinary.

'Karen knows about her because she has lessons from her. She can't pronounce her surname properly. She thinks it begins "Spess" something.'

'If she's trying to tell you she's Olga Spessivtseva you can forget it. She must have died years ago and even if she hadn't she'd be far too old to teach.'

'She is old. But anyway it wasn't Olga Spessivtseva, just someone who sounds like her.'

'Honestly!' Her mum pounced again, with her red pen. 'Drivel!' she cried. 'Total and utter drivel!'

Jessamy knew when she was beaten. If Dad had been here she could have asked him, though he didn't know all the local teachers as well as Mum did, but Dad was in New York staging a revival of Frederick Ashton's *Symphonic Variations* for ABT. (When she had mentioned it to Susan and Sheela they had thought she was talking about a television station. They had actually never heard of American Ballet Theater!)

Karen would be good in *Symphonic Variations*, she thought, reluctantly trailing upstairs to make a start on some homework. It was an abstract ballet, without any storyline. It was one of Belinda Tarrant's favourites (she had danced in it at Covent Garden with Margot Fonteyn) though Jessamy preferred

346

romantic ballets where you could do a bit of acting and give your emotions full reign.

Jessamy sometimes thought that if anything awful ever happened to stop her doing ballet – just suppose, horror of horrors, that she grew too big or the wrong shape – she wouldn't mind taking up acting. She always felt slightly wistful, when the school end-of-term productions were planned, at being passed over as a possible actress. It was always, 'Well, Jessamy! May we expect the usual contribution from you?' The usual contribution was a solo dance, made up by Jessamy herself, to fit in with the theme of whatever play they were doing. Maybe this term she and Karen could do it together? Or better still – she plumped herself down at her desk – maybe Karen could do it and Jessamy could act?

The trouble was, people were such snobs. Just because Jessamy came from a famous family and Karen didn't, or at least not as far as she knew, they were bound to insist that Jessamy danced the same as usual, so that they could write about her in the programme: 'Jessamy Hart comes from a famous family of dancers. Her mother, Belinda Tarrant', etc., etc.

Same old thing, every year. You'd have thought people would be sick of it by now.

Moodily, Jessamy unscrewed the top of her fountain pen and pulled a block of squared paper towards her. Mrs. Allan had actually gone and set them some homework. On their first day back! She would complain to her mum if they got too much. Belinda

Tarrant had chosen Coombe Hurst specially because it had a reputation for not pushing people too hard. Since Jessamy was going to be a dancer, ballet had to have first priority, particularly above beastly maths.

Fifteen minutes later, Jessamy had scamped through her decimal fractions, stuffed everything back into her school bag and was stretched out on her bed reading the autobiography of Gelsey Kirkland, whom Saul and Jacquetta had once been lucky enough to see dancing Juliet with the Royal Ballet. Jessamy had been too young, just as she had been for so many things. But that was why it was important to read about all the great dancers whom she had never been able to see. Far more useful than messing about with decimals and fractions and idiotic jumping dots (especially as she could never decide which way they were supposed to jump).

'I asked my mum about your Madame Olga,' said Jessamy, as she and Karen met up next day on their way to school. 'You were quite right. She hasn't heard of her.'

'She's very old,' said Karen. 'Practically retired. She only takes one or two pupils.'

'Did you have to audition for her?'

'Yes – well. Sort of. I hadn't started learning then.'

'But she could tell.' Jessamy nodded. 'My mum always says that she can tell almost just by looking at someone. She says you get a feel for it. I bet you were thrilled when she accepted you?'

'Yes,' said Karen, but she didn't actually sound very thrilled. Jessamy regarded her, doubtfully.

Maybe Madame Olga wasn't quite as good as she sounded. Too old, perhaps.

'If ever you want to change teachers,' she said, 'you could always come to my mum's school.'

'Do they do scholarships?' Karen asked it eagerly, her blue eyes alight and sparkling.

'Not scholarships exactly, but sometimes if people are deserving and can't afford the fees, Mum will only charge half price.'

The sparkle went out of Karen's eyes. Surely her parents couldn't be short of money? Not sending her to Coombe Hurst. Coombe Hurst might not be very academic, but it cost the earth, at least according to Jessamy's mum. Daylight robbery, she called it.

'I expect I shall stay with Madame Olga for a while,' said Karen. 'I've got used to the way she teaches.'

'Well, that is important,' agreed Jessamy, 'so long as she's good. *Is* she good?'

'I – I think so,' said Karen.

'Perhaps I should come and watch a class?' Karen looked startled. 'Then I could tell you,' said Jessamy. She didn't mean to sound boastful, but she had had enough experience to know a good teacher when she saw one.

Karen shook her head.

'Madame Olga doesn't allow anyone in,' she said.

Karen's special friend at Coombe Hurst was obviously going to be the serious-minded Portia, but nonetheless circumstances threw her and Jessamy together quite often. In movement class, Miss Shaw singled out Karen and Jessamy to demonstrate.

'Let's see what you two girls can do,' she said. They had been improvising to some beautiful music called Albinoni's Adagio, very slow and dreamy. 'Everyone sit down and watch Karen and Jessamy. I shall expect some real dancing from you two,' she added.

Jessamy was too busy with her own improvisation to see what Karen was doing, but it was obviously good for as the music came to an end there was a silence, followed by a burst of applause.

'Thank you,' said Miss Shaw. 'Thank you, both of you. That showed real feeling for the music.'

Quite often, because by now everyone knew that Karen was a dancer as well as Jessamy, people would come up to them and say, 'Can you do the splits?' 'Can you bend over backwards?' 'Can you lift your leg up behind you and touch the back of your head?'

'It's not really ballet,' Jessamy would say, 'it's just showing off.'

'So go on, then! Show off!'

Jessamy never minded obliging. Karen was shyer, but usually did it in the end.

'It's just acrobatics,' Jessamy would explain.

'And what,' demanded a big, fierce Year 8 on one occasion, 'is wrong with acrobatics?'

'N-nothing,' stammered Karen.

'In the right place,' added Jessamy.

'Don't you do those things when you have classes?' said Portia.

'Sometimes. Not always. Not like *plies* and *ronds de jambes* and – '

The Year 8 exploded.

'There they go! Spouting Frog! Why can't you just say knees bends?'

''Cause they're not,' said Jessamy.

The Year 8 made a rude noise. Jessamy had discovered that there were some people – not just Year 8s, but grown-up people, as well – who looked down their noses at the thought of anyone learning ballet. Her mum, only the other day, had exploded in rage at an article in the newspaper which said that ballet was 'anti-feminist and bourgeois'.

Jessamy wasn't quite sure what bourgeois meant (nor how to pronounce it), but it was obviously a term of abuse. She had shown the article to Karen, who read it slowly with puckered lips, and then said that she wasn't sure, either.

'I think perhaps what they mean is that only well-off people can do it.'

'Well, only well-off people can come to this school!' retorted Jessamy. 'That doesn't seem to bother them. Besides, it's not true. Lots of poor kids get accepted for the Royal Ballet School and Central.'

'Not lots,' said Karen. 'Only a few. It's much easier to get in if you can pay for it.'

Everything was easier if you could pay for it, thought Jessamy. That was a fact of life. 'It isn't our fault if we've got quite well-off parents,' she said.

Two little spots of pink appeared in Karen's cheeks.

Her skin was a delicate pale ivory, unlike Jessamy's, which was quite rosy and tended to break out into freckles at the first hint of sunshine.

'Perhaps it's just that people it's made easy for should be grateful and know that it's not the same for everyone.'

'Oh, well, yes. Of *course*.'

Jessamy said of course, but she was not, as a matter of fact, very often grateful for having a famous family. There were even times when she was tempted to think it a positive bore, like, for instance, when they were trying to sit quietly together in a restaurant enjoying a meal and idiot people nearby started staring and pointing and whispering behind their hands. Saul, who was the good-natured one of the family, said that it was 'all part and parcel', but it made Jessamy want to go and poke her fingers in people's eyes.

She accepted, all the same, that Karen was right. She *ought* to be grateful, because it wasn't the same for everyone.

She wondered if it were Karen's parents who had taught her to think like that – like a politician, almost – but when she asked her, Karen shook her head and said that she didn't have any parents.

'They're both dead. My mum died when I was born and my dad died afterwards, in a car crash. I live with my gran.'

Jessamy thought, that would account for the fact that in some ways Karen was strangely old-fashioned. She had never been to a sleep-over, knew almost

nothing about pop music (though everything about
ballet music), and even at weekends, when everyone
else dressed for fun, went round in sweaters and
skirts and sensible shoes. Jessamy bumped into her
one Saturday afternoon in the library, looking for
ballet books.

'I've got stacks of ballet books at home,' said
Jessamy. 'I've got all the ones that were my mum
and dad's and all the ones that were Saul's and all the
ones that were Jack's and all the ones that are mine.'

Ballet books, indeed, filled every available centi-
metre of shelf space in the Hart household, and then
spilled out across the floor.

'Do you want to come back and look at them?
You could stay to tea, if you like.'

'*Could* I?' said Karen.

She made it sound as if she were being invited to
Buckingham Palace to meet royalty. Jessamy always
had to remind herself that in the ballet world the
Harts *were* a sort of royalty. Only very minor, of
course; nothing compared to the all-time greats. But
her dad had been one of the finest Petrushkas in the
business until he had developed chronic tendonitis
and had to retire, and people even now talked of
Belinda Tarrant's Princess Aurora. Even Saul, at only
twenty, was dancing leading roles.

'Let's go back and you can look at the books and
then it'll be tea time and then we can watch a video.'

'Would it be all right if I telephoned my gran?'

'Of course,' said Jessamy, grandly. 'You can do it
from the phone in my bedroom.'

Karen picked out a great pile of books which she wanted to read — she kept asking, 'Is it all right? *Really*?' whenever she discovered that they had 'Ben Hart' or 'Belinda Tarrant' written inside them — and then she and Jessamy went downstairs to ask Elke, the German au pair, if she would do them some tea. They ate their tea with Elke, in the basement kitchen, trying to talk in German to her because you never knew when German might come in useful later on, when they were touring. After that, they went into the sitting-room to watch a video.

'Where are your mum and dad?' said Karen.

'Mum's gone to a conference. Dad's still in New York. What do you want to watch? Would you like to watch *Giselle*? We've got the *best Giselle* — well, I think it's the best. It's Carla Fracci and Erik Bruhn. I always weep buckets when Giselle dies. And Hilarion. I think it's so unfair on Hilarion. After all, he was in love with Giselle long before Albrecht arrived, and he really *was* in love.'

'But so was Albrecht,' pleaded Karen, 'by the end.'

'By the end it's too late. He's already done the damage. That's what comes of princes dressing up and pretending to be peasants.'

When Jessamy had shown the video of *Giselle* to Susan and Sheela they had irritated her by going 'Ooh' and 'Aah' every time anyone got up on their toes or did anything which looked in the least bit complicated. Susan and Sheela had no idea what was difficult and what was relatively easy. Karen was far more knowledgeable. She and Jessamy spent most of the first act passing comments to each other until they reached the mad scene, when they both sat spellbound with tears pouring down their cheeks.

'Carla Fracci is so wonderful,' snuffled Karen. 'And I see what you mean about Hilarion . . . he doesn't deserve to die!'

'Saul says I'm only sorry for him 'cause he's handsome,' said Jessamy, 'but it's not that. It's 'cause he dances it like a real person, not just a Jealous Gamekeeper.'

They watched as poor Hilarion, driven by the implacable Wilis, was finally hounded to death. Shyly, Karen said, 'He looks a bit like your brother.'

'Mm. I s'pose Saul is quite handsome. That's why he gets all these fan letters from people saying they're in love with him.'

'Women?' said Karen.

'And men.'

Karen looked at her, wide-eyed.

'You have to accept these things,' said Jessamy. 'It isn't any good being naive.'

'No.' Karen swallowed. 'Of course not.'

'Look! They're circling! I love this bit.'

The Wilis, victorious, wheeled about the stage and disappeared; and then a grief-stricken Albrecht came into the picture, clasping a bunch of flowers to place on Giselle's grave.

'I can't help feeling a *bit* sorry for Albrecht,' said Karen.

'Yes, 'cause he's Erik Bruhn and he's gorgeous.' Jessamy sighed and blotted contentedly at her eyes.

She always cried when she watched *Giselle*. 'Some people say he's the greatest dancer there's ever been . . . even greater than Nureyev.'

Karen looked shocked.

'Who says that?'

'Well, my dad for a start. My mum says she can never make up her mind. She says they had different qualities. I think they're both beautiful.'

'They are.' Karen nodded ecstatically, her handkerchief balled into her hand for the tears that were still to come.

'I adore the second act,' breathed Jessamy. 'It's almost my favourite in all ballet. I wish I could be Giselle!'

'Why can't you?'

'Not the type. You are. You're lucky. Look, that's Toni Lander as the Queen of the Wilis . . . isn't she heaven?'

It was dark by the time they had finished watching *Giselle* so Elke very kindly got the car out to drive Karen home.

'I'll come with you,' said Jessamy.

'You don't have to,' said Karen.

'I want to. There won't be anything else to do after you've gone.'

Watching ballet with a fellow enthusiast was so much more fun than watching it by yourself. She had one or two friends at ballet school, but nobody really close. There was too much rivalry and competition, and everyone was too aware of who she was: the daughter of Belinda Tarrant.

'You must come round again and we'll watch something else,' said Jessamy.

'That would be brilliant,' said Karen. She hesitated. 'I'm sorry I can't invite you back to my place, but my gran's a bit funny about things like that. And anyway,' she added, 'we haven't got a video.'

'That's OK,' said Jessamy. 'You can come to me. It's easier that way . . . I'll show you my collection of shoes next time.'

Jessamy had a whole collection of old ballet shoes, all worn and discarded and signed for her by their owners. Susan and Sheela had wrinkled their noses and said, 'Ugh! They're disgusting! Like old dishrags!' In their simplicity they had thought that ballet shoes lasted for performance after performance and still ended up all lovely and pink and shiny. They had been incredulous when Jessamy told them that quite often they scarcely even lasted for as much as one act.

'That is so *wasteful*,' Susan had said, severely.

What Karen wanted to know was whether Jessamy had one of Rudolph Nureyev's.

'No,' said Jessamy, 'but I've got one of Gelsey Kirkland's . . . You can try it on, if you like.'

Karen sighed, blissfully, as the car drew up outside a row of small terraced houses.

'Ask your gran if you can come next weekend,' said Jessamy.

On Monday, at the end of English, Mrs. Richmond asked Jessamy to stay behind.

'Well, now, Jessamy,' she said, 'I take it we can rely on you to come up with something for our end-of-term production, as usual?'

Jessamy's face obviously didn't quite register the enthusiasm that it should have done, for quickly Mrs. Richmond added, 'It is one of the high spots, you know. Everyone looks forward to it. The end of term wouldn't be the end of term without a contribution from you. You are, after all, our star performer!'

Jessamy forced herself to beam. It wasn't that she didn't want to dance for them, just that it would have been nice, for once, to be considered as an actress.

'We're doing a rain forest play,' said Mrs. Richmond. 'Look, I've brought a copy of the script for you. I thought a short solo at the beginning and another at the end might round things off rather satisfactorily.'

'All right,' said Jessamy. 'I'll think of something.'

That evening, after doing her homework (and after having her ballet class) she nobly sat down to read Mrs. Richmond's script. She would far rather have read a ballet book or watched a ballet video, but already, at eleven years old, Jessamy had the outlook of a true professional: if a job had to be done, then get on and do it.

The rain forest play was strange and rather beautiful, full of talking trees and choruses of frogs, but after she had read it Jessamy didn't mind so much about not being considered as an actress. She didn't regard it as acting to play a talking tree or be part of a frog chorus. Acting, to Jessamy, was being people. And even now ideas for her solos were rushing pell-mell into her brain.

The Spirit of the Rain Forest . . . a costume of leaves, deep, dark, shiny green, with a headdress of feathers in vivid parrot colours. Yellow, orange, scarlet . . . her shoes would have to be dyed. Green, probably, with green tights.

Jessamy reached out for a drawing pad. Already she was growing excited. Jack, who had escaped Coombe Hurst productions by starting off somewhere else and then going to the Royal Ballet School at the age of eleven, always dismissed Jessamy's end-of-term solos as 'tacky, if not downright naff'. In her heart of hearts, Jessamy sometimes agreed with her, but as her mum said, 'It's all good preparation . . . the more used to performing you are, the better. And the world needs new choreographers.'

Jessamy wasn't sure that her choreography was anything very amazing, but she did quite enjoy putting different combinations of steps together. Occasionally, if her dad were at home he helped her, but this year she was going to have to manage by herself.

Jessamy put down her pad and walked to the centre of the room. Slowly she went on *demi-pointe* and raised her arms in fifth . . . the Spirit of the Rain Forest!

3

Ballonné – extend – step forward – *dégagé derriere* and close in fifth.

Jessamy paused to look at herself in the long mirror which she had brought downstairs from mum and dad's bedroom. Critically, she readjusted her weight. That was better; try it again. *Ballonné* –

She had worked out her Rain Forest dance using some music by a composer called Villa-Lobos, which she had found on one of her dad's CDs. The opening sequence lasted three minutes, and the closing sequence five, which she thought was about right. All she had to do now was find time to practise it, and that wasn't so easy. She couldn't stay on at the Academy after class because the studio was needed for other lessons, and the sitting-room, which was where she was at the moment, was really far too small and cluttered even with all the furniture pushed out of the way. In any case, Elke grew grumpy when she had to come and move everything back again.

'I am not here – ' huff puff ' – as a removals person.'

Some of the furniture was quite heavy: Jessamy

went scarlet in the face when she tried to push it, so *that* couldn't be good for her.

Last year the sitting-room had been all right because last year she had only been ten and had done a really soppy, yucky sort of number full of silly little hops and skips such as befitted a ten-year-old. The Spirit of the Rain Forest was more ambitious, with proper jumps and even a couple of *pirouettes* (Jessamy rather fancied herself at *pirouettes*).

'I need somewhere to practise!' she moaned, as Elke came tutting into the room.

'Look at all this trouble you make! You move the furniture one more time, I leave it for your mother to see.'

'But I need to *practise*,' wailed Jessamy.

'Practise, practise! All I ever hear in this house,' grumbled Elke. 'Nobody thinks of any one thing but *practise*.'

In the end, Jessamy had an idea: she would go in early to school and practise in the gym. It wasn't easy, getting up early, but once Jessamy had set her mind to do something she always did it.

'Please, Elke, will you bang on my door at half-past six . . . please will you bang really hard?'

'What am I now?' cried Elke. 'An alarm clock person?'

But Elke was always up early. Jessamy had heard her singing pop songs in the bathroom before it was even light.

'Please, Elke!' she said. 'It's very important.'

Her end-of-term solos may be what Jacquetta called tacky, but they still had to be done well.

Next morning, Jessamy was down in the kitchen, washed and dressed and ready for breakfast by seven o'clock. By quarter-past seven Elke was driving her in to school.

'If Mum wants to know where I am,' said Jessamy, 'tell her I've gone in early to do some extra practice.'

The chances were Belinda Tarrant wouldn't even miss her. She was always too busy opening her post and sipping black coffee to notice much of what went on before midday.

Jessamy slipped into school by one of the side doors – opened by the caretaker for those who came in before school for extra music lessons or games practice – and made her way up to the gym. The gym was modern, with a good wood block floor, perfect for dancing. It wasn't until she had pushed open the swing doors that Jessamy made the discovery: someone else had had the same idea!

Karen, dressed in leotard and tights (the same as Jessamy herself under her regulation school blouse and skirt) was there doing *plies*, using the wall bar to hold on to. She stopped and spun round, her face scarlet, as Jessamy appeared.

'Great minds!' said Jessamy.

'P-pardon?' stammered Karen.

'Great minds think alike . . . I wanted somewhere I could practise my end-of-term solo.'

'That's all right!' Karen snatched up her clothes,

which she had draped over the back of one of the horses. 'I was just finishing.'

She obviously hadn't been just finishing: she had been just starting. Jessamy leapt forward, impulsively. 'You don't have to go! Why don't we practise together?'

Karen looked doubtful.

'But if you want to do your solo – '

'Not before I've warmed up,' said Jessamy. She stripped down to her leotard and sat on the floor to put on her shoes. 'Have you used the gym before?'

'Only this week.' Karen said it anxiously. 'I wanted to do some extra work and it was the only place I could think of. Do you think they'll mind?'

'Don't see why they should. It's not as if we're using any of their equipment.' Jessamy gazed round at the gym with its ropes and its wall bars. 'It's a pity there isn't any music . . . I might bring my portable CD player!'

'But suppose someone heard us?'

'Who could? There isn't anyone about.' The gym was at the back of the school, on the first floor; the staff room and Miss Shergold's office were both on the ground floor, at the front.

'We've got it all to ourselves! Our own private studio. How far had you got? Just *plies*?'

They went through *plies, battements tendus, ronds de jambes, battements frappes, battements fondus, grands battements and developpes*. Watching Karen, when she could (she couldn't watch herself: the one drawback of the gym was that there were no mirrors for

363

checking your position), Jessamy thought that whoever Madame Olga was and however ancient she might be she had certainly taught her well.

'Are you going to do your solo now?' said Karen.

'What, before we do any centre work?'

Karen looked at the gym clock.

'I don't think there'd be time for both.'

'All right. I'll just run through it quickly and show you what I've worked out . . . 'cause I've just had this really great idea,' said Jessamy, taking up her position in the centre of the gym. 'Why don't you learn it as well and we could make it a *pas de deux*?'

'They wouldn't want me doing it,' said Karen.

'Why not?' They could still have the great Jessamy Hart and her famous parents. 'It would be more fun than just me. I'm always doing it. Look! Watch and tell me what you think.'

Fortunately, Jessamy knew the music so well that she could hear it in her head as she danced. Karen sat quietly watching her.

'There!' said Jessamy. 'It's not terribly good yet, but that's what I'm planning to do. What d'you think?'

'I think it's brilliant,' said Karen.

'Really? Really and truly? You're not just saying it?'

'No, I mean it. That bit where you — ' Karen stood up and demonstrated. 'That works really well.'

'The *pas de chat*. I worked on that for ages. I couldn't get it to fit in properly.'

'It looks really good.'

'Yes, because it's a bit showy.' A bit showy, but actually quite simple to do. 'Like the *pirouettes*. They always like *pirouettes*. I wish I could do them on point! Have you gone on point yet?'

Karen shook her head.

'Madame says it's too early.'

'Yes, that's what Mum says. She says not until my feet are stronger. *I* think they're strong enough now.' Jessamy wriggled her toes inside their soft shoes. 'I'm really looking forward to buying my first point shoes. Aren't you? You don't feel you've properly started until you can wear point shoes.'

'I expect our toes will get sore,' said Karen.

'Jack's always used to bleed. She used to try stuffing things in her shoes to make it easier. Have you got good feet for point work?'

'Quite,' said Karen. She took off a shoe and displayed her toes: the first and second ones were the same length.

'Look at mine,' said Jessamy. She wasn't boasting: she just happened to have been blessed with good strong feet and ankles, and three toes the same length on each foot.

Karen sighed. 'You are so lucky,' she said.

'I know. I bet I could go on point right now if only Mum wasn't so pernickety. Anyway – ' Jessamy stuffed her ballet shoes back into their bag and pulled on her ordinary brown lace-ups. 'What do you think about us doing a *pas de deux*?'

Karen, still sitting on the floor, pressed the soles of her feet together. She bent her head over them.

'I don't think Madame would let me. She's very strict about things like that.'

'But it's good for you!' said Jessamy. 'It gives you experience of being on stage.'

'Y-yes, I know, but – '

'Why don't you give me her telephone number and I'll get Mum to ring her? I bet she'd be able to talk her round! Mum says it's important for a dancer to get the feel of performing. She says if you just slog away in class all the time you get stale, which is quite true,' said Jessamy. 'Doesn't your madame ever let you do performances?'

Slowly, Karen straightened up.

'It's not so much Madame, it's – it's more my gran. She wouldn't like it. She's funny about things like that.'

Jessamy frowned. Karen's gran seemed to be a very strange person, being 'funny' about things all the time. She was funny about Karen inviting friends home, funny about Karen performing on stage –

'She's a bit old-fashioned.'

Karen said it apologetically. Jessamy could see that it was difficult for her. Jessamy herself didn't have any grandparents. They had all died when she was still quite young. But once there had been a girl at school who was a member of the Plymouth Brethren and *her* parents hadn't ever let her join in with after-school activities, so Jessamy knew that these sort of people did exist.

'Is your gran a Plymouth Brother?' she said.

'What's a Plymouth Brother?' said Karen.

'A sort of religious person . . . very strict.'

Karen grew red and shook her head. 'No, my gran isn't like that. She's just . . . just old-fashioned.'

'Well, it's a shame,' said Jessamy. 'It would have been fun, dancing together. But if it's something that would really upset her – '

'It would,' said Karen.

Jessamy paused in the middle of tying her school tie.

'What's she going to do when you go to ballet school? You'll have to do performances then.'

Karen looked at Jessamy, gravely.

'I don't yet know whether she'll let me.'

'But that's *terrible*!' said Jessamy.

'I know.' Karen's eyes filled with sudden tears. She dashed them away and began peeling off her leotard. 'We'd better hurry or we'll be late for assembly!'

When once Jessamy took an idea into her head, she did not part with it easily. Karen *ought* to join her in the Rain Forest dance. It was sickmaking, Jessamy hogging the limelight every year just because she was the daughter of Ben Hart and Belinda Tarrant. And it was appalling if Karen's gran wouldn't let her become a dancer! Every morning now, the two girls met in the gym to do half an hour of class and to practise the Rain Forest dance – well, Jessamy practised the Rain Forest dance. Karen just shook her head when Jessamy suggested she should practise it with her.

'There isn't any point. I wouldn't be allowed.'

Something, thought Jessamy, would have to be done. She had seen enough of Karen's dancing to know that she had talent, and Jessamy had been brought up in a family which firmly believed that talent should not be wasted. They believed this as fervently as some people believed in God. Indeed, to them talent *was* a god – which was why they had been so angry with Jacquetta for tossing hers aside just as carelessly as if it had been an old glove or some worn-out article of clothing.

'Sacrilege!' had cried Jessamy's mum.

Jessamy wasn't absolutely certain what sacrilege was, but she believed just as firmly as the rest of the family (with the exception of Jack) that talent should be put to good use. Karen's talent, it seemed to her, was being stifled. Probably Karen's gran didn't realise that it wasn't something that could survive being shut up within four walls. It needed to expand; it needed to breathe. If Jessamy went round and explained this to her – very politely, of course – then surely she would see?

Jessamy made up her mind. She wouldn't tell Karen what she was planning to do, because Karen mightn't like it (though she would be eternally grateful afterwards), but on Wednesday, which was the day she didn't have a ballet class after school, she told Elke not to bother coming to pick her up.

'I'm going round to Susan's for a bit.'

'So I come and pick you up later from Susan's?'

'No, it's all right,' said Jessamy. 'I'll catch a bus.'

Elke raised her eyebrows.

'It may by then be after dark. Your mother will not like for you to be out after dark. I come for you.'

Really, thought Jessamy, trying to hatch plots and do things without other people knowing was extraordinarily difficult when you were only eleven years old.

'You say what time,' said Elke.

It wasn't any use arguing. Elke might object to moving furniture around, but she took her official duties very seriously.

'I'll give you a call when I'm leaving,' said Jessamy.

Susan didn't live too far away from Karen. She would go round to Susan's place and telephone from there. And it probably *wouldn't* be after dark. How long would it take to convince Karen's gran that Karen needed to dance? Five minutes? Ten minutes? Jessamy had great faith in her own powers of persuasion.

She walked out of school with Karen, who was, as usual, going to Madame Olga's. Karen turned left. Jessamy waited a moment, then turned right, in the direction of the buses. She knew how to get to Bolton Street, which was where Karen's gran lived: she had looked it up in the *A–Z*.

Quarter of an hour later, she was knocking at the door of Number Fifteen. Anyone else might have felt a little nervous perhaps, but not Jessamy. Overweening confidence was what Jessamy had (her brother Saul had said so).

The door opened on to a long, dark, narrow

passage. A little old lady stood there. She was tiny — hardly any taller than Jessamy — thin as a twig, and fragile like a bird. She was wearing slippers, and a flowered pinafore and was drying her hands on a towel.

'Good afternoon,' said Jessamy, in her best imitation of her mum. 'My name is Jessamy Hart. I'm a friend of Karen's. Are you Karen's gran?'

'Yes, my dear. What can I do for you? I'm afraid Karen's not here at the moment. She never gets back until about five.'

'I know,' said Jessamy. 'That's why I came, so we could talk on our own.'

'Oh.' Karen's gran sounded rather flustered. 'Oh! Well! You'd better come in.' She held the door open and Jessamy stepped through into the narrow hallway. 'Go into the front room, Jessamy . . . take a seat. Now, what was it you wanted to talk about?'

'It's about Karen dancing in the end-of-term show.'

'Karen dancing in the end-of-term show?' Her gran's face lit up. 'Oh! That is nice!'

Jessamy was thrown.

'You mean you don't mind?' she said.

'Mind? Of course I don't mind. I'm only too happy for her. I always feel a bit guilty, to tell you the truth, about Karen and her dancing. Obsessed with it, she is. I keep hoping it's just a passing phase — we all have passing phases, don't we, when we're young? I remember for years I most passionately wanted to be a jockey and ride in the Grand

National. Oh, dear! And we never had the money for a single riding lesson. But it didn't stop me dreaming. A bit like Karen, I'm afraid. She obviously takes after her gran.'

Jessamy listened with growing bewilderment. The conversation was not following at all the course she had planned. By now she should have been in full flood, exercising her powers of persuasion.

'So you really wouldn't mind,' she said, 'if Karen danced in the show?'

'So long as it's not going to put too much pressure on her. The only thing that bothers me is whether she would have enough time. What with all these extra bits and pieces she has to stay behind for – '

Extra bits and pieces? Jessamy wrinkled her brow.

'What extra bits and pieces?'

'Oh! I don't know. Netball, is it? Or gym? Something she has to do. And then there's some special class she has to stay on for twice a week . . . never home before five o'clock. They do seem to work you very hard at that school.'

Jessamy didn't know what to say. What were these special classes supposed to be? She wondered for a truly dreadful minute if Karen's gran were not quite right in the head. Maybe she was growing forgetful, as old people sometimes did, and it had slipped her memory that Karen had ballet lessons every afternoon with Madame Olga.

'Not that I'm complaining,' said Karen's gran. 'Don't think that! It's what her granddad always wanted for her. He was never lucky enough to have

an education himself, but he was determined that
Karen should. Dreamt of her going to university, he
did. I don't know whether she'll get that far.'

Karen's gran broke off and cocked a hopeful eye
in Jessamy's direction. Jessamy, who was never at a
loss for words said, 'Um – well – ' and was then at
a loss. To herself she thought, not at Coombe Hurst,
she won't. Coombe Hurst was not noted for its
academic success. You went to the High School if
you wanted that. Portia, probably, would transfer to
the High School before very long. She was far too
much of a genius for Coombe Hurst.

Karen's gran, as if reading Jessamy's mind, said,
'We tried for the High School, but she wasn't quite
up to it. Too much dreaming about ballet, I put it
down to.' Jessamy watched as the old woman pleated
the edge of her apron with gnarled fingers. 'She's
always pleading with me, but what can I do? When
her grandad said education he meant book learning,
not ballet. It wouldn't be right to use the money for
dancing. Not when he worked so hard for it.'

'But what about – about Madame Olga?' The
question was out before Jessamy could stop it.

'Madame Olga?' Karen's gran looked at her,
blankly. She had the same blue eyes as Karen, only
slightly cloudy now because of her being old. 'That'll
be one of her dancers, I suppose. All over her
bedroom, they are . . . Margaret Fonteyn, that Nooryeff. I can't keep up with them. I don't know where
she gets it from, there's no ballet in the family. Mind
you, her mother was musical; that might have some-

thing to do with it. But you can tell her — well, I'll tell her when she gets in. I've no objections to her dancing in the show so long as her school work doesn't suffer.'

'Actually — ' Jessamy stood up, suddenly anxious to be away. It had all gone most peculiarly wrong! 'Actually, would you mind terribly *not* telling her that I came? She might think I've been spying on her, or something.'

'Well, of course you haven't!' Karen's gran sounded indignant. 'You were just being normally friendly. I must say I'm very glad to have met one of Karen's friends at last. I keep asking her, why don't you bring someone home with you? All she does is make excuses. I hope she's not becoming too big for her boots, going to this posh school?'

'I'm sure she isn't,' said Jessamy, doing her best to slide out of the front door.

'You don't think she's ashamed of her old gran, do you?'

'I'm *sure* she isn't!' gasped Jessamy.

Karen wasn't ashamed of her gran. She was terrified that someone would discover her secret: that she was having lessons every afternoon with Madame Olga and that her gran didn't know! The mystery of it was, how was she managing to pay?

'Ask her to bring you to tea,' called her gran, as Jessamy opened the front gate.

'I will,' promised Jessamy.

She would, but she knew what Karen would say:

'My gran doesn't like me having people back. She's a bit funny like that . . .'

4

There was a mystery about Karen. You wouldn't have thought it to look at her, with her shy smile and demure manner, but she was obviously something of a dark horse. There was more to her, thought Jessamy, than met the eye, and one of these days she was going to discover what it was.

In the meantime, it had now become almost taken for granted that Jessamy and Elke would go and fetch her in the car after lunch on Saturday – Karen's gran didn't have a car – and that Karen would stay to tea and watch ballet videos, or look at Jessamy's collections of shoes and signed photographs. Karen had been gratifyingly impressed to find that she actually had a signed photograph of Rudolph Nureyev. (Even Susan and Sheela had heard of Rudolph Nureyev.)

'Mum got it for me,' said Jessamy.

'Did she ever dance with him?'

'Well, she wasn't actually partnered by him, but they danced on the same stage.'

'Did you ever meet him?'

'Oh, yes,' said Jessamy, airily. 'Several times.'

Karen's eyes grew big and round.

'*Really*? What was he like?'

Jessamy struggled for a moment. It would be easy enough to say 'nice', or 'funny', or 'friendly', but the truth was she didn't actually know. She giggled.

'I can't remember . . . I was only two years old!' She only knew about it because the family never tired of reminding her.

'At least you can say that you've met him,' sighed Karen. 'I've never met anyone great.' And then she blushed and added, 'Of course, you're used to it, with your mum and dad.'

'Mum and Dad aren't great like Nureyev was. Mum always says Rudi was in a class of his own . . . do you want to watch one of his videos? I've got one of him and Fonteyn. Shall we look at that?'

Karen nodded, blissfully. She couldn't have enough of watching ballet. She had already confessed to Jessamy that the only ballet she had ever seen live, on stage, was *Swan Lake*, which her gran had taken her to as a treat on her birthday.

'We'll go together, in the holidays,' promised Jessamy. 'Saul can get me free tickets sometimes.' She pressed the start switch on the remote control. 'Look! This is *Don Quixote*. Later there's the balcony scene from *Romeo and Juliet*, and then some of *Sylphides*, and then a bit from *Le Corsaire* . . . he's absolutely brilliant in *Le Corsaire*!'

They watched intently, Jessamy curled up into one corner of the sofa, Karen in the other, as Nureyev leapt and spun and bounded in great pantherine leaps across the stage. When he jumped, it was as if invisible hands held him aloft; when he turned, it was as if he were a coiled spring, or a top, unwinding. Jessamy was rather good at turns herself, but even she could only look and wonder. She *knew* how you could spin and spin and not grow dizzy; and yet the speed at which Nureyev did it seemed to defy all the laws of the human body. It simply wasn't possible that anyone could turn so fast for so long – but there he was, in front of them, young and arrogant and insolently beautiful, hair flying out and a smile on his lips as if it were a mere nothing.

Karen let out her breath in a deep sigh of ecstasy.

'He *was* the greatest, wasn't he?'

'He had animal magnetism,' said Jessamy. (It was a phrase she had read somewhere.) 'There'll never be another like him.'

Karen sighed again. So did Jessamy. A tear rolled down Karen's cheek.

'It's so awful that he's not here any more!'

'I know.' Jessamy nodded, solemnly. 'But at least,' she quoted her mum, 'at least his dancing days were over.'

'That's a terrible thing to say!' sobbed Karen.

'But it's true,' insisted Jessamy. She groped for her handkerchief. 'Think of the tragedy if he'd been young!'

'It's a tragedy anyw-way,' wept Karen.

'Oh, don't, I can't bear it!' cried Jessamy.

They were still sitting there, their handkerchiefs pressed to their faces, when the door opened and Saul's head appeared.

'What's this, then?' He jerked a thumb towards the television. 'One for the ghouls?'

'Shut up,' said Jessamy. 'Don't be beastly.'

'I'm not being beastly.' Saul crossed to the back of the sofa and leant over, between the two of them, watching as the dazzling figure of Le Corsaire soared, bare-chested and triumphant, through the air, curving and curling like a great golden eagle in effortless flight.

For a long while there was silence, then, 'By God, he was good!' said Saul.

'The greatest,' said Jessamy, scrubbing at her eyes.

'Certainly one of.'

'*The* greatest. Karen thinks so.'

Karen's face, still awash with tears, promptly turned itself into a glowing beacon.

'Karen thinks so, does she?' Saul cocked an eye, considering her. 'Well, she could be right. I'll tell you one thing . . . none of us could hold a candle to him.'

'He transformed the face of British ballet,' said Jessamy.

'He did. That's for sure.'

'Before Nureyev,' said Jessamy, 'idiot ordinary people thought that male dancers were soft. He made them realise you had to be a whole lot tougher than stupid footballers.'

'You bet!' said Saul. He straightened up. 'Well, I'll leave you to it.'

Jessamy turned to watch him go.

'Why are you home?' she said. 'Aren't you on tonight?'

'Knee injury. I'm out for a couple of days.'

'If you were any sort of a dancer,' yelled Jessamy, as Saul limped elaborately across the room, 'you'd dance through it!'

'Yeah, and cripple myself?' retorted Saul.

The sitting-room door closed behind him.

'Getting soft,' said Jessamy. The video had come to an end. She pressed the rewind button. 'That was my brother, by the way,' she said.

'I know!' Karen's face was still all aglow with pink.

'Fancy stopping dancing just for a knee injury!' Jessamy said it scornfully. 'I wouldn't.'

'You'd have to if it were bad.'

'Nureyev didn't,' said Jessamy. 'He danced through anything. So did all Balanchine's dancers. They *suffered* for their art. Gelsey Kirkland had tendonitis when she was only twelve years old.'

Karen looked at her, doubtfully.

'That sounds like bad training,' she said.

'Yes, he used to push them. Mum says he was a tyrant, but everyone worshipped him. What shall we watch next?' Jessamy went on hands and knees, scrabbling through a pile of videos. 'I've got one of Mum here. Do you want to see one of Mum? Or there's a bit of Dad, but it's not very good. It's a pirate version. Someone taped it when they shouldn't have. Let's look at Mum.'

'You're ever so like him,' said Karen.

'Who?' Jessamy sat back on her heels. 'Saul?'

379

She knew that she was like him for everyone was always telling her so – Karen herself had remarked on it even before she had met him. Jessamy really should have been used to it by now, but still she couldn't quite stop a pleased beam from spreading itself over her face.

Only last week, in a review, Saul had been described as 'this handsome and talented young dancer'. Of course, Mum and Jacquetta were the real *beauties* in the family; but if she grew up to look like a female version of Saul she wouldn't mind. *Jessamy Hart, this handsome and talented young dancer* . . .

'You are so lucky,' said Karen.

Karen was always saying that Jessamy was lucky. She didn't say it at all in an envious sort of way, though sometimes she sounded wistful, as if she would have liked parents who belonged to the world of ballet and understood the urgent need to express oneself in dance. Jessamy, who had always tended to take her ballet background for granted, was beginning to see that perhaps she *was* rather more fortunate than others. It must be truly devastating, for instance, to have as much talent as Karen and to live with a gran who insisted that education meant book learning and not ballet.

On the other hand, Karen was actually having more lessons than Jessamy, and private lessons at that, so perhaps she needn't feel too sorry for her.

'There are drawbacks,' said Jessamy, 'to having parents that are dancers.'

380

'I'd give *anything*,' said Karen.

'You wouldn't if you had to have lessons from your own mother and she was always holding you up as an example of how not to do things and expecting you to work twice as hard as anyone else and get better exam results than anyone else and fussing all the time about whether your feet are strong enough and how tall you're likely to grow and – '

Karen listened with shining eyes.

'You wouldn't think it so much fun then,' grumbled Jessamy.

'I would!' said Karen. 'I'd love it!'

Jessamy looked at her. She shook her head.

'You are bananas,' she said. 'Ballet bananas!'

'I've had an idea!' announced Jessamy, bounding into the gym one morning.

She and Karen always met there now, before school, just as they spent every Saturday afternoon together, though during the day Jessamy still went round with Susan and Sheela, while Karen and Portia stuck with each other. Jessamy suspected that quite soon – next term, maybe, if Portia transferred to the High – Karen would move in to make a foursome; and within the foursome it would be Susan-and-Sheela, and Karen-and-Jessamy; but for the moment none of the others realised how much time they spent together out of school hours. It was good to have someone to talk to who spoke the same language. Jessamy could confide things to Karen that she could never confide to the girls at ballet school – her growing certainty, for example, that she was going to turn into a dramatic dancer rather than a classical one. The girls at ballet school would immediately have latched on.

'Of course, *she*'s never going to dance the lead in *Swan Lake*. She might think she's the cat's whiskers just because of who her parents are, but it won't get her anywhere – not in the long run.'

All Karen said, very seriously, was 'But, Jessamy, some of the *best* dancers have been dramatic . . . look at Lynn Seymour!' And Jessamy did, and took comfort, and became a bit reconciled. After all, Lynn Seymour had danced with Rudolph Nureyev.

'Look,' she said now, as she burst through the swing doors into the gym, 'why don't I give you a class and then you give me a class and then we can tell each other all our faults?'

Karen looked dubious. 'Is that a good idea?'

'I think so,' said Jessamy.

It was all part of a cunning ploy to find out more about Madame Olga. Jessamy had several times in her life been accused of being pushy, but even she didn't quite like to ask outright, 'Where are you getting the money to pay for your ballet lessons?' Perhaps Madame Olga was giving them free because Karen had such obvious talent; or perhaps Karen had discovered a secret hoard of money under her bedroom floorboards – well, no, she didn't seriously think that; that was the sort of stuff that story books were made of. All the same, there *was* a mystery and

Jessamy wasn't going to rest until she had got to the bottom of it.

'Come on!' she said. 'Let's get started.'

'But what about your Rain Forest dance?'

'I don't have to do it every day. Now, come along, please!' Jessamy clapped her hands, as Mum sometimes did at the beginning of class. 'At the *barre*! *Plies* in first.'

She pressed the start button on her portable CD player. Karen obediently took up her position at the wall bars.

'And one, and two – '

Try as she might, Jessamy couldn't find a single thing to criticise, in Karen's *barre* work.

'Your *developpes* could be just a *teeny* bit smoother.' But really that was just nitpicking; not even Belinda Tarrant , would have found fault with Karen's *developpes*. Jessamy was only saying it for the sake of something to say. 'Just a teensy weensy bit. You'll have to work on it. OK, my turn!'

Jessamy sprang across to take her place.

'You can say what you like,' she said. 'I won't be offended.'

She wasn't really expecting Karen to say anything. After all, Jessamy had been taking dancing classes since she was five years old; far longer than Karen.

'Well?' As she reached the last of her *developpes* – as smooth as smooth could be – she turned, challengingly, to Karen. 'How was that?'

'Very good,' said Karen, 'on the whole.'

Very good *on the whole*? Jessamy bristled.

'What was wrong?'

'Nothing very much.' Karen said it soothingly. 'I just felt now and again that you were straining your neck just a little bit.'

Jessamy's cheeks grew red with indignation. Who did Karen Anders think she was, telling Jessamy Hart that she was straining her neck?

'I'm sorry,' said Karen, 'but you did say to tell you.'

Yes, and it was no more than her mum had pointed out to her last week, was it?

'You must take care, Jessamy, not to strain your neck . . . there's nothing worse than someone dancing with her head all poked forward.'

'It's 'cause my neck isn't as long and beautiful as yours.' Jessamy felt suddenly generous. 'I always feel I have to stretch it.'

'There isn't any need,' said Karen, 'honestly! It's a perfectly good sort of neck.'

Jessamy had to subdue an instinctive dancer's reaction to rush to the nearest mirror and look.

'Well, I suppose it will have to do,' she said, 'as it's the only one I've got . . . Your Madame has taught you really well. Does she have lots of other pupils besides you?'

'Um – not really.' Karen busied herself with the CD player. 'Just one or two.'

'How did you find her?'

'Oh . . . someone told me about her. Someone at my old school.'

'Someone who'd been with her?'

'No, someone who – who lived near her.'

'In Chiswick?'

'Mm.'

Slyly, thinking herself clever, Jessamy said, 'I suppose your gran had to go with you when you auditioned?'

Karen made a mumbling sound: not quite yes and not quite no.

'It must cost a lot,' said Jessamy, 'having classes every day.'

Karen made another mumbling sound. This time, she was pulling her brown school sweater over her head.

'I'd like classes every day,' said Jessamy, 'but Mum says not till next year. I think that's silly, 'cause if I were at ballet school full time I'd be having them.'

'Why aren't you?' said Karen.

Too late, Jessamy realised: she had let herself be sidetracked.

'Mum's scared I'll do a Jack on her. Jack was at White Lodge by the time she was eleven.' She didn't need to explain to Karen that White Lodge was the Junior Department of the Royal Ballet School: Karen knew these things just as well as Jessamy. 'Mum always reckons she resented it 'cause of never having had any other sort of life except ballet. She says she wants me to be old enough to make up my own mind. Maybe when I'm thirteen she'll let me go.'

'Did your brother go?' said Karen, blushing slightly as she said it.

Jessamy thought, ho ho, she's getting a thing about

Saul! She recognised the symptoms. She had seen it too often before: lots of girls had a thing about Saul.

'No,' said Jessamy, 'Saul went to Central. But Saul was different. He was fanatical from the word go. Mum says looking back on it she thinks she pushed Jack too hard. She says I'm half way between them. I'm more dedicated than Jack, but not as fanatical as Saul. Do you think you're fanatical? I mean, is there anything else you'd want to do other than dance?'

'Nothing,' said Karen. She said it in tones of almost tragic intensity. 'If I couldn't dance, I might just as well be dead.'

Jessamy nodded. 'You're like Saul; you're fanatical. I know you wouldn't *think* he's fanatical, all the fuss he makes about a silly little knee injury that anyone else would dance through, but it's because he can't bear the thought of having to give up early, like Dad did.'

'That would be *awful*,' said Karen. 'I'd die if I had to stop dancing.'

'I wouldn't,' said Jessamy. 'I mean, I wouldn't want to, but I'd still go on living.'

'But it wouldn't *be* living!' cried Karen. 'Dancing's like breathing. How can you live if you can't breathe?'

Jessamy looked at her, curiously.

'So what will you do if your gran won't let you go to ballet school?'

'I'll find a way.' Karen said it, for her, quite fiercely.

'If you want something badly enough, there's always a way.'

Jessamy thought, I am not very good as a detective. She was no nearer solving the mystery of Karen and Madame Olga than she had been before. There was only one thing for it: direct action was needed.

On Wednesday she said to Elke, 'I'm going to Susan's again. But I'll be back ages before it's dark so I can easily get a bus. You don't have to worry about me.'

'Your mother – ' began Elke.

Jessamy felt like screaming.

'Elke, I'm *eleven*,' she said. 'Loads of people that are eleven go home from school by bus!'

Elke pursed her lips.

'And the main road?' she said.

'I know how to cross the main road!'

Not even Karen's gran fussed and bothered the way Elke did.

'You must ask your mother,' said Elke. 'I take no responsibility.'

Belinda Tarrant, as usual, was busy when Jessamy tried to talk to her.

'Don't bother me now, Jess,' she said.

'So it's OK, is it?' said Jessamy. 'Elke doesn't have to bother getting the car out?'

'Elke doesn't have to do anything she doesn't want to do. She's not here for your personal convenience. She already does far more than she's supposed to.'

Jubilantly, Jessamy reported back: 'Mum says

387

you're not here for my personal convenience and you already do more than you're supposed to.'

Elke's forehead went into a confusion of ripples. 'But it is part of my terms of employment! To call for you from school – '

'Not all the time,' said Jessamy. 'Not on Wednesday. Mum says so.'

The fact that Mum hadn't been listening was neither here nor there. Jessamy had to have *some* freedom of movement. How could she be a detective with Elke dogging her footsteps?

That afternoon, at the end of school, feeling partly like a private detective engaged on a case and partly like a nasty common-or-garden snooper (but whatever she found out she would never let on that she knew) Jessamy raced through the school gates and positioned herself behind a conveniently parked car to wait for Karen to appear. There was a bad moment when Susan and Sheela's grinning faces came looming round the back bumper, demanding to know 'What on earth are you doing *there*?', but she soon despatched them.

'I'm spying on Elke,' she said. 'I think she has a boyfriend.'

'Ooh! Can we spy too?' said Sheela.

'No, it would be too obvious. Go away.'

Giggling, they did so. Seconds later, Karen came through the gates and turned left along Rosemary Avenue. Jessamy counted up to ten, then crept out after her.

There wasn't any cover in Rosemary Avenue, but

fortunately Karen soon turned out of it into Fairhall Road, which was full of shops that could be looked into, and cars that could be hidden behind, and people who sometimes got in the way and obscured your view but also served as camouflage.

Fairhall Road was a long one. If you walked along it one way you eventually came to Hammersmith; if you walked along it the other way you came to a horrible great motorway. Karen was walking in the direction of the motorway.

After a while the shops stopped and the houses started. Some of the houses had been turned into flats and some were empty, with boards nailed across the windows. Karen came to a halt at one of the ones which had boards nailed across it. Jessamy, lingering behind a pillar box, watched in amazement as Karen, after looking quickly to left and right, opened the front gate, walked up the front path, went through a side gate and disappeared.

Now Jessamy wasn't sure what to do. A real detective would have had field glasses, so that she could spy without being seen – except that not even field glasses could penetrate windows which had boards nailed across them. What would a real detective do?

Follow cautiously, thought Jessamy.

She stepped out from behind her pillar box and walked up to the gate. There was a faded sign over the front door which said THE NORAN SCHOOL OF DANCING. Jessamy remembered the Noran School. It had been run by two women called Nora Kline and Annette Pearson, and when it had closed down some of their pupils had transferred to Belinda Tarrant (the ones that were good enough). That had been almost two years ago; the house had obviously been empty ever since. What was Karen going into an empty house for?

Maybe Madame Olga had bought it and hadn't had enough money to put up a new sign. But surely she would at least have taken the boards away from the windows?

Jessamy crept round to the side gate, gently eased it open and slipped through into a dank, dark passage which ran between the Noran School and the house next door. The passage smelt of gunge and stagnant water. Somewhere a tap had overflowed and left a trail of green slime down the wall. At the end of the passage some kind of prickly bush had gone mad and tried to grow all over everything. Carefully, Jessamy picked her way through.

As she emerged from the coils of the prickly bush, she heard the sound of music. So this *was* where Madame Olga held her classes! What a very strange woman she must be.

Jessamy followed the music round to the back of the house. It was coming from a room with windows overlooking the back garden (what *had* been the back garden: it was more of a jungle, now) and double doors opening on to a paved area. Jessamy stood listening for a moment before risking a quick glance through one of the windows. What she saw so astonished her that it was a moment or two before she could bring herself to look again.

The room had evidently been the main studio of the Noran School. There were *barres* still attached to two of the walls, with mirrors along just one of them. At some time there had probably been *barres* and mirrors along the others as well, but now there were just gashes and areas of crumbling plasterwork.

Down the side of the wall, the outside wall by the passage, there was more of the yucky green slime. Beneath it, the floor looked boggy and spongy, while above it, part of the ceiling bellied out like a big water-logged balloon.

And holding on to the *barre*, as far away from the green slime as she could get, was a small figure in leotard and tights. It was Karen. No Madame Olga. Just Karen on her own.

Mesmerised, Jessamy stood on tiptoe, peering through the window as Karen put herself through her *barre* work. At the end of the *barre* work she moved out to the middle of the floor to begin centre practice. Jessamy continued to stand on tiptoe. She almost forgot that she wasn't watching a real class. She wouldn't have been in the least surprised to hear the voice of Madame Olga calling out instructions.

And then Karen stopped, and walked across the room to where she had left her clothes in a heap on top of her school bag, next to a small cassette player from which the music was coming. From the bag she took a book, which she opened at a marked page and spread flat on the floor. She squatted a while on her heels, studying it, then stood up, moved back to the centre of the floor, prepared herself in

fifth – and attempted a *pirouette*. Not very success-
fully. Again she tried, and again. The third time she
almost had it, but ended off balance and not quite
facing in the right direction.

Jessamy could see where she was going wrong. To
begin with, she wasn't spotting properly. She was
trying to, Jessamy could tell. She was fixing her eyes
on a point somewhere in the middle of the green
gunge, but because her head wasn't swinging round
fast enough, she kept losing it. Her body was arriving
first, leaving her head to follow; that was the
problem. Jessamy longed to wrench open the double
doors and go running in to set her right, but she
knew that she mustn't.

She watched in anguish for a few seconds longer
and then could bear it no more. It upset her to see
Karen, always so graceful, always so precise, making
such a hash of something which really and truly was
quite simple – well, Jessamy had always found it so.
But then Jessamy had not had to teach herself.

Thoughtfully, she picked her way back round the
side of the house, past the prickly bush, down
the dank and dingy passage, and up Fairhall Road
to the nearest bus stop. No wonder her mum had
never heard of Madame Olga. There was no
Madame Olga! Everything that Karen knew, she had
taught herself. It explained why she hadn't wanted
to join Jessamy in the Rain Forest dance, with its
couple of showing-off *pirouettes*: she would have had
to admit that *pirouettes* were something she had not
yet mastered. But I could have taught her! thought

392

Jessamy. I could still teach her – if only she would let me.

She had solved the mystery of Karen's ballet classes, but solving the mystery had created a problem, for how could she offer to help without betraying the fact that she knew? There had to be some way, she thought. Karen was never going to get to grips with those *pirouettes* if someone didn't explain where she was going wrong; and who else was there but Jessamy?

5

'Mum,' said Jessamy, 'do you think it's possible for someone to learn ballet without having a teacher?'

'Of course it isn't,' said her mum. 'What on earth are you talking about?'

'Well, could a person teach herself?'

'No.' Belinda Tarrant was very firm on the point. 'A person could not.'

'Hasn't anyone ever?'

'Not to my knowledge.'

'So maybe they actually *could*?'

'Rubbish! They'd get into all sorts of bad habits.'

Jacquetta, who had drifted up to town on one of her rare visits from the depths of the countryside, which was where she now buried herself in domestic bliss, leaned back amongst the sofa cushions and contentedly swung her legs up on to a footstool.

'You have to remember,' she said, 'that there is a vested interest at stake here.'

'What's a vested interest?' said Jessamy.

'Mum being a teacher . . . she's hardly very likely to admit that she might be disposable.'

Belinda Tarrant snorted. Jacquetta smiled happily and folded her hands over her stomach. Sometimes

Jessamy thought that Jacquetta went out of her way
to do and say things just to make Mum mad, like
this baby she was having. She bet she'd only done it
as a gesture of defiance. Who, after all, in their right
senses, would want to go round having babies when
they could be dancing? Jessamy privately suspected
she'd only got married for the same reason. Jacquetta's husband was short and dumpy and fifteen
years older than Jacquetta. He was called Neville
(stupid name) and he owned a company that made
bottles. Mum always referred to him as 'the Bottler'.
He had a lot of money, but he didn't know a thing
about ballet. What on earth did they find to talk
about?

'You don't think,' said Jessamy, 'that if you bought
a book which told you how to do all the steps, and
if you followed it really *carefully* – '

'You would end up with every fault under the
sun.'

Jessamy considered. As far as she could see, Karen
didn't have any faults at all – unlike some of the
pupils at the Academy. After three years of tuition
Lisa Marlowe still hadn't achieved a proper turnout,
and probably never would. As Belinda Tarrant said,
'You couldn't make a tutu out of a piece of old rag.'

'You might just about manage to stagger through
a few simple *barre* exercises, but after that you'd soon
come unstuck.'

Jessamy sighed. 'I suppose so.' It was true that
Karen *was* having difficulties with her *pirouettes*.

'Why, anyway?' said Jacquetta.

'I was just wondering.'

'Thinking of branching out on your own?'

'No! Not me. Someone else. They can't afford lessons and they've been trying to teach themself.'

'Can't be done.' Belinda Tarrant spoke briskly. 'A sure recipe for disaster.'

'So what can she do?' wailed Jessamy.

She waited for her mum to say, 'Well, she could come and see me and if she's good enough I might offer to take her on for nothing', but Belinda Tarrant was a professional. She was in business to make money.

'I am not,' as she had more than once rather crisply informed those mothers who had come to her with their mostly untalented daughters begging for favoured treatment, 'a charity institution'.

'What's she supposed to *do*?' demanded Jessamy.

'There are such things as scholarships. The Royal Ballet School, Central — '

'Yes, and how many people get offered them?' In any case, Karen's gran would never let her. She wanted Karen to have book learning.

'If a person has outstanding talent, it will not go unremarked.'

'Yes, but what about all the people with just ordinary talent that can afford to pay? *They* get to have lessons. They don't have to pass scholarships. It isn't fair!' cried Jessamy.

'Did anyone ever say that it was?' Jacquetta swung her legs down off the stool. 'Ballet, my dear Jess, is an elitist art.'

'No more so than anything else!' snapped Belinda Tarrant. She didn't like it when people said that only rich kids could afford to dance. Jessamy had never thought about it before, but she began to see that it was true. She bet there weren't many poor kids at the Royal Ballet School or Central.

'It's the way of the world, kiddo.' Jacquetta turned, and plumped up a cushion. 'Don't let it bug you – there's nothing you can do about it.'

There might not be anything she could do about the world in general, but there must be something, she thought, that she could do for Karen. She racked her brains trying to fathom a way that she could help her without letting on that she had discovered her secret. Karen would feel humiliated if she knew that Jessamy knew. It would be embarrassing, after all the stories she had spun about Madame Olga.

Jessamy thought it quite likely that in Karen's mind Madame Olga really existed. Once when Jessamy had been young and wanted a dog and hadn't been allowed to have one, she made one up. He had been called Toby and he had gone everywhere with her, even, occasionally, to school. If Toby had seemed real, she couldn't see any reason why Madame Olga shouldn't, which meant that Karen hadn't been telling fibs so much as living out a dream. Jessamy wouldn't want to shatter that dream but she had to find some way of making it come true.

After several days of wrestling with the problem – mainly in maths classes and during morning assembly – Jessamy came up with another of her bright ideas. It hit her quite suddenly, in bed at night. Wham, bang! It was brilliant! It was foolproof! The sheer stunning cleverness of it took even Jessamy by surprise. What a blessing she was a creative sort of person! It wasn't everyone who could keep coming up with ideas the way she did.

Now that she had a plan of campaign, she couldn't wait to put it into action – and went racing off first thing next morning to do so.

'Can I run through my Rain Forest dance?' she asked Karen, at the end of their *barre* exercises.

It was all supposed to have been so easy! She was going to run through the Rain Forest dance until she came to the *pirouette* section, and then – hey presto! – she was going to throw herself off balance. What could possibly be simpler?

What could be simpler, as she quickly discovered, was *not* throwing herself off balance. It was really most annoying, when she had been over and over it in her mind and was quite determined to carry it through, to find that at the last minute her body automatically behaved just the way it always did, just as it had been trained to do, taking not the least bit of notice of the new and confusing commands that were being thrown at it and, as a result, executing two very nearly perfect *pirouettes*.

'Bother!' said Jessamy, coming to a standstill.

'What's the matter?' Karen looked at her in surprise.

'Those *pirouettes* were *gruesome*,' said Jessamy.

'No, they weren't! They were fine.'

398

'They weren't. They were *gruesome*.'

'They didn't look gruesome to me.'

'Well, they felt gruesome. Let me do them again.'

The second time round, although still reluctant, her body obeyed her: she wobbled and almost fell, and ended up facing in the wrong direction.

'There!' said Jessamy. 'I knew there was something wrong.' Nobly (because she was proud of her *pirouettes*), she said, 'I do find them difficult sometimes, don't you?'

'I – I haven't really mastered them yet.' Karen said it in a great rush, her cheeks burning.

'I *thought* I had,' said Jessamy. 'Honestly, when you get them right they're dead easy. Do you want to have a go and I'll show you how to do it? 'Cause I know perfectly well in *theory*.'

'All right.' Karen scrambled eagerly to her feet.

'See, what you have to do, you have to find a spot and fix your eyes on it – '

'I already do that,' said Karen, 'but I keep losing it!'

'That's because you're not moving your head fast enough. You've got to let your body start turning, then your head comes after, but quickly – like this. Look!'

Jessamy executed three beautiful *pirouettes*, one after another.

'Slowly!' begged Karen. 'Do it slowly!'

They were five minutes late for assembly (which meant two punctuality marks), but by the time they left the gym Karen had mastered her first *pirouette*.

'It feels wonderful!' she said.

'It is,' said Jessamy. 'When you've got it right, you can go on turning practically for ever!'

'I'm going to practise,' said Karen.

It was a temptation to say, 'What will Madame Olga think?' but Jessamy knew that she mustn't. For once in her life, she was trying hard to be tactful.

'Why were you and Karen late?' said Sheela, as they went back to their classroom after assembly. 'Were you doing things together?'

'We were rehearsing my Rain Forest dance.'

'Why? Is she going to do it with you?'

'She might,' said Jessamy. She hadn't altogether given up on the idea. After all, now Karen had mastered *pirouettes* there wasn't any reason why she shouldn't.

'I suppose you like being with her better than you like being with us,' said Susan.

'I don't!' said Jessamy. 'It's just that I can talk about dancing with her.'

'You'll become a ballet bore,' said Susan, 'if you're not careful.'

'That's right,' said Sheela. 'You've got to have outside interests.'

Jessamy thought of her mum and dad, and Saul. They didn't have any outside interests. Lots of dancers didn't; they didn't have the time. She tried explaining this to Susan and Sheela but predictably they just shook their heads.

'You'll get narrow-minded,' said Susan, 'you will.'

Perhaps she already was. It was true that at the

moment she couldn't think of anything except the Spirit of the Rain Forest and how to help Karen. It was also true that when she wasn't thinking of those particular things she was thinking about how to improve her turnout or how to achieve the perfect *arabesque* or whether she would ever make as brilliant a Lilac Fairy as Colleen McBride (currently one of her two favourite dancers at City Ballet, the other being Alessandro Corelli, who partnered her).

Did that make her narrow-minded? Susan would say yes, and Sheela would agree, and maybe they were right – but what could you do? If you were going to be a dancer it had to occupy your thoughts every waking moment. Dedication was what Jessamy's mum called it.

The next day was Saturday. Jessamy met Susan and Sheela in the shopping centre and mooched round for a bit, trying things on in the Clothes Mart (until an assistant came up and told them to stop it), reading the magazines in WH Smith, putting their money together to buy a beanburger and chips, of which Jessamy ate only a tiny portion for fear of getting fat. At home she was never allowed chips. Susan, shovelling them into her mouth as fast as she could go, said, 'You know what? You'll get anorexia if you're not careful.'

'No, I won't,' said Jessamy. 'I eat loads more than most people.'

Some of the kids at the Academy practically starved themselves, even at the age of eleven. Jessamy thought that was stupid, and so did Belinda Tarrant.

She said, 'A bit of puppy fat never hurt anyone. If you look at pictures of Margot Fonteyn as a teenager she was quite moon-faced.' Jessamy wouldn't want to be moon-faced (even if it meant growing up as beautiful as Margot Fonteyn), but she certainly wasn't going to starve herself – she enjoyed her food too much. It was just that chips were definitely unhealthy.

'Yum, yum,' said Sheela, licking her lips. The maddening thing about Sheela was that she remained skinny as a rake in spite of stuffing herself with chips and crisps and chocolate. *And* having practically no exercise.

At midday Jessamy went home for lunch. It was Elke's weekend off and she had asked Jessamy to be punctual. She stayed just long enough to watch Jessamy eat and then set off in her best up-to-date gear (a big black cloak and hat bought from the Clothes Mart) to meet what *she* said was a girlfriend. Jessamy didn't believe a word of it.

'It's a boyfriend really, isn't it?' she said.

'You M.Y.O.B.,' said Elke, tapping a finger to her nose. 'And no mischief, please! You behave until your dad comes. If any problem, you call your mother.'

Mum was at the studio, as usual; Dad was due back home that afternoon. He probably wouldn't want to get the car out because he would probably be jet-lagged and fit for nothing but going to bed, so Jessamy thought she had better telephone Karen and tell her to come by bus. Not having an overconscientious Elke to fuss over her, Karen was quite used to jumping on buses and tubes by herself.

It was Karen's gran who answered the phone.

'Is that Jessamy?' she said. 'I'm so glad you've rung! I've been wanting to ring you, but I couldn't find your number. I'm getting a little worried about Karen. She hasn't come home yet. What time did she leave you?'

Jessamy, thrown, said, 'Um – oh! Ah – '

What fibs had Karen been telling now?

'She's never back later than twelve,' said her gran. 'Did she not meet you in the library the same as usual?'

'Um – n-no,' said Jessamy. 'We didn't actually – um – see each other.'

'So where can she have gone?' There was a note almost of panic in the old lady's voice. 'I said to her, lunch at twelve. It's nearly one o'clock!'

'I expect she'll be home soon,' said Jessamy. Karen had obviously gone to the Noran School to put herself through class and had forgotten the time. Too busy practising her *pirouettes*, probably, 'I don't think anything will have happened to her,' said Jessamy, trying to sound comforting and grown-up.

'I do hope not,' said Karen's gran. 'While you're on the phone, my dear, I wonder if I might make a note of your number? Just in case.'

Quarter of an hour later, the telephone rang. Jessamy thought it was probably her dad, calling from the airport, but it was Karen's gran again.

'Oh, Jessamy,' she said, 'I'm so sorry to pester

you like this, but that naughty girl still isn't back. I wonder . . . you don't have any idea where she might have gone, do you?'

Jessamy thought quickly. It was bad of Karen to upset her gran, but a secret was a secret and it wasn't up to Jessamy to give it away.

'She might be with – with one of our friends from school that isn't on the telephone, but lives quite near,' she said. 'Would you like me to go and see?'

'Oh, my dear, could you? If it's not putting you to too much trouble. The friend doesn't live too far away, does she?'

'No, not very,' said Jessamy. 'I can easily go round there. I'll tell her to come straight home.'

'And you'll ring me if she's not there?'

'I'm sure she will be,' said Jessamy.

She knew what it was like when you became obsessed with going over and over one particular step until you got it right. Time simply stood still. She wondered whether to take the bus down Fairhall Road or whether this could be counted as an emergency. She decided that it could – for after all, Karen's gran was old and might have a heart attack if she went on worrying for too long – and that it justified booking a cab through the cab company which her mum always used. Belinda Tarrant went everywhere by cab. She said that not having to drive oneself was one of life's little luxuries. Actually it was rather an expensive little luxury, but Jessamy reckoned her mum wouldn't mind one extra journey being added to her account. Going by bus would take for ever.

'Could you wait for me, please?' said Jessamy, in her best grown-up voice as the cab came to a halt outside the Noran School. 'I won't be a minute.'

'Right you are,' said the cabby. He knew Jessamy quite well; he had often taken her to places when Elke was sick or on holiday.

Jessamy pushed open the side gate and trod carefully down the passage to the back of the house. She couldn't hear any music so maybe Karen had already left – which would be all right, because it would mean she was on her way home.

Jessamy peered through one of the windows into the studio. At first she thought no one was in there, but then she looked again and what had seemed to be a shadow transformed itself into Karen, crouched on the floor at the back, clutching her ankle. Jessamy didn't hesitate: she threw open the double doors and bounded in.

'Karen! What's happened? What have you done?'

Karen's head came up. Her eyes, wide and startled, met Jessamy's.

'Have you hurt yourself?'

'I was – practising *pirouettes* and my – my foot went through the – the floorboards. I think I've d-done something to my ankle!'

'Let's have a look.' With cool professionalism, Jessamy dropped to her knees and took Karen's ankle between her hands. She knew about ankle injuries.

'Does it hurt when I do this?' she said.

'N–no. N–not specially. Just when I t–try to p–put any w–weight on it!'

'It's probably only a sprain,' said Jessamy. 'I don't think you've broken it.'

'It won't stop me dancing, will it?'

'Heavens, no!' said Jessamy. 'Well, only for a day or two. Not permanently. Listen, I rang your gran and she said you weren't home and she's dead worried 'cause she thought you were with me – ' two spots of colour appeared in Karen's cheeks – 'so I said I thought you might be with someone from school and I'd go and have a look.'

'How did you know?' whispered Karen.

'Can't tell you now – I've got a cab outside. I think you ought to go back to your gran before she thinks you've been kidnapped or something.'

'Yes.' Karen hobbled gingerly to her feet. 'I d–didn't mean to stay here for so long but I – I forgot the time and then – then the floorboards gave way and – '

'They're rotten,' said Jessamy. 'You're lucky it wasn't worse. Here!' She ran across and gathered up Karen's clothes. 'You'd better put these on. Your gran might think it odd if you turn up in a leotard.'

'You won't tell her, will you?'

'Not if you don't want me to.'

'It would upset her,' said Karen. 'She already feels bad about not having enough money to let me have proper ballet lessons.'

'She would have if it weren't for the book learning,' said Jessamy.

'I know; if she didn't have to pay for me to go to Coombe Hurst. But she thinks that's what Granddad wanted. She says it's what he left the money for and she c – ' Karen stopped. 'How did you know about the book learning?' she said.

'Tell you later. Can you walk all right, or do you want to lean on me?'

'I expect I can hop,' said Karen.

The cab driver didn't actually pass any comment about Jessamy appearing from a derelict house with Karen hopping on one foot behind her, though he probably wondered.

'What are you going to say to your gran?' said Jessamy.

Karen looked at her, stricken. 'I don't know!'

'You could always say you went round to see Sheela and forgot what the time was, and then I came and said your gran was worried, and you went tearing out in such a rush you tripped over and did your ankle in.' Jessamy was an expert in such matters. When you had someone like Elke clucking round after you you occasionally had to resort to making things up.

'Couldn't I have gone to see Portia?' said Karen. 'I really did go to see her once. It wouldn't seem such a terrible fib.'

'Yes, but I said whoever it was wasn't on the telephone.'

'Isn't Sheela on the telephone?'

'She is at the shop but not at home 'cause they've

only just moved and they're waiting for one to be put in.'

'Oh.' Karen heaved a sigh. 'All right,' she said. 'I'll say I went to Sheela's.'

'*I* don't know why you don't tell her the truth,' said Jessamy. 'I bet if she knew how desperate you were she'd let you leave Coombe Hurst and have ballet lessons instead.'

'Yes, but — ' tears sprang to Karen's eyes ' — then she'd feel she was letting Granddad down! He worked ever so hard to get enough money for me to have an education and then he died before he could see it happen. Gran wouldn't ever forgive herself if she spent the money on dancing classes.'

'But it's not fair on you!' cried Jessamy.

'I know, but the other way wouldn't be f-fair on G-Gran!'

Jessamy was silent a while.

'Sometimes you have to be ruthless to get any-where in life,' she said.

Karen hiccuped and pulled a strand of damp hair away from her cheek.

'That's the trouble . . . I don't think I am very ruthless.'

I am, thought Jessamy; but Jessamy didn't need to be. Jessamy had all the advantages that an aspiring ballet dancer could possibly want.

She would just have to be ruthless enough for the two of them.

6

'It wasn't that I was spying on you,' said Jessamy. 'I mean – '

She stopped. What else could you call it but spying? She *had* been spying; creeping round after Karen, trying to find out where she went. Jessamy felt her cheeks fire up. She turned away: she wasn't used to embarrassing herself.

'It's all right,' said Karen. She pulled out her handkerchief. 'I expect I shouldn't have t–told all those l–lies!'

It was the following morning. Karen and Jessamy were sitting on the bed in Karen's bedroom, the walls of which were entirely covered in photographs of dancers, including several of Saul. There was Saul as Albrecht, Saul as Prince Siegfried, Saul in *Les Sylphides*, Saul as himself, looking rather sleek and glamorous. Even Jessamy, who had seen him unshaven in his pyjamas with his eyes still glued together in the early morning, could understand how it was that some girls just went to pieces over him. When he wanted to, Saul could look quite devastating.

Jessamy heaved a sigh. 'They weren't exactly *lies*,' she said.

'Yes, they were! They were lies!' Karen mopped despairingly at her eyes with a damp patch of handkerchief. She was still inclined to be a bit weepy, not over her ankle, now swathed in a crepe bandage – the doctor had said it was only a very minor sprain – but over the loss of Madame Olga, for how could she go on pretending, even to herself? And how could she go back to the Noran School, after what had happened?

'I don't know what I'm going to do!' wept Karen.

'There's still the gym,' said Jessamy.

'It's not enough!' Karen blotted again at her eyes. 'I'll *have* to go back. I just won't dance on the rotten floorboards.'

Jessamy looked at her, frowning.

'I don't think you ought,' she said. 'I don't think it's safe.'

'It is if I just keep to one side of the room.'

'But what are you going to do when it's dark?' said Jessamy. 'You won't be able to see!'

'I'll take some candles.'

'Yes, and then you'll go and knock them over and set light to yourself!'

'No, I won't.' Karen sat up, straight-backed and cross-legged, on the bed. 'I'm not clumsy.'

'But suppose you were practising *pirouettes* and forgot they were there?'

'I'll put them on the windowsill.'

There didn't seem to be any argument to that.

Jessamy sat, brooding, by Karen's side. She was already discovering Karen's apparent docility was deceptive. She might *seem* meek and mild, but she didn't let anyone, not even Jessamy, push her around. It was true she wasn't ruthless, but still she had Mum's famous 'rod of steel' going up her back. Mum always said that you couldn't get anywhere without a rod of steel.

'If your gran knew what you were doing,' said Jessamy, 'she'd be dead worried.'

The tears came welling back into Karen's eyes. Her gran was a sure way of getting to her. 'That's why I c-can't tell her!'

'I bet if you did she'd say it was dangerous — 'cause it *is* dangerous.' Even Jessamy could see that. 'You could get *murdered*.'

Karen stared at her, wide-eyed. 'How could I get murdered?'

'All by yourself in the dark, in an empty house. It's almost as bad as getting into a car with a strange man.'

'But what else can I do?' cried Karen.

'I don't know,' said Jessamy. 'I'm thinking about it. If you really won't tell your gran — '

'No! I can't! It would upset her.'

'But it's your whole future that's at stake,' urged Jessamy.

'I know.' Karen twisted her damp handkerchief round a finger.

'It's not as if it's just some passing phase.'

Passing phase was what some of Mum's pupils at

the Academy suffered from. One minute they thought they wanted to be dancers and went rushing out to buy all the gear, the pink tights and the satin shoes and the shiny lycra leotards; the next it was too much like hard work and they couldn't be bothered any more.

'This is *serious*,' said Jessamy.

'I know, but – Gran loved Granddad s-so much and he k-killed himself making enough m-money for me to have an educ-cation! Gran would break her heart if I didn't have one.'

Karen's handkerchief was beyond redemption. Silently, Jessamy handed her a paper tissue from a box on the bedside table.

'She cried for months and m-months after Granddad died. Sending me to C-Coombe Hurst is the only thing that makes her happy 'cause she thinks it's what he w-wanted!'

'But she doesn't actually *know.*'

'Well, she d-does 'cause he used to talk of me going to university and that's something I'll n-never be c-clever enough to do!'

'Which is all right, 'cause you don't want to.'

'But he wanted me to!' Karen's tears burst out afresh. 'Sometimes I feel so g-guilty, telling Gran I'm s-studying when all I'm doing is p-practising ballet!'

Jessamy fell silent. She wondered how it must feel to love someone as deeply as Karen obviously loved her gran. Jessamy loved her mum and dad, of course, but it would never have occurred to her to consider their feelings above her own. Maybe it was because they weren't always there, as Karen's gran was. She was used to being without them for quite long stretches and to being able – more or less – to do whatever she wanted. She certainly didn't feel any pangs of conscience, or sense of responsibility towards them. Mum and Dad could take care of themselves.

She could see that it might be different for Karen with her gran. After all, Karen's gran hadn't *had* to look after Karen. Parents didn't have any choice. If they had a baby it was up to them to take care of it (as Jack would very soon discover. Jessamy bet *she* wouldn't be so happy when she had to keep changing nappies and getting covered in sick. Babies were always being sick. Nasty messy things). Karen's gran could quite easily, probably, have sent Karen to a children's home.

'I suppose you don't have any rich aunts and uncles?' said Jessamy.

Karen shook her head. 'Haven't got any aunts and uncles.'

'Oh, that's a pity. You could have asked them if they'd pay for your lessons. I mean, it would be an investment. One day when you're famous – '

'I'll never be famous at th–this rate!'

'You will,' said Jessamy. 'You've got to be! If I'm going to be, then so are you. You can't deny talent. There's got to be *some* way.'

'There isn't. Not if I haven't got anywhere to p–practise!'

'The thing is,' said Jessamy, 'even if you had you couldn't just go on teaching yourself.'

'I know!' Karen wept afresh. 'I couldn't even manage *p-pirouettes* until you sh–showed me!'

'This is it,' said Jessamy. 'You can't learn everything from books. You've done really well so far. I really thought there was a Madame Olga' (Karen blushed), 'but the more advanced you become the more difficult it gets. You really do need someone to help you.'

'There isn't anyone!'

'There's me,' said Jessamy.

Karen's tears stopped abruptly.

'You mean – y-you could teach me?'

'I could try,' said Jessamy. 'I taught you *pirouettes* OK.'

'But I haven't any m-money to p-pay you with!'

'I don't *want* paying.' Jessamy said it fiercely. 'I'd do it because you're my friend – and because you've got talent and it's a crime to waste talent. I wouldn't do it,' said Jessamy, 'if I didn't think it was worth it. It'll be fun – it'll be a challenge! But you'll have to do everything I say, like you would with a real teacher.'

'Oh, I will!' Karen nodded, earnestly. 'I'll work really hard, I promise you!'

'And you won't go back to that place any more? 'Cause I honestly don't think you should,' said Jessamy.

'Couldn't I just on a Saturday morning?' Karen said it pleadingly, almost as if, from now on, she had to ask Jessamy's permission before she could do anything at all.

'Maybe just on Saturday mornings,' agreed Jessamy, 'but not after school!'

'All right.' Karen gave her eyes one final blot with her paper handkerchief. 'And we'll meet in the gym same as usual.'

'Seven-thirty sharp,' said Jessamy. 'Then we can put in a full hour.'

Much though she enjoyed teaching Karen all that she herself had been taught – she enjoyed the sense of achievement when Karen finally mastered a new and difficult step; she also enjoyed the sense of power, of being able to say 'Do this. Do that' and of seeing that they were done – still Jessamy was aware that it was not the final answer. Sooner or later, and probably quite soon, Karen was going to need a proper teacher.

Half term was coming up, and Jessamy, ever resourceful, had another of her ideas. A good one, this time. This one was bound to work!

At half term, even the Academy closed for a few days. That meant that Mum would be at home.

'When you come over tomorrow,' said Jessamy, as she and Karen left the gym on Friday morning, 'why don't you bring your practice clothes and we could do a bit more work on your *battements fondus*.'

Karen looked at her, worried.

'Are they very bad?'

'They're not *bad*,' said Jessamy (feeling a bit mean,

since in fact Karen had perfectly respectable *battements fondus*. But it was all in a good cause). 'It's just that they could do with a bit more practice. So could mine, as a matter of fact. We could work on them together.'

'All right,' said Karen. She sounded happier now that she knew Jessamy had problems as well.

It was a pity they couldn't do centre work, which was what Karen really needed to practise, but either Mum or Dad was bound to be in the sitting-room and even if they weren't Karen would probably be too bashful to do anything where she ran the risk of being seen. Jessamy's bedroom wasn't enormous, but at least it was big enough for some simple *barre* work, *and* she had a proper portable *barre*.

'Are you going to be here at tea time?' Jessamy asked her Mum, on Saturday morning.

'Yes, I expect so,' said Belinda Tarrant. 'Why?'

'Karen's coming. She'd be ever so thrilled if she could meet you. Dad too, of course.'

Belinda Tarrant rolled her eyes.

'We are not exhibits in a zoo,' she said.

'It's the price you pay for being famous,' retorted Jessamy.

'Famous we are not. Famous we never were. Just slightly well known.'

'It's still the price you pay. *I* wouldn't complain,' said Jessamy, 'if I were dancing leading roles and people wanted to see me.'

'My dear Jessamy, I haven't danced leading roles

for over a decade. I'm nothing but a humble ballet teacher.'

'*Humble?*' said Jessamy. 'Huh!'

'Oh, get away!' Belinda Tarrant flicked at her with a scarf she was holding. 'Horrible child! In my day we never spoke to our parents like that.'

Cleverly – or so she thought – Jessamy engineered it so that she and Karen were still practising their *battements fondus* when Elke called up the stairs that tea was ready.

'We'll have to go down as we are,' said Jessamy.

'Like this?' Karen sounded doubtful. 'Won't anyone mind?'

'This is a *ballet* family,' Jessamy reminded her. 'They're used to it. Come on!'

Karen, obviously still not quite comfortable with the idea, pattered down the stairs after Jessamy. Everyone was in the basement – Mum, Dad, Elke, even Jacquetta and the Bottler, who were staying for a couple of days. Good. That was good. That was what she had hoped for. Jessamy held open the door for Karen and watched approvingly as she walked through. In her leotard and tights, with her hair pulled back into a regulation bun, Karen looked every inch a dancer. Jessamy felt proud of herself. Surely the family couldn't fail to notice?

She had underestimated them: Jessamy's family could be blind as bats to anything which did not directly concern themselves. Mum glanced up and said, 'Oh, hallo. You're Katie, are you? Sit down and have some tea.' Dad said, 'Jessamy, have you seen my *Beaumont on Ballet*? I can't seem to find it anywhere.' Jacquetta didn't even bother to look up. The Bottler was the only one who showed any signs of appreciation.

'What have we here?' he said. 'Another aspiring Fonteyn?'

Karen blushed. Jessamy said, 'This is Karen. Karen — ' she said it loudly, for her mum's benefit ' — this is my sister Jacquetta, and this is her husband, Neville.'

Someone in the family had to show some manners.

Dad said, 'Hallo, there, Karen. Now, look, Jessamy, about my *Beaumont* — '

'I haven't seen it,' said Jessamy. Why should she want his rotten *Beaumont*?

'Are you still doing your tacky little end-of-term number?' said Jacquetta.

'It's not tacky,' said Jessamy. 'It's all about rain forests and the environment.'

'Oh, how very earnest!'

'It's good,' said Karen.

Jessamy beamed at her, gratefully. Jacquetta said, 'Yes, I'm sure, but it's so *tacky*.'

'Jack gave up ballet to have babies,' said Jessamy, investing the word with as much scorn as she could muster.

'Only one,' said Jacquetta.

'For the moment,' added the Bottler.

Dad stretched out greedily for a hunk of cake. 'If

someone's gone and removed my *Beaumont* without telling me I'll poxy well flay them!'

'Wasn't me,' said Jessamy.

'It better hadn't be!'

'It wasn't.'

'Karen, have some scone,' said Elke. 'Scone with clotted cream and home-made jam. It's very good.'

'She can't have clotted cream – ' Jessamy said it angrily: you'd have thought Elke would have known, by now ' – she's a dancer!'

'She look to me like she's too thin,' said Elke.

'Dancers are thin. They're supposed to be thin.'

Elke made an impatient scoffing sound in the back of her throat: she had no sympathy with what she called 'food fads'. No one else took the slightest bit of notice. Dad piled a plate with cake and scones and carried it off to another part of the house with a cup of tea the colour of black mud, the way he liked it. The Bottler leafed through Elke's copy of *Elle* magazine. Mum sat and talked to Jacquetta about babies. She didn't even *like* babies. Jessamy felt quite sick with the lot of them.

Afterwards, back in her bedroom, she said, 'I really have to apologise for my family. They have manners like wart hogs. Dad was really *gross*.'

'He was cross,' said Karen, ''cause of his book.'

'Stupid book! I haven't touched it.'

At six o'clock they went downstairs to find Elke, to take Karen home in the car. As they walked round to the garage, they bumped into Saul on his way in.

'You again!' said Jessamy. 'What is it this time? Strained your big toe?'

'I am not on tonight, *ducky.*' Saul twiddled a finger in her hair. 'It's your beloved in *Swan Lake.*'

'Sandro?' She had seen him in *Swan Lake* loads of times. 'So when are you on again?'

'Monday, Tuesday, Wednesday matinee . . . that enough for you? Am I earning my keep?'

'What are you dancing on Wednesday?' asked Jessamy.

'*Spectre* and *Petrushka.* Why?'

Jessamy had yet another of her ideas.

'Could you get us tickets?'

'I daresay I might. If you asked nicely.'

Jessamy spun round to Karen, hiding scarlet-faced behind her.

'Shall we go and see him?'

Karen seemed too overawed to speak. She opened her mouth, but no sound came out.

'If you could very sweetly and kindly get tickets for us,' said Jessamy, 'we should like to come on Wednesday, please.'

'In that case – ' Saul turned and saluted them as he sprang up the steps to the front door ' – I shall pull out all the stops!'

When Jessamy arrived home after delivering Karen to her door, she confronted her mum in the sitting-room.

'Don't you think that Karen is the perfect shape for a dancer?'

'Is she? I didn't really notice.'

'Well, she is.'

'Good. That's nice for her.'

'It's not nice,' said Jessamy, ''cause she can't afford ballet lessons.'

'So what am I supposed to do about it? I'm not a charity institution. Honestly, you're like one of those awful ballet mothers, thrusting their pudding-like off-spring at me!'

'Karen is not puddinglike!' yelled Jessamy.

There were times when her family really were the *pits*.

7

'Go by yourself?' said Elke. 'To the *theatre?*'

'I've been lots of times by myself,' boasted Jessamy.

'This I do not believe!'

'I have, honestly! You ask Mum.'

It was true that Jessamy had sometimes *sat* by herself, while her mum or dad, or both of them, had wandered off backstage to talk to people; not quite true that she had ever actually gone there by herself. But it was easy enough! Jessamy knew the way. You took a tube from Chiswick Park to the Temple, and then you walked up Arundel Street to the Strand, turned right towards Fleet Street, and there it was, the Fountain Theatre. She had only once gone there by public transport, and that was with Saul, but she could remember it just as clearly as if it had been a sequence of ballet steps.

'I do not like,' said Elke. 'London is bad place for a young girl.'

It was really very tiresome, never being allowed to go anywhere by yourself.

'I never have any fun at all,' grumbled Jessamy.

'Fun? You think you don't have fun? I will tell you, young lady, you are most privileged person!

Spoilt is what you are, if you ask me. One big sulk because she is not allowed to go on the gallivant!'

'I don't want to go on the gallivant! I just want to go to the theatre!'

'So go! I come with you.'

'*You?*' said Jessamy.

Elke coming with them was the last thing she wanted. She had pictured it being just her and Karen, all cosy together, going up to the bar in the interval to beg lemonade and biscuits from old Mrs. P., discussing the performances, visiting Saul backstage afterwards. They didn't want Elke tagging along!

'Hah! See how that takes the wind from out of her sails,' said Elke.

'Well, but you don't even like ballet,' pouted Jessamy.

'So I make sacrifice for you. Like I say, you are spoilt child.'

'But I don't w – '

'Is part of my job,' said Elke. 'Is what I am paid for. And besides – ' did a slight pinkish tinge creep into her cheek or was Jessamy only imagining it? ' – maybe I see your brother dance, maybe I change my mind.'

Oh! So that was it! Someone else who had a thing about Saul. *Bother.* That would mean they wouldn't only be stuck with Elke sitting there with them, and shepherding them about during the interval, she would also want to come cramming backstage with them afterwards.

She complained bitterly to Karen, when she went round to visit her.

'It's such a *drag*. She only let me come by myself today 'cause it's the middle of the morning.'

'Mm. They get worried. But I suppose eleven is quite young still.'

'Not as young as all that. Some p – '

'Listen! I've got something to show you.' Karen snatched at her hand. 'Come and see what I've done!'

She went scampering off up the stairs with Jessamy in tow. Karen plainly didn't care that they were going to be stuck with boring Elke.

'Look!' She threw open the door of her bedroom. The bed had gone, and most of the furniture. 'I asked Gran if I could move into the spare room and use this for practice, and she said yes, if I really wanted, so long as I didn't thump about and bring the ceiling down, so I moved everything out, as much as I could – everything except the wardrobe.' Karen giggled, excitedly. 'Gran thinks I'm mad! The spare room's so tiny I haven't got room to breathe, hardly. But what's it matter, if I'm only sleeping there? I'm going to try and find a long mirror in a second-hand shop, then all I'll need is a *barre*. What I'd really like is one like you've got. Do you think they're very expensive?'

'Haven't the faintest,' said Jessamy.

She knew she ought to be showing more enthusiasm, but she was still smarting from Elke saying she was spoilt. How could she be spoilt when

Elke did nothing but nag at her and her dad was hardly ever there and her mum was too busy even to talk to her? Far from being spoilt, she was *deprived*. She wouldn't have minded so much if it were Mum or Dad coming to the ballet with them. In fact, it would be quite good if Mum or Dad were coming because then perhaps they would be forced to take notice of Karen. But of course Dad was going off again, to Frankfurt this time, and Mum was talking at a conference in Edinburgh, which meant staying overnight, leaving Elke in charge, so that now they were stuck with her whether they liked it or not. It was just absolutely *pathetic* that people of nearly twelve couldn't be trusted to go to the theatre by themselves.

' . . . every afternoon when I come home from school.'

Karen was still burbling on about her new studio. Jessamy gazed round, ungraciously.

'It's not big enough to do centre work.'

'Oh, well, no, of course! But I can do that in the gym.'

'What about school holidays?' said Jessamy. 'You won't be able to use the gym then.'

It was almost as if she had taken out a pin and physically burst the bubble of Karen's excitement. Karen's face fell. The light went out of her eyes.

'No, I know,' she said.

'And you won't be able to go back to the Noran School much longer, either,' said Jessamy. 'They're going to knock down all that block and put up a supermarket. I saw it in the paper.'

She didn't know why, all of a sudden, she felt the need to be mean. Just because Elke had had a go at her, she didn't have to have a go at Karen. Karen hadn't done anything to deserve it. It was just that it was so . . . so *idiotic*, imagining that you could ever learn ballet on your own, in your bedroom. If it were that easy, everyone would be doing it.

'When are they going to pull it down?' whispered Karen.

'Oh! I don't know. It didn't say. Probably not for ages.'

'I thought maybe, in the holidays, it would be all right if I went there – '

But what was the *point*? The gym, the studio, her bedroom . . . Jessamy felt a moment of angry irritation. It was just playing at being a dancer! It was nothing but make-believe. If Karen had any real backbone she would go to her gran and tell her, straight out, 'I don't *want* to go to Coombe Hurst! I want to go to ballet school.' So what if her gran were upset? Sometimes it was necessary to upset people. You didn't want to, but it couldn't be helped; it was either them or you. If you let yourself be trampled on, you'd never get anywhere – specially not as a dancer. The world of ballet might look deliciously frothy and foamy, but Jessamy knew, from growing up with dancers, that those who inhabited it all had Belinda Tarrant's rod of steel going up their backs.

'You're too soft,' said Jessamy, 'that's your trouble. Just because you don't want to hurt your gran . . . you'll never make it if you're not prepared to tread on a few toes. You'll just be wasting your time. *And* your talent. And that's even worse. Wasting talent is a crime.'

Karen looked at her, stricken.

'Don't you think I'm making any progress?'

'Why ask me? I'm not a teacher! You need to go to a proper school. You can't carry on like this – ' Jessamy waved an impatient hand round the empty bedroom. 'I mean . . . what do you think you're going to *do*?'

Karen, crestfallen, hung her head.

'I'd thought – perhaps – if you could go on teaching me until they let me leave school, then maybe – maybe I could get a – a scholarship, or . . . something.'

'That's just crazy talk!' Jessamy said it witheringly. 'It's *years* before you can leave school. And I'll be gone by then. I'm going to Central when I'm thirteen. I can't go on teaching you. You'd have to go back to doing it by yourself and by the time you left school it'd be far too late. Anyway, knowing your gran, she'd want you to stay on into the sixth and try for A levels, and then she'd want you to try for university, and – '

'I'll never get into university! I'm not clever enough.'

'So all this isn't just a waste of talent, it's a waste of your granddad's money, as well! It'd be far better

427

if it was spent on teaching you something you're good at. Because you *are* good.'

Jessamy's rage had burnt itself out. She felt ashamed, now. When she had arrived Karen had been happy and excited, eager to show off her lovely new studio. In just five short minutes Jessamy had managed to ruin all her pleasure and totally undermine her confidence into the bargain. Perhaps Elke was right and she *was* spoilt.

'Oh, look! Don't worry,' she said. 'We're bound to think of something.' Jessamy would think of something. It was the least she could do. 'Let's try out your new studio!'

'I haven't got a *barre*,' muttered Karen.

'Has your gran got a towel thing in her bathroom? One of those stand things you drape them over? We could use that!'

Jessamy went racing off down the passage to return triumphantly dragging the towel rack behind her.

'There! You can stand one side, I'll stand the other. It's amazing what you can do,' said Jessamy, 'if you just put your mind to it.'

The next day was Wednesday, when they were going up to town. Elke was nervous of driving in heavy traffic and she seemed to think it not right using Mum's cab service, so they collected Karen and all trailed down to Chiswick Park tube. Jessamy actually didn't mind going by tube – it made it seem more of an outing. It also made her feel pleasantly important, as Elke didn't know the way from the

Temple underground to the theatre and Jessamy did.
Jessamy also, of course, knew most of the front-of-
house staff – the ladies in the box office, the programme sellers, Jim the fireman and Mr. Waldron,
the front-of-house manager. They all waved at her
or came over to say hallo.

Because it was a matinee and out of the tourist
season, Saul had been able to get them seats in the
circle.

'This is good,' said Jessamy, settling herself down.
'I like being in the circle – you can see better from
here. Stalls are horrible. There's always some great
tall person in your way, and anyhow you can't see
the patterns properly.'

'What patterns?' said Elke.

'Patterns on stage. Made by the dancers.' She
hoped Elke wasn't going to show them up by asking
silly questions. Jessamy half turned in her seat towards
Karen. 'This is my very favourite theatre,' she said.

The Royal Opera House might be grander, but
Jessamy had grown up with the Fountain. She loved
its faded splendour – the beaming cherubs frolicking
about the ceiling (some had lost their arms or legs or
noses), the glittering chandelier precariously hanging
overhead, the blue and gold, slightly tarnished, of
the boxes (where she sometimes sat with Mum and
Dad), the musty smell of the old seats. Best of all
she loved the blue and gold curtain, with its loops
and its tassels, rolling majestically upwards at the start
of a performance, billowing down again at the end.

Jack, predictably, said it was 'tacky . . . place needs a facelift', but Jessamy loved it just as it was.

'So what are these ballets that we are to see?' said Elke.

'*Spectre de la Rose, Petrushka* and *Children's Games.* It tells you all about them in the programme.'

'I've always wanted to see *Spectre de la Rose,*' said Karen.

'It's one of my favourites,' nodded Jessamy. 'Jack says it's yucky, but I don't think it is.'

The curtain went up on *Children's Games*, a slight piece by Lloyd Parsons, one of the boys in the company. It was fun, though nothing very much more.

'Mum says it's just intended as a *bonne bouche,*' said Jessamy, applauding along with everyone else.

'*Bonne bouche!*' Elke clicked her tongue, disapprovingly. In spite of sometimes using German phrases when her English ran out (though that didn't happen very often), Elke held that it was nothing but affectation, not to mention downright bad manners, to sprinkle your conversation with foreign phrases. 'You have no English word for this?'

'Titbit?' said Jessamy.

'Titbit. So why not say so? Why always in French?'

'Well, because lots of ballet terms *are* in French.'

Elke sniffed. Jessamy sometimes had the feeling that Elke held the ballet and everything to do with it in total contempt, which was odd considering she worked for a ballet family. Maybe after she had seen Saul she would change her opinions.

430

'I hope she doesn't make fun,' whispered Jessamy, in Karen's ear.

'Make fun?' Karen looked at her, wide-eyed. 'What of?'

Jessamy nodded towards the stage, as the curtain rose on *Le Spectre*. Gemma Dugard was dancing the young girl who comes home after the ball and falls asleep, still in her ball gown, and dreams. Gemma was young and beautiful: just right for the part. Saul was dancing the spirit of the rose which she had worn at her breast that night.

On Jessamy's birthday last year she had invited Susan and Sheela to an evening performance of *Spectre* – *Spectre, Sylphides* and Act II of *Swan Lake*. They had all sat in a box with Belinda Tarrant. Susan and Sheela had spent the evening passing Mum's opera glasses to and fro between them, making personal remarks about the dancers – 'Ugh! She's ever so ugly!' 'Heavens, look at his *make-up*!' It had been a mistake to bring them; but the biggest mistake of all had been to bring them to *Spectre*. The sight of a man – even one as handsome as Saul – dressed up in pink petals pretending to be a rose had been too much for them.

'He looks as if he's got a bath cap on his head!'

'Is he *naked*? Apart from the petals?'

'He is! He's naked!'

He wasn't, of course, but that didn't stop the two of them goggling and giggling and snatching at the opera glasses. Mum had said afterwards, 'It's the last time I take any of *your* friends to the ballet. Little philistines!'

Karen didn't giggle. She sat forward, enthralled, on the edge of her seat. Elke didn't giggle either, which perhaps wasn't surprising since Elke was not really a giggly sort of person, but Jessamy had braced herself for the odd derisive snort. She could understand that a ballet with a man dancing a rose, with pink petals all over him, might not perhaps be the best introduction for a person who wasn't sympathetic, but, after all, she hadn't planned on bringing Elke. If she had planned it then she would have picked something a bit more butch and obviously masculine – *Le Corsaire*, for example, or *Prince Igor*.

'That was *wonderful*,' breathed Karen, as they made their way up to the bar during the interval.

Elke looked at her. She seemed amused.

'I think maybe the costume is not help.'

'That costume,' said Jessamy, angrily, 'is a copy of the original.'

'So, but fashions change.'

'Not in ballet.'

That wasn't strictly true – today's ballerinas wouldn't be seen dead in some of the costumes worn by, say, Anna Pavlova or Adeline Genee. Too cluttered. Too frilly and fussy. But there were some ballets where the costumes were traditional, and *Spectre de la Rose* was one of them, so Elke could just go and – and drown herself! Jessamy turned rather huffily away.

'Maybe *Petrushka* is better,' said Elke.

Jessamy humped a shoulder.

'More of a story . . . what does your brother dance? He dance Petrushka?'

'No.' Look in your programme if you want to find out. *Daring* to criticise! Elke, who knew nothing about anything. The cheek of it!

'Saul's dancing the Moor,' said Karen.

Saul never danced Petrushka, probably because Dad had made his name in the role. Strictly speaking he wasn't really tall enough to dance the Moor, who ought to tower over poor lovelorn Petrushka, but it didn't matter since Petrushka was danced by Piet van den Berg, one of the shortest dancers in the company. Gemma Dugard was the Ballerina, pert and pretty with her rouged cheeks, running along on her points, with her doll's jerky movements, as she blew her toy trumpet. The Ballerina was one of the roles which Jessamy longed to dance: already she knew it by heart. If only Mum would let her go on point!

Petrushka was a success even with the sceptical Elke. It could hardly be anything else, thought Jessamy, watching as the braggart Moor, in his bright silks and satins, chased Petrushka round the stage, scimitar in hand. The Ballerina teetered after them, a fixed smile on her lips, still blowing her trumpet. She was a flirt, thought Jessamy. An inflamer of passions. There was poor Petrushka desperately in love with her, and there was she flaunting herself in front of the Moor, even to the extent of sitting on his lap and having a cuddle with him. (Jessamy

wondered if Saul enjoyed Gemma sitting on his lap
and cuddling with him, or whether he just accepted
it as part of the ballet. She thought probably he just
accepted it. Mum had once said that ballet was 'really
quite sexless in spite of all the bare flesh'.)

Of course the true villain of the piece was the
heartless puppet master. He didn't believe that
puppets had feelings and wouldn't have cared even
if they had. He enjoyed setting the Moor and Petrushka against each other, just to entertain the crowds.
He thought it amusing that Petrushka should lose
his heart to the Ballerina. It was all part of the
show when the jealous Moor finally caught up with
Petrushka and slashed at him with his scimitar.

The people who were watching (the people in
the ballet, that is) all gasped in horror. They thought
that Petrushka was a real person – they thought he
had been killed – but the puppet master contemptuously picked up the limp body and showed them:
nothing but a sawdust doll! No need to shed any
tears. Poor Petrushka!

It served the evil showman right when at the end
of the ballet Petrushka's ghost suddenly appeared
over the rooftops, amidst the swirling snowflakes. A
sawdust doll come back to haunt him! Maybe in
future, thought Jessamy, he would treat his puppets
better.

Elke nodded judiciously as the applause broke out.

'This one I do not mind so much. Though it is a
pity,' she added, 'that Saul had to paint his face. It
could have been anyone dancing it.'

It could not, thought Jessamy, crossly; not if you knew Saul. Jessamy would recognise her brother from the way he moved even if he had his head tied up in a sack.

'Let's go back and see him,' she said.

Karen's face, predictably, turned tomato red.

'*Can* we?'

'Of course we can! I always do.'

'Won't he mind? It's all right for you, you're his sister, but – '

'You're a fan,' said Jessamy. 'Everyone needs their fans.'

'But they do not perhaps always want them crowding in their dressing room,' said Elke. 'I think it best maybe we go straight back.'

Jessamy looked at her, haughtily. She might have to do what Elke said at home, but here in the theatre Jessamy was in command. What did Elke know about anything? Why, she wouldn't even know where the pass door was!

'*I'm* going backstage,' she said, 'and so's Karen. You can wait for us outside.'

Elke pursed her lips. 'Jessamy, I really think your brother will not wish to be bothered at such a time.'

'Pooh!' said Jessamy, rudely. *Amateurs* – she couldn't stand them. She pushed past Elke, pulling Karen with her.

'See you outside!' she called, but of course Elke had to follow. When it came to it, she couldn't resist.

Because it was a matinee, there weren't too many people in Saul's dressing room.

'Hi!' Saul was busy wiping his face clean of black make-up. 'So you dragged Elke along as well, did you? How did she like it?'

'Very nice, thank you,' said Elke.

'Except that it was a pity you had to paint yourself black,' said Jessamy, 'as it could have been anyone dancing.'

Saul grinned. 'I see! That puts me in my place, doesn't it?'

'No! Really!' protested Elke. (That would teach her, thought Jessamy. Saying Jessamy was spoilt.) 'Really, of course I am knowing it is you.'

'She knew in *Spectre*,' said Jessamy. 'Could hardly help knowing there, considering you had hardly any clothes on.'

Elke's face grew red as a ripe tomato. 'Jessamy!'

'What there was of it,' said Jessamy, 'your costume, I mean, she thinks is old-fashioned.'

'She's dead right,' said Saul, 'it is! I've been fighting a battle for years to have it junked.'

'But it's *traditional*,' said Jessamy, shocked. 'It's what Nijinsky wore!'

'So were a lot of other things that you'd be laughed off stage for if you appeared in them today. Either laughed off stage or arrested. How about you, K – ' He stopped. 'Katrina?'

'Karen!' snapped Jessamy.

'Karen. How did you like it?'

'I thought it was lovely,' said Karen.

'She didn't think the costume was old-fashioned,' said Jessamy, 'did you?'

Karen blushed, shaking her head.

'She probably did, but doesn't like to say so.'

'To me,' said Elke, 'this man is the *spirit* of the rose, not the rose itself. So my view, if this is the case, he should be a young girl's dream – '

'Not a ponce in a pink petal bath hat. Precisely.' Saul nodded. 'I couldn't have put it better myself. Jess, chuck us that towel, will you? Ta.'

Because of Elke being there, Saul hardly spoke to Karen and Jessamy at all. He hardly even noticed Karen. It simply wasn't fair.

Jessamy telephoned him next day, at his flat in town that he shared with another dancer in the company. (Saul could quite easily have lived at home, but he said it 'cramped his style', whatever that was supposed to mean. Jessamy privately thought it meant that he was having love affairs, which wouldn't surprise her in the least.)

'Saul?' she said. 'You know my friend Karen?'

'Do I know your friend Karen? Oh, yes! Your friend Karen. The little blonde who likes the pink petal bath cap. What about her?'

At least he had noticed that she was blonde. Encouraged, Jessamy said, 'Did you think she looked like a dancer?'

'I don't think I thought anything at all. Should I have done?'

'Yes, because she *does* look like a dancer. She's really got talent, she's taught herself out of a book, but now she needs proper lessons and her gran can't afford them. Do you think – '

'What? The answer, I should warn you, is almost certainly no.'

'Do you think – ' Jessamy said it doggedly ' – that if you came and gave her a lesson – '

'*Me?*'

'So that you could see her dance and tell Mum she's a deserving case.'

'Oh, come off it, Jess! You know what the old girl'd say . . . "*I am not – *" ' Saul mimicked Belinda Tarrant's light, crisp tones to perfection ' " – *a charity institution.*" '

'But, Saul, Karen is really really good!'

'Yes, I'm sure,' said Saul. 'Just like Tracey and Donna and Sharon and my-little-darling-who-went-up-on-her-points-at-the-age-of-two. Forget it, kid! The world is full of 'em!'

The trouble with her family, thought Jessamy bitterly, was that they were all too *cynical*.

8

'Right! Across the diagonal, one at a time. Jessamy, will you lead the way, please?'

Jessamy, positioning herself for a *pirouette*, caught an exchange of glances between Selma Chadwick and Donna Fletcher. She knew what they were thinking: *favouritism*.

Just because Jessamy was Belinda Tarrant's daughter. Well, it wasn't true. Mum never showed favouritism; if anything, she tended to be harder on Jessamy than anyone else (though some might have said that that in itself was a form of favouritism. Better to be taken notice of, even if it did mean constant criticism, than to be ignored). But one thing Mum hardly ever did and that was put Jessamy at the front of the class or ask her to take the lead. She was only doing it now because Jessamy's *pirouettes* were indisputably the strongest. Oh, what bliss it would be when she could do them on point! How fast she would move! How she would spin and dazzle!

Jessamy reached the far corner of the room, taking care to end neatly, as she had started, in fourth position. She stood, leaning against the *barre*, watching as the rest of the class followed. Selma, with her fat thighs. Donna, off balance as usual. Wendy Adams all over the place. Dawn Collier travelling in the wrong direction.

There wasn't a single one of them likely to make the grade – well, no, perhaps that was a slight exaggeration. Jennifer Ellis and Lucy Skinner weren't too bad. If Jenny didn't grow too tall and Lucy could keep her weight under control they might stand a chance. *Just*. They were more likely to end up as teachers. They weren't anywhere near as good as Karen, either of them.

It wasn't fair! All these no-hopers with their wrong-shaped bodies and their lack of talent cluttering up the studios and people like Karen, people with *real* talent, condemned to struggle alone in their bedrooms. Selma's mum worked all week on the tills in Marks & Spencer, up in Oxford Street, just to pay for Selma's ballet classes (and much good they did her. With thighs like that. Like *tree* trunks). Why couldn't Karen's gran go out and work? She wasn't as old as all that.

She knew what Karen would say. Jessamy had hinted once before that maybe if Karen's gran got a job then she would be able to pay for Karen to have both ballet lessons *and* go to Coombe Hurst. Karen had been shocked.

'I couldn't ask Gran to do that! She gets these terrible pains in her knees, so bad she sometimes can't even walk. She couldn't go out scrubbing floors.'

Jessamy hadn't said anything about scrubbing floors. Surely there were other things that Karen's gran could do?

'But why should she?' had said Karen.

Why shouldn't she, was what Jessamy thought. She had chosen to bring Karen up. Surely it was her responsibility to make sure she had the opportunity to use the talent God had given her? After all, it wasn't everyone who was blessed with talent. You only had to look at Mum's Tuesday class to see that. Even Jenny and Lucy were only a bit better than average; they were never going to be star material.

Belinda Tarrant never discussed her pupils in front of Jessamy, but Jessamy had once overheard her talking to Dad. She had said that 'apart from Jessamy, of course, and Marcia Eagling, there really isn't anyone I'd call promising'.

Marcia had won a place, last term, at the Arts Educational in Tring. That only left Jessamy. Which did *not* make her big-headed, as some of the others tried to claim. Jessamy knew her strong points, but she also knew her weaknesses.

'*Line*, Jessamy! Focus your eyes — watch those shoulders. *Smoothly*, please! No jerking.'

Allegro was her forte: adage all too often her downfall. Ignorant people tended to judge a dancer solely by the number of *pirouettes* and *fouettes* they could do, and the speed at which they did them. Those who knew, the true ballet enthusiasts, looked for something more. The line of an *arabesque*, the carriage of head and arms: balance and control and poetry. Jessamy knew she still had a long way to go.

'Don't stand there like a garden rake! Put some feeling into it!'

The others liked it when the great Jessamy Hart had her knuckles rapped. But when she did something well, like today's *pirouettes*, they put it down to favouritism: implying that if she had been anyone else she would have been roundly criticised along with the rest.

'All right for some,' muttered Donna, as they filed into the changing room at the end of class.

'Yes, it is, isn't it?' said Jessamy. Donna's dad was some big pot in industry. Donna not only learnt ballet, she also studied piano, owned her own pony and had a television set and a video in her bedroom. Even Jessamy didn't have that (in spite of Elke saying she was spoilt).

'What are you talking about?' said Selma.

'What she said.' Jessamy jerked her head in Donna's direction. 'It's all right for some.'

'Yes, and we know who,' muttered Donna.

Selma stripped her tights away from her horrible fat thighs. 'I bet we could all get noticed if we had the right parents.'

They were so jealous it was unbelievable. Karen wasn't jealous. If she had been, Jessamy wouldn't have bothered with her, no matter how much talent she had. She was sick of all the spite and backbiting; she'd had enough of it at ballet classes. What did they have to complain about, Donna and Selma, compared with Karen?

'Four classes a week,' said Selma. 'Some of us have to make do with only two.'

'Yes, and some people have to make do with none at all,' snapped Jessamy.

If Karen could have just one class a week, it would be something. Not enough, of course; but at least she would be able to show what she could do. How much did one class a week cost? Maybe if Jessamy took money out of her building society account . . . but Elke would never let her. She would go and tell Mum and Mum would tell Jessamy to stop being so silly.

'I am not a charity institution, and neither are my daughters! That money was put there for you. For your future. Not to go throwing away on pudding-faced nobodies.'

Mum had more than a rod of steel going up her back: Jessamy sometimes thought her heart was made of steel as well. Naturally she had to defend herself against all the dreadful pushy ballet mothers thrusting their offspring at her, Jessamy could quite understand that. She had seen enough of people's mothers to know that ballet teachers had to arm themselves against them. Selma's mother, for instance. She was a big solid woman with huge thighs, who simply didn't seem to realise that Selma was going to grow up just like her, and that thighs like giant oaks had no place on a ballet stage. She still kept buttonholing

Mum and trying to get her to say that Selma was the greatest thing since Anna Pavlova.

She had to take pupils like Selma, if only because pupils like Karen were so rare. Marcia Eagling had been her last success: she was looking to Jessamy to be the next. So wouldn't you think, if talent were so scarce, she'd listen when Jessamy tried to tell her about Karen? It wasn't as if Jessamy were a ballet mother (though she was almost beginning to feel like one). She was *Belinda Tarrant's daughter*. Didn't that count for anything?

It seemed not, in spite of what her fellow pupils at the Academy chose to believe. Belinda Tarrant had heard too many tales of second Anna Pavlovas and of Margot-Fonteyns-in-the-making. It had made her cynical, so that now she wouldn't trust anyone or anything; only the evidence of her own eyes.

Shortly after half term Mrs. Richmond asked Jessamy how her solo was coming along.

'Had any ideas yet?'

'Yes, it's all worked out,' said Jessamy. 'I've been practising it for weeks.'

'Oh, splendid! I knew we could rely on you. When shall we be able to see it? At the dress rehearsal? Or would you like to unveil it before? Perhaps you should come along next week — we're rehearsing on stage for the first time. Doing a full run through. Two o'clock Saturday. Could you manage that?'

'Yes, that would be all right,' said Jessamy.

'In the meantime, I'll get Mrs. Markham to come and measure you up for a costume. You can tell her what sort of thing you had in mind.'

Karen was obviously disappointed, though she tried not to show it, when Jessamy explained that she wouldn't be able to see her on Saturday as usual.

'Why don't you come to the rehearsal?' said Jessamy.

'Oh, but I couldn't!' said Karen. 'I haven't been invited.'

'Yes, you have . . . I've invited you!' Karen really would have to learn to be a bit more pushy. It didn't do to be too nice in the world of ballet. 'Look, you've got to come,' said Jessamy. 'I need someone to be there, to tell me how it goes. I've never done it on stage before – it might be disastrous.'

'It won't be,' said Karen.

'Well, but I still need someone there who knows about ballet. Everyone else just goes ooh and ah and says why don't I dance on my toes. They don't know the first thing about it. I need a proper dancer's opinion.'

Karen, though plainly flattered, said, 'Couldn't you ask your mum?'

'Mum's busy teaching.' And anyway, Belinda Tarrant always kept well out of anything to do with ordinary school. She never came to parents' days or open days, or even end-of-term shows. She just didn't regard it as important enough.

'You're the only person I know,' said Jessamy. 'The only one I can rely on.'

Susan and Sheela were both at the rehearsal – they were part of the chorus of frogs. They sat out front with Karen while Jessamy did her Rain Forest dance and afterwards took it upon themselves to criticise. They never had any qualms about voicing their opinions on subjects about which they were totally ignorant.

'We thought it was very good,' said Susan.

'Except for just one small thing,' said Sheela.

'What we can't understand – '

'When you've been doing ballet for so long – '

'Is why you can't go up on your toes yet.'

'We feel,' said Sheela, 'that it would be better if you went up on your toes.'

'Yes, because otherwise you're going to be dwarfed by all those hulking great tenth years standing around being tree people.'

'It can't be that difficult,' said Sheela, 'surely? I mean, even I can do it. Look!'

She demonstrated, wobbling on to her points (securely cushioned in their expensive Nike trainers) and grabbing hold of Susan to maintain her balance.

'I mean, I expect you'd have to practise a bit, but – '

'If Sheela can do it – '

Karen caught Jessamy's eye and giggled.

'If you go on point before you're ready for it,' said Jessamy, rather coldly, 'you can ruin your feet.'

'Well, my goodness,' said Susan, 'how long does it take to be ready for it?'

'Years,' said Karen. 'Everything in ballet takes years.'

'Well, it just seems a pity, that's all . . . if no one is going to *see* her. Because the dance itself,' said Susan, 'is very nice.'

'Very effective,' said Sheela.

'And will be even better, of course, when she has the costume.'

'Ah, yes, well,' said Sheela. 'The *costume*.'

Fortunately at this point, before Karen could choke herself or Jessamy choke someone else, Mrs. Richmond came up and told Susan and Sheela to hurry along or they would miss their entrance as frogs. As they scuttled away, she turned to Jessamy.

'Well, Jessamy! What can I say? That was marvellous! Exactly the sort of thing I wanted. Quite the budding choreographer, aren't you? I thought it was most ingenious. Well done!'

'Was it really all right?' said Jessamy, when she was alone with Karen.

'It was terrific,' said Karen.

'But what about that first *arabesque*? Didn't I wobble?'

'Only a bit, but you don't usually. I expect it was just stage fright.'

'And d'you think I'll really be dwarfed by the trees?'

'Of course you won't! That's just Susan and Sheela being silly.'

'Whatever you do – ' Mrs. Richmond had come back. She tapped Jessamy on the shoulder as she passed ' – for goodness' sake don't go breaking any bones or twisting any ankles before we get to the end of term! We're relying on you . . . you're our star turn!'

That night in bed, Jessamy had yet another of her bright ideas. (To be fair, really, it had been Mrs. Richmond's bright idea – not that Mrs. Richmond was aware of it.)

It came to Jessamy just as she was falling asleep. It niggled at her for the rest of the night and stayed with her all day Sunday.

'It is the *best* idea,' thought Jessamy, 'that I have ever had.'

It might have been the best idea, but sometimes even the best ideas have a big BUT attached to them. In this case it was a particularly big but. Jessamy wrestled with it right through Sunday night and into Monday morning. She was still wrestling as she walked into the gym, to find Karen, as usual, already hard at work. Karen paused in her *plies* and turned a tragic face towards her.

'They've started,' she said.

'Started what?' said Jessamy, still wrestling.

'Pulling it down.'

'Pulling what down?'

'The house! I passed it on the bus. They're taking the roof off!'

Bother, thought Jessamy. They would have to go and start this morning, wouldn't they? This was emotional blackmail. Now she wouldn't have any choice.

'I was hoping they'd leave it till after Christmas. Now I won't be able to go there any more!'

'Yes. Well. Never mind that.' Jessamy drew herself up in regal fashion, like Belinda Tarrant. 'We have work to do.'

Karen's lower lip trembled: she had obviously been looking for sympathy. Well, she wasn't going to get it. There were more important things at stake.

'I have decided,' said Jessamy, 'that instead of just doing exercises all the time you ought to learn my Rain Forest dance.'

'B – '

'For one thing – ' Jessamy held up a hand, imperiously silencing whatever objections Karen might be going to voice ' – it will be something different. For another thing it will extend you. And for another thing, I'm the teacher and you promised to do what I say. And I say,' said Jessamy, 'that we shall do a twenty-minute *barre* and then we shall start on the Rain Forest.'

Karen had watched Jessamy so many times that she almost knew the Rain Forest dance by heart. (Jessamy secretly thought that she had probably practised it in the studio at the Noran School. It was what Jessamy herself would have done.)

'I'll never be as good as you at *pirouettes*,' sighed Karen.

'No, but your *arabesques* are far better. You didn't wobble once. We'll work on it again tomorrow,' said

Jessamy, as she took off her shoes and put them in the special red shoe bag that Jack had made for her (Jack having time on her hands now that she was a lady of leisure).

'What sort of costume are you going to wear?' Karen wanted to know.

The costume was going to be almost exactly as Jessamy had envisaged it – a headdress of brightly coloured feathers and all the rest a deep dark emerald green. Green shoes, green leotard, with sleeves and a high neck – even her face and hands were going to be covered in green make-up.

'It sounds wonderful,' sighed Karen. 'Will they send the local papers to take photographs?'

For a moment, Jessamy felt a slight pang. She reminded herself firmly that she was *making a sacrifice*. And what, after all, was a local paper?

'I expect they'll send someone,' she said, carelessly. 'They usually do.'

And then they had these really yucky captions – YOUNG BALLET STAR, LITTLE BALLERINA – which made Jessamy cringe and enraged everyone at the Academy. Really, not being in the local paper was only a very small part of the sacrifice.

'Will your mum and dad come and watch?' said Karen, wistfully.

'Dad might not, but I'm going to make sure that Mum does!'

Mum coming was the whole point of the exercise: Mum had to have the evidence of her own eyes.

Jessamy cornered Belinda Tarrant that same evening, when she arrived back from teaching.

'Mum – '

'What do you want, Jessamy? Can't it wait till morning?'

'I never see you in the mornings!'

'Whose fault is that? If you will get up at some unearthly hour – '

'I have to. Mum! Listen.'

Belinda Tarrant groaned. 'Must I? All I want is my hot bath and my dry Martini!'

'It won't take a minute. I want you to come to the end–of–term show.'

'What, at Coombe Hurst?' Belinda Tarrant rattled ice cubes into her Martini glass. She sounded surprised, and rather put out. 'What do you want me to come to that for? I thought you said it was tacky.'

'Jack said that, not me.'

'So isn't it tacky?'

'Well – yes; I suppose it is, quite.' Coombe Hurst didn't have a reputation for drama. The only reason the papers came was because of LOCAL BALLERINA'S DAUGHTER DANCES IN SCHOOL SHOW.

'In that case – ' slosh, gurgle went the Martini into the Martini glass ' – why do you want me to come? I never have before.'

'Yes, well – that's why,' said Jessamy. 'If you and Dad – '

'Oh, it's no use trying to rope your dad in! He's

off to Winnipeg. He won't be back till Christmas Eve.'

'All right, you, then. I want *you* to come. I want you to see my Rain Forest dance. It's — it's very important,' said Jessamy.

'Why? Is it a choreographic masterpiece?'

'No, but I want to know what you think of it.'

'You could dance it for me in the studio.'

'*No*! It's not the same. I want you to *be* there. It's only short,' said Jessamy. You could be home again by nine o'clock.'

'Oh, very well! Anything for peace and quiet. Get me a ticket and remind me nearer the date. I'll do my best. I can't say fairer than that.'

Was it really so much to ask? wondered Jessamy. There were moments — not very often, just now and again — when she was almost tempted to wish that she had ordinary parents. *Normal* parents. Parents who automatically came to the end-of-term show. Parents who didn't keep flying off to Winnipeg and Frankfurt and New York. Parents who behaved like parents.

She grumbled about it to Karen, next day in the gym.

'They're not normal, my parents aren't.'

'Well, of *course* they aren't.' Karen said it reverently. 'They're famous dancers.'

'I don't see why that has to make them abnormal.'

Karen thought about it.

'I suppose perhaps famous people aren't ever the same as ordinary people.'

'No, they're a *pain*.'

'I bet you wouldn't like it if they were ordinary.'

'No, and I bet you wouldn't like it,' retorted Jessamy, 'if you had to live with them!'

'I would.' Karen's face had gone all rapt and dreamy, the way it often did when Jessamy talked about her family. 'I'd give anything to have parents like yours.'

Jessamy snorted.

'Is your gran going to turn up for the end-of-term show?'

'Yes! She wants to see you dance. She's really looking forward to it.'

'There! You see? That's what I call a *normal* parent. Not like mine, having to be bullied into it. And she's only your gran. I bet you wouldn't swop her . . . if you could have my mum and dad and go to ballet school, and I could have your gran and not go to ballet school . . . I bet you wouldn't, would you?'

'I – ' Karen opened her mouth and closed it again. Her cheeks grew pink. Jessamy could see the struggle going on inside her.

'*Would* you?' said Jessamy.

'I suppose I wouldn't if it meant not having Gran.'

'So there you are, then!'

Karen hung her head.

'I'm not tough enough,' she said, 'am I?'

'Doesn't matter.' Jessamy picked up her school bag and slung it over her shoulder. 'It'll all work out.'

'I don't see how it can,' said Karen.

'It can 'cause I'm telling you it can.'

'How?' Karen hurried after her. 'How can you be so sure?'

'Just wait,' said Jessamy. 'You'll see!'

9

The end-of-term show had two performances, one on Friday, one on Saturday. The reporters from the local newspapers always came on the Saturday, because everyone reckoned that the second perform-ance was the better one. Belinda Tarrant had rolled her eyes at the thought of giving up her Saturday evening to watch 'a bunch of untalented amateurs – present company excepted, of course', but Jessamy had bought her a ticket and marked the date in her diary in enormous red letters that couldn't possibly be missed, so now she had no excuse for not turning up.

Karen's gran, originally, had been going to come on the Friday. 'She has her friends round on Satur-days,' said Karen, 'and they play whist.'

'Tell her to bring her friends as well,' had said Jessamy.

Karen had looked at her, doubtfully. Jessamy realised that it did sound rather big-headed, instructing Karen's gran to bring her friends along just so that they could watch her dance, but that couldn't be helped. It was essential she came on the Saturday. Unless, of course –

But no, that wouldn't be any good, even if Jessamy *were* prepared to sacrifice herself totally and utterly, which she wasn't sure that she was. After all, she was the one who had gone to the trouble of choreograping the dance; it wasn't fair to expect her to give up everything. She was giving up quite enough as it was. And anyway, she had bullied her mum into coming on the Saturday she couldn't change the day now.

'Honestly,' said Jessamy, 'Saturday is the *only* day. Friday will be dreadful, it always is. *Please* ask her to come on Saturday . . . *please!*'

It was the first time Jessamy had ever asked anything of Karen. She could see that it put Karen in an awkward position, but if she wouldn't be ruthless on her own behalf then someone had to be ruthless for her.

'I mean, she can play whist any Saturday,' said Jessamy, 'can't she?'

Karen, reluctantly, admitted that she could.

'So will you ask her? *Please*? Tell her it's for me.'

'All right,' said Karen.

So now not only Karen's gran but two of her gran's friends were coming, as well. Jessamy rubbed her hands, gleefully. How easy it was to talk people into doing what you wanted them to do!

The dress rehearsal was a disaster, but dress rehearsals always were. Sheela, leading the tree frog chorus, led it on in the wrong place, in the middle of someone else's scene; a great hulking brute of a sixth former crashed into a rather fragile piece of scenery and crushed it; the stage manager (another sixth former) brought the curtain down before Jessamy had done her second solo.

'Doesn't matter,' said Susan, cheerfully. 'A bad dress rehearsal means a good first night. That's what they say in the theatre, isn't it?'

'Is it?' said Jessamy, gloomily.

'Well, you ought to know!' said Susan.

Karen, who had come to watch the rehearsal, suppressed a giggle. She found Susan and Sheela a perpetual source of amusement. Jessamy said nothing. She rather suspected that at Coombe Hurst a bad dress rehearsal might quite likely mean an even worse first night, but the first night didn't really matter. It was the second night that was important.

'You will be here nice and early,' she said to Karen, 'won't you?'

'Gran always gets everywhere early,' said Karen. 'She's terrified of being late.'

'Good! Do you want to try my costume on?'

'Yes, please!' said Karen.

The costume fitted Karen perfectly. Apart from having slightly longer legs than Jessamy, her measurements were almost exactly the same. Even the green-dyed ballet shoes, being soft, were the right size. (Just as well they weren't using point shoes. That would have been more difficult.)

'Goodness!' said Mrs. Richmond, coming into the dressing room. 'I thought for a moment you were Jessamy!'

'She looks really good,' said Jessamy, 'doesn't she?'

'She does,' said Mrs. Richmond. (How was it Mrs. Richmond could see it and not Jessamy's lousy rotten family?) 'Are you another dancer, Karen? I didn't realise that. Why didn't we have a *pas de deux*? It would have been rather nice.'

'Next year,' said Jessamy, 'we will.'

Apart from a piece of scenery collapsing and one of the tree frogs tripping over its own feet, the first night wasn't as bad as Jessamy had feared. Her Rain Forest dance went well – her *arabesque* didn't wobble, her *pirouettes* were spot on – and everyone came gushing up afterwards, the way they always did.

'So this is Belinda Tarrant's little girl?'

'Chip off the old block, eh?'

'Following in mother's footsteps – '

'They say it runs in families.'

All the things that Jessamy had heard a million times before. Once she had lapped it up and been in danger of growing big-headed, but now she was used to it, and was old enough, in any case, to know that people will always come flocking round the child of famous parents. Of course she enjoyed being the centre of attention; that was only natural. And of course any artist was always anxious to be reassured at the end of a performance: Jessamy was no exception. But for all that, there wasn't a single person whose opinion she really valued; not as she valued Mum and Dad's.

It would have been nice, reflected Jessamy, rather wistfully, as she removed her green make-up, if just for once her mum *had* come to see her. For a moment she almost wavered – but then she thought of Karen's gran giving up her Saturday evening whist, and Karen's gran's friends giving up *their* Saturday evening whist, and why should they be expected to do that just to watch the great Belinda Tarrant's spoilt brat?

It's true, thought Jessamy, confronting her image in the mirror: I have been spoilt. Dancing lessons practically the moment she could walk, kissed by Rudolph Nureyev (not that she could remember it), best seats at the theatre, Gelsey Kirkland's ballet shoe (just one of many), signed photographs, autograph book filled to the brim with famous signatures, all the great ballets and many of the greatest dancers there for her to see on video, just whenever she wanted. When you looked at it like that, you wondered how other people – ordinary people – ever stood a chance.

Firmly, Jessamy replaced the lid on her tin of cold cream (full stage make-up box, given to her by the grateful director of one of the ballet companies her dad had worked for. Dad was always bringing her back these little presents from his trips abroad). If she had really been so desperate to have Belinda Tarrant come and watch her she could have talked her into it last year. Last year it hadn't occurred to her – and if she was to be honest it wouldn't have occurred to her this year either, if it hadn't been for Karen. Mum saw Jessamy dance almost every day of the week; it was someone else's turn, now.

Jessamy set off early in the car with Elke for the Saturday evening performance. Belinda Tarrant was talking on the telephone to America. She had been talking for the last half hour. Jessamy mouthed urgently to her, 'You will come, won't you?'

'She will come,' said Elke. 'I remind her.'

'You promise?' said Jessamy.

Elke nodded, gravely. 'I promise.'

There was one good thing about Elke: you could rely on her.

Jessamy was dropped at the school gates. It was too early yet for any of the audience to be arriving, and even too early for most of the performers. She made her way into school and along the empty corridors until she came to the music rooms, which had been turned into dressing rooms for the occasion. Cautiously, she opened the door of Room C – Tree Frogs, Humming Birds and Jessamy. Good! No one there.

Jessamy sat down and waited.

A humming bird from Year 8 was the first to arrive. She looked at Jessamy tenderly cradling one bare foot, and obviously decided that this was just something which ballet dancers did. Jessamy said nothing, but ostentatiously massaged her ankle.

A group of tree frogs then turned up, including Susan and Sheela. No one took the least scrap of notice of Jessamy massaging her ankle. Dancers were always prodding and poking at bits of themselves, especially their feet. Susan and Sheela were having an argument about whose fault it was that last night half the tree frogs had ended up with their backs facing the audience.

'I told you, it's because they *turned* the wrong way.'

'Yes, but *why* did they turn the wrong way? You're the one that's supposed to be leading us!'

'I did lead you. It's not my fault if people don't watch what I'm doing and can't tell left from right.'

Jessamy stood up, on one leg, carefully lowered her other to the ground and let out a loud yelp. The argument stopped. Everyone turned to look at her.

'Now what's the matter?' said Sheela.

'What have you done?' said Susan.

Jessamy sank back, groaning, on to her seat.

'I think I've ricked my ankle.'

'Ohmygod!' said Sheela. 'That's fatal, isn't it? For a dancer?'

'Shall I get Mrs. Richmond?' said Susan. 'I'll see if I can find her!'

Susan galloped off. Sheela, morbidly hopeful, said, 'Have you broken it?'

'Twisted it,' said Jessamy, 'I think.'

'How?' said a humming bird.

'Coming down the stairs . . . I tripped over something.'

'If it's ruined your career,' said Sheela, who had plans for becoming a solicitor, 'you could probably sue.'

'It won't – ruin my career,' said Jessamy, heroically wincing as she probed at herself, 'but I don't think I'm – going to be able to – dance – tonight.'

If she had expected a horrified hush to fall upon

461

the room, she was disappointed. (*Amateurs*. They were all *amateurs*.)

'Not to worry,' said a humming bird, comfortingly. 'It's not that important. After all, you're only a sort of extra.'

Jessamy gave her a look of cold contempt. She might only be a sort of extra – though embellishment was the word she personally would have chosen – but without the Rain Forest dance the show had no pretensions to quality at all. Just a gaggle of tree frogs who couldn't tell which way they were supposed to be going, a few moth-eaten monkeys, some humming birds that squawked about the stage like chickens, and half the sixth form hanging about with creepers while the other half solemnly intoned ecological messages in blank verse. They needed Jessamy's Rain Forest dance to wake the audience up.

'Fortunately,' continued the idiotic humming bird, 'it's the play that people have come to see.'

'Yes, you mustn't worry,' said Sheela, in soothing tones. 'It's not as if anything depends on you.'

Jessamy began to feel rather alarmed (as well as indignant). They were sabotaging her plans! At this rate they would simply do away with her dances altogether.

Mrs. Richmond came hurrying in, with Susan and the school nurse. (What was she doing here? Come to watch the performance, presumably. Jessamy hadn't been expecting that.)

'Jessamy!' said Mrs. Richmond. 'What's all this I hear?'

Jessamy pulled a suffering face.

'I tripped coming down the stairs . . . I think I've twisted my ankle.'

'Let Nurse have a look at it.'

'There's nothing to see, but it hurts when I stand on it,' said Jessamy.

'Does it hurt when I do this?'

'Ow! Yes.'

'How about this?'

'Mmm . . . a little bit.'

'Well, I don't think you've actually sprained it, but I'll put a bandage on for you and you'd better not risk dancing.'

'I would risk it,' said Jessamy, 'but I just can't stand on it.'

'Oh, dear!' said Mrs. Richmond. 'What a thing to happen! I do feel guilty . . . I shouldn't have gone putting ideas into your head.'

'It was an accident,' said Jessamy.

'I'm sure it was! I'm sure you didn't do it on purpose. Never mind, it can't be helped. We'll just have to – '

'Karen could take over.' Jessamy leaped in quickly before Mrs. Richmond, like the rest of them, could decide that the dance was dispensable. 'She knows it by heart – we've practised it together.'

'Really? Where is Karen? Is she coming tonight?'

'Yes, with her gran. I should think they're probably already here. She said her gran always gets to places early.'

'And you really think she could do it?'

She'd better be able to do it, thought Jessamy, after all the trouble I've been to.

'I know she could,' said Jessamy. 'She's a really good dancer.'

'Well — ' Mrs. Richmond hesitated. 'We could just cut it out, though it seems a shame, when it frames the work so well. And it would seem a pity to waste your lovely choreography. I'll go and see if Karen's out there. I'll see how she feels.'

This, thought Jessamy, was the real test. If Karen let her down — but surely she wouldn't?

'Oh, you poor *thing*!' said Susan. 'This is what dancers hate most, isn't it? Other people getting to dance their roles.'

'Doesn't really bother me,' said Jessamy, bravely. 'I danced the first night.'

'But the press is here,' said Susan. 'They'll get pictures of her and not of you. That's not fair!'

'I don't mind,' said Jessamy. 'I've had my picture in the paper loads of times.'

A few minutes later, Mrs. Richmond arrived back in the dressing room accompanied by an apprehensive but excited Karen.

'Jessamy! What have you done?'

Jessamy pulled a face.

'The same as you did. It's nothing very bad, but it hurts to walk on. It's just as well I made you learn those steps.'

'Do you really think you'll be all right, Karen?'
Mrs. Richmond still sounded doubtful.

Karen exchanged glances with Jessamy. Jessamy
nodded, vigorously.

'I'll try,' said Karen.

Nurse Rendall insisted that Jessamy stay in the
dressing room, with her leg propped on a chair, until
just before the curtain was due up.

'We'll smuggle you in at the last minute; you can
sit at the back with me. Or have you got someone
coming? Would you rather sit with them?'

'No, I'll sit at the back,' said Jessamy.

If she sat at the front with her mum, Belinda
Tarrant would quite likely decide to leave there and
then. 'I didn't come here to waste my time watching
some pudding-faced nobody!'

If Jessamy sat at the back, she wouldn't discover
until the curtain went up and by then it would be
too late. Jessamy didn't think that even her mum
would be rude enough to walk out once the curtain
had gone up.

'I'm scared,' whispered Karen, as Jessamy helped
her on with her costume. 'I can't remember any of
the steps!'

'You will,' promised Jessamy. 'As soon as you're
on stage you will. It's something that happens.'

'Has it ever happened to you?'

'Lots of times,' lied Jessamy. It never had, but she
had read enough books to know that it happened to
other people. 'All you've got to do is just remember
the *first* step – ' She sketched it out, as best she

could, with her bandaged foot. 'Once you've done that, the rest will come.'

'I hope s–so,' said Karen, through chattering teeth.

Jessamy hoped so, too. Karen didn't realise how much was depending on her performance. Suppose she made a complete mess of it? It didn't bear thinking about!

So I won't think about it, thought Jessamy, hobbling into the hall on the arm of Nurse Rendall seconds before the show was due to start. What was the point of torturing yourself when the worst might never happen?

The lights were already dimming as Jessamy and Nurse Rendall took their places, so she didn't have a chance to pick out Belinda Tarrant in the front row, though she thought she caught a glimpse of her red hair. Good old Elke! You could always count on her.

The curtain went up with a satisfying swoosh (at the dress rehearsal it had become stuck half way) and there, in a pool of green light, arms symmetrically framed above her head, stood the Spirit of the Rain Forest. Jessamy took a deep breath.

Slowly,, Karen lowered, her arms. *And* –

Echappe – *releve* – *releve devant* –

Jessamy let out her breath. She would be all right, now. It was the first steps which mattered.

Karen's Spirit of the Rain Forest was different from Jessamy's. It was more mystical, for a start. Jessamy, when she was dancing it, always felt that she was fighting a battle – a battle for the rain forest.

With Karen you felt that she *was* the rain forest. Harm the forest and you harmed her. Her *pirouettes* might not be as diamond hard and precise, but her *arabesque* was a perfect line from fingertip to toe.

Jessamy, sitting next to Nurse Rendall, had the double satisfaction of seeing her own work performed by her own pupil. She felt almost as proud as if she had performed it herself. Not even Belinda Tarrant could fail to be impressed!

As soon as the curtain came down for the last time (and a bashful Karen had taken her curtain call), Jessamy sprang up from her seat.

'Watch your ankle!' cried Nurse Rendall.

'It's a bit better now,' said Jessamy. 'Sitting down seems to have cured it.'

'Well, don't go rushing about. You can't afford to take any chances.'

Jessamy forced herself to walk slowly and carefully down the rows of seats. Mum was right at the front, in the centre (special treatment because of being Belinda Tarrant).

'Mum, d — '

Jessamy stopped. Where had she gone? Surely she hadn't *left*?

'Excuse me, was there someone sitting in this seat?' she said to the lady who had the seat on the other side. The lady shook her head. (She was wearing a red furry hat that looked like hair.)

'No,' she said, 'there wasn't.'

Jessamy swallowed.

'Not even . . . at the beginning?'

'No, not all evening.'

Jessamy's cheeks turned crimson. Mum hadn't come! She had let her down! After she had *promised* –

'Jess?'

A familiar voice made her spin round. Saul was forging his way towards her.

'Why weren't you dancing?'

'I twisted my ankle. Where's Mum? Why isn't she here? Why are you here?'

'Second-best. I got home and found Elke in a flap. It seems our twitty-minded sister decided to start having her baby and your twitty-minded mother couldn't resist the opportunity to go dashing off to participate.'

'*Mum*? You mean she'd rather go and watch a baby being born than – ' Jessamy's eyes filled with self-pitying tears. After all the sacrifices she had made! 'How *could* she?'

'My sentiments precisely,' said Saul. 'There's a baby being born every second.'

'She doesn't even like them!'

'So she says. Beneath the flinty exterior there obviously beats a heart of pure marshmallow. So, anyway, I came instead, albeit twenty minutes late, expecting to see my littler and less twitty-minded sister performing miracles of her own devising, and what do I see instead? Some other child performing the miracles on her behalf . . . who is she, by the way?'

Jessamy blew rather fiercely at her nose.

'Karen.'

'Who's K – oh! I remember. Wasn't she the one who came with you that day? The little blonde?'

Jessamy sniffed.

'Who's her teacher?'

'Hasn't got one.'

'Well, who used to be?'

'No one used to be. She's never had one.'

'What do you mean, she's never had one? Who taught her to do all that?'

'She did, mostly.'

'By herself?'

'*Yes*. By herself. What everyone says is impossible.'

'I'd have said it was.'

'Well, it's not,' said Jessamy, ''cause she's done it. All I did was help her with her *pirouettes*.'

'Yes, they are her weakest point. She needs to do some work on those. But other than that – ' Saul shook his head. 'I don't believe it! She's having you on.'

'She is not,' hissed Jessamy. 'She's never had a proper lesson in her life, she j – '

'All right, all right!' Saul backed away, hands held up in protest. 'You don't have to get shirty!'

'Well, but – ' Jessamy's eyes filled again with angry tears. First Mum letting her down, now Saul not believing her!

'Hey, hey! What's all this?' Saul tilted her chin with a finger. 'Just because Mum didn't turn up?'

'She promised that she would!'

'Yeah, I know. Elke said – she seemed to think it

469

was important. But does it really matter,' said Saul, 'since you weren't able to dance anyway?'

'I didn't want her to see me dance! I didn't care about her seeing me dance!'

'Ah! You wanted her to see the choreography? Well, I've seen it. I'll tell her. I th – '

'I didn't want her to see the choreography! I wanted her to see Karen!'

'To see *Karen*? But – ' Saul stopped. 'Hang about! Just what exactly happened to that ankle of yours?'

'Nothing, if you must know!'

'I see.' Saul nodded, slowly. 'The penny begins to drop . . . all part of a grand plan, eh? Foiled at the eleventh hour by our twitty-minded sister . . . well, look, cheer up! All is not lost. *I* came – I saw. I can report.'

'You mean about – about Karen?'

'Sure. Why not? Any kid that can get that far on her own deserves a break. Leave it to me. I'll have a word with her.'

Jessamy said breathlessly, 'With Mum? Or with Karen?'

'I meant with Mum, but if you think Karen would like me to have a word with her, too – '

'She'd be delirious!' said Jessamy.

'Very well. Lead me to her. Let's go and make her delirious.'

Karen blushed so fiercely fiery red when Jessamy appeared backstage with Saul that Jessamy almost expected her to burst into flames.

Saul said, 'That was very good, young lady. I

congratulate you! But we must do something about those *pirouettes*.'

Karen blushed even deeper.

'They're better than they were,' said Jessamy. As an afterthought she added, 'She couldn't do them at all before.'

'Before what?'

'Before I taught her,' said Jessamy.

Saul pressed a finger to Jessamy's nose.

'You,' he said, 'stick to dancing. And to choreography. That wasn't half bad. Leave teaching to those as knows how.'

'But th – '

'Enough,' said Saul. 'Have faith. I will do what I can.'

Jessamy paused only long enough to whisper in Karen's ear – 'He was really impressed! He couldn't believe you'd never had any lessons. He's going to talk to Mum!' – before springing joyously up the stairs after Saul. She just managed to put in a little hobble at the last minute.

'Now, look here,' said Saul.

It was Sunday evening, in the kitchen. Belinda Tarrant had arrived home full of baby talk. Jacquetta had had a little boy. He weighed nine pounds two ounces and looked just like Saul had when he was born. He was obviously going to be a dancer.

'He has a dancer's feet!'

Saul looked at Jessamy across the kitchen table and

471

shook his head. Elke, serious as ever, said, 'How can one tell? When so young?'

'One can't,' said Saul, 'is the answer to that.'

'I can,' said Belinda Tarrant. 'That child is a dancer if ever I saw one.'

'Now, look here,' said Saul for the second time. 'Can we stop babbling about babies? Can I get a word in edgeways? I've got to get back to town in a minute. But before I do – '

'Yes, yes! Before you do? You can always tell a dancer's feet. At least, I can.'

'Before I do,' said Saul, 'talking of children born to be dancers, last night I watched an eleven-year-old who's never had a dancing lesson in her life and has more talent in her little toe than most of your Academy brats have in all their great clumsy feet put together.'

'Oh?' Belinda Tarrant sat up straight, babies abruptly forgotten. 'Where did you see her?'

'At Jess's school. Taking Jess's place because Jess had – um – how can one phrase it? Temporarily put herself out of commission. On purpose. Only you'd gone off babying so it was a bit of a wasted effort, except that fortunately I was there, and I'm telling you, you ought to take a look at this child because in my opinion she could well be star material.'

'Really?' Belinda Tarrant turned, accusingly, to Jessamy. 'Why haven't you ever mentioned her?'

'Oh, *Mum*!' wailed Jessamy.

'What, you have mentioned her?'

'Over and over!'

'I gather,' said Saul, 'that in your usual inimitable fashion you said you were not a charity institution for other people's pudding-faced offspring. Or words to that effect.'

'Yes, I very likely did. Because I'm not. On the other hand, if it's a question of real talent – '

'It is,' said Saul. 'You can take my word for it.'

'I see. Well, in that case – ' Belinda Tarrant turned back to Jessamy. 'I take it you have her telephone number? You'd better give her a ring and arrange for her to come round to the studio some time.'

Jessamy hesitated.

'She can't afford to pay anything,' she said. 'She lives with her gran and her gran's really poor and her grandad killed himself so she could have an education only her gran thinks he meant book learning and – '

Belinda Tarrant waved a hand.

'The money is immaterial. Let me see the child dance.'

Jessamy thrust her chair back.

'I'll do it right away! When can she come?'

'Tomorrow, if you like. You might as well bring her with you after school. And Jessamy – ' Mum reached out a hand, pulling Jessamy towards her. 'I'm sorry, darling, that I let you down. It was naughty of me. I can only say that it's not every day one becomes a grandmother – but that's no excuse! It was most unprofessional. And what was worse, it upset you.'

'That's all right,' said Jessamy.

'Am I forgiven?' Mum held up her face for a kiss. Jessamy pecked, perfunctorily, at her cheek. She just wanted to rush now and tell Karen.

Belinda Tarrant laughed. 'Oh, I can see you're impatient! Go on, off you go, and break the good news.'

Like a bullet from a gun, Jessamy shot across the room, up the stairs to the hall, up more stairs to her bedroom. She could have used the telephone in the kitchen, but she didn't want to talk in front of the others. This was between her and Karen.

She snatched up the receiver and dialled Karen's number.

'Hallo?' said Karen.

'It's me,' said Jessamy. 'Listen! Saul's spoken to Mum and Mum says I'm to bring you with me after school tomorrow! She wants to see you dance.'

'Oh, Jessamy . . .' Karen's voice was hardly above a whisper. 'If this works out I'll be in your debt for ever and ever!'

'It will work out,' said Jessamy. 'I have good feelings about it. And you won't be in my debt – you'll be in Saul's . . . *I* didn't do anything.'

'You taught me how to do *pirouettes*!'

'Didn't even do that very well, according to Saul.'

There was a pause.

'So how is your ankle?' said Karen.

'My ankle?' Just in time, she remembered. 'Oh, that's all right.'

'Goodness! It got better quickly.'

'Yes, well, it wasn't very bad.'

'Like a sort of one–hour sprain, really.'

'Well – yes. I suppose it was, really.'

'Just enough to stop you dancing.'

'Oh, I couldn't have danced,' said Jessamy.

A sound suspiciously like a giggle came down the line.

'What are you laughing about?' said Jessamy.

'Nothing,' said Karen. 'See you tomorrow, in the gym. Do you think we ought to work on my *pirouettes*?'

'Yes,' said Jessamy. 'I think we'd better!'

FANDANGO!

As soon as Jessamy gets her first experience of Spanish dancing she is hooked, but Karen and her mother seem to disapprove.

'That was just so incredible!' declared Jessamy. 'The way they use their whole body – the way they express themselves! It couldn't be more different from the ballet!' It makes ballet seem almost – ' she searched for the word ' – almost like – like *tinsel*. Like – froth! As if it doesn't have any substance. This is all earthy, and bloody, and – and primitive!'

Jessamy talked, excitedly and non-stop, all the way to Chiswick. Karen said very little beyond the odd 'Mm' or 'Ah,' but then she was not given much opportunity. It wasn't until the cab had turned into her road and they were nearly at her gran's house that she said carelessly, 'Maybe we should go again.'

Jessamy was definitely going to go again. 'But I thought you agreed with Mum that it was only glorified tap?'

Karen's cheeks glowed pink in the semi–darkness. *Now* what was she blushing for?

ISBN 0 09 925111 6   £3.50

NICOLA MIMOSA

The riveting sequel to HI THERE, SUPER-MOUSE! in which Nicola is faced with some big decisions to make about her future.

'What are you up to?' the door was pushed open and Mrs French came in carrying a tray and three coffee mugs. 'I hope you're not trying to talk Nicola into becoming a model?'

'Why not? She'd make a very good one, she's exactly the right build, got exactly the right type of bone structure.'

'That's as may be. I happen to have other plans for her.'

Oh? Nicola spun round, wonderingly. This was the first she'd heard of Mrs French having any plans.

'How would you like to try for a place at Kendra Hall?'

'*Me?*'

'Yes, you!' Mrs French laughed, as she set down her tray. 'Who else would I be talking about?'

ISBN 0 09 921321 4   £2.99